A TWIST OF FAITH

MITCHELL'S CROSSROADS: BOOK 1

BASHAM

Faith and family add depth to this heartwarming tale of brokenness and second chances. Basham weaves a unique tale sure to please the romantic at heart.

~**Denise Hunter** Bestselling author of *Married 'til Monday*

Eliza Doolittle digs her heels into the Appalachians in this witty and delightful charmer by Pepper Basham. A beautifully written tale that will sweep you away to a cozy spot in a mountain cabin. Highly recommended!

~**Janice Hanna Thompson** Author of the *Weddings by Bella* series

Pepper Basham updates the beloved classic tale of "My Fair Lady" with a fun twist: this time the professor is a woman with something to prove as she tries to prep and polish an Appalachian farmer for a big-city job interview.

~**Beth K. Vogt** Author of *Wish You Were Here* and *Take Another Look*

Pepper Basham throws us into the culture of Appalachia with a cheeky grin, promising we'll love it... and we do. This romance hits all the right notes with a prickly heroine on the verge of having it all but has no one to share it, and a wounded hero on the verge of losing it all but surrounded by a steadfast and loving family. Sweet, light-hearted, and enough romance to make Eliza Doolittle give up her flower stand- this one is a keeper.

~**Mary Jane Hathaway** Author of *Pride, Prejudice, and Cheese Grits*

With seamless writing and effortless charm, this unlikely romance will remind you that love often finds us where we least expect it. And somehow that makes the journey even sweeter. Pepper Basham's mastery of 'happily ever afters' may incline you to race ravenously to "The End" yet each word might as well be the finest chocolate, filled with warmth and sweetness meant to be savored.

~**Amy Leigh Simpson** Author of *When Fall Fades*

Romance filled with sparks, country twang and Blue Ridge spice, Pepper Basham has spun a story sure to engage hearts and leave the most hopeless of romantics with a heady sign at the close of the last page, yearning for more from the Virginia hills and Reese and Adelina.

~ **Casey Herringshaw Apadoca** Author and ACFW Carol Awards Coordinator

To my family, Dwight, Ben, Aaron, Lydia, Samuel, and Phoebe, who have prayed with me before I've submitted manuscripts, encouraged me through rejection, and provide daily inspirations to my life. I am blessed beyond measure with your love.

CHAPTER 1

Remember that you are a human being with a soul and the divine gift of articulate speech: that your native language is the language of Shakespear and Milton and The Bible; and don't sit there crooning like a bilious pigeon."
(Pygmalion, Act 1)

PhD was *not* supposed to smell like this.

Adelina Roseland dropped a box of research articles onto the floor and stifled a deep breath as the strong aroma of naturally fertilized farmland wafted in from the open window. The small room with, apparently, no air conditioning, defied any prestige the brass placard on her mahogany desk could have given:

Adelina. N. Roseland, PhD
Assistant Chair
Department of Communicative Disorders, Blue Ridge University

SHE TOSSED her bag on the desk and contemplated closing the window, but a cool morning breeze blew in for a moment's respite from the stuffy warmth in the room. Stale heat or the scent of country charm? She sighed in resignation to the irony of life and kept the window open. Country charm it was.

The view from the window paused—an indefinable pull from a horizon of Blue Mountains almost irresistible. They shouldn't draw her or provide any comfort. The memories of her childhood should snuff any longing the fog-covered sea of mountains encouraged, but instead of pain, she heard the gentle hum of her granny's voice. The soft song from the past threatened to awaken feelings and memories she avoided like black-eyed peas and family reunions. But it called her to remember—to soften the sadness, loss, and grief.

Her throat tightened as unbidden memories peeked into the present. She pushed them away, determined to leave her unsavory past in the place where all bad memories go: one-on-one intensive psychotherapy.

With a deep breath, she turned her back to the window, to the memories, and faced her future. The office. *Her* office. Two massive bookshelves lined the nearest wall across from her mahogany desk, and an armchair sat near the window as if in invitation to sit and gaze out at the rolling green vista. Another bookshelf stood behind the desk next to a floor lamp and a leather desk chair.

She sighed and placed her plant and calendar on the nearest shelf. The office might lack Charlottesville's class and appeal, but it was hers —and it was temporary. She'd been handpicked for this experimental satellite program from her coveted University of Virginia, and if she succeeded, her dream job dangled like a prize at the end.

Running wasn't an option.

She'd worked much too hard. Focused. Driven. A bit obsessive, if her previous ex-boyfriends had anything to say, but not a runner. She smoothed a hand over the front of her plum suit jacket and infused her thoughts with courage she didn't feel, drawing in a defiant deep breath of stale air. Maybe an element of prestige hung somewhere between the farmland and fertilizer after all.

Her smile quivered as her dad's old adage echoed in her head, strengthening her will. *Everybody starts somewhere, Dee.* Ransom, Virginia, was a *start* but certainly not an end.

She reached into her bag and claimed the desk with one single item—her father's picture. His intense eyes stared back at her from the woodgrain frame, reminding her not only of their shared hazel hue but their shared dream for her life—full professor at UVA Charlottesville.

Remembering him, the usual ache around her heart flared to full sting. She could *almost* hear his baritone voice, *almost* smell his scent of English Leather and pipe tobacco. Determination fisted her hands. She'd prove herself, even now. Make him proud. At least she could do that one thing for him.

"I see you've found your office."

Dr. Alexander Murdock's voice sliced into her solitude like missed high notes on a fiddle. And straight to her last nerve. She steadied her expression and turned to face him.

He stood framed by the doorway. Every piece of his six-foot-two frame blared *flawless*. From his dusty-blond hair sculpted to Michelangelo-like perfection, down to the pristine lines of his navy suit. Pretty is as pretty does, her granny used to say—and Dr. Murdock embodied the perfect descriptors of the last three men in her life: gorgeous, arrogant, and self-absorbed. Oh, why did he have to be her immediate supervisor? Hadn't four years as his research assistant been enough punishment for one lifetime?

"Dr. Murdock?" Dee tightened her arms across her chest, his annoying presence the possible root of her often-recurring migraines. Oh, well, it was either clench her jaw and instigate a headache, or say something she'd live to regret a long time, like the length of her freshly-signed contract. She bit back a sigh, refusing to give him the satisfaction. "What might I do for you?"

He advanced into the room as if waiting for a drum roll to begin. Or had it already started pounding a rhythm inside her head? She almost prayed for strength. *Almost.*

"Dr. Murdock?" He raised a questioning brow above one of those pale green eyes of his and walked past her, taking his eternal smirk and overpowering Polo cologne to the window.

The ache deepened at the edge of her forehead. Yep, migraine cause confirmed.

"Adelina," he said slowly. "We're colleagues now. Call me Alex." He frowned. Then closed the only source of fresh air. "Besides, as much research as we've done together, we already have the start of a good friendship. Right?"

Adelina forced a smile and hoped her expression wasn't as sardonic as it felt. "In that case, you should call me Dee." *Not really.* "I didn't expect to see you so soon."

"Ah, well, I had to personally deliver some paperwork to Dr. Russell to finalize this little university's new connection with Charlottesville. It's already starting several weeks behind schedule, so we don't want to have any more delays." He picked up her father's picture, stared a moment, then carelessly placed it back on the desk. "I thought I would go ahead and drop in while I was here."

She caught the frame before it toppled over the edge and pulled it close to her chest. "How often, by the way, should I expect your visits?" *Please say never.*

"Monthly as agreed upon by the program committee." Dr. Murdock pulled his iPhone from his jacket pocket and thumbed over the screen, dropping his comment in silence.

Dee swallowed the little taste of envy in her throat. PhD—check; iPhone—no. She had her priorities in order. Keurig machine and a new car before an iPhone. Surviving on coffee and microwavable mac-n-cheese through college deserved *some* rewards.

"Emails will do for the rest of the time." He returned his phone to his pocket and stepped to one of the bookshelves, examining the two lone items she'd randomly placed there: Her faithful plant, Despereaux, and her *Calvin and Hobbes* year of quotes calendar.

His fingers drifted over the peace lily, which had survived all four of her moves in the past five years. If nothing else, the poor plant deserved a consistent owner, even if it couldn't get a permanent

4

home. Then he tilted the *Calvin and Hobbes* calendar up toward him. She'd just read the one for today as she'd unpacked it.

"So, is this a lucky underwear day?" Alex waved the calendar at her, condescending humor undeniable.

"A lucky *underpants* kind of day." The correction popped out before she could catch it.

His delayed reaction confirmed his disbelief. "You have these memorized?"

A swell of warmth burst into her face. She spanned the distance between them and retrieved the book. "Of course not."

Liar, liar, pants on fire.

She cleared her throat and thumbed toward a plastic tote of books on the floor nearby in an attempt to divert his attention from her drowning embarrassment. "I haven't even been to my rental house and ... as you can see. I still need to unpack."

"I noticed." He turned abruptly, then sidled over to sit in the office chair. *Her* office chair. "Always work before comfort, right, Dee?"

She pushed a loose piece of her dark hair back into her bun and placed her father's picture back on her desk as she tempered her retort. "Well, one of us has to work."

He laughed and threaded his hands behind his head as he stretched back in her chair. "Being on your home turf is bringing out your country charm." The green gaze took an impish turn. "Didn't you grow up somewhere near here?

Placing distance between Alex's cologne and her assaulted sense of smell, Adelina shelved a few books and rearranged her Calvin and Hobbes calendar. "Yes."

"Quaint."

Quaint? She turned. He had no idea about the Appalachian culture. Quaint described little of her experience within the folds of the rural Blue Ridge. Lonely. Hostile.

"There's something about it." His softened voice drew her attention back to him. He was staring out the window. "I never imagined a real place like Mayberry."

Alex loosened his tie. The edges of his hair matted against his damp forehead.

Maybe the heat would send him all the way out of her office.

"What's it like?" His expression took on genuine interest that put her on guard. He only sobered from the confident-rich-kid routine when he was serious about something—usually women. "You know? Coming back home."

Maybe the heat *was* going to his head? "This isn't home for me." Growing up in the culture singed any desire to return. The lure of the mountains beyond her window already had her heart palpitating a retreat rhythm.

Alex cleared his throat and stood, casting another glance out the window. "The town seems idyllic—something from a movie set. I've never seen anything quite like it. I just thought maybe it was a good place to call home, that's all." The contemplative look on his face evaporated with his shrug. "Who needs to worry about home when we have our work, right?"

His declaration shook her. Was he right? Was her job all she had?

Alex flipped through a random phonology text on her desk. "And while I'm here, I need to get a copy of those last ten cases you completed."

"My cases?" Her contemplation ground to a lurching halt. "Why?"

"I'll need the information for my presentation at ASHA in November."

The temperature in the room vaulted to volcanic proportions ... *He wouldn't.*

"ASHA?" The annual speech-language pathologists' and audiologists' convention? "You're going to present *my* research at the national convention?"

"*Your* research?" Alex's head shook, as if to console her. "You wouldn't have your research had I not agreed to supervise it. I set you up for success with my contacts. My name is on all the documentation."

Adelina placed her hands on her hips. "Your signature gives you the right to steal my work?"

"Supervisor clearly gives me specific rights, Adelina. You know that."

"Perhaps technically." She lifted her chin in challenge. "But ethically?"

Alex drew out a long sigh. "You are a very bright woman, and no doubt you will be in top form to present at the National Conference soon. But you lack an important ingredient for the success associated with such an honor." He sobered, like he just might have found a heart. "You have excellent theory, you're a solid clinician and researcher, but you have practically no experience. This presentation is part of a round table discussion with the experts. You just received your doctorate in May, Dee." He tapped her desk as he rounded it, sat on the edge, and then offered her another consolatory smile. "You're not ready for that."

Her eyebrows and blood pressure shot skyward. *Not ready?* "It took me six years to finish my PhD, and four of those years were spent devouring research on accent modification. *I* followed through with all the protocol. *I* found the subjects to evaluate and treat. *I* wrote the papers. And *I* should present those findings at ASHA." She marched around him and jerked open the window. "It's *my* research."

Well, that got his attention. He stood to his full height, eyes narrowed. "Self-promotion has never been your strong suit. Do you think you're prepared for the pressure of researchers grilling you?" He held his palms out toward her. "By all means, if you're ready, you need to prove it."

"I can prove it."

"You've not shown a lot of personal initiative so far. You've been more of a follower."

Her cheeks flamed hot enough to evaporate her makeup. "During the past two years, I've helped over forty clients reduce their accents. Two native Appalachian speakers even went on to land jobs in Fortune 500 companies. I *have* experience and saw faster results with my clients than …" She snatched more books from the tote and tossed them toward a shelf. One clipped the edge and fell to the floor.

Alex stepped closer to retrieve the textbook, green gaze never leaving her face. "Finish your thought, Dr. Roseland. You saw faster results than me? Isn't that what you were about to say?" Placing the book back on the top shelf, Alex brought his face and every ounce of his cologne into her personal space. "This isn't a contest, Dee."

His use of her nickname tightened her spine. She hated how he towered over her. Even on tiptoe, she barely reached that Grecian nose of his.

"I've seen over three hundred clients and presented at ASHA on four separate occasions, as well as at several other national conferences." His voice gentled, almost coaxing. "My expertise isn't as focused on accent modification as yours, because I've spread my research out with the Aphasic population, but I am clearly more qualified to—"

"It's *my* research, Alex." She shoved her finger into his chest. "I have the knowledge *and* skills, and I *can* prove it."

"Really?" His tone almost mocked her ability—or at least it sounded that way to her nagging insecurities.

Adelina stepped past Alex to the other side of her desk. She looked at the picture of her father—and with new confidence continued. "I can take any hillbilly in this town and pass her off as a Harvard grad in twelve, maybe even ten weeks."

Alex sat back on the corner of the desk bringing them closer to eye level. "Ten weeks?" He didn't try to hide his amusement. He laughed. "I'll admit you're good, but not that good."

"You pick anybody. I can do it and *when* I do, I'll present at ASHA in your place."

"What? That's ridiculous."

"And if I don't ..." She racked her brain for an ultimatum, something powerful. Something worth the fight. "You can take all of my former research and use it as you will."

"'S'cuse me. I'm sorry to interrupt." A deep rumble of words pulled her attention to the doorway and away from their heated discussion.

A rugged looking man stood framed by the doorway, muscular arms tan against a pale blue shirt half hidden underneath dark overalls. His jaw line was shaded by a five o'clock, no, more like ten o'clock shadow. Midnight hair in a disarray of curls topped his head and spilled over his forehead, enhancing a pair of chocolate-brown eyes. The nervous movement of the cap in his hands came in direct contrast to the strength and confidence in his size, but it also told her something else. He was as out of his element as she was.

"Need any help, ma'am?" He spoke the words to her but focused his attention on Alex.

Adelina blinked out of her trance and snagged a breath, casting a glance back at Alex whose jaw was set with purpose. The last thing she should feel toward the burly farmer in the doorway was safety, but something about her knight-in-overalls almost had her stepping closer to his side to take cover.

"No, thank you." Adelina smiled. "May I help you?"

His gaze—alive and intense—focused back on her face. There was a gentleness in those eyes that caused her to pause, to wonder for just a second what might hide behind them. His eyes were dark, rich brown, more like milk chocolate.

"I'm real sorry for presentin' myself like this. I wasn't plannin' on comin' into town today." He patted a tanned hand against his chest and offered an apologetic grin that didn't quite match the farmer motif—a perfect row of white teeth. "You know a Dr. Roseland?"

Adelina worked to keep the surprise from her expression. "Dr. Adelina Roseland?"

"Adelina?" He tried the name on his tongue, a kettle drum of consonants. "Well now, Mama ain't said nothin' about the doc being a lady."

How on earth could he make the word *mama* sound so sweet, even with his vowel-mutilation? In her experience, the two rarely fit together.

Adelina pushed away from her desk and extended her hand. "I'm Dr. Roseland."

His dark brows tilted ever so slightly followed by another glimmer of teeth. "Nice to meetcha." He stepped further into the room, all two hundred-something lean pounds of him, and took her hand. His skin was rough, but not his touch. She looked up from their clasped hands and a sudden sense of safety washed over her.

Heat drained from her face and she pulled her hand from his. She hadn't felt safe in a long time.

"Name's Reese Mitchell. Welcome to Ransom." The poor man could injure more vowels in a single sentence than all the Beverly Hillbillies combined.

"Thank you, Mr. Mitchell." Dee gestured to Alex. "This is Dr. Alex Murdock."

The men exchanged a nod, measuring each other like two dogs. Well, in this standoff, her odds were on the mountain man.

"I didn't mean no bother. I was sent to help you with your boxes and things."

He ran a hand through his hair, upsetting more curls. Something just wasn't fair about a man with hair that pretty.

"You were sent?" Several huge boxes of books still waited in the trunk of her car. Had Dr. Russell sent her some help? Maybe country manners weren't so bad. The only thing Alex offered to take off her hands was her research. "I do have a few more boxes in my car."

He plopped the cap back on his head, and his eyes lit with boyish humor. "I can get 'em."

Dee squelched a reflexive smile, forcing professional distance she usually had no difficulty maintaining. Mr. Mitchell's thought stopping gaze captured hers again, almost as if he was gauging if she was fine or not. Could he tell? What did he care if her life ended in the next five minutes? Or worse, her career?

"That's very kind of you. Thanks." She kept her attention away from Alex and turned for her purse.

"Are you a farmer, Mr. Mitchell?" Alex asked.

"I am."

"Have you been in Ransom long?"

Dee needled Alex with a stare as she pulled her purse close. As if Mr. Mitchell's six-inch-long accent said anything else? Couldn't the brilliant Dr. Murdock tell from all his "experience?"

Alex's brow took on a playful wiggle. That man was a puzzle. She'd tried her best to keep her distance because his reputation came with a disclaimer: charming, unpredictable, and commitment free, but sometimes he left her wondering what really went on behind that megawatt smile.

Mr. Mitchell's grin stilled. "Most of it. I finished some schoolin' in other places, but mostly I've stayed close."

"Schoolin', eh?" Alex did nothing to hide the humor in his voice. "I guess farmin' is a close-to-home kind of job."

Mr. Mitchell's eyes narrowed and he stood a bit straighter. He was even taller than he looked at first. "Home is a good place to be, Dr. Murdock. But I don't mind some adventure now and then. Got myself an interview up near Chicago soon."

Dee braced herself for Alex's reply.

"Do you? For farming?"

"Agricultural engineering firm. Seems that even big city folks want experienced hardworkin' country folks. Or at least I hope so." He looked back at Dee, no smile in his eyes. "How 'bout them keys, Doc?"

Doc?

"Well, that's interesting." Alex's words came out slow, almost premeditated.

She risked a look at Alex. He looked happy. *Too* happy.

"Besides, Dee." Alex stood from the chair and adjusted his jacket. "We needed to finish our discussion so I can be on my way."

From the mischievous expression on Alex's face, Dee wasn't too sure she wanted to finish their discussion. Perhaps keeping Mr. Mitchell as a human shield wouldn't be a bad idea. At least he looked pretty solid.

She glanced at her farmer-protector and hesitated, keys in hand. "It's a blue Jetta out in the front lot of the building. Two boxes in the trunk are labeled 'office.' Oh, and there's one box in the back seat too, but the back left door handle is broken, so you'll have to come through the right."

A shaded grin quirked up one side of Mr. Mitchell's moustache. "Yes, ma'am."

"And you might have to jiggle the key a little in the keyhole to get the doors to unlock." His hand bumped her fingers as he took her keys and sudden warmth moved up her arm.

"Got it."

She released her keys and stepped back. "Thank you."

With one last look at Alex and a quick glance back to her, the farmer stepped from the room.

Dee braced herself as she turned.

As soon as the door clicked close, Alex was ready. "We have a deal."

"What?"

"*You* and Mr. Cowman. Ten weeks." He readjusted his tie.

"No. You can't be serious. I am not going to bring Mr. Cow ... um ... Mitchell into this."

Alex pulled keys from his pocket. "Too much of a challenge?"

"No, I—"

"Oh, I see. You planned on picking someone who couldn't roll their 'r's?" He shoved his hands into his jacket pockets and walked passed her to the closed door, head down. "Pity."

"You know that's not—"

"Once you gain more experience, right?"

"Okay, fine. Deal."

Alex spun around and extended his hand to shake.

Dee folded her arms in protest.

A slow, steady grin spread across his face like *The Grinch Who Stole Christmas*. "Ten weeks, which should make the great unveiling at the department Autumn Leaves Gala in Charlottesville. Perfect. By then *if* you can pass him off as a sophisticated intellectual, no hint of the cowboy who just walked in this room, I'll even buy you dinner at ASHA after your presentation." Alex saluted her then walked toward the door.

Her eyes shuddered closed. *What had she done?*

"Adelina?" He stopped in the doorway and looked over his shoulder at her. "You may not believe it, especially coming from me, but you're more than capable of succeeding in this position."

She hesitated at another view of this gentler side of the usually self-assured Dr. Murdock. "Why would you say that?"

"Just because I have an ..." He looked to the ceiling as if searching for the word. "... eclectic reputation doesn't mean I don't value hard work and talent. You have both." He tapped the doorframe with his keys and tossed a genuine smile her way. "I look forward to you winning this bet, Dr. Roseland. Good luck."

She nodded, unable to respond to his authenticity, let alone his compliments. Maybe, just maybe, there was something more to Dr. Alexander Murdock than a perfectly pressed suit and a trail of broken hearts. She shrugged off the curiosity. Her cup was already overflowing with more trouble than she cared to taste—this wager foaming at the very top.

She collapsed into her desk chair. Her father's framed face looked back at her. Trailing a finger along the edge of the frame, she studied the photo, wondering what he would do or say about the desperate deal she made with Dr. Murdock.

Mr. Mitchell provided a perfectly timed distraction from her internal lecture of guilt. He moved into the room, a book box under each arm as if they *didn't* weigh seventy pounds apiece. "Where would you like these, Doc?"

She flinched at his pet name for her, its familiarity. "By those bookshelves would be fine, Mr. Mitchell. Thank you."

The T-shirt stretched taut across his broad shoulders as he placed the boxes on the floor. She quickly looked away and stood, reaching for a stack of files from a box nearby.

"Is that all?"

"For now. I still have some boxes to sort through once I reach my rental house." She had a list of important things to accomplish during her first six months at this tiny school, and reforming Reese Mitchell was not on the list.

Until now.

If she truly went through with this wager, she'd practically be married to him for ten weeks. Ten weeks of intensive speech therapy with a backwoods, mountain cattle farmer? A prayer came to mind out of nowhere. *Help me, God.*

Mr. Mitchell dusted his hat against his overalls. "Again, I'm real sorry 'bout showin' up like this. I usually clean up better when I come into town, but I had to run Mama to the hospital."

Dee stood. "Your mother?"

"There ain't nobody with the blend of sweet and stubborn like my mama. Fell off a ladder 'bout four hours ago while she was paintin'. Bruised a few ribs. Didn't tell nobody for two hours." He offered a crooked smile and her heart stumbled into a different rhythm. "Mama didn't want to miss her appointment with ya."

"Her appointment? With me?" Dee's thoughts tinkered to a crawl.

"Yeah, to take you to your house."

"My house?" The spot above Dee's right brow throbbed.

Reese leaned toward her. "The house you're gonna live in while you're here?" He slowed his speech. "The one at Mitchell's Crossroads."

Mitchell's Crossroads? Reese Mitchell. A sudden sense of dread whooshed through her and drained her face of heat.

"It's our family's old house, spittin' distance from the new farm. My mama's yer landlady."

"My landlady?" She knew he spoke English, after all speech clarity was her specialty. But his words and her expectations weren't matching up. "Your mother is my landlady?"

His smile quirked into a fake, this-woman-is-crazy-grin. Could he tell she was fighting the impulse to run away and never return? A sudden uncertainty quivered from her neck all the way down to her secondhand heels, which she was tempted to click together three times and repeat *There's no place like home*. But the problem was … she didn't have a home.

"We'll take good care of ya, Doc. The last professor who stayed with us didn't leave for eight years."

Nobody could take care of her *that* well.

Dee steadied herself with palms to her desk and stared at Reese Mitchell, willing him to disappear or tell her it's all a joke or provide some ruby red slippers. Something. Anything.

Scanning the room, he took in a deep breath and shrugged. "Well, Doc, if yer ready, let me take you home."

CHAPTER 2

Yes: in six months—in three if she has a good ear and a quick tongue—I'll take her anywhere and pass her off as anything. We'll start today: now! this moment!
(Pygmalion, Act 2)

Her lips were as tight as her jeans, and both a distraction. Shucks, everything seemed tense about Dr. Adelina Roseland, even the dark bun at the nape of her neck. Reese released a sigh and shifted his truck into a lower gear as he turned off the main road and hit the gravel stretch toward his grandfather's house. He didn't need any distractions.

Doc followed close behind in her beaten-up blue Jetta. Not the type of car he'd expected for the high heeled, fancy-faced sort. Course, he hadn't had much time to think about women lately, between his kids, the farm, and his brother's illness. There were more important things to worry about than dark eyes and long legs. And she had both.

Reese checked his rearview mirror. A large patch of scuffed paint on the hood of Doc's car, a sick sounding engine, along with the secret door opening technique he mastered while removing her boxes told him her car had a life expectancy of six months maybe, not including a hard winter.

Reese rubbed his chin. She had old eyes, without any wrinkles. Weary, and maybe a bit lonesome, but tough as nails. Except her hands. They were soft.

Reese shook away the surprising thoughts of dark eyes and soft hands. Clearly, three late nights in a row with the cows turned his brain to mush. Besides, Doc probably kept the view of most city girls: the notion that country boys lacked charm, smarts, and a sense of class. He couldn't blame her for such thoughts today. He hadn't exactly made the best first impression. Muck covered overshoes, dirty overalls, and enough hair on his face to clothe a dog. He cringed as the trail of dirt clods on his floorboard basically confirmed any assumption. She probably thought he couldn't count to fifty, let alone get a job in Chicago.

He hoped his mom's advice held true in this situation. *City folk only get smarter about country folk the longer they live in the country.*

Well, that'd take a long while with Dr. Adelina Roseland, and it didn't matter nohow. Bet she'll be out of here in a year, maybe less. City mindsets didn't belong in places like Ransom. Didn't appreciate it.

The road ahead split the forest and opened up to a small field with his grandparent's white house at the center. Oaks and pines—planted generations ago—towered over and around the farmhouse like guards. Grandpa told him once how old they were, but Reese couldn't recall. Since his grandpa's death, he'd been losing the memories of the smaller things, even though the patriarch's presence breathed over the property like a warm summer breeze. Through all of his childhood, Reese knew no better place.

He jerked the truck to a stop in the dusty driveway. All eighty pounds of his black lab vaulted off the back and charged Doc's Jetta.

"Mavis! Git on back here."

The dog slid to a halt just as Doc opened her door.

"Back in the truck, girl. You ain't stayin' long."

Mavis hightailed it back into place, head down as if he'd scolded her beyond bearing.

"Excuse me?"

Reese turned his attention to Doc. She looked fightin' mad, and he almost grinned. Why did sass and spunk look so attractive on a woman?

Doc's dark gaze shifted to Mavis, a look of understanding dawned, and then she sighed. Must be tired. She kept rubbing her forehead. He'd better get her settled in quick, before she collapsed right there in the driveway and got her fancy designer jeans dirty.

"How 'bout we get you inside. I can unload your car."

Doc bumped her car door closed with her hip. "No, thank you. I can manage." She nodded toward the house. "If you'll show me around, then you can be on your way. I don't want to trouble you further."

Reese adjusted his cap and turned. He took the porch steps two at a time like he always did, tossing a glance over his shoulder to see if Doc kept up. Nope, she stood stone still at the bottom of the porch with Grandpa's old hound sniffing at her heels.

"That's Haus." Reese offered a smile.

Doc grimaced.

Seemed 'bout right.

He placed the key in the door and opened. Somehow, the place still smelled like pipe tobacco, mint, and home.

"What is he ... doing?" Doc's voice sounded small and a little scared.

Reese followed her wide-eyed stare to Haus' grin.

"Well, he's smilin' at ya."

"Smiling at me?" She pressed her body against the wooden rail and finished her ascent up the stairs, never taking her attention from the dog.

"Yeah. He's real friendly."

"Where does he live?"

"Here." Reese leaned against the doorframe keeping the screen open with his foot. "We ain't been able to get him to realize Grandpa's dead. So he lives here and somebody usually stops by once a day to check on him. No better dog in all of Virginia."

Doc shrugged past Reese, stumbling over his foot. In one fluid motion, he steadied her in his arms. Her hands gripped his shoulders and momentum pushed her forward until her nose grazed his chin, fanning warm breath down his neck. Heat rumbled to life in his chest, and if she hadn't pushed him away so fast, he'd have beaten her to it. *He had to get out of there.* She was causing way too much noise in his head.

"I'm not much of a dog person," she said.

Reese backed out the door, half falling. "That's alright. He don't mind none." The threshold of the door stood between them like an invisible wall, but it couldn't hide the faint bloom of color in her face.

He cleared his throat and pointed toward the staircase inside. "There are two bedrooms upstairs and a ladder to the attic. Not much room for storage up there, 'cause it's full of old stuff of my grandparents Mom ain't gotten around to piddlin' through yet. There's a study beside the kitchen with Internet—but we only got dial-up way out here, so if you're needin' to do anything with speed, you'll have to use computers at the school. There's talk in town of WiFi comin' back here in a month or two, but I wouldn't hold my breath."

No reply, but she did blink a few times as she took in what she could see from the doorway. She did have pretty eyes. Not that he was looking.

His mama and sister had replaced all the outdated furniture with something they called a 'cozy cottage' style and though Reese preferred a more practical house, he had to admit it looked good. Probably too simple for Doc's big city tastes, but a whole lot nicer than faculty housing at the university.

She approached the fireplace. "Is that a mountain dulcimer?"

Reese didn't have to look, but the sheer fact the woman knew what to call the Appalachian instrument had his brain in knots. "Sure is. Was my granny's. Grandpa kept it out 'cause he said Granny's soul whispered in her music and he wanted to keep it at the center of his house to remind him of her. I reckon that's why we keep it there too."

Doc raised her hand as if to touch the dulcimer, but then dropped it back to her side. "Music is an intimate thing."

The lost look on her face drew on his compassion. Seemed more like a wounded critter on the farm than a college professor … and critters he knew somethin' about. "Do you play?"

"It's been a long time since I've had much to do with music, I'm afraid." She pulled her gaze away from the instrument. "My education has taken up most of my time."

"Education is important." Reese nodded. "But I reckon a person can't get by without some food for the heart."

Silence swept between them and Doc's gaze searched his. For answers? Understanding? He couldn't say, but as quickly as it came, it disappeared into a frown. "Thank you, Mr. Mitchell." She shifted her attention to the door, then turned her face toward the fireplace, dismissing him like he was a young'un. "I appreciate your time and assistance."

"I reckon you can manage on your own?"

He thought at first she didn't hear him, but then she nodded, almost like she was lost in a trance or something. Well, how's that for gratitude. Reese headed to the door. He didn't want to see those eyes again nohow—and the fact that he was even thinking about them was a downright nuisance. The screen slammed behind him.

"Wait, Mr. Mitchell."

He stopped at the bottom of the porch steps, hands on his hips readied for her complaints. She pushed the screen open. "There's food on the kitchen table."

Reese returned to the top of the porch and glanced around her through the doorway. "Mom and Rainey, my sister, have been by, I reckon. That's their way of sayin' welcome."

"They brought me food?" She placed her hand against her stomach, her voice weak.

There he was, lost right smack dab in the middle of watery mix of cedar-brown and honey-gold eyes. Did her bottom lip quiver? Maybe she was lonely in this new place after all and that's why she acted like a loon? *He was a jerk.*

He stepped closer and kept his voice soft. "Listen, we're gonna be neighbors, so I reckon you should call me Reese. Neighbors take care of each other 'round here. I'm sure my mama and sis figured you'd be busy with unpackin' and didn't need to worry with fixin' food too. Country folks sure do like to eat."

He chuckled at his joke, but her brows crinkled into a deeper frown. Even that pretty rose color left her cheeks. Nope, there was no winnin' any favors with this one.

"Thank them for me, will you? It's very kind." She paused in her turn and sent a passing look to Haus. "Oh, and please take the dog with you when you leave."

Reese looked from Doc, back down to Haus, and up again. "Take the dog?"

"There's no reason to keep him here."

Haus lost his smile.

"No reason?"

She paused at the threshold of the doorway. "As I've told you, I'm not a dog person. In fact, I prefer my solitude when I'm away from work. And I'll forget to feed him."

Reese shifted his weight and gave the woman a measured look. Naw, she wasn't lonely. She was crazy. "He'll just come on back, no matter where I take him. This is his home. Besides, you won't have to feed him. One of the family will come by and check on him."

"I can assure you, I won't pet him either. I'm allergic to dogs. He'll probably grow to dislike me as much as I'm sure I'll dislike him."

Nobody'd ever disliked Haus. "Well, Doc—"

"My name is Adelina."

"Adelinuh." He deliberately mutilated her name and gave her a pointed look. "He'll be around here for now, and it's a good thing too. He'll keep the 'coons and coyotes away."

A look of horror dawned on Adelina's face, enough to lighten his step a little. He patted Haus on his gray head, and with a self-satisfied turn stalked to his truck and left a dusty cloud in his wake.

ADELINA RUSHED to the porch steps with the strong temptation of plucking out every hair on Reese Mitchell's beard. Impossible man! It probably didn't help that she wanted to take out all her crazy emotions on someone, and he happened to be the closest person available. Oh … and to stoop so low as to try and scare her with the bit about coyotes?

His truck disappeared up the gravel road.

"I'm not afraid of coyotes."

The open space swallowed up her grand declaration. Haus tilted his head to one side as if examining whether her statement was true or not. Her shoulders slumped forward with a sigh. Now she was trying to guess the thoughts of a dog?

She walked into the house, pressing the door closed behind her. She'd imagined a lot of scenarios for this move, but nothing prepared her for a stubborn cattle farmer, an impossible wager, and a grinning dog. How on earth was she going to spend two months giving that man therapy? An accent was one thing. Reese Mitchell gave a whole new meaning to country born and bred.

Closing her eyes, she pressed her head back against the door. But he was a means to an end … and she didn't have a lot of time. Besides, he would gain quality skills for free. Who wouldn't want that?

She drew in a deep breath and the full scent of the table's contents hit her, awakening her hunger, and something much deeper. A spot inside no one had touched in a very long time, a tender place which tempted her to believe in a place of love and baked bread and goodnight kisses and … home. But she didn't believe in fairytales anymore.

She sniffed back another sting of tears—ones she'd almost shed when entering the house. Pipe tobacco. Her father's signature scent. And then the dulcimer? Memories of her granny's knotted hands strumming over the strings sent a jolt to her fingers and an ache through her heart. Thinking of Granny Roseland conjured a few soft memories from her childhood, summers at her cabin buried in the hollows of Keene, Virginia.

The sudden rush of feeling almost shook her knotted-up emotions loose right in front of Reese Mitchell. And looking like an emotional mess in front of the cattle farmer wasn't on her to-do list, even if it felt painfully true at the moment.

No, this place couldn't be home. She'd lost too much in these rugged mountains. Her father had lost too much. The beauty and tranquility mocked her with their secrets. She ground her memories to a halt and turned from the mantle's view. She'd sworn to leave this mountain life and all its narrow-mindedness behind. Even if it meant working with Mr. Cattleman.

If there was a God, he had a ruthless sense of humor.

The sound of a slamming vehicle door brought her back to the front door. She pushed away the soft cream folds of curtain veiling the sidelights. Mr. Mitchell stepped from his truck and walked around to the other door. What was he doing? Providing some raccoons or coyotes to prove his point about the dog? She snickered at her internal sarcasm. As if coyotes ever came close enough to anyone's house to bother them.

He walked back around the truck with a five- or six-year-old little girl in his arms. Dee's breath caught. The girl's dark hair curled around her cherub face and framed a set of large eyes. Mr. Mitchell smiled down at her, his expression so filled with love, it squeezed Dee's emotions to the melting point. He wasn't so very bad looking when he smiled.

As soon as he set down the cherub-in-jean-overalls, she ran straight for the mangy hound at the foot of the porch steps ... even wrapped her arms around him. Adelina cringed. The dog produced his eerie grin again. How could Mr. Mitchell let her snuggle up to the smelly, creepy creature?

Mr. Mitchell ruffled the little girl's head, sending curls much like his bouncing. With a gentle nudge, he broke the little girl's hold on the dog, and then lifted the dog into his arms. His long easy strides took him to his truck, where he deposited the mutt in the back and then knelt down to gather up the little girl, nuzzling her neck until she squealed. She grinned up at him, her dimpled cheeks and glowing eyes conveying sheer adoration. Dee pressed her palm against her chest, warmth vibrating around her heartbeat. If he loved a little girl like that, maybe Reese Mitchell wasn't so bad after all.

He looked up, then, and caught her staring at him through the window.

She couldn't move. His dark gaze held her, fastened to the spot as if glue was attached to her shoes. She should be indifferent to him, unaffected, but he carried an air of easy confidence. And gentleness. A combination she'd never seen before. And Reese Mitchell was her one-way ticket out of this backwoods place. She *needed* him.

She pushed open the screen door and stepped out. "Thank you, Mr. Mitchell."

He nodded and placed the little girl in the truck. "Haus will be back, you know."

"Thank you all the same."

His brow lifted. "Yer welcome."

Dee drew strength from a deep breath and pushed the doubts as far away from her dreams as she could get them. She could win this wager. She *had* to win it. "Mr. Mitchell, I'd like to help you."

"Help me?" His hand paused on the open door. "With what?"

"I can get you ready for your interview. I have an excellent track record. I could offer you therapy services, you see. Accent modification, it's called." She stepped farther out onto the porch. "It's my specialty."

An unshackled look of disbelief crossed his face. "You wanna give me lessons on how to talk right?"

"Well, lessons on how to talk more conventionally. Pronunciation and grammar. An accent isn't right or wrong, it's just a difference." She lifted her finger and used her best 'teacher' voice. "Yet it is a difference that could cost you a job, I'm afraid."

He removed his cap and ran his hand through his hair again.

"How badly do you want this job?"

He squinted up at her and shrugged. "It's more of a need than a want."

She clapped her hands together in an awkward attempt at selling her plan. Oh, what a tangled web ... "Perfect. All the more reason to make your interview count. Right?"

"Daddy, look. I made Mavis smile like Haus."

The little girl in the truck pressed the black dog's mouth back into a crooked grin. The poor animal sat in contented stillness during the entire experiment. Dee almost let herself laugh.

"That's sweet, honey." Reese nodded to the little girl and then turned back to Dee. "You're offering to give me lessons to help with my interview?" He tilted his head. "How much will it cost me?"

Dee opened her palms and smiled. "How does free sound?"

"Right." He laughed and closed the truck's passenger door. "What's the catch, Doc? Ain't too many things free."

Dee shuffled through excuses in her mind and finally landed on one. "You're right, Mr. Mitchell. I would like to use you as research. Accent modification is my area of expertise, and therapy with you would only prove to strengthen my work. We both win."

"You do research on accents?"

"Whether you recognize it as a reality or not, in more metropolitan areas your accent can be the kiss of death to your career. With it comes a preconception, which may or may not be true." Her saleswoman persona returned to the conversation. "What you want is to display your quality skills and not allow your accent to detract from those."

She hoped he had some quality skills. From the looks of those dusty old jeans and dirt clod boots, fashion was not one of them.

"I don't know."

The knot in her stomach twisted tighter. Waiting. "Think of it as a way that I can be neighborly right back to you and your family, and in the process continue to hone *my* skills."

"Listen, Doc, I just don't see how this'll work. It's clear as day that you don't really wanna be around me, and I ain't up for feeling like an idiot just to learn how to speak my own language better. If the folks up in Chicago don't like what they see and hear as I am, then I'll just look for something—"

"I can help you." She moved to the top of the steps. "I could almost promise you that job, if you'll let me work with you. Not just your accent, but your professional presence."

He looked about as convinced as she felt. "I'm sure you're real good at what you do, but I can't ride into town for therapy more than once a week. I have a farm to run and two young'uns to care for."

He doubted her? Oh, no ... she would convince him now. She'd become an expert at fighting for herself. "I can see you here or at your home. It doesn't have to be at the university. Besides this isn't a professional arrangement, it's ... a favor." She smiled, but it felt awkward, kind of like her offer. "Since we're neighbors and all."

"I don't know, Doc," He shook his head. "I mean with two kids ..."

Two children? His words finally registered. So he was married? A father of two? The adorable dog loving girl was *his* daughter ... of course.

"Listen, I gotta go pick up my boy and get on back home." He placed his cap on his head and stared at her, long and hard, like he knew she was petrified ... or lying. "Me or Mama will stop by in a couple of days to see how you're settlin' in. I'm sure Mama left her number by the phone, in case you need somethin'. Good evenin', Doc."

He touched the tip of his cap and slid into the driver's seat. His truck disappeared in a haze of dust over the hill and the vacancy, even from Reese Mitchell, picked at her loneliness. She twisted her frightening feeling into one she could control—frustration. With Reese Mitchell. He doubted her abilities? She rested her hands on her hips and stared in the direction his truck vanished ... for the second time. "We'll see about that."

By the time his interview came in November, not even his Mama would recognize him. He would have his new job, she'd earn her one-way ticket to Charlottesville, and with every piece of her research in tow. No strings attached.

CHAPTER 3

Women upset everything. When you let them into your life, you find that the woman is driving at one thing and you're driving at another."
(Pygmalion, Act 2)

"You gonna marry that girl?"

"What?" Reese's daughter's question shocked him so bad he almost slammed on the brake. "You've been hanging around your Aunt Emma too much and we can only handle one matchmaker in the Mitchell clan."

"You don't think she's purdy?"

He scratched his chin and glanced sideways at Lou. Just the thought of marrying anybody tensed him from eyebrows to bootstraps. "I think you're purdy and I ain't gonna marry you."

Lou shook her head of curls until they bobbed around her face. Even at seven, she was starting to leave the little girl behind and the thought sent a wrench-squeeze to his chest.

"You can't marry me. I'm your daughter." She sighed back against the seat. "Besides, I don't have no job yet."

Reese pulled the truck to a stop in front of his mama's cabin, a grin twitching at the corner of his mouth. "Well, if you're hankerin' for a job, I think we can fix you up just fine." He tapped her nose and leaned close. "I have a felled tree up in the pasture that's gonna turn into some firewood and I can always use help with the load."

Lou's face scrunched. "Daddy, princesses don't load firewood."

"Is that so? Any princess who lives on a farm should be able to load firewood."

She grew quiet as if considering his statement. He took the opportunity to snatch her by the waist and pull her out his door. "Are princesses ticklish?"

Lou's bright blue eyes grew wide and she squealed as Reece buried his head in her shoulder.

"You're scruffy! You're scruffy, Daddy."

He growled and her giggle hit him square in the heart. Life hadn't been easy, but he sure was blessed.

"There's a whole bunch of noise out here."

Reece's mama hobbled forward onto the porch, her cautious steps reminding him of her injuries. White and gold hair swept up in a bun, with wild strands flying all directions.

"How you feeling?"

"Nothing worth all this fuss." Grace Mitchell gestured with her head toward the inside of the house. "Rainey won't leave me be and keeps following me around like I'm a young'un. I didn't know if she'd let me go to the bathroom alone or not."

"I heard that, Mama," Rainey called from inside.

Mama lowered her voice, gray eyes a-twinkle. "I don't know where in the world she gets that stubbornness from."

Reece looked heavenward and laughed. "It's a wonder."

"Dada home?" Brandon rounded the corner of the doorway, blond hair haloed by the sun. His toddling legs wobbled in the turn, but he caught himself and offered his cherubic smile until it dimpled in each chubby cheek. The boy looked too pretty really, and was a painful reminder of all Reece had lost. Jana's ultimate betrayal.

"Right here, little fella." With Lou still pressed to one side, he knelt to lift Brandon with the other arm. The boy snuggled up next to Reece's face and planted a sticky kiss on his cheek. Yep, he didn't need nothing else, especially some high-class city girl. "What's Granny been feeding you, boy?"

"Granny couldn't move as quick as usual, and Brandon got into pie innards before I could swipe them." His mama held open the screen door to the kitchen, with Reese close behind, a kid in each arm.

The scent of fresh baked apple pie warmed him from the outside-in. There was no place like Mama's house.

"He's a smart boy." Reece dropped Lou to her feet and used his free hand to ruffle Brandon's head. "Food before play."

"More like play with the food." Mama nodded to the white handprints decorating one row of cabinets. "That boy reminds me of his daddy."

In actions only. Brandon's pale hair and Scandinavian green eyes looked nothing like Reese, and sometimes, the ache from that truth bothered him still.

"Well, did you get Dr. Roseland settled in?"

Reece slung Brandon over his shoulder and leaned against the counter, snatching a cookie. "Did you know the doc is a woman?"

His mom shuffled, stiff and stubborn, to the counter and started peeling potatoes. "Sure I did. Been talking with some contact person in Charlottesville for over a month about her. What's she like?"

Brandon squirmed until Reece placed him on the floor. The boy took off to the living room after his sister, so Reece pulled up a stool and gave himself some time to sort through his answer. What *was* Adelina Roseland like? Those remarkable golden eyes flashed into his mind. "She seemed nice."

Mama stopped peeling and looked up, keen as a hawk. "That's good."

"I think this might be her first job. She's real young."

"Mmhmm," his mother replied and returned to her slicing.

"I don't think she'll be here long. She don't fit, and knows it."

"How can you tell?"

Reece tried not to give his mom an "I'm not stupid" look, but she caught him.

"I ain't sayin' I don't believe you. It's just you only met her today and already seem purdy sure about her not belonging. Just wanted to know why."

"Mama, she's dressed up like a movie star, with shoes that wouldn't last one day outside that university. I bet she ain't never changed a tire or hauled wood in her life, and I thought she might cry over at Grandpa's house. I'm not sure why." Would a grown woman cry over dial-up Internet?

"It's always hard adjustin' to a new place, Reese." Her words came soft, but he felt her meaning down to his overshoes. *Not all city girls are like Jana.*

How on earth did his mama do it? With one hard look, she still made him feel like he'd gotten a whippin'—or at least needed one.

She opened up an old paper bag and placed it on the counter like she always did when peeling potatoes. Her first row of peelings landed in the middle of the paper. "Who knows what the woman's come through? High class don't mean pain-free."

"I reckon not, but I'm pretty sure about one thing, Mama. She ain't going to be here for long." He shook his head, still befuddled. "She must be a bit desperate for research too. She offered to give me lessons."

"Lessons? For what?"

"She said she could help me get ready for my interview in November. The one for the position *Farm and County* is developing for the southeast I was telling you about last week. Offered to give me lessons for free to help her research or something like that." Reese laughed and lifted the lid of the nearby cookie jar. "Crazy woman. There ain't no way that could work."

Mama scooped the sliced potatoes into her palms and dumped them in the sauce pot. "It's a real good idea, sure 'nough."

"Good idea?" Reece about dropped the cookie he'd just picked up. "Some city woman who thinks the only thing I'm probably good for is unhaulin' book boxes? Don't sound like such a good idea to me."

29

"This ain't worth your pride, Reese. The woman up in Charlottesville said somethin' about Dr. Roseland bein' an expert on accents or somethin'."

Reese pressed a heel of his palm to his head and wondered if Doc's headache was contagious. "Well, it won't work, no matter what kind of expert she is."

"You and I both know we can't keep the better half of this farm unless more money's coming in. Even if Trigg's next report comes back good, he ain't gonna be able to do his part for a while yet. More strength he saves to fight cancer the better, but we'll still have to pay hired hands."

"I know, Mama." And boy did he know. The gaunt look of his brother's face after surgery, and then nearly a year of meds kept the thought fresh in mind. Seeing his big brother weak and broken not long after their stepfather's death to cancer upended all the pain like reinjuring an old wound. They'd lost enough in the last two years. All of them.

"I don't plan to sit back and let the bank take any of our land to pay those bills. I'll find a way."

"God's provided a way. That Chicago job pays good money. More in a few weeks than what you make in a couple months on the farm. You can't afford to make a bad impression, son. It's too important."

"Then I'll get Rainey to teach me."

"Teach you what?" His sister marched into the room, blonde hair pulled back in her usual ponytail, and a dusty pair of jeans to show she'd already been out to the barn.

Rainey was born and bred for this type of life. Strong. Independent. Tough. Not some city girl with heels sharp enough to cut up Mama's potatoes.

"Reece wants you to give him speech lessons."

"Speech lessons?" Rainey laughed as she slid onto the barstool next to him at the counter. "I can think of a host of other lessons he needs, but speech?"

"It might help me with my interview."

Rainey rolled her eyes, picked a raw potato slice from Mama's pot, and popped it in her mouth. "I'm not giving you speech lessons.'"

"Why not? You do the same thing Dee does."

"Dee? Who's Dee?"

Reece almost kicked himself for using her name—not even her name, some nickname he'd heard Dr. Murdock call her. Fit her better than Adelina, though, and was a whole lot easier to say. "Dr. Adelina Roseland, the woman staying in grandpa's house."

"Oh, yeah, the new assistant chair." Rainey nodded. "Did you ask *Dee* to give you therapy or something?" Rainey's eyes narrowed. "What'd you do to her?"

"Do to her?" Reece looked to his mother for support, but she only raised her brow clearly in agreement with his sister. Women! "I didn't do nothin' to her. As a matter of fact, *she* asked *me* about therapy. But there ain't no way we'd be a good pair for working together. She don't even like dogs."

That argument alone should have set the record straight, but Mama just stared back unmoved, and Rainey's eyes took on a mischievous glimmer.

Reece pushed away from the bar and pointed toward the window in the direction of grandpa's house. "I was as nice as could be. I helped her find her way out here, offered to unpack her car, and even brought Haus over 'cause she *don't like dogs.*"

Maybe they didn't hear him the first time.

"Well, you're gonna have to be nice to her, Reece Mitchell." Rainey snuck another piece of potato from Mama's pot and gestured to him with it. "Lest you forget, I work with the kids who speak very little or not at all. Accent modification and speech sounds are not my area of expertise." She popped the slice in her mouth and shrugged. "Though the idea of getting to boss one of my big brothers around has lots of merit."

"I bet it does." Reese ignored her wrinkled-up smile and stared through the doorway of the living room, where Lou and Brandon sat watching cartoons with Rainey's girl, Sarah. "I'll take my chances with your bossiness, sis. I've fended it off for years; figure I can handle it for a few mo—"

"What's the matter, brother?" Rainey gave a playful nudge to his arm. "Are you afraid of her?"

Oh, that spilled through him like hot coffee. "I was just thinkin' it'd be less trouble on everybody if you tried to teach me all that accent stuff, than some citified foreigner. She doesn't want to do it."

"She said that? She said she didn't *want* to help you?"

"With everything but her mouth." The thought of her pouty bottom lip nearly distracted him. He groaned and looked back over at the kids. Life was much simpler then. Cartoons, capes, and good old-fashioned hard work. "She kept trying to convince me. Win-win is what she said, but all I see is trouble. Trouble, and probably a whole lot of frustration for both of us."

"Here, son, try a piece of this apple pie." His mom walked over, fork brimming with the golden sweetness she'd just pulled out of the oven.

The scent of cinnamon tickled his taste buds as he accepted her offer. Mama's eyes teemed with mischief, the kind that made him a little nervous. Brown sugar, apples, and butter melted onto his tongue. "It's good, Mama."

"Did you pick those apples for this pie?"

The apple pie turned bitter in his mouth. "Now Mama, you know I—"

"Or make the crust?

"That has nothin' to do with—"

"You realize I put six sour apples in there? Six? And they were sourrr." She drew out the word and winced. "But it don't taste sour, does it? All that good ol' sugar sweetens up them apples. Makes the pie worth its sass."

"Are you sayin' you want me to make her a pie?"

Rainey burst out laughing and hit him with a dishtowel. "How on earth did you ever manage to get a master's degree from Virginia Tech?" She sighed as if his ignorance caused her pain. "Be kind to her and your kindness will rub off, idiot. But heaven help us if you speak more than three sentences to the poor woman. She might realize what a big job she has ahead of her and quit on the spot."

His mama shoved another piece of apple pie into his mouth before he could reply to Rainey's unwanted comments. "Kindness don't take no words." She nodded toward the door. "Sometimes, you can speak more when you don't say nothin'."

Reece growled while he chewed. Ganged up on by the womenfolk. He should have been used to it by now, but it stung every time—probably because they were usually right.

"Son, there's no tellin' what Dee's past has been like. No knowin' if she's had a lovin' family or struggled for long years to make it where she is. Sounds like there's a lot more goin' on than we can see. Usually is." She pushed a tall glass of milk to him. "Time and gentle stirrin' brings the cream to the top."

Reese closed his eyes so Mama didn't spy his thoughts. She believed everybody could change for the better with a spoonful of sweetness, but it wasn't so. His wife never fit in that 'everybody' category, and she was just as much a city girl as Adelina Roseland.

"Gonna git cold tomorrow. I think our new neighbor might need some firewood."

He glanced from his Mom to the door. The homestead and an unwanted lesson in humility stood just beyond the tree line. A grin twitched below his moustache as he caught sight of a four-legged gray hound dog running across the field toward the scattered row of trees. Knowing Haus was on his way back lessened the irritation of going to ask for Dee's help … a little.

A CRASH OUTSIDE jerked Dee from her dreamless sleep. She slid to the end of her bed and pulled her robe about her as she stumbled to the window, forcing her drowsy eyes wide. She'd chosen to use the only bedroom downstairs for now. It made the house feel smaller and not quite as empty, but chills trembled across her skin at the thought of someone on the other side of the wall. Moonlight afforded little answer to the cause of the noise, but another crash followed and the rim of a trashcan rolled into view. Her breath eked out in a tight stream.

Something lurked outside the garage. She slipped into the hall. A pale glow filtered through the windows and haloed the room in ghostly white. Her muscles tensed. She edged across the cold floor on tiptoe, as if the intruder could hear her noiseless footfall. The culprits were probably some mangy raccoons—the kinds that chew through wire or steal the stuffing from inside the seats of people's cars. As she stepped through the kitchen to the back door, she took a frying pan from the stovetop and gripped it like a baseball bat. Whatever it was, it would end up with a concussion if she got a clear shot. She'd never liked furry bandits.

The door slid open without a sound, evidence of some good care to the hinges. Dee kept her body against the open door. One quick move would put her back in the house with locked door between her and whatever spilled the garbage cans. The forest crept in from all sides, shadowed and strange, highlighted by a cascade of ghostly moonlight. She'd forgotten how dark it was in the country. Dark and lonely.

Another crash shook her from the top step and she stumbled forward, the back door slamming behind her. She teetered on the edge of the porch step, suspended in time and moonbeams, like a ballerina on stage. Unlike the ballerina, though, her poise only lasted a second before she lost her balance and tripped with a bump to the ground. Her cast iron weapon thudded to the grass in a rather anti-climactic thump beside of her.

A shuffling sound drew her attention to the shadow beyond the wrecked trashcan. Four legs, and definitely too big for a raccoon. Maybe raccoons weren't such mangy creatures after all. Actually, they were cute. Funny, even. And much smaller than the animal walking toward her.

Coyote. A chill settled across her skin and she froze.

It had been a long time since she'd seen a coyote, but one thing she remembered from her dad. They traveled in packs, or at least pairs.

Her breath thickened with dread. Which meant she was already outnumbered. Another shadow prowled from her left, confirming her fear. Two.

She slid her hand across the ground to grip the handle of the frying pan and the coyotes responded with guttural growls. Icicles of fear tingled over her skin and the frantic pulse in her ears added a soundtrack.

"Get out of here." Her words, meant to command, sputtered out on a whisper, like trying to scream in a nightmare. Nothing. She pushed herself up to her knees and lifted the pan in front of her, pointing it from one mangy beast to the other. "Get out."

Even though her voice gathered volume, the sound only halted the animals' approach for a moment before they stalked closer. Their eyes glowed like spectral orbs in the night, fueling the tremor running through her hard enough to shake her knees. How had it come to this? Dying in backwoods Appalachia in the jaws of coyotes? The thought straightened her spine and she stood, daring the canines to get closer.

"Listen here. There is no way I'm going to die in the middle of nowhere before I get my chance at tenure." The frying pan shook at the same tempo as her words. "So if you want a fight, then bring it on."

The closest coyote crouched to the ground readied to jump. Maybe she'd been a little overconfident. She gripped the frying pan tighter and lifted it up in the air, when all of a sudden another shadow charged from the darkness toward her.

She tried to scream, but her vocal folds didn't even flutter.

Reese Mitchell's grinning dog leapt forward.

He planted himself between her and the coyotes, teeth bared for battle. Her black protector looked bigger than he had this afternoon, stronger—his fur lifted at his neck and ears flattened against the sides of his head. Haus! Haus was his name.

The closest coyote backed away a few inches, but kept his growl as warning. Haus didn't appear fazed. In fact, his vicious snarl grew into an impressive bark. She and the coyotes both flinched. There was a big difference between his smile and his snarl. Big.

One coyote backed further away, still staring for a few more moments before he turned on his heels and ran toward the forest, followed by his companion.

Haus' growl rumbled low until the coyotes disappeared from sight. Just in time for all the strength to leave Dee's weakened legs. She collapsed on the porch steps, body shaking so hard she dropped the pan back into the grass. Haus moved toward her. He kept his head low, as if he knew the creepy smile on his face wouldn't win any favors. Smart dog.

In complete contrast to the mamba rhythm of her pulse, Haus sat on the ground a few feet away and yawned. Yawned? She sniffled through a nervous laugh. Well at least one of them would be sleeping. Her nerves were so raw, she wouldn't be able to calm down for hours. With a hand to the porch railing, she pulled herself to her feet, snatching the pan as she stood. Haus' head perked up.

"I'm going inside now, Dog."

He licked his jaws and placed his head down on his crossed paws, big brown eyes staring up at her. Dee looked around the back yard for a dog's house, but there wasn't anything except the overturned garbage can and miles of darkness.

She took the last two steps up to the covered back porch and sighed. "Well, I suppose you should stay on the porch so you can keep an eye on things." She pointed a finger at him. "But don't get used to it."

Haus' head popped back up and one ear tilted upward.

Dee bit the inside of her lip studying the problem of breaking her own rules about dogs. She cast another glance to the forest and squeezed her eyes closed in resignation. "Come on, then."

As if English was his first language, the dog lifted himself from the ground and ambled to the top of the stairs, taking a place in the shaded corner of the porch. She almost smiled at the big bundle of curled-up black, and for the first time since stepping into her new world, she didn't feel quite so alone.

Haus closed his eyes and snorted into the night, emotions clearly not as high-strung as hers. The dog had to be male. She walked into the kitchen and rubbed her palms down her arms to ward off the residual chill the coyotes left behind. The fireplace glowed with a dying flame, flickering light across the cozy living room furniture. Dee snuck a cookie from the plate on the counter and snatched the brown blanket from the back of the couch—draping it across her shoulders.

Silence whispered a lonesome tune with the thrums of a familiar ache. She tossed in an extra log from the wood stashed nearby and sparks danced a magical mixture of light and smoke into the air.

The flames highlighted the silver strings of the dulcimer, tempting her heart with a taste for something she'd ignored a long time. Ransom's quaint world kept doing that—drawing her mind into vulnerable territory. In the two days she'd spent alone at this house, everything from the morning birdcalls to the fresh smell of dew awakened her mind to a few of the beauties of Appalachian life she'd chosen to forget ... or ignore. She took a deep breath and stepped to the fireplace, resting her fingers against the mantle.

The fretted dulcimer shone with a cherry finish, dark and smooth. The small size hinted the sound would have tenor tones, unlike her uncle's larger one which carried more bass. She smoothed her fingers over the strings, the dulled song soft and familiar, sending a tremor from her fingertips to her heart.

Sting.

She drew back, the touch too painful. If she accepted the small beauties of her past, she'd have to accept it all—wouldn't she? She cleared her blurred vision with a blink and backed away, picking up her newest professional journal on the coffee table. She didn't have time for the past when her dreams waited on the other side of Ransom, and listening to the silence only widened the awareness of her solo path.

Career first.

Success waited on the other side of one handsome cattleman and a ridiculous wager.

Well, she could handle the wager. Her thoughts settled on Reese Mitchell, but her heart responded with anything but a steadied beat.

CHAPTER 4

Oh, men! men!! men!!!
(Pygmalion, Act 3)

Dee turned her car up the gravel road away from her house and began to climb a hill through pastureland. After she found Reese's number and directions, it took the entire day to convince herself to go through with this crazy plan. Traveling to a man's house she barely knew to give him accent modification therapy? Out in the middle of nowhere? What was she thinking?

Desperate times and coyote-filled dreams forced acts of insanity.

From the sound of his commitment over the phone, he was as thrilled about it as she.

Maybe his wife would be there.

As she crested the hill, a two-story farmhouse came into view. Its cream siding and wrap-around front porch stood in contrast to everything she expected from Reese Mitchell. A porch swing rocked in the breeze, inviting a moment's pause from the hectic push-and-pull of her emotions. Empty flowerpots stood to each side of the porch steps—waiting for a bunch of red mums, maybe?

The dark burgundy front door, a simple berry wreath hung for welcome, inched open a floodgate of regrets. Home? Family? Love? Her grip tightened on the steering wheel, forcing the weak feelings to subside. Looks were deceiving—a truth engraved on every chapter of her childhood. Anyone could pretend to have it all together. And in her experience, Appalachian secrets came with drunken nights, dangerous arguments, and enough hypocrisy to cover a lifetime of sins.

As Dee stepped from her car and glanced back toward the way she'd come, her breath caught. The view stretched out over the valley, a splattering of houses decorating the verdant countryside. Various shades of green rolling hills spanned out to the gray-blue mountain ridge in the distance and the horizon beyond. Majestic and marvelous, it called to a hidden place in her soul. She shuddered. Even the scenery hinted at pretense—a shallow beauty.

"You Doc?"

Dee shaded her eyes and looked up to the porch where a young girl with a dark ponytail stood. Grass stains smudged the knees of her jeans and a strip of dirt smeared down one side of her face. Was she the same little girl Reese had with him a few days before?

"Yes, I'm Dr. Roseland."

With one hand hitched to her side and her dimpled chin low, she stretched out a welcome palm with the confidence of an adult. "Daddy told me you'd be comin' today. I'm Lou Mitchell. But Lou ain't my real name. My real name is Louisa, but everybody calls me Lou. You can call me Lou too, if you want. I don't mind none."

A strange mix of fear and warmth fogged Dee's emotions. In grad school her nervousness always impacted the treatment she gave to children—stiff and emotionless. Or worse, she fumbled around with her words and materials as if she didn't have control of the situation. Heat swelled to her cheeks at the memories. One of her graduate supervisors had strongly encouraged Dee to stick with adult therapy.

And Dee had gladly obliged. Like father like daughter.

But Louisa or Lou boasted an easy confidence with the carefree knowledge of a child. Dee stepped closer. "Is your daddy or mama here?"

Lou scrunched up her nose. "I ain't got no Mama. She died."

Her atrocious grammar hit Dee first and then the blow from the little girl's words stopped her steps. No mother? Dee knew that feeling. The rounded blue eyes didn't mirror the loss, or the gaping silence of loneliness—but that would come later. Or maybe the complete absence of a mother left more possibility for hope than the lifelong presence of a bad one.

"I'm sorry."

"Well, Uncle Trigg says Mama probably didn't make it to Heaven for what she and Uncle Gray done." She sighed from a weight much too big for her little shoulders. "But Daddy says God forgives little sins and big ones. So maybe I'll get to see her in Heaven one day after all." She looked up to the sky. "It's gonna rain."

The change in subject merged so matter-of-factly with the rest of her conversation, it took Dee's mind a full five seconds to catch up. How could children state such complex and large things so plainly? And God's forgiveness? Well, Dee didn't even want to go there. Some sins were too big for forgiveness, and if not, God had some explaining to do.

"May I speak to your daddy?"

"Sure, you can. Come on in, it's gonna be a while."

"It's going to be a while?" Dee followed Lou up the porch steps and into the house. "Isn't your Dad here?"

The faint hint of cinnamon met her as she crossed the threshold. Reese Mitchell didn't strike her as the baking type, but if she wasn't mistaken, the delicious aroma matched the scent of cinnamon rolls. Dee swallowed back the mouth-watering thought and continued down a hallway of clean beige walls—bare as if freshly painted. The little girl led the way across rug-covered oak floors and made a half circle through the kitchen into a long living room with a fireplace similar to the one in Dee's house. Furniture, pictures, and decorations looked pretty scarce. Dee almost stopped to examine the one portrait in the room. One of Reese and two children—a little boy and then Louisa, but she shook off the curiosity. She didn't come here for personal information—business. Strictly business.

"Your dad's not here?"

Louisa sat down on the living room rug in front of an exquisite wooden dollhouse. "Nope. He had to go and help Gypsy in the field."

Gypsy? Who on earth would name their child Gypsy? "And he'll be gone a while?"

Dee's hope plummeted at the little girl's dark-headed nod.

"Ain't no tellin' how long he'll be gone. We got some lemonade if you want something to drink."

"He left you here alone?" A seven-year-old, all alone? *Not impressive, Mr. Mitchell.*

"He's just out in the field. That ain't but a hop-skip." The girl looked up, nonplussed. "Emma's in the back room with my brother, Brandon, so we ain't alone. Granny's just down the hill." She went back to her dollhouse. "And Mustard and Mavis are in the back yard too."

Dee must have heard wrong. "Mustard?"

"He's our 'coon dog."

The dog's name was Mustard, and the cattleman left to help some poor woman named Gypsy? Dee looked heavenward for help in clarity ... or strength. Could her predicament get any worse?

"Ms. Doctor, you up for playin' dolls with me while you wait?"

The simple request compounded with the news of Lou's mother's death turned Dee's heart and well-laid plans to mush. Even if she didn't like children, how could she refuse? "Maybe for a little while."

The bittersweet moment plunged Dee into memories she'd ignored for years. An absent mother, a father who worked hard to counteract her mother's illness, and two children who hid from the rants of a drunken madwoman. She couldn't recall playing dolls, but as Louisa gave her assignments, she found herself taking a mental snapshot for later. Her therapists would have been proud. Building positive memories to replace the bad ones became an overarching assignment—one she'd tried to perform by making top scores in school and a myriad of awards. But something in this simple moment fed a barren place.

"Now the family's gonna pray before they go to bed," Louisa said. "They need to thank God for the new mommy God brought 'em." Louisa looked up. "You got the mommy. She's supposed to kiss the young'uns good night and tell 'em she loves 'em."

Dee's fragile grip on control unwound with a drop in her stomach. Tears swelled into her vision and she blinked them away, following Louisa's instructions.

"Ms. Doctor, you don't have to cry because Daddy's not here." Lou stared up at her and offered a reassuring smile. "He always comes back."

The words tore Dee's raw emotions. This was ridiculous! She pressed a palm to her stomach and stood to her feet. "Thank you, Louisa. I think I need to use your bathroom, though."

"Well, sure, it's right down the hall."

Dee almost ran to escape. Tears quaked her shoulders, building until the bathroom door snapped closed behind her. She released her pent-up grief into balled-up tissues, muffling her sobs. A mother who will stay? A father who always comes back? Pain knifed to the marrow of her soul, opening wounds hidden beneath denial and secrets. Her mother spent too much time away to play dolls with her or even kiss her goodnight. But her father? She sniffed against the tissue. No, she couldn't remember her father giving goodnight kisses either. He'd always been working—hard, long hours.

Had she ever known the tenderness of love that Louisa acted out with her doll family? Her thoughts paused on Granny Roseland and the way her wrinkled hands smoothed across Dee's forehead at night before bed. Those summers at her house provided brief and beautiful respite from a home-life turned on its head. Was that a taste of what love could be? A gentle hand? A good-night kiss? The grief and anger washed over her in quiet waves until her feet landed on firm control again.

She stood and pressed her fist to her chest. What sort of grown woman cried over playing dolls? She forced her mind to wrangle in the spiraling questions. The hard thrumming of her heart slowed along with the tears, and self-preservation veiled the pang of heartache like a shield. With a quick check to the mirror, and a grimace at her blotched reflection, she re-twisted her dark hair into a bun and left the room.

A young woman, maybe early twenties or younger, knelt in the floor by Lou, helping her pick up doll pieces. Honey-colored hair fell in straight layers across the shoulders of her upscale floral blouse. She looked up and smiled, her caramel eyes brimming with welcome. "Well, hi," she offered in her easy drawl. "You must be Doc."

Adelina.

"Yes, Dr. Adelina Roseland."

"Nice to meet you." Her long legs unwound into a stand and she held out her hand. "I'm Emma, Reese's youngest sister. I was just in the back taking care of Brandon's diaper before I hauled the kids over to Mama's house while Reese finishes up in the field." Her accent came out slow and gentle. "Said he's havin' some trouble with Gypsy."

"Is he far?"

"Who? Reese?" Emma leaned down and placed the last doll furniture pieces away. "Not far. Just up on the next ridge. We got our cows back there."

The sky outside the front window sent mixed signals. From the hilltop view, puffs of cloud and dimming rays of sunlight moved across an aging afternoon sky. She really didn't have time to waste, and he couldn't be very far. After all, country treks made up her early life too. Why couldn't she work on his accent while he did his farming? It's how she'd studied for tests through high school and undergrad. And those times weren't *that* long ago.

"You can wait here until he gets back, if you want?" Emma offered. "Or you can come have some fresh-baked chocolate chip cookies with me and the kids. Brandon's already in the car so we have room for at least one more."

"I think I'll just walk over and see if I can help Mr. Mitchell."

"Help Reese? In the field?" Emma swept a glance from Dee's suit

43

down to her heels and shoved her hands in her pockets. "Okay." She drew out the word and quirked a brow. "Um, do you want some boots?"

A row of grungy farm boots lined the back wall of the kitchen. Dee stilled a tiny cringe in her shoulders. "I think I'll be fine. Thanks."

Emma's eyes widened for a minute. "Alright, Doc. Just hate to see you ruin those nice pumps. Are those Michael Kors or?" Emma gasped. "Chloe?"

Dee stared down at her shoes and back to the country girl who really shouldn't be able to guess her shoe type. "Um ... Chloe."

"Wow. I have a pair I bought at this fantastic designer consignment shop in town. If you ever want to check it out, let me know." Her smile brimmed with appreciation as she waved her fingers to Dee's suit. "Of course, you probably don't shop in places like that."

"Thanks for the tip ... Emma, was it? I might have to take a look."

Lou's attention volleyed between both ladies and she finally released a massive sigh. "All this talk about shoes havin' names is plum crazy. Shoes is shoes."

Emma laughed, a lovely trill, took Lou's hand and walked toward the door. "Oh, just wait, Lou. When you try on your first pair of Audrey Brookes," Emma sighed and fluttered her fingers in the air. "Or even better Adrienne Maloof, your life will never be the same."

With Emma's persuasive adoration, Dee felt compelled to drop everything and make a mad dash to this little consignment shop. Oh, how long had it been since she splurged on something frivolous and beautiful?

"Come on, Lou, let's get over to Granny's." Emma held the door for Dee to exit and tossed another grin. "You'd better take your phone with ya, Doc, in case you get lost."

Dee followed the two outside, still contemplating her degree of desperation and the magnetic pull of a promising good deal. As if in answer her phone buzzed with a text from Alex Murdock. *Hope all is well. 11 weeks until show time. Is the game still on?*

Dee looked over the countryside again and groaned. In surrender, she texted back.

Yes.

She slipped her phone into her pocket. No turning back now.

"Nice to meet you, Doc." Emma rested one hand on the car door and gestured with the other. "The trail goes through the back pasture and then up the hill. Reese should be in the next field."

"Thank you."

Lou reached up and gave Dee a quick hug. "Thanks for playing dolls with me. You have a good mommy voice."

Dee stood frozen in place as she watched Lou skip off to her aunt's Camry. The sweetness of the comment paired with the hug nearly sent Dee racing back to the tissue box. She turned away from the car and squeezed her eyes closed. This was ridiculous. She was an emotional wreck over a dollhouse, cinnamon, and a little girl's hug? Maybe Appalachia *did* drive people to distraction!

With one last glance at the cloudy sky, she turned and marched around to the back yard. A gold and white beagle charged forward, sounding out his welcome. *Mustard.*

"I'm not going to bother you, Dog. I only want to find your master."

The dog cocked his head as if listening to each word. Dee walked around him, keeping a safe distance from his muddy face and her pantsuit. "I should not have to resort to this to find Reese Mitchell."

The dog's head perked up at the name and then he charged down the hill, stopping halfway. He looked back to Dee and waited. She stared at him. He stared back. There was no way that dog understood her, was there? The animals here were crazy. One smiled, and both spoke English. Maybe it all really was one long bad dream.

As she neared the dog, he took off running further down the hill and then stopped for her to catch up again. Her heels sank into the earth a few times, leaving clods on the backs of her shoes and slowing her forward momentum, but she'd come too far to turn back now.

Reese's beat-up truck sat at the bottom of the hill Mustard started climbing, so Reese had to be close. She followed the dog up the short but steep embankment, more than once relying on her heels as scaffolding in the earth to keep her from falling backward. Oh, yes, this was another reason she wanted to get out of Ransom as quickly as possible. Civilization. Sidewalks. Escalators. Air that didn't smell like dank and pungent manure.

Her Calvin and Hobbes proved almost prophetic as it referred to reality spinning life out of control.

Oh, what she wouldn't give for a tall, single-shot, caramel latte right now. She grabbed the next tree, a clearing in sight. *On a veranda overlooking the Shenandoah Valley.* A branch snagged her bun and sent half of her hair into a frenzy. *Eating a chocolate donut with cream in the middle.* She took another valiant step. *Without one cow, tractor, or cattle farmer in sight.*

Her gaze rose above the tree line to the cloudy sky. *God, is this some funny and somewhat sadistic dream to torture me for not going to church in ten years?* What else exhibited the wrath of God on a wanna-be high class professional more than hiking up a soggy bank in heels to find an Appalachian cattle farmer who was helping some poor woman named Gypsy? Judgment produced an acute sting, or was that the slap of a branch to the back of her head?

With the painful nudge of the tree-branch and the determination of promotion spurring her on, she crested the hill. Trees parted to reveal a large pasture with a one-hundred-eighty-degree view of the countryside—and right in the middle of the field bent Reese Mitchell in a position she'd never hoped to see anyone in again.

He stood covered in mud, OB chain in hand, assisting in birthing a calf.

REESE HAD to be seeing things. Maybe fighting with the cow for the past hour caused him to lose his mind. That was his only explanation for visions of Dr. Roseland stomping toward him in a navy pantsuit and heels, eyes narrowed for a fight. Mustard led the way.

She looked downright fascinating.

"There you are." She hissed and wobbled a little on her heels. Her hair fell in wild strands from her bun around her pink face. "What are you doing?"

If it was a dream, he'd play along. "I'm sipping tea and eating bonbons. What does it look like I'm doin'?"

Her face turned all shades of red. "Listen here, Mr. Mitchell, I didn't walk all the way up here to be insulted. We had an appointment and you didn't—"

Her foot landed smack in the middle of what the cows left behind. Yep, it must be a dream, 'cause that'd be exactly something he'd imagine. He laughed. She sent him a look to curdle his insides. The cow made a mournful sound and Reese tightened his hold on the OB chain he'd just fastened to the unborn calf's ankles. He'd pulled on the chain for the past fifteen minutes, hoping to get the calf out before he lost both the baby and the mama.

"I'd love to hear all about how much you need to fix my speech, but right now I have a cow in trouble. So, I'll have to pass."

"I'm beginning to think fixing you is way out of my league. A team approach might be more fitting."

Daggone it, even her little snarl looked cute.

Focus, Mitchell—and not on the brunette.

"I didn't take you as a quitter, Doc."

"I am not a quitter. It's just that—" She placed her hands on her hips and stared hard enough to wipe his smile clean off his face. "You could have called me. Said something like" —she put on her best imitation— "I ain't got no time to meet with you today, Doc. I gotta go birth a cow."

Reese's grin stretched wide. "You do that real good. Makes me like you more."

If he didn't know better, she almost relaxed those tight lips of hers into a smile.

"I don't really care if you like me or not. I'm here to help you with your job interview and me with my research, not be likeable."

Reese held the chain with one hand and used his other to wipe his brow. "You beat all, woman. You come all the way up here to work on my speech? I thought at least the house was afire or something' worth all the effort."

"I was under the impression this interview *was* worth something to you. And my name is Adelina, not *woman*."

He groaned but didn't dare agree out loud. In fact, this job made the difference between keeping the farm together and selling it off in pieces. The thought about broke his heart.

Another contraction tightened the chain and pulled his attention back to the cow. "Come on, Gypsy. You can do this, girl."

"Gypsy? The cow's name is Gypsy?"

"Alright, Doc, either stop your yappin' or come help me. Unless you ain't got the stomach for it."

She took the minor challenge with a lifted chin. Marching closer, she reached down into his bag and drew out a pair of his sterilized gloves. With the ease of familiarity, she snapped them onto her hands and walked over to him, wiping her filthy heel against the grass in front of Reese, no doubt out of pure spite. "Ain't is not a word."

Now he *knew* he wasn't dreaming.

"What are you doin'?"

"You said either stop talking or come help." She ran her hand along the side of the cow's abdomen. "She's having another one. Pull."

The chain in Reese's hand tightened with Gypsy's contraction. It was a good thing one female in his presence was the gentle sort, and he wasn't thinking about the Doc. Gypsy was about as close to a pet as a cow could get, which was a blessing in disguise if trouble with birthing arose. At least she'd stay put so he had a chance at helping her. He pulled down on the chain and a pair of black front hooves came into view. About time. He was exhausted. The mama had to be worse.

Blessed silence followed for a minute while Dee examined the hooves.

"Words that end with 'ing'?"

"Yeah?"

"The 'ing' is there for a reason. Use it. Pull."

Reese grunted but complied with her command about the cow.

The calf's front ankles emerged. The little thing was gettin' a whole lot closer to daylight. He replayed his own sentence back in his mind, *'getting a whole lot closer.'* Good grief, he was even thinking with more 'ings.

"She's so close." Dee took hold of the chain above Reese's grasp. "Pull."

As she leaned back to help tug, her gloved hands slipped over the chain. In a flash she'd landed firmly against him and all that wild hair pressed right up onto this face. The silky dark mess smelled like lemons and green apples. Both sour. He fought his grin.

"Sorry." She pushed away and dusted off her suit as if she'd landed on something dirty. "I slipped."

A beautiful rush of rose spread across her cheeks and he liked it a little too much. She was one weird puzzle to figure out. For being a high-class city girl, this woman sure knew a thing or two about cows. "Where did you grow up?"

Doc rubbed the cow's side again. "Keene, VA."

"Keene, VA?" He almost let go of the chain. "That ain't." Reese caught himself. "That isn't a city."

"I never said I was from the city." Dee stepped back to the cow. "I see the head. Oh, it's a little black head."

For somebody who didn't like animals, she seemed awful excited about the calf's head. Did the woman even know what she liked and didn't like? Reese pulled again and the head popped through.

"You got a good look at him?"

"Have. Do you *have* a good look at him?" She examined the calf's face with her fingers. "He's not responding. His tongue is dark. We have to get him out of there."

Reese pulled again and took hold of the sides of the calf to help the shoulders slide out, Dee beside him all the way. The crazy woman in a blue pantsuit and heels knew how to birth a cow? Reese couldn't even find words to speak, and even if he could, she'd probably correct them. He was going to beg Rainey to teach him, possibly pay her.

Another tug and he caught the calf as it slid from its mama to the ground. It lay motionless on the grass. Reese passed a handful of hay to Doc and she waved it under the calf's face without one directive. As she swabbed the calf's nose and mouth, Reese took the calf's front legs and pressed them into its body, in and out, working the new lungs. The calf sneezed. Good sign.

"Oh! The little thing is breathing." Dee smiled up at him and the entire awkward scene slowed down.

She'd been pretty before, but when she smiled, a genuine smile, she literally took his breath—her face flushed from exertion and framed by a wind-blown halo of dark hair. Man, in all his life he'd never imagined city and country could mix so well, even more surprising than Jana.

The calf sneezed again, drawing Reese out of his embarrassing trance. The little thing moved its head and even tried to push himself up. Gypsy turned and nuzzled her baby, animating the calf even more.

"So, Keene, Virginia, is where you learned about birthing cows?"

Dee took off the gloves and nodded. "My father used to own a farm in Keene. He had a few hired hands because the farm was more of a hobby than a job for him. His *real* job was as a professor at UVA."

Reese digested the new information for a minute. So, country-born Adelina Roseland wanted to leave her roots and be a city girl? Why would such a smart woman want something like that? "I don't know of too many folks who have farming as a hobby. It's a livelihood for most."

"He'd inherited it. It was family land."

Family land? Now *that* he knew a lot about. "You have any brothers to help your Dad on his farm?"

"Are you implying that I wasn't enough?" She firmed her palm against one hip.

Reese tried to hide his grin, but it must not have worked.

"A girl can't work as well on a farm as a boy, Mr. Mitchell?"

Reese's palms flew up in surrender. "Now I ain't sayin' that, Doc."

"Ain't is not a word."

"My sister Rainey's worked as hard on the farm as either me or my brother. Emma? Well, she came along so much later, she ain't." He took a deep breath to control his frustration. "She hasn't had to do as much." He shrugged an apology. "You're just not like Rainey."

A round of thunder interrupted her sure-fire rebuttal.

"Better get this little 'un out of the rain."

"Rain?"

Reese gestured toward the sky. "We're gonna need to hone those country girl skills of yours, Doc. You're a bit out of practice. Now ..." He adjusted his cap on his head. "Unless you can do some impressive running in those fancy shoes of yours, I think we're about to get wet. Come on."

Reese wrestled the calf away from its mama and started a slow pace to his truck. The calf made quiet calls in his arms, urging Gypsy to follow. Dee grabbed the bag of OB tools and came alongside him as if she'd always belonged. Somehow, in a weird sort-of-otherworldly-kind of way, she fit.

Another blast of thunder quickened Reese's pace. The mama kept up, and so did Dee. Just as they reached the tree line, the heavens opened. Dee tripped, but caught herself before landing face first in the damp grass and earth.

"I should have taken Emma up on her offer."

"What was that?"

"Boots."

Maybe she wasn't such a smart woman after all. Whatever country-girl-sense flowed through her veins likely disappeared along with her accent. A pantsuit and heels in a cow pasture? He almost chuckled from the absurdity. One look at the steep grade of the hill down to his truck and he swallowed the chuckles right back down his throat. Especially with the rain.

"Doc, grab my arm and hold on so we can save that purdy suit of yours."

"Pretty. The word is pretty, not purdy."

He looked down, her face so close it made him feel all warm inside. "I have a hankerin' to leave you and your *purdy* suit right back in the woods to get some peace and quiet."

Her eyes widened and she snatched his arm tight. "You wouldn't."

His grin made no promises. "You got anything else you want to say about my vowels and consonants right now?"

She offered him a smile so sweet it had *danger* written all over it. "I have a wealth of vowels and consonants I'd like to use, but since I'm a lady *and* I like this suit, I'll refrain. For now."

The rain crashed against them in torrents. He was wet clean through, but barely felt it. Dee's hands wrapped around his arm and her face buried in his shoulder, little shield from the blasts of the storm. Despite her sassy disposition, a protectiveness welled up inside him. He hadn't felt such a strong attraction in a long time, a connection. And now? To some country-turned-city girl? Why didn't life make sense more often than not?

Once they reached flat ground, she rushed ahead to the truck. Reese followed, placing the calf in the back and starting the engine with the heat wide open.

"We made it." Doc leaned back in the seat and sighed. Her hair fell in little wet curls around her face, and the cab got a whole lot hotter than it ought to be. Reese put the truck in gear and moved forward at a slow pace to the barn so Gypsy could keep up.

"What took you from Keene to here?"

"This job." She stared out the window. "When daddy died, the farm was split between me and my older brother. Jason didn't want the old house on the property, so he took a little more of the land and built his own place. He still runs the farm."

"There are a lot of good farms up there. My uncle owns one. I used to spend summers with him helpin' out. He's been trying to get me up there for three years." A little dream he fed every once in a while, when no one was lookin'. A smaller farm of his own in the middle of farming country so he could still do research and consulting sounded good—a little too good to hang much hope on it, though. "I've had several consults up that way. It's a good place."

"Consults?" Doc tried to brush some of the rain off of her jacket sleeves.

"Just so you know, I wasn't consultin' them on how to speak proper English."

He won her smile. "What a relief."

"I consult on cattle care and management. Been doin' it for years to supplement the farm income. With the economy like it is, though, I hadn't had as many private pays, so the Chicago offer is good." He pulled the truck up to the barn, rain still spinning rivulets down the windshield. "Be right back."

Once he got the calf and its mama settled in a cozy corner of the barn, he ran back to the truck. "Miss me?"

Dee stared at him a moment and then looked away. "You sounded just like my dad. It must be a country boy thing."

"Your dad must have been a good fella."

"A hard worker, like you." Dee nodded and stared back out the window, her profile sober "You're more jovial. He was a pretty serious man." She gave a humorless laugh. "Definitely long-suffering and driven. Some of the qualities that took him to full professor at UVA."

Reese let the silence sit for a minute. Loneliness tinged her words. Loneliness and determination. "You want to return to Charlottesville? Be like him?"

"As soon as I can."

Reese pulled his truck up beside Doc's car. Any thoughts of attraction for Dee Roseland died with the engine. She was passing through, and his family didn't need any more emotional roller coasters.

"Thank you for the ride, Mr. Mitchell." Doc placed her hand on the door and turned his way. "I can honestly say it's been the most interesting speech therapy session I've had in my life."

"Glad I could liven things up a bit for you, Doc."

She grinned. "See you Friday at my office?"

"Yes, ma'am."

"Without the cow."

"I'll do my best, but I ain't promising nothin'."

Her frown didn't match the glint in her eyes. "Mr. Mitchell, *ain't* is not a word."

With that, she slammed the door, leaving the faint hint of apples behind. He couldn't help notice her uneven walk from the dirt clods clinging to her shoes. Well, he probably could've helped it, but didn't. A figure like hers rarely went unnoticed.

Heat crept up the back of his neck. Rainey *had* to give him speech therapy. There wasn't any other option. Dr. Adelina Roseland hit upon his weakness for smart, witty, brunette city girls, but he'd learned a lot in the past two years. A painful lot. Neither he nor his family needed another woman with a restless heart.

CHAPTER 5

*You must be reasonable, Mr. Higgins: really you must. You can't walk over
everybody like this. (Pygmalion, Act 2)*

D ee pushed open her office door, bone-weary from a late
night of class preparation, and the scent hit her. Blueberry
muffins and coffee. The piece of toast she'd crammed in
her mouth as she ran out the door barely made a dent on her appetite.
A muffin waited on her desk on a paper plate complete with napkin,
and the coffee sat beside in a Styrofoam cup with a note attached.

*Hope you didn't catch cold from the rain. The best way to start the
morning is with a full stomach.*

Mama Mitchell

Dee blinked twice and reread the note. Mama Mitchell? Who was
Mama Mitchell and how did she get into Dee's office? Dee collapsed
into her desk chair and reread the note while her computer booted
up, the fresh-baked aroma causing havoc with her growling stomach.
Reese's mother? The same lady who left the magnificent feast at her
rental house?

Hunger overcame caution. She pulled the muffin from the bag and took one slow, tantalizing bite. Her eyes fluttered closed as buttery warmth and blueberry sweetness melted across her tongue in fresh, homemade uniqueness. Good heavens, that woman calmed Dee's nerves with a combination of sugar and flour like nobody else. Dee reread the card, wondering if Mrs. Mitchell looked or acted anything like her scruffy son.

The rolling hills outside her window brought Reese Mitchell to mind. Despite her best attempts, a smile slid onto her lips at the memory of him and the calf. His raw authenticity appealed to her wounded spirit. He certainly wasn't someone to escort her around the gilded halls of UVA, and formal gatherings probably made him cringe, but he left a very different impression with her heart than she'd anticipated … or wanted. She wanted to trust him.

She drew her attention from the window to focus on her university email account. The third message made her choke down her next bite of muffin. It came from Dr. Shaye Russell, chair of the department, and reminded her of their first faculty meeting at 8:30. *This morning.*

Dee looked down at her clock. 8:29. Brilliant. If only the Internet made some sort of connection at her house. She could work out a word-math problem faster than a Google search on her ancient digital connection. With a sigh, she shoved away from the desk, snatched up her laptop, and halfway ran down the hallway, praying the meeting was in the one conference room she remembered from her brief tour.

Voices reached her from the conference room, adding another thrum or two to her heartbeat. She slowed her pace, took a few deep breaths to calm down, and stepped into the doorway. A small group of three men and four women gathered around an oval table in the small room. One man, with a very Richard Gere-ish sort of professional look, sat in deep conversation with a younger woman, blond hair pulled back in a ponytail. Another gentleman sat at the end of the table, fingers flying over the keyboard of his laptop. The typing only came to a halt as he glanced up to note her presence.

"Good morning, Dr. Roseland."

Dee met the gray-blue eyes of the woman at the head of the table, a woman who commanded attention with the lift of her chin.

Dee extended her hand as she approached the obvious leader. "Good morning, Dr. Russell."

They'd only met twice, and both times in a group of two or more, but Shaye Russell gave off every intimidation-vibe known to man ... or woman. Her short, classically spiked salt-and-pepper hair fit the direct shift of her expression. To the point.

"Welcome. I hope you are settling well?"

"Yes, thank you for your recommendation on the house."

Dr. Russell's expressions softened almost imperceptibly. "Grace Mitchell is a one-of-a-kind lady. She always takes care of her tenants."

"Yes." Dee shifted her weight and scanned the room again, forcing the lie out of her mouth. *Think promotion. Think promotion.* "It's a pleasure to be here."

The admittance hurt less than she thought it would, but Dr. Russell's keen attention seemed to pick up on Dee's reservation ... or maybe Dee was paranoid. The Chair's searching stare sent a warning tingle down Dee's spine. The room grew quiet.

Dr. Russell turned to the others. "As you know, I am spearheading this collaboration with our department at UVA and Dr. Adelina Roseland has come to join us from Charlottesville to assist me. Our first year is somewhat of a trial—to gauge interest and the effectiveness of the idea. The grant is for two years, as we find our feet, so to speak." Her gaze grew intense. "And we *know* the need in this part of Virginia to offer such a program, so we are going to *make* it work. Isn't that right, people?"

A swell of verbal consents followed. Dee shifted on her feet again and placed her laptop on the table in front of her.

Dr. Russell focused on Dee, the directness of her attention a bit disconcerting. "All concerns, questions, and complaints can come to me and we'll tackle this opportunity together." There was a hint of challenge in Dr. Russell's last sentence, almost as if she expected Dee to test her. "As a team."

Dee nodded and took the proffered seat. "I look forward to being a part of the team."

Dr. Russell hesitated, gaze still searching Dee's face before she gestured to the others in the room. "Some of us have worked together for a few years developing prerequisite courses so expansion into a graduate program wouldn't be as large a transition. Dr. Theodore Ryken began teaching a few introductory courses for a Communicative Disorders minor about three years ago."

The Gere-ish gentleman's bright blue eyes crinkled at the edges as he offered her a broad smile. Not exactly the two-hundred-year-old geriatric she'd pictured in her mind. Another kick to her negative presumptions.

"Nice to have you, Dr. Roseland." The gentleman's accent placed his origin somewhere in the New England states. Hmm, another outsider? "If there's any way I can assist you, all you need to do is ask."

Dee nodded her thanks and gripped the edge of her laptop to calm the slightest tremors to her hands. Maybe she wasn't ready to be an Assistant Chair, if only for this grant. She couldn't even meet new professionals without shaking like jelly on a plate.

"A list of projected teaching assignments is on your agenda and should concur with the previous list I sent out last week." Dr. Russell tilted her chin toward one of the young women across the table from her. "Dr. Ryken and Dr. Elizabeth Simpkins will assist you with covering the adult courses."

"Glad to have you." The woman with caramel-colored hair framing a set of similarly colored eyes grinned. "And I ought to offer my condolences. I'm sorry you're trapped at Mitchell's Crossroads with that crazy clan."

"Like you can say anything, Liz." The blonde next to her rolled her eyes to the dark-haired woman at her right as if everyone understood the subtle innuendo of her comment. "Lizzie spent most of her childhood at Mitchell's Crossroads, Dee. She's practically part of our crazy clan."

Did everyone assume her name was Dee? And did the woman say our *crazy clan?*

With a light laugh, the blonde stood and offered her hand. "I'm Rainey Mitchell. Kept my maiden name."

Dee paused in her handshake. Mitchell? Another one?

"Ms. Rainey Mitchell is our child language specialist." Dr. Russell interjected. "Along with Paige Ramsey, whose area of expertise is early intervention and pediatric feeding."

"Welcome to Ransom, Dr. Roseland." Paige's voice came soft and somewhat reserved. Maybe a bit of kindred spirit lived in those walnut brown eyes of hers.

"Glad to have you here." Mrs. Mitchell responded with a well-cloaked accent, only a few hints in her vowels. "Lizzie, Paige, and I will be happy to show you around when you have the chance." Rainey nudged Dr. Simpkins; their obvious camaraderie nursed Dee's ache for friendship. "We've been here most our lives, well, except Paige. But we've inaugurated her so now she knows all the best places too."

A magnetic pull stemmed from the warmth in Rainey's eyes—sheer friendliness. It reminded her of Reese, but the similarities stopped there. Instead of Reese's milk-chocolate gaze, Rainey's eyes shimmered with hues of pale blue-green, her honey blond hair in direct contrast to her brother's black. But they smiled in the same way. Generously.

"Thank you."

"I'm sorry you had the unfortunate opportunity to visit my brother yesterday." Rainey shook her head with mock sympathy from the crook of her lips. "Not exactly the way we'd planned on welcoming you to the community—a cow birthing and a rainstorm."

Several heads popped up with Rainey's comment and Dee's face grew warm. She squeezed her hands together in her lap. The temptation to bury her face in her hands sent a twinge through her fingers. Not exactly the type of information she hoped to build her reputation in academia. Her stomach twisted another knot of discomfort.

"It's certainly been memorable."

"Memorable?" Rainey laughed, full and without reserve. "Well, we can offer you memorable if nothing else."

"Amen to that." Dr. Ryken added.

"Oh, you poor thing. What an introduction," Paige added.

"Just don't come to my house, Adelina." Lizzie shook her head. "My mother is bent on marrying off as many single women as she can before God takes her home. And she's not too picky about the matches either."

"Might I interject?" Dr. Ryken lifted a hand. "She doesn't focus solely on single women."

"Oh, that's right, Teddy." Rainey flatted her palms against the table with a chuckle. "The Irish organist."

Lizzie waved her hand like a warning flag. "Don't worry, Dee. I'll keep Mom away from you, but I can't promise the same kind of protection from Rainey's family."

Dr. Russell cleared her throat. "Ladies, I believe this conversation can be continued at your lunch break."

"Right, Shaye." Rainey slid Dee a look. "Lizzie's mom scares Shaye to death too."

The group laughed together. The collegiality bounced off the walls and hit her with the renewed sense of her place as an outsider. Nothing new. She'd been looking *in* for years, it seemed. But maybe now, with an earned doctorate, she'd find her place? *Prove* her place.

"In the back, we have Dr. Devansh Khatri, whose specialty is voice and adult swallowing."

"Call me Devan." He stood and took her hand, devilishly handsome with his dark olive skin and jet-black hair and eyes. *Yep, he gives off all the bad boy vibes.* "It's easier to say in America." His Indian accent curled his vowels in an intriguing way that reminded her of Dr. Kadakia at UVA, the cognitive language professor who captivated every graduate student's attention with his suave personality.

"Nice to meet you." She took his hand.

"And finally, we have Dr. Maxwell Roberts. He is our resident audiologist who will provide some adjunct courses for our students."

Dee pulled her hand from Dr. Khatri's and focused on the copper-haired man at the end of the table. He sent a nod of recognition before returning to his computer.

"We have a challenging year ahead of us and I expect everyone to be ready to give one hundred percent to this program." Dr. Russell turned to Dee, her gaze needling her point. "Though we are collaborating with UVA, we need to succeed in our own right as a department and program."

Dee swallowed down the sour taste of fear and breathed in confidence. She could do this. She *would* do this. One small step for Ransom's program, one giant leap for Dee's future.

"All faculty members must create their own clinics for graduate training." Dr. Russell continued. "As many of you know, The Tolliver Center is a solid resource for clients, particularly the pediatric population, and might prove a helpful starting point for those of you who are newer to the area. Caseload numbers should be accounted for by the end of next month with clinics ready to begin in January."

Dee's throat closed. Caseload? How was she supposed to develop a caseload? She didn't have any contacts in Ransom, let alone the names of facilities that treated adults with speech disorders or accent modification needs.

"No problem, Shaye." Rainey Mitchell perked up and turned her attention to Dee. "I would guess you don't have a lot of contacts yet, Dee. The Tolliver Center has loads of kids who need services. I can take you over to start some screenings next week, and Lizzie's clinic at the rehab center would be a good place to pick up some more clients. Adults, even. We all have a lot to do, you know. It's good to have some help when you're new and green to all this."

A defensive edge rose in response to Rainey's words. She wasn't *green*. Simply because she was new at being a professor didn't equal new to giving therapy. Dee's budding frustration sprouted horns. "I'm certain to be tasked with learning the ropes of my advanced position, so your help would be most appreciated, *Ms.* Mitchell."

Dee inwardly cringed at the sound of condescension lacing her words. Had she really just drawn attention to Rainey's mere master's degree? Out loud? In front of the whole room? She sounded like Alex Murdock on a really bad day.

Her stomach dropped. She never wanted to be like him, not even a little. That mental acknowledgement sent Dee's emotions reeling into shameful regret. Perhaps Rainey didn't pick up on the tone?

No such luck. Her golden brows perked high and the smile in her eyes faded. Dee wanted to cry on the spot. Rainey Mitchell didn't deserve the wrath of Dee's insecurities.

"Right. I see." Rainey tapped the notebook in front of her, gaze unswerving. "Let me know if you change your mind. We're always in need of people who want to serve others at the Tolliver Center, but only those willing to get dirty and make a difference need apply."

Dee squeezed her eyes closed a moment and prayed to sink into her chair. She could practically feel the heat from Dr. Russell's disapproval.

"And since you are the liaison for us to the main campus in Charlottesville," Dr. Russell added, "we'll need to schedule regular meetings so we can send reports once a month to note progress. The grant has specific protocol for success—and *friendly* collaboration is key to that success."

Notes of resentment with a crescendo of warning highlighted each syllable of Dr. Russell's speech. *Perfect.* Stuck in the middle of nowhere with an enemy who had more power than she did, an offended coworker, and a cattle farmer with enough vowel changes to take-up yodeling. This didn't bode well at all. What was the old saying about catching more flies with honey?

She needed to buy stock in honeybees.

"I look forward to sharing all the opportunities we'll provide to the people in rural Appalachia. I'm certain Charlottesville will be impressed." She focused her attention on Rainey, hoping her efforts to make amends might be noted. "I know I can learn a lot from you all." She'd make a note to apologize in person later, after she hid in shame for three days. "Thank you for your offer."

The meeting moved forward with the comfort of nails on a chalkboard, but besides Dr. Russell, the other faculty members seemed pleasant at most, indifferent at least. Except for the gnawing look of disappointment on Rainey's face, and the deeper root of it in Dee's heart.

She bit her bottom lip and kept a firm stare on the screen of her laptop. No wonder she'd never kept friendships long enough to develop the depth of intimacy evident in Lizzie Simpkins and Rainey Mitchell's. Pain knifed straight to her heart. Another pinch of failure —no, this was more like a slap. Maybe she didn't know how to make friends—or at least keep them very long.

She ached through final discussions of courses, start dates, and menial administrative changes. When Dr. Russell reiterated the importance of clinic numbers, the Chair's gaze shot Dee an exclamation point.

The whole population of Ransom, Virginia, could benefit from accent modification therapy, but she doubted volunteers waited at her door to sign up. The thought of working with children added another item to her list of reasons to leave Ransom and another kick to her self-confidence. Children didn't like her. Lou Mitchell's sweet face popped to mind, unbidden.

Okay, maybe there was one very small and cute exception. But only one.

Dee slipped from the room as soon as the meeting adjourned, without one glance at her colleagues to confirm her humiliation. She sprinted a direct path to her office at an Olympian speed-walker pace.

"Dr. Roseland."

The commanding voice brought her to a stop in the middle of the hallway. She drew in a deep breath for strength and made a slow turn to face Dr. Shaye Russell. "Yes, Dr. Russell?"

The woman folded her hands in front of her and offered a tight smile along with a piece of paper. "I have asked *Ms.* Mitchell and Dr. Simpkins to make a list of possible contacts for you to build a clientele."

There was no mistaking her emphasis on the *Ms.* part. The seed of panic blossomed into sweaty palms. Dee took the piece of paper and tried to return her smile, tight and all. "Thank you."

"I'm certain you want to keep Charlottesville's opinion of you very high, since you wish to return there as soon as you can."

Dee drew in a quick breath at the sting.

"But remember, Dr. Roseland, your promotion to Charlottesville has as much to do with my recommendation of you as it does with your skills. *Team players* impress me. *Team players* who care about the welfare of the clients and students we serve, and not just their own advancement in academia."

"Of course. I'm sorry I—"

"You'd do well to take your position as, not only a superior, but as a *service* provider into serious consideration."

Dr. Russell left the comment hanging in the air as she turned and disappeared down the hall. Dee's morning had taken an impressive downward spiral from Ma Mitchell's delicious blueberry muffin and it was only ten a.m. No amount of rocket-ship underpants could fix this mountain of self-inflicted trouble. She pressed a hand to her forehead to stay the tears.

The warmth in Reese's conversations, the welcome in Rainey's eyes, all encouraged her to lower the carefully constructed wall around her heart and trust them. A piece of her craved it. Another part, the one scarred with a million painful memories, trembled with the possibility of being wounded all over again.

Her mind drifted to her father. Empty evenings with her brother, night after night, sent an uncomfortable wave of doubt. She'd created herself into a person quite capable of living alone—safe from the disappointment and pain of others. But did she want that empty childhood to turn into a lonely adulthood?

Her heart squeezed a resounding no.

She fisted the list in her hand—a list with about six contacts Rainey Mitchell helped develop.

The *Rainey* she'd offended.

What a way to start off her school year.

THE CONSISTENT SWING of the axe set a rhythm for Reese's thoughts—slow and steady, working through the kinks of the wood. Things looked up for his family. Trigg even helped with the feeding that morning, confirming the doctor's latest report. His brother was getting better. Stronger. A few more months and he could be as good as new—nearly, except for a few adjustments to his plans of having a family.

More than an older brother, Trigg was Reese's best friend, but neither proved ready or willing to talk about those modifications to Trigg's future yet. Reese stopped chopping and glanced up at the sky. God knew how much he loved his brother—enough to give up his dreams and return home, but how could God fix this one? It hit at the core of a man.

And the endless medical bills? Reese wiped the back of his hand across his forehead and glanced out over the pasture toward his brother's house, barely visible beyond the tree line. Insurance was pricey for a farmer, and a year of treatments added up big time.

He had to put his best foot forward for this Chicago job.

Had to. Even if it meant accent modification sessions with Dr. "Ain't is not a word" Roseland.

He rubbed the back of his aching neck and looked over at his grandpa's house. Dim sunlight skittered over the horizon and framed his grandpa's house in an orange glow. A haven for travelers, his mom called it. His thoughts drifted to the dark-haired professor. She sure did work long hours. About as long as him.

Well, he reckoned the university got a winner when they hired Doc. Single-Minded. Motivated. Career and advancement over the needs of a family—or at least in her case. Rainey seemed to make it work—even as a single-mom. But did Doc really want her job to be her whole life?

He slammed the blade back into the wood with extra force, slicing through the logs with new fervor. *Stop thinkin' about Adelina Roseland.* But his mind went right back to the cow-birthing madness and her sour-apple hair. He needed to finish up before he came face to face with the brunette when she returned home. Maybe he'd just leave the firewood on her porch. Would she remember how to start a fire?

A rumble from the gravel road warned him thinking proved a poor substitute for action. Her blue Jetta came into view, hobbling down the dusty road like a wounded calf. Poor woman needed a new car. He turned to finish up the last few pieces of wood, tossed a large pile in his wheelbarrow, and met her as she stepped from the car.

"Mr. Mitchell." She nodded her greeting.

Her red jacket brought out the soft white of her skin and the rich hints of caramel in her hair. There wasn't much else to do but stare just a second longer to admire the view, since all he'd seen the last two hours was the handle of an axe and the inside of a split tree.

He jerked to attention, shocked at his traitor-mind. "Doc."

They stood in awkward silence.

"Brought you some wood." He lifted a load from the wheelbarrow into his arms.

"Yes."

Great, Mitchell. As if the woman didn't have eyes in her head. "It's supposed to get cold tonight."

"Well, thank you." She spoke softly and the sound made him do a double take.

An expression he'd mistaken as aloof suddenly transformed into something fragile upon deeper inspection. She even looked close to tears. He turned to mush on the inside and took a step back to protect her. He wasn't too good with fragile things.

"Mama left you a casserole on the counter. Chicken. Thought you might be ready for another meal." A good dose of Mama's cookin' helped everybody.

"Another meal?" Doc walked passed him to the front door, entranced, words nearly lost in a whisper.

Maybe she really *was* crazy. Pretty and fragile, but crazy. That would explain a whole lot about this country-turned-city-girl who didn't like dogs. Of course, Mama's cookin' did have a strange effect on folks sometimes.

He tried to follow Dee, but his wood-laden arms blocked the door. When Doc looked up from the casserole and saw him struggling, she snapped out of her food-induced stupor and rushed to help.

"I'm sorry, Reese."

She blinked. So did he. She'd called him Reese? Something warm and dangerous flickered to life right around his heart. *Daggone-it.*

"Um, I think formalities are past since we're neighbors, don't you?"

"Makes sense." He stepped around her and took a few strides to the fireplace. Some distance between him and those large-and-lonely eyes would do him good. "I ain't too good with formalities anyway."

"That's a shock." Her sarcasm slapped him in the face.

He dumped the firewood with a noisy crash by the fireplace and restacked it as loudly as possible. Getting soft with the likes of Adelina Roseland proved her craziness was either rubbing off on him or he was just plain stupid.

"I didn't mean it the way it sounded." Her sigh drew his attention. "I'm just not very good with ..." She waved a hand toward him. "... um... people."

He wasn't certain how to respond. The admission closed in on an apology and he wasn't inclined to hold a grudge—unless it involved Jana and a certain no-good former brother-in-law.

Dee stared at some sheets of paper, shaking her head. One looked like a long row of words.

"If you need some groceries, Mama or Rainey can show you some of the best places." He rested an arm on his knee and offered another smile. A peace offering?

"No, thank you. I mean, this isn't a grocery list. One is my teaching list, the other is my clinic list, and this third one is a list—" She bit her lip. "Never mind. I'm sure those things aren't very interesting to you."

"You like lists, don't ya?"

"It helps me remember and stay on track." Her shoulders stiffened. "You have no idea the stress and responsibilities of a university position."

Moody too. One minute she spoke right near friendly and the next ... He asked one question and she jumped to all high and mighty again. Fine. He'd start this fire, finish his therapy with her the next two months, and try not to talk to her again. Reese slammed more pieces of wood into the pile, positioned a few in the grate, and pulled a lighter from its place near the hearth. "Want me to light your fire tonight?"

She turned from the casserole so fast he thought she might fall over. "Excuse me?"

When Reese replayed the question in his mind, he was pretty sure he'd already started the fire—on his face. "I mean, do you want me to heat things up in here for you."

Her eyes grew wider. His face got hotter.

"Let me fix you up a fire." He pointed to the fireplace just to rule out any doubt. "Right here. In the fireplace."

She stood there staring, so he got to work. Anything to keep from opening his mouth and proving his stupidity out loud. Changing the subject seemed like a good idea.

"Why don't you warm up some supper? I bet you're hungry after a full day."

He shuffled through some kindling and beat himself up in his head. What an idiot. He needed a whole lot more than accent therapy. He needed brain therapy. This particularly woman crossed-up his thinking. Proof-positive he should steer clear of her as much as possible.

A strangled noise from behind took his attention off of his self-beating. Doc had her back to him, one hand on the counter, and the other up near her face. The sound came again. Louder.

Was she choking? Could she breathe? Her shoulders started shaking. He jumped up and quickened his pace. The sound grew into something resembling ... laughter?

"Dee?"

She swung around and brought a full laugh with her.

"You're laughing?" He pushed a hand through his hair to keep from shaking her. "I thought you was chokin'."

She laughed harder. Her dark eyes glimmered. Evidently dying-by-choking wasn't such a bad idea in her book. Well, since she was crazy anyhow, it made perfect sense.

"What is so daggone funny?"

She snorted a reply in a cute-unladylike-kind of way and then leaned forward, bracing her shaking body with a hand to her waist. More of her dark hair fell around her shoulders.

"You need help, woman."

Her shoulders shook harder, but she managed a broken reply. "Help? With lighting my fire?" She lost her laugh again. "No, thanks, mountain man."

He'd thought she was pretty before, but when her eyes lit with humor, her cheeks glowed ruby, and her smile spread full and beautiful across her face. He turned plum befuddled. He couldn't help but grin back. Crazy sure did look good on her.

"Proves my need for speech lessons, don't it?"

She snickered behind her palm. "I don't know if my degree reaches to that level, Mr. Mitchell."

He stared at her a little too long, trying to figure out how the glow on her transferred heat to his chest. And arguing with himself to leave the house immediately, before all that warmth forced him to say more dumb things. He'd kept attraction at bay a long time—and this type terrified him. It tempted to spill over into something a lot deeper with the ease of another laugh.

Her eyes sobered. Her smile faded. She kept looking at him … and he looked right back like the loon he was.

Getting to that fire was probably a good choice. And *not* the one starting in his chest.

He stepped back until his heel hit a chair.

"It's good to see you laugh, Doc. I gotta feeling that needs to happen a whole lot more than it does."

"I haven't laughed that hard since …" She paused and touched a finger to the corner of her lips. "I can't even remember. And after the day I've had, I needed it. Badly."

He bent down to the fireplace. "Rough start?"

"Of my own making, I'm afraid. I was mean." She lifted the lid on one of the dishes on the counter and paused to take a deep breath of its contents. The large open room, with living room spilling into the kitchen, gave him a clear visual of her. "Have you ever wished you could rewind an entire day, maybe even an entire year, and start over?"

Reese tossed another log on the fire then leaned his arm against his bent knee, studying her. "I'm pretty sure everybody's been there some time or other."

She put a hand to her head and leaned back against the counter. No doubt the woman was tired and probably pretty hungry. And if those eyes of hers got all fragile again, he might do something they'd both regret. Like kiss her.

The thought drew his attention to her pouty bottom lip. He shot to his feet. "I'm gonna leave so you can go ahead and eat. A little thing like you is bound to fall over if you don't eat something."

Her dark brows shot to attention. "I am not weak."

"I didn't say you was weak. I said you was little." The growing flames crackled behind him.

"You *were* little."

"Woman, I ain't little."

"I'm *not* little. Not I *ain't* little." She pointed the serving spoon in her hand, not looking one bit tired. "And do not call me *woman*."

He grinned at the wild-eyed spitfire. "Second lesson?"

She stared a minute and then her expression softened again. "We have to start somewhere. Can you come to the office this week?"

"I'll be in town on Wednesday. Could you see me then?"

She scooped out some casserole onto her plate, and then looked down at the counter where a little book lay next to her lists. "Wednesday morning would be great." She took a bite and nodded, then closed her eyes. "Mmm, your mom is a fantastic cook. She really shouldn't keep bringing me food."

Reese dusted his hands off on his jeans and stepped toward the door, watching her enjoy his mama's cooking suddenly made him jealous of a casserole. Yep, he was bona fide crazy, but he liked *this* Adelina Roseland a whole lot better than the tight-bunned professor from a few days ago.

Sunset's orange light fell pale across the floor. Time to head home and take solid control of his wayward mind again. Most likely his mama, sister, and brother kept a close watch on the house from their windows. No need to get tongues to waggin'.

He walked to the door. "I'm off to get the young'uns and start up my own fire."

She snorted.

Heat shot back into Reese's face and he nearly tripped on the threshold. "Anyhow, I reckon I'll see you Wednesday?"

"Will nine o'clock be okay?"

"Nine o'clock, it is."

"And maybe I could come out to your place on Friday? In the afternoon? The more practice, the sooner we can get you ready for your interview."

Getting therapy from her was still a bad idea. And after the *fire lighting* incident, it blazed bad for a whole new set of reasons.

Haus greeted him on the porch.

"Hey, boy." Reese scratched the dog's head and was rewarded with a smile. It did look kind of eerie at night. "Don't worry, Doc. I'll load him up the in the truck before I—"

"No, no," Dee nearly ran to the door, but stopped at the threshold. "Um, it's okay if he stays." She shrugged. "I mean, this is his home. As long as he stays outside."

Reese looked down at the dog, who grinned wider, and back to Doc, who studied the floor with a sudden intensity. If dogs spoke English, no doubt Reese would hear a good tale.

"Alright." He nodded. "Good night, Doc. See you on Wednesday."

"Good night, Reese Mitchell." She met his gaze and the smallest of smiles dawned on her expression. "Thanks for ... um ... lighting my fire."

He slammed the screen door on her laugh, stomped down the porch stairs, and tried real hard to ignore the sparks in his heart for Dr. Adelina Roseland.

CHAPTER 6

You see, I've got her pronunciation all right; but you have to consider not only how a girl pronounces, but what she pronounces;
(Pygmalion, Act 3)

Adelina's smile refused to tame itself and her wayward thoughts twisted out of control. The picture of Reese Mitchell's broad arms, muscles taut underneath his blue shirt as he carried in her firewood, kept popping up at the most inconvenient times. Like in the middle of her first private meeting with Dr. Russell. Dee was pretty sure Dr. Russell caught some stupid smile on her face while she discussed the importance of oral hygiene in swallowing patients.

Or while sliding some leftover scraps to Haus when it was still dark outside so none of the neighbors could see. Or just now, when reading Alex's recent email and wishing she'd never made the stupid wager.

And though she'd never admit it out loud, something close to sparks ignited in more than the fireplace when he stopped by. Lighting her fire?

She caught her laugh and then looked up at the beautiful degree hanging on the wall as she took another bite of Mrs. Mitchell's strawberry crepe. Dee's parents must have been attracted to each other at some point, even if their marriage didn't turn out with a happy ending—especially with an alcoholic mother bringing the entire family down. The constant example of how mountain people couldn't change their ways, so her father said. Narrow-minded and simple, right?

She took another bite of the crepe and sighed. For the first time since her father died, the prejudice failed to settle. Reese and Rainey didn't fit that preconception.

Her Calvin and Hobbes calendar's quote for the day nudged her not to lose sight of the joy in the moment, the day. Hope spun a thread around her heart and gave it a little tug, but the image of her father's lifeless face snipped the string.

No! She tossed the remaining crepe into the trash and pushed the thoughts of Reese Mitchell from her mind. This type of irresponsible thinking led to poor, impulsive decisions. Even if the Mitchells proved an exception to the rule, she belonged somewhere besides Ransom.

Reese's visit caught her tired and off guard after a horrible day, but she wouldn't allow it to happen again. From this point on, it was strictly professional.

She stared at her to-do list and slumped forward from the weight of her responsibilities.

None of the contacts on her client list returned any calls, which left her with no clinic. None. The meeting with Dr. Russell only reiterated her loss. What would she do if she failed at this position?

And she *still* needed to apologize to Rainey. Even if Rainey forgave her arrogance, it was highly unlikely she'd want someone like her working with kids. Besides, Dee *never* worked with children, but her choices were limited—even if Rainey showed mercy.

She left her office and turned toward Rainey's, the walk down the endless hallway bringing up the exhausting memories of making apologies to her father. His usual reaction included a long diatribe recounting Dee's past, similar disappointments, and a reminder of how deceit only mirrored her mother's sins...and she never wanted to be like her mother. After a half hour of reviewing her guilt, her father would finally put her out of her misery with a pat to her shoulder and a nudge out the door. The end.

But it never felt like an ending, merely a long succession of unhealed wounds.

How long would Rainey make her pay for her mistake? Dee's pace slowed as she braced herself for the inevitable. Rainey's office waited at the end of the corridor, tucked near a large play area with mural-covered walls known as the Language Room.

The open door emboldened her with needed courage. Rainey sat at her desk, face bent low over a book, absorbed. Her long golden hair tied back in a low ponytail, and she pushed the limits of "professional casual" with her khakis and long-sleeved blue t-shirt. Half of a strawberry crepe nestled at the corner of her desk.

Mrs. Mitchell made her rounds.

Unlike the barren cavern of Dee's office, unruly colored art and various posters littered Rainey's walls. A sign for Autism Awareness hug on one wall and nearby, a picture of Albert Einstein with the caption *Think Differently*. Kid-art took up some space, brightening the olive walls with pastel rainbows, neon cats, and misspelled words.

The sweetness of it carved a deeper ache in Dee's heart. Not everyone's life fit into the perfect little world the Mitchells knew—rainbows, neon cats, and all, but the simplicity of it must be the secret of the Mitchell's kindness. People who've known hardship kept more somber attitudes, at least in Dee's experience.

Rainey's desk pointed to the right toward the large window in the room giving Dee a full view of her paper and picture-strewn work area. Three framed photos graced Rainey's desk. One held the picture of a grinning, golden-haired girl and the other appeared to be a family photo. Reese stood on one side of Rainey, a lady who must have been Mrs. Mitchell hugged Rainey's other side, Emma stood beside her, another young, dark-haired man came next, and then an older man closed off the other end. Family.

"Hey, Dee, I didn't see you standing there."

Dee looked up and gestured toward the desk. "Yes, well, um, I see you have strawberry crepes too."

Rainey's grin unfurled as she swiveled her office chair around to face Dee. "Mom's notorious for spoiling people with food." She patted her stomach. "It's a good thing I have farm work to do, a four-year-old to chase, and like to run."

"What are you reading?" Dee nodded toward the book, procrastinating a little until she worked up the courage and the words to apologize.

Rainey flipped her book over to show the cover. *You're Gonna Love This Kid.* "It's an older book about teaching kids with autism," Rainey explained. "But the author does a fantastic job of laying the groundwork for more positive perspectives. I love her thoughts." Rainey's expression darkened. "But I doubt you'd be interested. The author only has her master's degree."

Dee cleared her throat and touched the corner of one of the photos on Rainey's desk. "About that ... I wanted to apologize for making such generalized assumptions, for my...arrogance." She looked up. "It was wrong of me."

Rainey remained silent, but didn't look away. Her direct blue gaze searched Dee's in a way similar to Reese's. Uncomfortable. Honest.

"I'm not usually ... well, there's really no excuse for it and I'm sorry."

Rainey tilted her head, as if clarifying Dee's sincerity, and then without another pause, she stood and offered an outstretched hand. "Apology accepted. Let's start over. What do you say?"

Dee hesitated out of sheer astonishment. No emotional manipulation? No groveling? Clearly, Rainey Mitchell didn't follow in Dee's father's footsteps. Was there a hidden agenda behind her ready forgiveness?

"That sounds ... good." The usual edge of caution rose its ugly head. Was there a hidden agenda behind her ready forgiveness? Dee took Rainey's hand and quickly released her hold, looking back at Rainey's cluttered desk to give her stinging eyes another place to settle. "Your pictures are nice."

"That's my daughter, Sarah. She's four and a sweetheart. Like her Mama, of course." Rainey sat and leaned forward, lowering her voice. "Just don't clarify that last statement with either of my brothers, okay? They'll give you false information."

Dee chuckled and sat, trying to sort out this woman. "She looks exactly like you."

Rainey tapped the desk with her pencil and leaned back in her office chair. "Well, she has her daddy's nose, but since he has a perfect nose, I don't mind so much."

"And that is your other brother?"

Rainey picked up the framed picture, her expressions softening. "Yeah, that's Trigg. His real name is Edward, after Daddy, but everyone's always called him Trigg." She wrinkled up her face. "And it fits him *much* better than Edward."

"And the older man? Is that your father?"

"Yep. Tall, dark and handsome." Rainey picked up the family picture, her smile sad. "He died a few years ago of cancer. About a year afterward Mama and my dad's best friend, Ezra Drake, started … courting." Rainey lifted her brow at the apparently scandalous notion. "They even called it courting. They weren't married a year when Ezra had a massive heart attack while out in the field."

Dee's breath hitched. "How sad."

"I loved my daddy." Rainey's eyes glistened with unshed tears, the sudden kind grief brought. "But we were really blessed to have Ezra in our lives too." She set the frame back down. "Life isn't easy."

The understatement of the century. "It's a beautiful family."

Rainey's perceptive stare started working again. "Family is a good thing. Do you have any?"

"A brother." Dee looked away and decided for another change of subject—safer ground. "You offered to help me earlier, and I could certainly use it now. I know I don't really deserve your help after what I've said, but …?"

"No luck with everyone else, eh?" Rainey's grin turned wicked and then she laughed off Dee's sudden tension. "The Tolliver Language Center is my pride and joy. Besides Sarah, of course, and chocolate chip cookie pie fresh from the oven. I started TLC five years ago to help underprivileged families in our county who couldn't afford services." She winked. "TLC? Get the double entendre?"

Rainey Mitchell definitely didn't fit any mold Dee expected. Her ready friendliness, even after Dee's rudeness, confused her.

"There's always a need for extra therapists at TLC." Rainey snapped her fingers and reached for her purse. "Do you have time this afternoon? I have a two-hour break. I can show you the place."

She'd drop everything to help her? Dee stumbled over her reply without even checking her day planner. "Umm, yes, actually I do."

"Maybe we can swing by and visit Lizzie's clinic too. I bet she can scrounge up a few adult clients for you so my brother isn't your only example of small town crazy. Although I'm sure he causes enough trouble for an entire caseload." Rainey tossed her giant, blue bag up on her shoulder and stepped forward as if Dee never offended her at all. "Lizzie has several post-stroke clients who are working on their speech. I bet that would tickle your fancy a whole lot more than kids who don't speak at all."

Dee fingered her jacket sleeve, no experience with complete and unshackled forgiveness. She sat staring at the floor. "How can you be so ... Why are you helping me so ... easily?"

"Why am I helping you?"

Dee didn't answer.

Rainey moved to sit in the chair next to her. "I don't know what kind of hurts you've had, or what sort of people you're used to, but from my perspective we're all in this world together. Life's way too short to hold grudges. Besides, there are bigger offenses than status-envy." She grinned and patted Dee's arm. "We all screw up. It's in the human DNA."

"You've shown me nothing but kindness and I was rude to you. Egotistical, even." Dee glanced up. "You can't just let it go like that."

"Are you saying you *want* me to stay mad at you?"

When stated so plainly, Dee's request sounded rather ridiculous.

Rainey dropped her bag on the floor beside her seat. "Listen, we're both human, both need Jesus, and both desperate for the same things at the core of who we are. Hope and love." She folded her hands in front of her and leaned forward, bringing her sincere expression directly into Dee's line of vision.

Jesus? What did Jesus have to do with any of this?

"You don't think I've had my share of rude moments? Heaven help the people who worked near me two years ago when Gray walked out the door and left me with a little girl and a broken heart. I still struggle with that one on a regular basis."

Dee barely kept her mouth from dropping open. Maybe the Mitchells' lives hadn't been so easy. Another dose of healthy shame warmed Dee's face, proving all the more her understanding of Appalachia needed reconstruction.

"Talk about a dragon lady." Rainey's shoulder shook with a mock-shudder. "Unforgiveness never brings anything but a sad life and a hard heart in the end. The last thing I need is bitterness eating away at my confidence." She touched Dee's arm, a simple act which moved all the way to Dee's heart. "It's not easy, but without forgiveness of the big or the small, we'd all lead a pretty sad and lonely existence. I believe God places us in each other's lives for very specific purposes. For good or bad, we need each other to become the person He wants us to be." Rainey's brows wiggled. "Accents and all."

Dee looked down at her folded hands, her emotions creating a frustrated knot in her stomach. This was *not* the Jesus her father preached for years. Be good. Do right. Make your list and keep it, and only *then* God would bless you with a job in Charlottesville and the prestige you deserve.

Rainey's declaration painted God as someone who took her brokenness and mended it, even though the brokenness came from her own making. It seemed too simple. Too frightening. Too amazing. What would she do with a God like that?

Dee reminded herself Reese gave a perfectly legit excuse for cancelling their session. If a cancer patient spikes a fever, you get him to the doctor. Especially if the patient is your brother. Her response was less understandable. Sunday lunch with the entire Mitchell family? How did Sunday lunch wind up on her list alongside therapy?

Friday's Calvin and Hobbes' quote had been about surprises. Something about there being so many of them, but never when you needed them. Surprises rarely boded well for her. They never fit on a list. Unfortunately, her move to Ransom started an avalanche of surprises piling in a heap of accents, cow fields, and mountain people. Meeting a handful for lunch in their home sent her nerves on end. The few family dinners she remembered passed in strained silence or ended in a screaming match between her parents.

But Reese and Rainey Mitchell already upturned most of her assumptions, so perhaps another *good* surprise, right after Rainey's unexpected forgiveness, was worth having. Dee's chiseled experience told her to keep her hopes bound tight—and her expectations low.

At least Reese didn't press the issue of going to church. It would take more than a forgiveness chat and some bonding over laughter to see her inside the walls of a church again. She left God a long time ago when God never answered her prayers and Granny Roseland died. How could He care about her and let her childhood fall into such massive shambles? But even as she delved into an internal argument, Rainey's words, her actions, hinted at doubt. Something seemed uncomfortably inviting about the God of whom she spoke.

A small cabin at the top of the hill came into view, snuggled between a wealth of aged pine trees and an endless sky. The porch stretched the length of the house, with potted plants dangling a welcome sway in the breeze. A simple rock path lead to the front door, lined by a few yellow mums and fire-red shrubs. The house resembled something from a family Christmas movie with every imagination of Mrs. Mitchell fitting to idyllic proportions as hostess extraordinaire.

As soon as Dee stepped from the car, Mustard bounded forward pursued by the other dog she'd seen in Reese's truck, and then Lou followed with a small blond-headed girl trailing at her heels. The mismatched welcoming party doused a little of her nervousness with a soft touch of sweetness—unfamiliar and welcome sweetness. Dee recognized the other cherub face from Rainey's desk pictures. Sarah, was it?

"Hey, Ms. Doc. Granny said you'd be comin' today." Lou placed her hands on the hips of her jean jumper dress and offered a snaggled-tooth grin. "She's makin' her famous chicken casserole." Lou licked her lips. "Ain't much better than chicken casserole, unless it's chocolate chip brownies."

Dee's mouth started to water. "Sounds fantastic."

"Did you notice I lost my top two teeth?"

Dee barely controlled a laugh as the little girl's grin stretched to comic proportions to show off the gaping hole where her teeth belonged. "I see that."

"That means I can stick my tongue clean through the hole. Watch."

She proceeded to demonstrate, and Dee knelt down to get a better look. If all children proved as delightful as Lou Mitchell, maybe working with kids wouldn't be so hard. Lou didn't seem to mind Dee's discomfort one bit.

"That's impressive. Are you ready for something funny?"

Lou's eyes brightened and Dee wanted to reach out and hug her for making the conversation so easy.

"What?"

"Try to say the special sound *th*."

Lou attempted it, but with her top two teeth missing, her tongue filled the hole and produced a whistle. Lou's eyes grew wide and then she burst out in a giggle. "It tickles my skin."

"I bet it feels funny."

She tried it again. "I sound like an old whistlin' grandpa."

"A rather cute old whistlin' grandpa, I'd say."

The little girl at Lou's side almost smiled too, but with one look at Dee, she pinched her lips closed and blinked through her round glasses. Sarah's response felt familiar. More like Dee's expectation of children.

"We got a whole crowd comin' over." Lou turned to the little girl. "Ain't that right, Sarah?"

Sarah slid further behind Lou, but kept those curious sky blue eyes fixed on Dee.

"Sarah ain't too friendly with strangers, but she'll be alright." Lou patted the little girl on the head. "Remember what I told you about Ms. Doc. She can play dolls real good."

Dee cringed a bit from Lou's grammar but a gentle smile to the shy little girl. Sarah's lips didn't even twitch, but her eyes grew wide. Who was she kidding? Dee's mother's voice whispered in her head. She wasn't a kid-friendly person.

"Lou, would you show me the way inside?"

Lou's little shoulders perked up, ready for action. "Well, of course. Granny's been hankerin' to lay eyes on you for two weeks."

Lou skipped her way up the stone steps, through the front door, and into the warmth of baked bread and laughter. Dee's stomach responded with a reflexive growl and tightening apprehension. A massive rock fireplace formed the centerpiece of both the kitchen and living rooms, but most people gathered in the far living room area. Laughter and the happy hum of conversations came from all directions, warm and inviting.

They certainly didn't act like a group of wounded humans.

"Oh, bless me, you must be Dee."

A middle-aged woman, soft curls of gold and silver wrapped back in a loose bun, walked forward with arms outstretched. Before Dee could prepare herself, the woman swept her into the sweetest hug she'd known since Granny Roseland died. Ms. Mitchell smelled of a homespun combination of roses, dishwashing liquid, and fresh-baked chocolate chip cookies. Those scents mingled shockingly well together on the right person.

She pulled back but continued to keep her hands on Dee's shoulders. "I'm just tickled pink you could come today, honey. Now I finally get to meet you."

Welcome brimmed from Mrs. Mitchell's smile to her warm touch.

"I hope it's fine."

"Fine? Well, it's plum perfect." Mrs. Mitchell patted Dee's shoulders again and then moved to a place behind the kitchen the counter. "I can't promise you a quiet lunch, not with the crew we got, but I can promise you some good company and ..." She winked. "Pretty good food too."

Dee stepped close to the counter. "If it's anything like what you've left in my office or house, good isn't a strong enough word."

"Just wanted you to feel welcome. It's mighty lonesome moving to a new place all by yourself."

"One gets accustomed to it after a while." Dee gripped the back of a nearby barstool and nodded in an attempt to display more confidence than she felt.

Mrs. Mitchell dusted her hands on her yellow sunflower apron. "You're a tougher woman than I am, Dee. I don't reckon I'd ever get accustomed to being alone after life with a gang." She nodded toward the other side of the room. "Here come a few of 'em now."

"So glad to have you here, Dee." Rainey walked into the kitchen and linked her arm through Dee's. "Let me introduce you." She pulled Dee toward the throng. "Meg, come here and meet Dee."

A woman by the window turned striking jade eyes in their direction. Her hair fell in locks of mingled shades of dark and light brown, and she rested her hand on the back of a wheelchair, where a young man sat.

"That's Meg." Rainey nodded toward the woman. "Her brother, David, is with her. He was born with cerebral palsy. One of the happiest guys on the planet though, no thanks to their parents." Rainey huffed her displeasure. "Mom's kind of adopted them since their mother gave them up years ago. They grew up about a mile away with their grandmother. Meg takes care of all of them now. Well, her brother started college this year, so maybe less care of him."

The look Dee gave Rainey must have held questions.

"Long story," Rainey replied, golden head shaking. She turned to include Meg with a smile. "Come meet Dee. She's our new Assistant Chair at the university. Dee, this is Meg Reynolds, secret-keeper extraordinaire and one fantastic nurse. She's been the *go-to* girl on questions about Trigg's health since the ugly fiasco started."

"Thank you, Rainey." Meg's gentle smile matched her voice. "I should probably ask for a raise since putting up with your brother for so long."

Meg glanced toward a tall, dark-haired man standing by Mrs. Mitchell in the kitchen. Dee recognized him from the picture on Rainey's desk. Trigg. He looked up from sniffing a pie and showed off some striking cobalt blue eyes, his pale face and lean frame the only indicators of an illness.

"Meg's telling Dee how much trouble you are."

Dee shot a look from Rainey to Trigg. Wasn't he the one with cancer? And that's how they talked to him? The power in his stance spoke of a man who still held a great deal of strength, like Reese.

He leveled Meg with a steel cold look. "I'm nothin' but sweetness itself."

Meg turned back and lowered her voice to a whisper. "Actually, he can be pretty sweet."

"Don't say it too loudly, Meg." Rainey shook her head, warning in her tones. "We'll never hear the end of it."

A pink hue bloomed in Meg's cheeks for a moment. "He knows it already, Rainey. There's no hiding it."

Rainey took a few steps toward him and patted him on the shoulder. "We're celebrating his good report on Friday. The fever had nothing to do with his cancer. In fact, the doctor feels good about next month's reexamination to prove it. He's pretty sure all the cancer's gone."

"That's great news."

"Hey Doc, you came," a familiar mountain-man's voice entered the room.

Dee turned to see Reese walk in with a sunny-headed toddler tucked under one arm like a football. The little boy's trill-like giggle lit the room and zoomed right into Dee's heart. Oh, what a beautiful child in the arms of a handsome man. She'd never seen anything on earth more endearing ... even attractive.

The mountain man had donned a red polo with a pair of dark jeans hugging him at the hips. His trimmed beard and hair gave him less of a grizzly bear-look and more of a Stetson cologne appeal. Dee's breath hitched. The sight of him combined with the tender look he sent Lou as he passed sent a tremor of warmth through her.

Her entire body tensed to the defense.

She survived research statistics for an entire semester, Dr. Richards's adult swallowing disorders class *and* lab, plus the travails of working as Alex Murdock's research assistant for four years—she could withstand her attraction for Reese Mitchell. Only nine weeks. Besides, what could really happen in nine weeks?

"This here is Brandon." Reese lifted the boy high causing another explosion of giggles. "He's about as rotten as boys come."

"He's beautiful," Dee whispered and touched a soft tendril of gold curl on his head. She blinked back to attention and dropped her hand, but not before she caught Reese watching her. His intense gaze sent those tingles stuttering throughout her body with renewed strength. *Nine weeks. Only nine.*

"Supper's ready. Everybody to the table," Mrs. Mitchell called from the dining room.

Dee waited for directions, but the crowd swarmed in a chaos of chatter following the scent or tradition. No order or plan, but mass exodus from one room to the next. She slid into the chair between Rainey and Mrs. Mitchell, still watching in awe as the big family unfolded to their spots. Grace Mitchell orchestrated it all without drawing any attention to the process or the preparation, almost as if everything magically appeared on the table.

As Mrs. Mitchell led the group in prayer, Dee's assumptions about Appalachia and her mother's generation of women shifted a little more. Absentee alcoholic and comforting servant? Somehow, she had to rectify the picture of her mother with Grace Mitchell … and maybe she needed to refigure her definitions and expectations too.

REESE'S ASSUMPTIONS had been dead-on. Dee barely spoke during the whole meal, and *aints* flew around like gnats at a picnic. She didn't correct one *'ing* and the only people using those were Meg, Rainey, and himself. Truth be told, she lived only to make *his* life miserable, not anyone else with mile-long vowels.

Though, he couldn't complain too much. Sitting across from her, he got a chance to see her smile a whole lot more too. Brandon took a shine to her, and for someone who wasn't too fond of kids, she grinned and cooed over him like he was the prettiest thing she'd ever seen.

Her posture stayed fence-post-straight and she didn't break out into laughter, but her quiet countenance and occasional smiles confirmed something. She kept a firm hold on her feelings, which suited him fine because weeping women made him nervous, but she couldn't hide the longing in her eyes for what his family shared around that table.

Reese tucked Brandon close, as he sat out on the front porch watching Lou and Sarah play in the yard. He looked down at his son sleeping against his chest, golden hair haloing his face and pink cheeks, and he agreed with Dee's earlier statement. Too pretty for a boy, but Reese didn't have the heart to cut off all those curls. It kept him looking like a baby, *his* sweet, little baby boy.

He readjusted Brandon in his arms and looked out over the valley before focusing his attention back on Dee, who was in a deep conversation with his little girl. Dee's hair fell long and dark down her back today. Silky. Like chocolate pie. Suited his tastes just fine.

With a pair of jeans curved to her petite body and an oversized, button-up blouse, he almost forgot the high-class PhD who wanted to beat the wrong vowels out of him. Jeans looked good on her. Real good.

He jerked his mind out of the ditch and back to her face, which was no hardship. She had a pretty face too, prettier by the day in fact.

Man, he needed help for his runaway thoughts, and that was the truth.

She walked over and sat beside him, leaning back with her palms to the porch, not helping his thoughts one bit. "I don't think I've eaten so well in a long time."

"If there's one thing my mama enjoys, it's entertainin' folks."

Dee quirked a brow. "Entertainin'?"

Enter the professor. "Entertaining. But I don't see why my 'ings are so important if you understood me just fine."

"It's the difference between sounding professional and not." She shook her head and the scent of apples came with the breeze. Chocolate and apples? Just like Mama's chocolate chip apple pie? No complaint about that combination either.

The front door slammed and Trigg walked down the steps. He carved his usual path across the front yard trail toward his house, giving Lou a toss over his shoulder for a second and tugging one of Sarah's braids before continuing his trek. The light bounce in his step gave Reese a jolt of hope. Trigg's house sat on the back part of the family land, about a half mile's walk, down the hill and by the pond that had some pretty good bass fishing.

Reese snuck a peek at Dee. Had she ever been fishing?

"Your brother seemed in good spirits."

"He's a whole lot better than he was a few months ago. The surgery, then medication wore him out. The doctor says it'll take a while to get back to normal."

Or a new kind of normal without kids in the future.

Reese instinctively pulled Brandon a little tighter. Well, not every young'un had to be blood-related to be your child. Lou and Sarah ran passed them up the porch steps and into the house, laughing all the way.

Dee hugged her shoulders and tilted her head to look at him. "You have a great family."

The setting sun bathed her hair and face with golden light, bringing out the earthy greens of her eyes. His pulse jumped into a stampede. "They are crazy in their own way, but I wouldn't take any other."

Dee looked back at the horizon, her smile fading. "Some kinds of crazy are much better than others."

"You have a brother, right?"

"Jason. He's a writer who also happens to farm." Dee's smile twitched wider. "And one of those brooding reclusive types."

"Sounds like Trigg, except the writing part."

Dee nodded. "I can see that. Jay has a good heart, but isn't around people to show it. His imaginary world and friends seem good enough for him."

"And he's older?"

"By a year." Dee reached a finger out and stroked Brandon's cheek. Her sigh seemed to come from deep inside. "So sweet and peaceful."

A puzzling play of emotions crossed her face. Awe. Sadness. Resignation? "He's perfectly content in his father's arms. That's a beautiful thing."

Reese's chest tightened along with a return of the stampede. He kept his voice low. "Kind of like God, ain't … isn't it?"

Her brows pinched and she shifted her attention back to the horizon. "God and I don't have a lot of conversations, so I can't say I've ever felt content with Him."

"Maybe you just don't know Him very well."

Dee pressed her lips together and released a long stream of air through her nose. He wasn't sure whether she was trying to control her anger, or tears, or just plain tired. She had talked a whole lot more in the past two hours than he'd ever seen her talk.

Lou burst from the front door and danced down the porch steps, her giggle at full volume. Sarah followed on her heels, fingers wiggling in *tickle* motion. Life at its finest. Lou was happy—unshackled by the weight of her mother's betrayal. Would another woman in Reese's life shake Lou's confidence? Break her heart as Jana had broken his?

He felt Dee's stare on him, but ignored it, slowly moving to stand, worries itching his insides. Brandon shifted in his arms and his stuffed bear landed on the porch floor. Dee bent to retrieve it. The tension in Reese's shoulders eased as she gently wedged the bear in between Brandon's arm and Reese's chest. Her fingers trailed along Brandon's cheek and ended on one of his curls, her lips softened by a smile. Reese kind of liked the looks of those lips—especially in a smile. Wonder what they tasted like.

He almost winced. *Idiot brain.*

"You know, it's funny. Your kids aren't so scary."

Her whispered words drew him closer, head bent to hear. A full scent of apples hit him. He caught her gaze. "Maybe it just took getting to know them better. Time can clear up all sorts of confusion." He shrugged. "If you take it."

She searched his face, locking him in place. He didn't even breathe, just in case it might break the spell. Unspoken questions surged between them as doubt and hope wrestled over her expression. Who was she? Why had God brought her in his life, awakened his heart, at just this time? It didn't make sense.

"If you're right about God being a father and holding us in his arms, then He has a lot of explaining to do."

Reese rubbed a palm over his spreading grin and then nodded. "I'm pretty sure He can handle all of your questions."

"How about my anger?"

Without a second's hesitation, Reese nodded. "I have firsthand knowledge He can handle that too. The real question, Doc, is if you can handle His answers."

CHAPTER 7

I've a sort of bet on that I'll pass her off as a duchess in six months. I started on her some months ago; and she's getting on like a house on fire. I shall win my bet.
(Pygmalion, Act 3)

Reese slammed his truck door and revved the engine. He'd had about enough of Doc's bellyaching. Maybe they shared a few sweet moments at his mama's house on Sunday. He'd talked about his family, she'd talked about her dad, but then—*wham*—Tuesday started right back into *fixing Reese* with a fury. When she came to his house on Thursday, it wasn't no better. And now, Friday, he'd spent the last hour practicing *r* words.

For one whole hour. Didn't make no sense to keep practicing something he learned in first grade. That woman really needed a hobby. Maybe fishing—one of the best calming activities in the world. It didn't hurt if you caught your dinner either, and the word *fish* didn't have one single *r* in it.

But Dee didn't seem to remember any of their sweet moments

from Sunday. In fact, the last three visits with her were all business. And *all* bossy.

"Ain't is not a word."

"Put your 'ing on the ends of words."

"Light is made up of a diphthong, not one long, flat vowel."

"Stand up straight."

"Put away your toothpick."

He shifted his truck into reverse to pull out of the university parking lot and caught sight of Dee leaving the school building. Her gray skirt highlighted the length of her legs and Reese looked away. Trouble, with a capital T, underlined, and in italics. That's what she was. One minute he wanted to kiss her and the next he wanted to run from being schooled on his *alphabet*. She'd probably even correct a compliment if he gave her one.

He watched her until she sat safely in her car, and then he backed out, scared to even think of any words for fear they'd be wrong in his head. A loud bang sounded from his right. In one split second, the cause for the blast came into full view. He swiped a hand across his mouth to keep his grin covered. Smoke rolled from the hood of Dee's car, obscuring much of the windshield view.

Wonder what vowels and consonants the Doc yelled about now?

He steered his truck beside of her and parked, planning a perfectly enunciated sentence in his mind. Before he even reached her, her hand swept out to stop him.

"Don't say anything." Her index finger shot up as warning. "Not one word."

Palms up in surrender, he stepped forward, grin itching to break free. Dee popped the lid of her car and more smoke poured out, sending her coughing. Reese released a low whistle.

"I told you not to say anything."

"I didn't." He looked over into the car and recognized a lost cause. Oil sputtered from one place, darkening various spots across the engine and spark plugs.

"It made a weird noise when I pulled into the parking lot today, but I hoped—" Her shoulders slumped forward and she swiped her hair back with shaky fingers, leaving a long smudge of black along her cheek. "I hoped letting it rest would fix it."

Reese shoved his hands in his pockets and nodded, not daring to say one little word and certainly not fidgeting to clear the mark off her face.

Dee moaned and stepped back, giving the underbelly of the dying vehicle a glance. "Look, there's something leaking from underneath too. What on earth is that?"

"Do you want me to answer this time?"

She propped her hands on her hips and waited, brows up to her hairline. He took that as a yes.

"It looks like antifreeze. Which ain't ... isn't a good sign."

"No, no, no." Dee's eyes rounded and her bottom lip dipped into a pitiful little pout. "It can't die right now. In one more month, but not right now."

Reese put a hand to her arm and she leaned into it for a second, resting on his strength. He kind of liked it. Made him feel strong and brave—a hero, even for the likes of a high-class city girl like her, but she seemed to think better of it and righted herself.

"Are there any mechanics open at five?"

"I know one we can call. A good buddy of mine. Hold on." He grabbed his phone and turned with a wink. "And you can add him to one of your lists."

"WHY CAN'T the mechanic fix it," she asked for the third time.

Reese thought Dee's dead engine might take some of the bossiness out of her for a little while. No such luck. He focused on the road as she sat beside him in his truck, pouting.

"He *can* fix it, but it's going to cost more to fix the car than what it's worth. Your best bet is to buy a new car."

Her palm covered her face and she groaned. "I can't afford a new car. It's not on my first purchases list."

"Your what?"

"I have a list of things I want to buy with my first check and a car isn't one of them."

He stared at her as long as the drive let him and then shook his head. "I reckon you're going to have to move it up on the list or you won't have a way to work for another paycheck."

"But I have loans to start paying back, items I've been waiting to purchase until now ... this was *not* in the plan."

"Not in your plan?" Even when he said it out loud it sounded weird, and it had nothing to do with his accent. "I guess you're gonna have to rearrange your plan. Life's full of adjustments, big and small."

She looked at him so hard, he felt slapped.

"Does everything you want always fit in a plan?"

She sighed back against his seat and stared ahead. "That's why I like plans, I guess. I can know what's going to happen and try to make those things happen. Maybe not fail so much?"

She grew quiet. Nothing but the hum of the truck's engine rumbled between them. Afraid to fail? The stubborn woman probably had never failed at anything in her life. He tried to ignore the softening around his heart, and would have completely, if her chin hadn't wobbled a little.

"I think there might be something we can work out."

"What?" Her words sounded hoarse, a sure sign she was trying not to cry... or scream. "Do you have a car hidden away somewhere? A friend in need of some extra money for their pickup?"

There was an idea. Reese pulled off on Mitchell's lane and stopped the truck. "I do got a really nice Accord up at the house—"

"You *have* a really nice Accord, not you *got* a—"

"I'm trying to help you here, woman, and you go off and correct my grammar?" He banged the steering wheel with his palm to emphasize his words. "Do you need a car or not?"

"Well yes, but—"

"Then stop giving me therapy when you're off the clock and listen a minute."

She pinched her mouth closed and crossed her arms, like Lou did when she didn't want to listen. Girls! But it did take the wounded look right out of her eyes, which kept him from taking her in his arms.

"I *have* a nice Accord up at the house. It's about seven years old, but in good shape. Nobody's driven it in two years."

Her brows crashed together. "Why would you keep a car you don't drive?"

He rubbed his jaw and took in a deep breath. "It was my wife's car."

"Oh, I'm sorry," Dee whispered and touched his arm. "I shouldn't have—"

He swallowed past his tightening throat. "This pickup fits my needs on the farm a lot better than a car, so I don't drive it none. I could give you a real good deal on it."

"None?"

She opened her mouth to say more and he stopped her with a look. "Now here's what I figure. You need a car and I need the money, so it's a win-win situation."

"You're really not a good salesman."

"Listen here, Doc. I shoot straight." He turned his body toward hers. "I wouldn't be interviewing for a job all the way up in Chicago if we didn't need the money. Trigg's got doctors' bills up to his eyebrows, and since he's been sick I've had to hire help to run the farm. It all costs."

Dee's eyes lost their frustrated glint and sobered like a sensible person. "I can imagine."

If she knew anything about farming, she realized the seriousness of losing a strong hand. And the farm stood as their daddy's legacy. Important. Especially to his brother.

"Family's worth whatever sacrifice I need to make. Chicago is a small price to pay."

A tender look softened her expression and pulled him closer, dark eyes searching his. But he wasn't immune to failure either. He'd promised Jana they'd only move to Ransom long enough to help out when his stepdad died, but she'd never given him the chance to fulfill his promise. He'd planned to move her back to the city-life she loved. Charlotte or Knoxville, maybe even Atlanta, but waiting pushed her too far. She never gave him a chance to do right by her. It was impossible from the start—and he'd never had sense enough to know it.

What was he thinking trying to encourage any relationship with Adelina Roseland?

He jerked back a little and cleared his throat. "So, do you want to look at the car or not?"

Dee blinked those large eyes of hers and bit at her bottom lip. "Okay."

"Okay." Reese nodded and put the truck in gear. "And since you'll be up at Mama's house, you might as well stay for supper."

Why on earth did he just invite her to supper? He was going to force Trigg to give him a mean fist to the head. Maybe it would knock some sense into him.

"Supper?"

He looked at her out of his periphery. "Last I recall, you liked Mama's cooking pretty good."

"Well."

"Pretty well," he ground the corrected phrase out through clenched teeth and focused on the narrowing dirt road. "And I think it's meatloaf."

"Does she cook for you every night?"

"Naw, but about three nights a week she does. She's spent so many years cooking for a herd of people, it's hard for her to get out of the habit."

"It's nice that you all stay so close."

"I reckon we've always been close. Even when I lived in Charlotte for a time."

Her head spun his direction. "You lived in Charlotte?"

"You make a whole lot of assumptions about me, don't ya?"

She flat out ignored his question. Tough little thing sure hated being wrong. His lips scratched a grin.

"Why were you in Charlotte?"

"I did some consulting there for a few farms. Ran a construction company too." He gripped the wheel more tightly as he rounded the next bend in the road. "You'll want to be careful of this curve coming up. Especially in fog or bad weather."

Dee followed the direction of his nod. Every time Reese passed the turn, it made him nervous. He'd even considered moving his house to the other side of Mitchell's Crossroads before Lou started driving so she could avoid the curve altogether.

"That's a steep drop."

"It sure is." Reese controlled a shiver. "And it comes right up on you when you least expect it. The road narrows here where the bank's eroded from rain. Just be careful."

"Why do you sound so angry about it?"

Stubborn woman. "Do you have to question everything?"

"Don't you?"

"Some things I take on faith that a person is thinking of my welfare, trying to help me."

"I'm sorry if I'm not a Pollyanna." Her words tensed. "But I haven't had a lot of people in my life I can trust, and certainly not a family like yours."

Reese got a sight of her in his peripheral vision, arms crossed and chin tight. Few people ever experienced a family like his—and it was easy to take it for granted. He sighed. "There have been three accidents off that drop." Reese slowed the truck to a crawl, visions flashing through his mind. "The one in our family was two years ago. And the driver wasn't a stranger to this road."

THE PAIN CREASING Reese's forehead confirmed the serious tone in his voice. Dee almost reached out to touch his arm again, share his hurts, but good sense kept her hand firmly planted in her lap. The last time she'd touched him, the tenderness of his look urged a knotted spot in her heart to unwind. He offered something her soul craved and it frightened her to her core.

She moistened her dry lips. "What happened?"

His brows pulled tighter and he focused on the road ahead. "Tom,"

Reese stopped and shot Dee a sideways look. "Lizzie Simpkins' husband. I reckon you met Lizzie at work?"

"Yes."

"He'd found, I mean … he was driving my wife home." Reese grew quiet, hesitated. His fists clenched and unclenched on the wheel, as if working up the words to say next.

But he didn't have to. Dee read the end of his story in the emotions on his face.

"Nobody knows what happened to make him lose control of the car. I came upon the scene, first. Not sure how long they'd been down there. They were already—" He paused again and took a few deep breaths.

Dee's stomach twisted, replaying the pain of loss she knew so well. She pressed her eyes closed, as if not seeing his pain might make the words mean less, but every syllable he spoke weighed down with his loss. He understood.

"There was nothing anybody could do. Maybe, if I'd been there a few minutes sooner."

"At least you didn't have to watch her die, Reese." Her throat squeezed out the confession. "Nobody wants that memory in their heads."

A fact she knew all too well.

"No, I reckon not, but I saw her lifeless face staring back at me from under the water. I was completely helpless to change any of it." Reese's voice broke and he shook his head. "A person never forgets a moment like that."

Her hand covered his forearm, the kinship with him deepening. "I'm so sorry, Reese."

"Mama and me has—" He started over. "Mama and I have written letters to the state about fixing this road, but nobody's done nothing." He took a deep breath. "I mean no one has done anything." He pulled the truck up to his Mama's barn and turned to face Dee, arm stretched along the back of the seat almost touching her shoulder. "Be careful, alright?"

He held her gaze and a wordless connection joined them together.

No accents. No corrections—and for the first time in a very long time, she embraced the attraction. The shared understanding.

Quivering inside, she bathed in the sweetness of this unfamiliar tenderness. "Thank you."

His hand moved ever so slightly and she thought he might touch her. Her breath stopped. His fingers flexed then fisted and he moved his hand back to the wheel, jaw tight. "Well Doc, let's see what you think about this car."

THE CAR WAS PERFECT. Silver and small. Classy. Everything she wanted. She kept circling it, her fingers aching to take it for a drive, which she did once Reese found the keys in some *junk drawer* in his mama's barn where the car stayed parked. She tried to curb the excitement, but when he placed the keys in her hand, she danced a little jig right in the middle of the barn. She was woefully out of practice with happy dances.

Reese's grin twitched up on one side, the grin that did strange things to her heart. It had become increasingly easier to let her guard down with him—with all of his family. Their friendliness and open acceptance etched away at her guardedness and suspicion. Like opening a rusty door in her soul, she gave into the trust. Trust never came without a price tag of some sort, not in her history. The Mitchells enticed her to believe in family—a real family—and trust, but at what cost?

She test drove the Honda to town, even joined the Mitchells for some leftover meatloaf. Brandon shared his brownie with her, complete with leaving a trail of chocolate on her blouse. Mama Mitchell told a few humorous stories about Reese and Trigg as boys, leaving Reese a little red-faced. The entire process, from car keys to dessert, carried a strange cathartic quality. Even with all of her Dad's support and guidance, she'd never known the authentic kindness and care of the Mitchells.

She smiled up at the starry sky on her walk to her house after dinner. Millions of stars blanketed the inky night canvas, their twinkles more brilliant in the middle of the country. No competing lights. An awe stilled her and for a brief moment she wondered if God watched, if maybe ... just maybe, he smiled at her. Could He really care for something as simple and practical as a silver Honda? The Mitchells thought so. They believed God worked in everything, the big and the small.

Reese insisted on walking her home, with Brandon up on his shoulders. Lou held her hand, to "keep her from getting lost". She swung their braided hands back and forth, matching the pace of their steps. The sweetness of it poured over deep-set wounds in Dee's heart, offering something she'd believed to broken for her future to possess.

The stars and the company called her to reconsider so many things —about family, about faith—and another dream she'd long since discarded.

Motherhood.

Her idea of motherhood lay marred under years of neglect and manipulation, but Rainey and Ma Mitchell proved not all families matched her history. The hidden shame of her mother's alcoholism and erratic behavior kept Dee close to home during her childhood, and the possibilities of making the same mistakes killed any of those little girl wishes. The daydream of wrapping her own children in her arms fell to ashes and one goal replaced all others: Charlottesville.

But motherhood?

Haus ran to greet them as they came into the light of the porch and Lou reached out to take him into her arms.

"I think Haus is gettin' fatter, Daddy." Lou grinned up at them, her eyes sparkling in the porchlight.

"Well, if Dee's been givin' him any of Granny's leftovers, I'd imagine he's enjoyin' them."

Reese winked at Dee and she turned away, pretending not to notice. Now if she could pretend away the heat waving over her skin it might not burst to fire-engine red on her face. Attraction or not, she still needed a hint of composure. Lack of control was her mother's trademark.

"He smells good too, Daddy."

A fresh rush of warmth invaded Dee's cheeks for a new reason. What if they discovered she'd actually shampooed the stinky dog?

"Thank you for walking me home." Dee placed her hand on Lou's head. "Can you find your way back in the dark?"

"Ain't no trouble. I've walked it for a long time." The way she drew out the word *long* made it seem a whole lot longer than her seven years.

"Well, then I won't worry about you." She turned to Reese and focused on Brandon instead of the handsome face staring down at her. "Good night, little one."

He waved a chubby arm at her and even added a *Night, Dee*.

Dee backed away, distancing herself from them, her head and heart vying for a solid landing. Her gaze flitted to Reese. He cared about her. From his tender look to the tilt in his smile, there was no mistake. Oh, how she could bathe in that look for years! "Thank you."

"Sweet dreams, Dee."

Her smile wobbled into place and she turned, barely making it inside. Memories, regret, and anger poured out with her tears. It would be so easy to let go. So easy to trust her heart to the hope Reese offered, but trusting always disappointed—or ripped a scar so deep she couldn't recover.

Trusting her mother. Trusting her father. Trusting God?

It meant the ultimate sacrifice—her plans, her control.

Was she willing to pay whatever price Reese cost, or worse, whatever price his God demanded of her?

CHAPTER 8

Happy is the man who can make a living by his hobby!
(Pygmalion, Act 1)

The silver Honda sat waiting in the driveway in the morning, with a note in the driver's seat.

Try it out for the week. There <u>ain't</u> no taxis back here anyway.

– *Reese*

Ain't was underlined.

Dee touched the card to the corner of her grin and shook her head, a thrill pumping up from her fingertips. She really shouldn't get this excited over a car, or a note from Mr. Cattle Farmer, but both added a pleasant spin to her typically ho-hum day.

The car fit in so well with the other nice cars in the university parking lot, shiny and stylish. Not even Dr. Russell's email reminder about clinic numbers got her down. It was the perfect car for Charlottesville, not too stingy, not too haughty. As Goldilocks said … just right.

Even her attitude about her first attempt at therapy with children since grad school remained positive. She walked into the Speech & Hearing Clinic ready to face whatever those four kids threw at her. Armed with nervous energy and enough articulation cards to wallpaper a room, she forged ahead. Her first day of classes had gone well, why not clinic too?

The good feelings didn't last long. Simon Reynolds defied gravity. Dee couldn't get him to sit in a chair longer than two seconds, let alone try to produce any of the ten sounds he couldn't say. And little Christy Painter pitched a royal tantrum so loud and high, Dee wondered if she heard dogs barking outside from the intrusion. And no matter how hard she tried to encourage Dominique to make an *r* sound, it ended in tears—for both of them.

The only lesson ending without drama or trauma was with Julie Blake, who didn't speak at all. The entire forty-five-minute session.

She just sat in the kid-chair and stared as if Dee were an imminent threat.

So much for feeling like Charlottesville-quality material. She failed … again.

Who was she kidding? Motherhood? She rolled her eyes to the ceiling of her cute little car and stifled a royal tantrum herself. She needed an outlet for pent-up frustration. Rainey used running. Reese had the farm. Slicing up articulation cards with a sharp pair of scissors only ruined perfectly useful clinic tools—if emotionally therapeutic, nonetheless.

Not even her Calvin and Hobbes calendar helped. Though it did result in a laugh before her mass failure. Maybe a sombrero would have helped!

With the thought of her disaster, Reese Mitchell came to mind. She had eight weeks left. *Only eight.* And she hadn't even started talking about his presentation, just his accent so far. Clopping into a room full of businessmen and sitting down like he was straddling a barstool wasn't going to make the best first impression, even with his heart-stopping grin.

Dee took the steps down from the third-floor clinic to the parking lot, making a list of things to research on child treatment before she'd allow herself to go home for dinner. The sight of the cute Honda soothed her disappointment a little, but if she couldn't keep her clinic numbers alive and well, she wouldn't have a job to pay for the adorable, professor-car.

A multitude of insecurities attacked her during the ten-minute drive from the clinic to her office. She'd planned this moment for years—something her father would be proud of and something to separate her from her mother's reputation. She'd dedicated hundreds of hours to research and high grades, forgoing simpler things like trips with friends and holidays with her brother.

And now? She couldn't even get a child to pay attention for a thirty-minute therapy session? No one wanted a failure.

She pushed through the glass doors of her building and marched down the hall toward her office, every step more determined than the last.

"Adelina."

She froze in her tracks as Alex Murdock met her in the hall outside her office. "Dr. Murdock?"

"Just thought I'd drop in and check on your progress. Dr. Lindsay and I came down for a meeting with Dr. Russell, so I thought I'd see how you're settling in."

"It's only been three weeks since your last visit, Alex. I'm still adjusting."

Dead car, clinical failure, and a visit from the current bane of her professional existence? This was turning out to be a stellar day. Perhaps a sombrero was the only logical solution.

"Would you like to come into my office?"

He followed her inside. "You look well."

She distanced herself with a desk between them. *Her* desk. "Thank you." Looks can be deceiving. "Please sit down."

"Your email reports all sound good, great in fact." He sat back and laced his hands in front of him. "Did you teach your first class yesterday?"

"Yes, it went well. It's a small number of students to start, but I'm sure with the creativity and motivation of the faculty here, those numbers will improve." Her own statement surprised her, and she meant it.

He smiled, in an almost genuine way, his face not nearly as haughty as she remembered. Or maybe the Mitchells influenced a new view. The thought stuck uncomfortably in place.

"You always covered my classes well. I've no doubt you'll excel with your teaching and I'm happy you find the other faculty members equal to your standards."

She shifted in her chair, uncomfortable with the subtle criticism to the faculty in her department, but hadn't she shared those exact sentiments a few weeks ago? No wonder people found her difficult and controlling.

"Are you enjoying the natives?"

Visions of the Mitchells around their family table forced their way through her self-examination. "They've been very kind to me."

"Have they?" His eyes grew wide. "Well, that's a surprise, isn't it? Even the interesting landlady you were worried about?"

Heat rose to Dee's cheeks. Her own thoughts reflected back in vivid and arrogant detail hammering the truth of her revelation into place. She was on the fast track, all right—to becoming a person she despised. *Bitter, arrogant, and alone.*

She focused on her desk and blinked at the papers in front of her. No, she didn't want to be that person. She shook her head and pushed a file toward Alex. "Here are my adjusted plans based on my new clinic opportunities."

"Thanks. I'll give these to Dr. Lindsay."

He nodded, stood, and flipped open the file, pacing the floor in his infuriating way which resembled a vulture. Circling prey.

No, wait. Dee brought her criticism to a halt and reexamined Alex Murdock: designer slacks fit to perfection, green oxford with the top button left fashionably undone, and golden hair sculpted to DaVinci precision. He really wasn't a vulture. Arrogant, condescending, fairly selfish, but three weeks ago, his lifestyle and goals would have matched hers without question.

And now? She wasn't the same. Not inside. Or maybe, she'd finally seen herself. But who was she? Beyond the years of focused study, self-denial, isolation, and lonely memories, who was left? She almost shuddered at silence's answer.

Perhaps, more hid beneath Alex's behavior too.

Alex turned to her, as if he'd read her thoughts, his green gaze direct. "You shouldn't be surprised at your progress, Dee. You're married to your work, like me. Without family to distract us, we'll become one of those great researchers we admire in record speed."

The swell of pride ebbed in Dee's chest. *Then what?* Her father wasn't here to share in her success, her brother remained distant at best, and her mother? She'd barely spoken to her mother since she graduated from high school.

"And speaking of research ..."

Dee looked up.

Alex returned to the seat across from her and leaned in. "I still haven't received those remaining cases from you."

Nope, he was a vulture.

She closed in to meet his challenge, hands flatted against her desk. "I have seven weeks."

His lips twisted into a lopsided grin which probably proved to dissuade quite a few ladies in the past. She remained unmoved. "So you're still going along with our little wager?"

"I thought the agreement was clear. Do you want to forfeit?"

Surprise flickered in his eyes and slowly transformed into an elfish glimmer. "Not at all. In fact, I have a gesture of goodwill." He pulled two tickets from his pocket and tossed them on the desk. "A trial, so to speak."

"Trial?" Dee picked up the tickets and frowned. *Football?*

"Dr. Lindsay's husband is good friends with Virginia Tech's head coach. She gave me four tickets to the UVA/Virginia Tech game in two weeks. Seats in the VIP box."

Dee smoothed her thumb across the tickets. Her heartbeat stuttered. Trial? No one mentioned anything about a trial.

"Show up. Give him a practice run." He shoved his hands into his pockets like a cheerful schoolboy and walked to the door. "Put him under pressure, and see how he does. Then you'll have an idea if your treatment is really working or not."

"I don't need to prove anything to you."

"Prove anything to *me?*" His brows shot skyward. "I could care less, but Dr. Lindsay will be right beside you in the box. Plenty of time to chat about your plans. Your research. Charlottesville?"

A knock turned both of them toward the office door. Rainey leaned in, her smile more welcome than Ma Mitchell's cooking … at present.

"Hey, Dee, sorry to interrupt. I just wanted to see if you had lunch plans."

Alex strode to the doorway, pearly whites in full gleam. His orthodontist must be proud. "No trouble at all." He offered a hand. "Alex Murdock."

Rainey shot Dee a humored glance before taking Alex's hand. "Rainey Mitchell."

"Mitchell?" Alex looked back at Dee for clarification. "I met another Mitchell when I was here last. Reese Mitchell?"

"He's my brother. Small town—big families." She pulled her hand free and braced it against the doorframe. "What brings you to Ransom, Mr. Murdock?"

"Dr. Murdock," he corrected, gently.

Man, with the proper motivation Mr. Charmer's skills rivaled Casanova's. His soft look, a tilt to his head, and any other woman except Rainey Mitchell would probably be swooning. "But please, call me Alex."

Dee rounded her desk, ready to step in and protect Rainey, if necessary. "Alex came down to check up on me."

"Ensure she was settling in, you know," He added.

"From Charlottesville?" Rainey's brow lifted. "That's quite a drive just to check on her."

"*Important* people are worth the time."

"Right." Rainey nodded, her lips stretched into a knowing smile. "*Important* people."

"What is your position here, Dr. Mitchell?"

"Clinic coordinator of the Tolliver Speech & Language Center and instructor for childhood language disorders. By the way, it's *Ms.* Mitchell, not Doctor." She confronted him with a look. "Important enough for you?"

Alex didn't seem to note the hint of fire in Rainey's words. She'd seen right through him in less than a minute. Not one flicker of attraction reflected in her eyes, merely a quirk of mischief in the challenge. Ooh, Dr. Alexander Murdock met his match.

"I'm interested in finding out, Ms. Mitchell." He drew another ticket from his pocket and placed it in her hand, attention focused on his target.

Rainey did a double take at the ticket and then laughed. "VIP tickets for UVA versus the Hokies. You have got to be kidding? This is awesome."

A smile so pure spread across Alex's face, Dee hardly recognized him. All façade fell away, replaced by … admiration? The charmer charmed? Maybe a heart pumped underneath the playboy after all.

"I … um … I'm glad you like them." He hesitated, a tiny *v* forming in his brow as he studied Dee. "I gave more to Adelina—one meant for your brother."

"Oh wow, thanks, Alex." She squeezed his arm, and Alex's grin spread wider. He looked like a six-year-old on Christmas morning—genuine, amazed, and a little too strange for Dee's past experiences. Who was this guy?

"Reese is going to flip. He's never been to one of the games before, even when he attended there."

"He went to UVA?" Dee stepped closer to the pair, another kick to her pride. Reese was right. She did make too many assumptions.

"No way. He's a Hokie through and through. So is Trigg." She looked back to Alex who hadn't taken his attention from her face for a moment. "Are you sure I don't need to pay you something for this, Alex?"

The elf returned. He placed a palm on the doorframe and leaned close. "Your time?"

Rainey's expression froze, then slowly her eyes narrowed. "I think you like games, Dr. Murdock."

"There's always time for a worthy opponent, wouldn't you agree, Ms. Mitchell?"

She hitched a grin. "Farm girls always watch where they step, Dr. Murdock. It's an occupational hazard and fabulous life lesson. Besides, I think this game is much too expensive for me. VIP?" She pressed the ticket back into his hand. "I'm a low-maintenance-type gal. Bleachers and binoculars."

"Keep it." He covered her hand with his. "In case you change your mind."

"Um ... thanks." She turned to Dee and barely cloaked an eye roll. "So, lunch?"

"No plans."

"Then I suggest we go over to Daphne's," Rainey said and turned to Alex, smile crooked to match his best mischievous smirk. "And since you're here for a visit, we might as well give you a taste of the good food and culture you're missing up in Charlottesville."

"My pleasure, Ms. Mitchell."

"But Dr. Murdock, play nice." She paused in her turn and leveled him with her turquoise stare. "You're on *my* home turf here, and I've played this game before."

LUNCH PROVED to be fairly uneventful, except for Alex declaring Daphne's café quaint, hitting it off with the waitress, Rainey's sister Emma, and unreservedly flirting with an unresponsive Rainey. Scratch that. Rainey responded with wit and sarcasm to make the mighty Alex Murdock squirm in his Ralph Lauren loafers.

How could Rainey live with such confidence and contentment in this little town? Maybe...maybe it wasn't about a place. Appalachia. Charlottesville.

Maybe it was about something much deeper.

"Is he always so obvious?" Rainey waved as Alex drove away from the café after lunch.

"Pretty much."

"And arrogant?"

"Yep."

"And you worked as his assistant for four years? Ugh." Rainey closed her eyes and released a long-suffering sigh. "I pride myself on being forbearing, but I don't know how long I could handle him. It's like talking to a cologne salesman or something."

"A cologne salesman?"

"You know, those guys who dress in sexy suits at the cologne counter in posh department stores." Rainey snagged a grin. "They look like they walked out of GQ. Every line, every compliment has *buy more cologne* written between the lines."

Dee grinned and watched Alex's car disappear out of sight, taking her place on the passenger's side of Rainey's jeep. Rainey brought an ease to friendship, a genuineness which encouraged Dee to relax and enjoy the process. "He'd probably benefit from being in Ransom for a while. A little authenticity would do him good."

"Ooh, and expose all of the flaws behind his perfect appearance?" She wiggled her brows, turning the key in the ignition. "Sounds like *my* kind of game." Rainey sobered. "So, is he your competition?"

Dee's stomach dropped. How much had Rainey heard of Alex's conversation? "What do you mean?"

"Well, I know you don't have plans to stay in Ransom forever. Is he the man who determines where you'll be next fall? Do you have to impress him or something?"

Dee worried her lip, weighing her words. "His opinion could influence the Chair's and Dean's decisions, but most of the responsibility for advancement falls on me."

"You don't like small towns?" Curiosity seemed to fuel her question, not accusations, so Dee released her worry on a sigh.

"A more rural community really doesn't meet my plans or interests. It's like trying to imitate a foreign accent. It doesn't come naturally, so I have to work at it to make it fit."

"I get that. Country life isn't the right place for everybody." She stared ahead as they drove through the quaint downtown streets of Ransom. "And you can't force someone to fit." Rainey shrugged off whatever shadow darkened her countenance. "So, what *do* you like? You're interested in researching accent mod, enjoy learning, and you seem to like teaching?"

"I *do* like teaching." The thought lured a smile. Watching students come alive earned one of the top spots on Dee's favorite-things list.

"What else? Besides speech pathology?"

"What do you mean?"

"You know, hobbies? Movie interests? Music? Favorite vacation spot?" Rainey turned the jeep into the university parking lot. "If you didn't have to worry about fitting into those designer clothes, what dangerously delicious food would you eat all of the time?"

"I don't know that I've thought a lot about it." Dee laughed her surprise but when the humor settled, her mind drew a blank. "I've been focused on getting through school."

"Come on. That's not an answer." Rainey brought the jeep to a stop and killed the engine, turning to face Dee. "You're not a country music fan, I'll bet."

Dee grimaced.

"Okay, and I'd say going to this football game has a much higher purpose than watching a bunch of three-hundred-pound men fall on each other over a pigskin. Do you even know what a touchdown is?"

"Ha, ha. As a matter of fact, I do." Dee crossed her arms in front of her chest and then relaxed her shoulders in assent to the truth. "But that's about all I know."

"If you were trapped in an elevator, what music would you want to listen to?"

Heat drained from Dee's face and she turned to open the jeep door. "I don't take elevators."

"I mean, if you were in one and—"

"No, I mean I don't *ever.*"

Dee slammed the door on Rainey's next question, a chill of terror pinpricked up her spine. Rainey met her around the front of the jeep.

"Never?"

Dee shook her head and started walking toward their office building.

"Oh, so there's something else I know about you. You're claustrophobic."

Let her think what she will. "I like classical music. I think it's soothing."

"I would have guessed that." Rainey slapped her hands together. "Are you a tennis player?"

Dee's jaw slacked and she stopped on the sidewalk to stare at her colleague. "How did you know?"

"It fits you. Isolated sport." Rainey winked. "I bet you were a dancer when you were younger too."

"Okay, now you're scaring me." Dee waved a hand in the air, resuming her walk. "Am I that obvious?"

"I just have to pay attention with you. You don't talk about much else besides your job." Rainey held the building door open, her sobered gaze pulling Dee's attention. "You know, Dee, you can always come to my house or Mom's if you want company. It's not good for people to be all alone—not when you don't have to be. You *do* have friends here."

The old caution rose with icy fingers around her heart. Trusting someone? Believing in them? Opening oneself up to them? Rainey offered a new type of friendship, exquisite and rare like holding a masterpiece. The Mitchells meant their friendships to the core of who they were.

"Thank you, Rainey."

Rainey hitched a half smile, but her gaze stayed intense, adding potency to her words. "You got it. Any time." She followed Dee through the door and toward their offices. "Now, let's talk about giving kids therapy."

Dee groaned and reached for her office keys. "I know, I'm horrible."

Rainey laughed. "No, you're just very well-planned. For adults.

Your lesson plans were impeccable. I've never seen reports so detailed, let alone lesson plans."

"I have a PhD for heaven sake. I should be able to do this." Dee sighed and opened her office door. Total helplessness lodged like a giant pill in her throat. "I've always known I wasn't meant to work with children."

"Really? I wouldn't have guessed that."

"Even after today?" She hadn't pegged Rainey as a bold-faced liar.

"I've seen you with Lou and Brandon. You're great. It's just with therapy you're trying to force things to happen, to make kids fit into some sort of plan without taking their learning style or age into consideration." Her smile held an apology. "Great intentions, poor follow-through."

"I just can't manage that sort of behavior. The bouncing-around, the lack of attention." She slumped into her office chair and placed her face in her palms. "The crying."

Hands rested on her shoulders and Dee looked up in to Rainey's compassionate face. "This may be hard for you to hear, but sometimes, you just have to *go with the flow.*"

Dee peeked through her fingers. "You sound like your brother."

"I will try not get be offended by such slander."

Dee grinned and dropped her palms down to her desk. Go with the flow? Her throat grew bone-dry. "I don't think I can do that."

"Sure you can. Mind you, there are some times and some kids that you toss everything into the air and start from scratch—but not the ones you have. You've just got to get inside their heads. Think … play."

"Play?" Ten times easier said than done.

"Right." Rainey sat down on the chair across from Dee, eyes narrowed. "You did used to play at one point in your life, didn't you?"

"Who can remember?"

"Okay, that does it. On Saturday, we're taking you on a family hike and picnic. It's obviously been way too long since you did something besides work, and helping my brother deliver cows doesn't count."

Dee's smile spread until it turned into a laugh. "When you put it that way, my life does sounds pathetic." Pathetic and painfully true.

"It needs a little spicing up, I think. Mitchell-style." Rainey rubbed her hands together, a sparkle in her eyes. "But first—let's talk about giving children therapy and having fun doing it."

"No, Emma Mitchell." How many times would Reese have to repeat himself? "Dee and me are not dating. That's the last time I'm gonna say it."

Emma's sneaky brow shot north along with one side of her lips. "Sure you aren't, bro." She placed her palms on the restaurant table and leaned over him, her little white apron almost dropping into his coffee. "You two make a wonderful couple. I can tell."

Reese gestured toward the pair at the back of the restaurant. "Just because you matched up Widow Edwards with Old Man Parker, doesn't mean you've grown some kind of pink matchmaking thumb. You got lucky."

She shrugged in a *whatever* sort of way, but her golden eyes kept their mischievous glint. "They happen to be the second couple I've successfully encouraged into matrimony."

"Isn't there some famous story about a young girl who wouldn't mind her own business? Kept matchmaking and the like?"

Her smile brightened. "You mean Jane Austen's Emma?"

"Good grief, you even have her name?" He slapped his forehead and groaned. She'd stepped into her role with prophetic zeal, no doubt. Not so great for the singles of Ransom.

"I think I've found a gift."

"Well keep that gift of yours to yourself and top off my coffee instead of wasting my time."

Emma slid into the booth seat across from him instead. Weren't little sisters supposed to listen to their older and wiser brothers? No chance with his sisters—even this prissy one. He got the same response as talking to the back end of his tractor. Nothin'.

"You should really shave off your beard."

"Now listen here, little girl." He palmed his chin, protecting his fuzz. "I don't tell you how to cut your hair or shave your face, so don't you be tellin' me."

She harrumphed. "I'm sure there's a handsome man underneath all that fuzz somewhere. You look the most like Daddy of any of us."

Reese pointed at her and nodded. "And Daddy had a beard too."

"And *Daddy* was born back when houses had dirt floors and phones were scarce in these parts. You wanna live like that now too?"

Reese growled.

"Who knows, you might even catch Dee's attention if you shave. Maybe even wear a suit or something. You look like an old grizzly bear in overalls."

Reese's BLT turned in his stomach. He reserved his only suit strictly for funerals and weddings. No wonder bellyachin' was called bellyachin'. What had happened to his nice, sweet baby sister? The one who looked up at him like he was the best thing on the planet? His stomach clenched with another spasm. Would Lou grow up to bellyache too?

"Why is it so all-fired important that I shave my face?"

Emma rolled her eyes to the ceiling as if only Heaven could help her bear with such a brother. "How many fuzzy-faced heroes are there in movies, Reese?"

"A whole lot. Most of them, in fact."

"I don't mean westerns. Women aren't watching a whole lot of westerns. They're watching primetime cop shows, or romantic comedies, or historical dramas; and ninety-five percent of those men are clean shaven or pretty close."

Reese sat a little taller and grinned. "Then I'm a nonconformist."

Emma didn't laugh. "No, you're a stereotype. Grizzly, uneducated, narrow-minded mountain man."

"The only one I resemble in that list is mountain man."

"And grizzly." Emma looked past him and her face suddenly brightened. "Oh, boy! Look who's coming in for her evening dessert. I call this positively providential."

Reese didn't have to turn around to know exactly who walked through the café door. Why did God get the blame for everything?

And, of course, his brain stopped working and his eyes took over and pulled his attention right toward the front door. Dee entered, hair up in a fancy twist and little red coat blowing around her from an evening gust of wind. She looked like Christmas—and he'd always liked Christmas. He rubbed his beard and examined his overalls. He was not grizzly.

"Well, hi there, Doc." Emma slid Reese her sweetest smile. "I was just taking a break for a minute talking to my big bro. Care to take my place?"

If Emma felt the heat from his stare, she didn't show it. Not one hint of smoke. Her smile only grew wider. Meddlin' female.

Dee's eyes popped wide. "Well, I wasn't planning to stay. Just wanted to pick up something sweet for home."

Emma's gaze shot to him, filled with enough mischief to shame an elf.

Before he could answer, she jumped in with both feet and a cupid bow. "We have a fresh apple pie nearly done. Maybe ten more minutes. How about you sit yourself down right here until it's finished and I can serve you up a piece while it's still warm?"

"I bet she's tired from a full day of work, Emma." Reese firmed his words to get his sister's attention. "She might want to go on home."

"Fiddlesticks." Emma brushed his suggestion off with a wave of her hand. "Who wants rest when there is a fresh, warm apple pie only minutes away? Eat first—rest later."

The back end of the tractor listened much better.

Dee smiled and Reese's heart responded. Maybe he'd get a slice of apple pie too.

"Maybe a scoop of vanilla ice cream to sweeten the deal?"

Dee laughed, which seemed to be coming on a more regular basis lately. Especially when she wasn't tormenting him through a session. "You've sold me. I probably wouldn't rest well knowing I'd missed such a remarkable apple pie anyway."

Emma snapped her fingers. "Now you're talkin', Doc. Have a seat and I'll bring a piece out once it's finished. A la mode."

Dee loosened the belt of her jacket and Reese nearly jumped to a stand, offering to help. She stared up at him as if he'd grown a horn from his head. Or maybe it was the beard. She didn't seem like the western-loving type. She hesitated, then allowed him to slide the jacket from her arms and hang it on a nearby coat rack.

Even when he tried to be a gentleman, he screwed up—without even saying a word. Maybe he was getting worse instead of better.

"Sorry, did I do something wrong?"

She blinked out of her stare. "You keep surprising me. That's all."

His grin started slow and stretched across his face as he sat back down. "You don't like surprises?"

Dee cleared her throat and adjusted her sleeves, a tactic to avoid looking at him, he guessed. This was getting a little bit fun. He was versatile. He liked mysteries too.

"Surprises are fine, just unexpected." She pinched her eyes closed. "You know what I mean."

"They're not on a list or somethin'?"

Her lips twitched. "Or some*thing,* yes. Where are the children?"

"With Rainey. She took them to some sort of children's festival about Dr. Seuss."

"She has an amazing amount of energy—all positive. I've never known anyone like her, or your mother, even after what Rainey's been through."

The confession must have slipped out because Dee pinched her lips closed and studied the table for a minute. Reese didn't mind her admission one bit. He took pride in both his sister and mom, even if both were as stubborn as Emma. Dee's acknowledgement just showed good sense.

"It takes a lot to suffer loss and come out smil*ing.*"

Dee titled her head and studied him a moment. "It does."

One of those deep quiet moments passed between them again, before Dee stared back at the table, her fingernails carving a line across the wood grain. She wore lonely like a raincoat.

"What about your loss, Dee? Your daddy died when you were young, and your mama?"

Her finger curled into a fist and her gentle expression hardened.

She flipped a cold stare up to him, not directed at him maybe, but he still flinched from the chill. "My mother hasn't been a part of my life in a long time. End of story."

Reese sat back in the booth and allowed the silence to distance her anger. She stored a heap of hurt behind those words, recoiling into the pain like a shell. The last thing the woman needed was more time away from people.

She looked up and offered a fake-smile. "Did you like living in Charlotte?"

"You're real good at deflecting those personal questions, aren't you?"

"Some things are best left unsaid."

"And some things only heal when you say them." He tapped her fingers that lay on the table. "Or have others help you carry 'em."

Her expression remained closed, but that pouty lip of hers appeared. "Thank you, Mr. Mitchell, but I find I handle things much better privately, on my own."

"Where people won't fail you? Or where you won't fail them?"

She flinched. "How can you possibly know anything about it, Reese? Loneliness? Rejection? Crying out to a God who wasn't listening?"

The emotions waved across her face from soft to hard. But the softness came first—a small breach in her stubbornness, but one all the same. Hurt, deep and painful, etched in the lines on her face. She *needed* somebody to show her what love really looked like—how much God listened. How his strong arms held weak people.

The big question now was why did Reese care about Dr. Adelina Roseland discovering those things? Why did this woman draw him in with such curiosity, with such need? Just maybe he was as stubborn as the backside of a tractor too.

Reese softened the blow of his words. "People are going to fail, Dee. It's human nature. The real issue is what we do when they fail that matters most. Do we hold it all inside or do we let it go?"

Her chin stiffened. "I've spent thousands on counselors. I've had hundreds of hours of sleepless nights. If I want another opinion about how I should manage the emotional affairs of my *private* life, you'll be the first to know." She released a shaky breath and pulled her hand away from his on the table. "Until then, vowels and consonants remain safe topics. Okay?"

And she did it again—threw him headlong right out of her business, but not before giving him more information in one admission than she had the previous weeks. She opened the door to her past and, for better or worse, his traitor-feet and heart, pushed him right through it.

CHAPTER 9

But you have no idea how frightfully interesting it is to take a human being and change her into a quite different human being by creating a new speech for her. It's filling up the deepest gulf that separates class from class and soul from soul. (Pygmalion, Act 3)

Reese turned from the sink in time to hear a knock at the door. Last night's conversation with Dee still hung in his mind, sparking more interest with each memory. She harbored some mighty big wounds to cause such a violent reaction. Wounds he should leave alone if he was smart.

The knock came again. Without hesitation, Lou ran from the living room to the front door, Brandon close behind. Dee's voice greeted him before he even saw her. "What a sweet welcome, guys."

"Daddy says you've come to work on his words some more," Lou bounded into view.

Dee looked up from his little girl, her smile broad and beautiful. She'd worn her hair pinned back at the sides, but the length of it fell around her shoulders in the back. Soft, like the brief glimpses behind the wall of her heart. Good grief, he was thinking in poetry. He could practically hear Trigg laughing at him like a fool, but it didn't stop his fingers from aching to scoop up a handful of those locks. He stiffened his jaw. Nope, he'd never been very smart.

"Oh, yes, we have to get your daddy ready for his big meeting."

He tossed the dishtowel over his shoulder and met the ladies in the living room, trying to ignore the added scent of apples she brought with her. Good enough to taste.

Heat trailed up his neck and he swallowed a groan, the Trigg-in-his-head still laughing.

Lou looked up at him. "They don't speak English where you're going, Daddy?"

"Not mountain English, Lou." He touched his daughter's cheek and nodded to the living room. "Would you go ahead and put the movie in for Brandon while Doc and I work in my office?"

Lou leaned close, cupping her words to a whisper. "I ain't picking the dinosaur movie again, Daddy. It's about ready to drive me plum crazy."

He matched her volume. "I don't think Brandon will care which movie you pick so long as it has lots of songs on it."

Lou heaved a ten pound sigh. "Yeah, it's always about the songs."

He looked up to find Dee watching them, all the frigid energy from last night gone. Her gaze melted into his, soft-like. He cleared his stuck voice and grinned. "Ready to work?"

At her nod, he led the way to his office, which he'd rushed through cleaning before she came. It still looked like a tornado hit it, but at least now it was a little tornado. The room boasted all the things he loved. Family photos, favorite books, a few old-fashioned maps, and a prize bass he'd caught three years ago and mounted to the wall.

"I heard we were going on a picnic this weekend." Reese weighed each word, using all those *ings* and final consonants.

"That's what I heard too."

"Rainey's real good at them." He stopped and ran his hands through his hair, biting down on each syllable so he could get the session off to a good start—maybe even impress her. "Does every word matter that much, Dee? I mean, it ain't–"

Her brow shot up.

"It isn't like I'm speaking a foreign language or something. Surely those men up in Chicago can get the gist of what I'm talking about."

Dee took a seat and folded her hands in her lap. He'd already learned what that meant. She didn't agree. "Do you want to take that chance? Let's say we put aside the whole notion of saving your farm. You said yourself this is a great opportunity to not only increase your income, but stretch yourself professionally. If you're thinking of bigger things …"

"I don't think I said it quite so well as that."

Dee clasped her lips into a smile. "No, you said it more like *the farm needs the money and I wouldn't mind the challenge none.* Does that sound about right?"

He rubbed his jaw and studied her. "Well now, I'm not sure you had enough twang in your speech."

Her smile came loose and brightened her entire face. "I'm pretty sure you'll beat me hands down on twang."

Their gazes held a moment too long. She looked away but not before his heart jumped like a scared rabbit. Any woman who flipped from one emotion to the next in half a second, shouldn't be on his list of possible wives. *Stupid man.* He should run while he had the chance, but there he was, staring like an idiot—and enjoying what he saw.

"I'm sorry about last night."

His pulse settled into a pleasant thump. She kept her gaze to the ground. He'd take a heart-felt apology any day. It neutralized the *crazy* a little. "No harm done, Dee."

She lifted her eyes, forehead puckered with remorse. "Yes, there is harm done. I'm perceived as a witch or prima donna. You and your family have shown me nothing but kindness." She looked back down at her hands. "I was harsh. I don't *want* to be harsh."

"I bring it out in you, don't I?"

Her expression softened. "It must be the accent."

He chuckled and Dee went right into the session, starting as usual:

a list of words and phrases for him to repeat with proper speech. It was like reliving first grade, with a much cuter teacher than baggy-cheeked Mrs. Milner.

Dee's focus lightened a little at the end, as he read off some *Calvin and Hobbes* quotes using his best speech. Her intensity and focus fueled his. Teaching brought her to life, brightened her face with a ferocity it turned a man's thoughts in rascally directions. Heat skimmed his collar as his rebel gaze took in the beauty of her from hairline to heels—when she wasn't looking, of course. If she redirected some of her energy into loving a man, it'd knock him clean into next year.

"What do you get out of all this?"

She placed her *Calvin and Hobbes* book back in her bag and looked up. "What do you mean?"

"Well you're putting in a whole lot of time and energy on me, and though I'd like to think you're here because of my rugged good looks and magnetic charm, I don't think that's quite it."

She tilted her head back and laughed. A great sound, but the thought wasn't *that* funny.

"As I've said before, it's part of my research. And it's not so much *therapy* with you as it is … er … tutoring." Her sweet smile sent cupid's arrow directly through his chest. "Besides, it feels good to know I'm helping your family."

"So you spend all this time and energy tutoring me out of good will and for research? Seems extreme. I think I know your real secret."

EVERY OUNCE of warmth drained from Dee's face and landed on her unsteady pulse. Had Rainey overheard her conversation with Alex and put the pieces together somehow?

"Reese, it's really—"

"You like a challenge."

Warmth rushed back into her extremities with the surge of relief. "I do love a good challenge." She straightened, tamping down the near panic. "But research helps guide practice, so it's vital as well."

"Yeah, I know it's important, but there has to be something else pushing you along besides research." He cradled the back of his head in his palms and stretched his legs out in front of him. "When I do research I have to feel like I'm either helping people with what I'm learning or sharing information for productivity and awareness later on. Not just the research."

She didn't quite catch her scoff in time. "You've done research?"

"Sure I have." He stood and walked to a bookshelf, taking a handful of paperback magazines.

Several slipped from his grip so Dee bent to collect them. They were journals, fairly prestigious looking too from the binding. Journal of Agricultural Economics? National Journal of Farming Science? She caught a surprised burst of air with her hand and held out the journals to him.

"You're published? In these?"

He winked and a responsive flutter erupted in her chest. "Shocking, ain ... isn't it?" He flipped through one of the journals and stopped in the middle. "See, here's my favorite."

She couldn't take her eyes from his face. This burly farmer, lifelong mountain man, was published in a research journal? And more than once?

Would he never cease to disprove all her preconceptions? Her mind scrambled to piece everything together. Not only was he strong, a loving father, and kind ... but intelligent? How had she not known about his degree? How could she stay so stuck in her misperceptions? Maybe because throughout school she surrounded herself with people who held the same prejudices to make her feel right? She sighed. The arguments against Reese crumbled further, loosening her emotions and the strength in her knees. She'd seen the hurt in his eyes last night. The memory kept her awake, forcing her into further self-reflection, and as she dug deep into her heart, she found him. Waiting.

Was she ready? Willing to be as authentic as him? Would he want her if he knew all of her little secrets? "I … I just didn't expect. You seem so—"

He took a step closer, voice low. "Ignorant? Crass?"

She couldn't pull her gaze from his. "No."

He edged another step. "Pigheaded? Backwoods?"

"No … um," her words crept out slow, heavy with uncertainty. The interest in his gaze fogged up clear thoughts. "You've surprised me again. You—"

"What? I don't make it on one of your lists?" His gentleness teased her forward. He folded the book together. She rested a hand on his chest, the cotton fabric warmed by his skin beneath. Her breaths grew shallow and utterly useless.

His hand to her waist didn't help matters. "What do I seem like to you, Dee?" He brushed back a stray hair from her cheek with the back of his fingertips. The sweet depth of his voice chased a row of tingles down her neck. Would he kiss her? She craved it and feared it all at once.

Her fingers wrapped around the cloth of his shirt, pulling him nearer.

The fire in his eyes ignited sparks in her chest. His right brow and corner of his mouth turned upward in question. "How about we try some nonverbal communication?"

His feather-light touch cascaded across her cheek to cup the back of her head. The gentleness in his caress glided across her skin, leaving liquid warmth in its wake. Her eyes flickered closed to focus on the sheer pleasure of his touch. Such a sweet embrace, so sweet it whispered of hopes buried. How long had it been since someone brought her emotions to life? Had anyone ever? Like this?

Deep yearning in her soul awakened with a fury, uncontrolled and beautiful, silencing her reservations.

His hand left her waist and moved to stroke her other cheek, thumb brushing against the dip below her bottom lip. She opened her eyes and lost any fears in the desire in the depths of his coffee-colored eyes. His gaze trailed to her lips and back to her eyes, his brow jotting up as if to ask her permission. In answer, she tugged him closer. He tilted his head slightly, inching nearer, and deepening the sense of wonder spiraling through her chest. *So much trust.*

His lips barely brushed hers. Dee held her breath.

The truth knifed into the moment's tenderness. *He trusted her.* What was she doing?

"Daddy," Lou called from down the hall. "Daddy, Brandon stinks."

Reese didn't move, just looked down at her lips like a hungry man. His lips didn't look so bad either. Her knees weakened. Her grip on his shirt tightened. His palm swept down to steady her at the waist and he leaned in again.

"Daddy?"

Dee's mind cleared and she forced herself away. He dropped his hand, but didn't move, a smile forming slow and easy. He trusted her —and he shouldn't.

"You wanna trade places for about five minutes?"

The fog in Dee's brain slowed comprehension. "What?"

"Daddy, I think you're gonna need a dump truck for this one."

His heated gaze hovered on her lips and left a fire trail of anticipatory tingles. "Okay, we might have to trade places for ten minutes."

Dee cleared her throat and stepped further away. "I ... I need to go."

His expression intensified, confident. "I'd run from this too, Dee." He grabbed her hand before she slipped out of reach. "Grumpy farmer, stinky son, and a bossy little girl? It can only lead to trouble." He brought her palm to his lips and then let go, turning to the door. "Comin' Lou—and I'll bring the dump truck."

He glanced her way before leaving the room. "Did I mention another of my many good qualities?"

She steadied herself with a hand to the table, but couldn't look away.

"I'm a patient man. Very patient." He winked one more time. "And I'm pretty fond of challenges myself."

He walked out the door and Dee collapsed into the chair. Seven weeks? Who really would win this wager? Alex? Herself? Or Reese Mitchell?

It took three conversations with Rainey and one visit from Grace Mitchell to convince Dee to join the family picnic. After the near emotional breakthrough she had with Reese a few days earlier, where his lips teased all sorts of daydreams out of her, she'd tried to convince herself of two things:

One—getting out of Ransom remained her primary purpose, not building confusing relationships. Two—if Reese really knew her, if he scratched beyond the surface, he wouldn't like what he saw. Rainey was witty and charming. No wonder people liked her. Mama Mitchell's generous nature and homespun appeal endeared others to her. But Rainey's personal questions and Reese's personal touch shook her to the soul. Underneath all the education and the years of denial, who was left? A skeleton of a frightened little girl clinging to a dream that didn't exist? And three—she'd made a wager, and if he ever found out it would probably ruin any good feelings he had for her.

Fear of his rejection secured her distance, but broke her heart. When she closed her eyes, she sensed his fingertips stroking her cheek and the mere thought of his bass voice near her ear had her pulse doing the samba. As Calvin said, *Getting an inch of snow is like winning ten cents in the lottery.* A near kiss from Reese Mitchell evoked the same reaction ... enough to make her mad, or crazy.

Rainey pulled into the driveway with her blue SUV, Sarah's pixie face evident through the back window. Dee met her at the porch steps, a list of excuses readied. "I have a lot of work to do for classes next week. Maybe I should just stay—"

"I have the same number of classes as you." Rainey's lifted brow brooked no refusal.

"But there's a new assessment on Wednesday I—"

"Nope. Won't work." She shook her head. "I have *three* new

assessments on Monday and one on Thursday. All the more reason to have some fun today."

Dee opened her mouth with another excuse and Rainey cut her off. "Nope. Not listening. You obviously don't know what's best for you, but lucky for you, friends do." She jerked her head to the passenger seat. "In."

"I haven't been hiking or on a picnic in ..." Dee looked up at the cloudless autumn blue sky. "I can't even remember." Everything after her father's death meshed her high school years into a constant blur with one goal: move out of the house. Before, laughter wasn't a common occurrence, let alone picnics. After nearly kissing Reese Mitchell, spending time near him terrified her because ... it didn't make sense in her plans.

"All the more reason to go today. If you can survive a Mitchell family outing, you can survive anything."

Surviving wasn't the issue. Chocolate-colored eyes and mountain charm struck up a confused chorus of fear and hope with an entire emotional orchestra screaming *run!* Dee reluctantly made her way to the passenger side and climbed in, thankful her jeans and long-sleeved t-shirt matched Rainey's casual look.

Rainey steered down the gravel drive, the high-pitched chorus of children's music playing in the background. Sarah swayed her golden head to the tune, a smile spread from one plump cheek to the other.

"I brought cream puffs for the picnic." She held up her offering wrapped in Tupperware.

Rainey gave it a solid nod. "Thank you, Dee. I'll have to jog an extra mile today because of you." Her grin turned wicked. "Unless you want to challenge me in a tennis match?"

"You play tennis too?"

"Nah," Rainey shrugged. "Well, I mean, I can play enough for people to make fun of me, but that's about it. You'd get a nice laugh out of it."

Dee looked out the window, thoughts turning to Reese. "I didn't know your brother did research. He's even published."

"Oh, Dee, to be such a smart lady, you sure have a lot to learn."

Rainey chuckled and turned the music down a little. "Just because people in your past were a certain way, and chose to live as they did, doesn't mean everyone in Appalachia is the same."

"I recognize that."

"Right." Her tone said otherwise. "Here's a good test. What would you say if I told you I got my Master's Degree from Vandy?"

Dee's jaw came unhinged. "You got into Vanderbilt University?"

"Crazy, right?" Rainey shrugged, the green jacket turning her eyes more green than blue. "Loved it—and proved my point, by the way. You have some pretty wild misconceptions about Appalachian folks."

It took five seconds for Dee's brain to catch up with the news and muddle through a fresh flush of shame. If Rainey only knew … "Why did you come back *here?*"

"You make the choice sound like a bad thing."

Dee smoothed her hands over her jeans. "I'm sorry. I didn't mean—"

"There's a lot to be said for a place called home, Dee. I guess for someone who is used to bigger towns and cities, it's hard to imagine."

Dee tried to keep her expression neutral, but evidently failed.

"I know it's not Charlottesville, but it works for me and my family. Home isn't a certain place, it's the peace in knowing that I belong. And here?" Her smile grew. "I'm going to be loved just the way I am—crazy and all. When I've won, when I've lost. Even when I don't know where I'm going, I still have a place called home." She shrugged. "It's more than enough."

"Your family makes people feel at home." Dee braided her fingers together in her lap.

Home. The word, so long an uncertain, dark place, found residence in her imagination again, and from a distance, it looked a little bit like Ransom. But only a little.

THE PATH WOUND through the forest. Sunlight sprinkled the veil of pines and cast pinpoints of light along the way. Moss and pine needle scents mingled with the cool mountain air, and the freshness in the breeze awakened all of Dee's senses.

Their trek brought them over a ridge and into a view of endless mountains. They rolled up to see the hazy horizon tinted a million hues of blue. The vastness of the view struck Dee with a sense of wonder.

Dee turned and watched the group pass her, a humorous entourage of women and children, with Reese as the lone adult male representative. And what a representative. His ball cap was delightfully absent allowing her full view of his dark curls. With the hunter green windbreaker and Brandon riding on his shoulders, his appeal grew. He loved his kids and mother so well—which only proved he'd do the same with any woman in his life.

Lou held her hand, swinging it back and forth, as naturally as if she'd done it a hundred times before. It fit so well, drawing her into their sweet world like another fixture. Dee's long list of reasons why a relationship with Reese could never work, number one being the simple fact she was using him for professional advancement, was reason enough to quell any attraction.

But it wasn't working.

At all.

"Sure does make you think about how small we are and how big God is, don't it?" Reese stood beside her, Brandon on his shoulders flapping at Reese's hair.

She stared back over the panoramic scene. *So big He didn't even care about her?*

"I got an idea."

Dee shielded her eyes from the mid-morning sun and looked up at him. "You *have* an idea?"

"Yep." He tilted his head, clearly ignoring her correction. "Mama's birthday is tomorrow and I'm sure she'd love for you to come. What if you rode with us to church and then joined us for lunch?"

Dee's throat tightened around her response. Had he been reading her mind or did God really hear her thoughts? His spies must be everywhere. She scanned the view for clues.

"That'd be great, Ms. Doc. Granny loves company." Lou added, swinging their hands wider. "And you don't have to work on Sundays like Aunt Rainey neither."

Dee might have tried to gently correct Lou's speech if the thought of church hadn't put breath in limbo. Years of pushing God as far away as possible, shuffled among the unanswered questions and prayers. She looked out over the horizon and almost *felt* Him there too, nudging her. She shuddered.

When she turned back to Reese, his grin broadened. "You said you liked a challenge. Maybe your idea about God is about as correct as your idea about me and my family?"

She narrowed her eyes. "You're one sneaky sort, Reese Mitchell." She shook the notion from her head. "Besides, one doesn't have anything to do with the other."

"Then you're scared?"

Dee sighed in resignation. "Maybe, I'll go just this once, if I remember."

"I can write it on your list for you."

His teasing tone relaxed her shoulders. "You're impossible."

He leaned in close, his whiskers tickling her ear. "Just something to ponder—You can't fail him so badly that He won't love you anyway."

She kept her face forward. If she looked at Reese, in the quiet awe of the moment, tears threatened to rise. Then, as if the most natural thing in the world, he reached down and wrapped his fingers around her free hand. His gaze took in the view, apparently unaware of the effect of his touch. Her breath support pittered away to nothing, her face warmed, and something inside her broke free, all because his touch awakened the sense that *Someone* else might not be as far away as she'd believed. Someone cared.

"Why did I agree to this?" Dee washed her breakfast dishes and looked over at Haus on a rug by the back door. His ears perked up as if he knew exactly what she was saying. Crazy dog.

"But I'm not afraid. I just don't see any reason in talking to Someone who is not interested in my life. If He ever was with me, He left a long time ago."

She peeked at her reflection in the oven-range microwave and smoothed her hair around her face. "So, I'm only doing this for Lou and Mama Mitchell."

Haus' scary grin settled in place.

"It's the truth. You can grin all you want."

An engine rumbled at the front of the house. Dee pushed Haus out the back door onto the covered porch, just as a knock came to the front. "I'll never hear the end of it if they know I've let you inside, boy."

She eased her walk across the house, taking a deep breath before opening the front door.

Reese met her, beard trimmed, and a white oxford tucked into a pair of dark jeans. Good heavens, her thoughts dipped into areas inappropriate for church—whether God read her mind or not.

Reese gave her a healthy, painfully slow appraisal before adding a whistle at the end. "Well, Doc, you sure do clean up well."

The unshackled admiration in his gaze brought heat to her face, and the whistle fanned the flame. "You're not so bad yourself, Mr. Mitchell."

"I'm wearing a button-up shirt and there isn't a wedding." He tipped his head closer, voice purring an octave lower. "You *must* be pretty special."

Her face spiked to feverish temperatures. "I see it as a good sign for things to come, don't you?"

"Do you think it will help me act fancier too?"

"I'm not sure if the clothes truly make the man, Mr. Mitchell." She snatched her purse and lifted a brow. "But if you use the techniques I've taught you, I'm certain you are less likely to offend God's ears with your prayers."

He laughed and held the door for her to exit. His appearance paired with his scent nearly had her swooning. *Cedar and spice and everything nice.* She cast a look toward heaven and shook her head. If

God could see everything, then her heated thoughts added another failure to her list. Well, one thing was for certain: Reese Mitchell would be a much-needed distraction from the guilt-laden sermon awaiting her. God hadn't been interested in her as a fourteen-year-old crying for help. Why would He be interested now?

CHAPTER 10

The hardest job I ever tackled, make no mistake about that, mother...
(Pygmalion, Act 3)

Maybe Dee wasn't such an idiot at child therapy. After adding more research with Rainey's tips, she not only had fun but the kids did too. Finding words posted on the walls of a dark room with a flashlight kept them engaged and begging for more. A scavenger hunt for words instead of thirty minutes of forced repetition proved to be more resourceful with time, effective, and enjoyable for everyone. A little miracle in her life.

Good planning mixed with play really worked. Who knew? One of the children even gave her a hug on the way out. Why had she talked herself into disliking kids? She hadn't been around them very much growing up, so lack of practice bred some insecurity, but how had the general negative decisions become so ingrained?

Her father disliked kids. No one knew, of course. He'd smile and talk to them when they came near, but afterward he'd complain about their loudness and make comments about *people who work with children do so because they can't work anywhere else.*

But it wasn't true.

Why hadn't she seen his inconsistencies before? Did the Mitchells bring out the comparison? Her father's truth wasn't truth at all?

Church on Sunday sparked more doubts. *The God of lost things?* In her fourteen years of church visits, she'd never heard the story of the lost sheep or the lost coin. Unshed tears burned her eyes as she recalled the preacher's words. Or the lost son.

The thought of the son coming home to his father whispered through her barren soul and urged her to reconsider her previous assumptions. Had her father influenced such prejudice? Perhaps that possibility frightened her the most. Had her entire life been built on faulty vision?

Uncertainty pierced like a blade, slicing one memory and conversation after another. What if she gave into the new hope Mitchell's Crossroads offered? What if she even reassessed her ideas about God?

When she'd walked into Mrs. Mitchell's house after church, birthday balloons and laughter all around, the tiny taste of being *found* rattled her senses. How long did it take the lost son to realize his lostness?

She couldn't shake the questions, even as the rich warmth of mocha, cinnamon, and pumpkin bread enveloped her with one step into Daphne's. Her entire body relaxed into the decadent aroma— carb-therapy at its finest. She passed an old-fashioned counter lined with various local novelties, like hillbilly sticks, and then beyond a display case revealing a myriad of delectables. Her anxiety subsided with each step deeper into the fragrance of baked bread and melted butter. Visiting Daphne's was therapeutic … and needed to happen more often.

"Well, hi there, Doc." Emma scrunched up her nose with a perfect princess smile. "Did you notice the baguettes and Focaccia bread? Aunt Daphne's letting me try out some of my chef skills on the locals." She shook with excitement. "I'm in my second year of classes and absolutely loving it, but it's going to be a hard sale for my aunt." Emma lowered her voice to a whisper, exuding enough energy to light the restaurant. "She has the *if-it-ain't-broke-don't-fix-it* mentality." She blinked back to attention. "Hungry?"

"With smells like this, it's impossible not to be."

Emma's wink held the same mischief as Reese's. "Aunt Daphne's secret ingredient to keeping this place at the top of the Blue Ridge hot spots. De-licious food. One step in and a sample of homemade goodness satisfies every time."

"What do you suggest? I'm on my way up to Reese's for another speech session. Maybe I could take something to the kids?" She bit her bottom lip and tried not to appear too obvious. "And what might Reese like?"

Emma's smile inverted but still flickered at the corners of her eyes, in true pixie form. "I don't know if you want to do that, Doc. Reese has been awful sick since the day of the picnic."

"What? He hasn't called me about it?" Of course, why would he? They weren't dating or anything.

"Well, I think he's been way too crummy to chat." Emma shook her head slowly. "Mama said something about dizziness and a bad cough. Sounds pretty rough."

"Dizziness? Does he have a fever? Has he been to the doctor?" Dee pressed her palms against the counter. "Does he need anything?"

Emma's lips pinched in a sad smile, but her eyes clung to the glimmer. What was she up to?

"That's awful nice of you. Mama's been off to Roanoke with Rainey today for her doctor's checkup about the ribs and all. I'm sure Reese could use a touch of kindness about now? Maybe take him something to help him feel better?"

Emma's intentions clinked into recognition. A setup emerged, as plain as the chocolate icing on the cake under her nose. "Well, I wouldn't want to intrude. Maybe *you* could take something?"

"I don't get off until nine." An exaggerated sigh pulled at Emma's shoulders. "Aunt Daphne's just finished a fresh pot of chicken noodle and rice soup, and Reese *loves* Aunt Daphne's soups. It's never quite as tasty as when it's fresh."

Dee drew in another deep breath of the intoxicating aroma and stared over at the plates of freshly baked cookies sitting atop the counter. She hadn't been around a lot of sick people, let alone a sick, single man.

"I'll throw in a half dozen chocolate chip cookies." Emma's impish grin returned. "And a raspberry scone from my special *new items* stash?"

Dee surrendered with a smile. "You're definitely a saleswoman."

She laughed. "You should have met my dad. He could have sold milk to a cow. One bat of those coffee-colored eyes of his and my mama was a goner every time."

Yep, Dee knew all about the intoxication of coffee-colored eyes.

Someone either knocked at the front door or the pounding in Reese's head had started up again. He couldn't remember the last time he'd been so sick. If people listened to him once in a while, everyone would be a lot better off—but no, the womenfolk insisted on a picnic. *Insisted.* He told them it was going to rain. Checked the Farmer's Almanac to be sure, but nobody listened, as usual.

And who was suffering for it?

Him. Of course. Blasted females.

The pain hammered in his head again, louder. He squeezed his head to keep it from dancing clean off his neck.

"Somebody's at the door, Daddy."

Lou's words sifted through a tunnel of fog to his brain. Door? Hammer? Person? Yeah, it still didn't make sense in his head either.

"Daddy," Lou's voice got louder, his headache grew meaner. "Somebody's at the door and I ain't supposed to answer it after dark, remember?"

His sassy little offspring had one hand on her hip and a finger pointing toward the front door. When he felt better, he'd let her know just how unladylike such sassiness was, but for the time being, her words finally sifted through the sickly mire to comprehension. He stood from the couch and the world took a spin. He'd never liked roller coasters.

"You look all woozy, Daddy." Lou pushed at his belly. "Just sit back down and I'll get the door."

He hadn't figured his little girl was so strong, but the pressure from her hand and the dizziness from the spinning room pushed him right down on the couch. He pulled the fleece blanket back around him and closed his eyes. "I think I need to feed the fire. I'm freezin'." The front door opened. "If it's a salesman, Lou, just tell 'em I have a contagious disease and see if it will run 'em off."

"It's Ms. Doc."

The words entered his thoughts like syrup dripped off of 'em. Mrs. Doc? Dee. He tried to stand back up, but his vision hit the spin cycle again and he collapsed with a moan. Not the best way to impress a lady.

"Oh, Reese, you *are* sick."

Her voice split into his fuddled thoughts like a sweet dream. "It's just a cold or something. I'll be fine."

He didn't know what her new perfume was, but he liked it. Smelled like chicken noodle soup and chocolate chip cookies. He studied her as her steps passed him to the kitchen table, her navy slacks a little too snug for even a sick man not to notice. She deposited whatever she had in her arms and gave the house a quick glance.

He inwardly cringed. Tissue piles left a trail from one room to the next, laundry waited to cause an avalanche on the other side of the wall, and the dishes in the sink probably had enough life in them to talk back to her.

Yeah, he needed a makeover from accent to tissue trail. He wouldn't have to worry about her wanting to kiss him ever again.

"Whatcha got in them bags, Ms. Doc?" Lou stood on tiptoe. "Smells like it's from Aunt Daphne's."

"Good guess, Lou." Dee smiled down at his little girl, probably gritting her teeth behind the grin. His house was a wreck. "Emma sent some things to help your dad feel better."

Reese grinned. Food and a lovely lady? Well, his little sister did know a thing or two about the right kind of medicine for her sick brother. Reese stared up through watery eyes as Dee drew closer, barely raising his head in greeting.

"That was awful nice of you to bring it up."

"Awful nice, was it?" The soft light in her eyes contradicted her pointed brow.

"You're not gonna make a sick man work on his accent now, are you?" Reese's heavy head plopped back against the couch. "That wouldn't be awful nice, Ms. Doc."

She leaned over him and touched a hand to his forehead, cool and soft. "Reese Mitchell, you're burning up."

"No I ain't. I'm freezin'. I need to start a fire." He tried to rise but Dee's hands went to his shoulders and pressed him back down. How were all these women getting so strong all of a sudden?

Her cool palms rested against his cheeks, face close. Man alive, she was pretty. "Have you taken some Tylenol for your fever?"

"I ain't no baby, Dee. I don't need—"

"Lou, honey, do you know where the Tylenol is?"

"Sure do, Ms. Doc."

Dee smiled a sugary sweet smile directed at Reese. Way too sweet for comfort. She straightened and directed the same dangerous grin to Lou. "Go get it for your Daddy." Her gaze zeroed back on him, all sweetness gone. "Who *will* take it for his own good."

"Woman, I don't need—" His argument disappeared in a tirade of coughs that clawed at the inside of his chest, but there was no way he'd tell Dee about it. She'd probably force some awful tasting purple goo down his throat. He squirmed like Lou.

"Exactly," she said with a nod. "You have a fever, your cough sounds horrible, and you can't even stand up straight. You are not okay *and* you do need someone to help you."

"I'll be fine."

Her palms cooled his cheeks with their soft touch again, eyes examining his face. She smoothed back some of his hair, which probably resembled an uncut field. "Is this from the picnic and the rain? You weren't out in the rain long, Reese."

He liked the way she said his name, all warm milk and honey.

"I had to mend a fence after I got home because the cows got out."

"You went back out in the storm?" Dee lowered herself to the edge of the couch. "For how long?"

"I don't know. It wasn't exactly on my list of things to do." He closed his eyes and leaned back, his grin easing onto his face.

She gave his arm a light smack, getting his attention again. "You need to see a doctor." Concern wrinkled across her forehead and the worried look in her eyes softened his stubbornness a little.

"I hate going to the doctor."

"Nobody likes going to the doctor." She tapped his knee, pink highlighting her cheeks. Man, concern looked real good on her. "If people liked going to the doctor it probably wouldn't cost as much … but you're going. As soon as you can stand, I'm helping you out to my car." Dee turned to Lou and took the pill box. "Where's Brandon?"

"He's takin' a nap, Ms. Doc."

"When he wakes up we're taking you to the doctor and that settles it."

Reese tried to argue again, but ended up coughing so hard his throat burned and the top of his head throbbed. Dee tucked the blanket up around him and then walked to the kitchen, returning back with a glass of water. If getting sick meant a pretty lady would come and fuss over him, he shouldn't complain too much. Kind of nice, for a change.

"Take a few of these." She pushed the Tylenol into his mouth and lifted the water to his lips, her gaze thoughtful. "I thought Emma was just trying to—"

"What?"

"Nothing." Dee turned away from him and placed the glass on the coffee table.

Reese tried to sit up straighter. "What? Is she alright?"

Dee sat in a chair nearby, hand perched on the arm of his couch.

"Yes, she's fine. I just thought she was trying to trick me into coming up here."

Reese squeezed his forehead with his fingers and kept his eyes closed. "Now why would she try to trick you into—" Reese peeked over at her from under his hand. "You think Emma's matchmaking?"

"Silly, I know."

"Let's say she was. What do you think about that sort of thing?"

She folded her arms and gave him a direct look. "I think people need to mind their own business."

Reese's grin stretched wide and he closed his eyes again.

"Why are you grinning like that?"

"Like what?" It felt good to close his eyes.

"Like … like you know something I don't."

Reese yawned and rested his head against the back of the couch. "I know a whole lot of things you don't."

"That's not what I mean." Her voice held a fighting edge, and fighting with her was a whole lot more fun than fixing his speech. "Stop grinning like that right now."

Darkness hovered on the edges of his periphery. Sweet, warm darkness, scented with apples. A chill trembled up through his chest. "Dee, I'm a might bit cold."

"That's normal with a fever," came her clipped reply.

He forced his words out on a whisper. "Will you do something for me?"

A shift in the weight of the sofa let him know she'd moved closer. She sighed and the blankets readjusted around his shoulders. "What do you need?"

He peeked through his lashes to get a glimpse of her reaction. "I need you to light my fire."

Her eyes widened and then narrowed, even as her lips tilted ever so slightly to hide a laugh. With one fluid movement, she jerked the pillow off the couch beside him and hit him upside the head with it. "Not on your life, cowboy."

He fell asleep? She'd hit him with the pillow and next his deep roaring snore responded. Incredible. Dee looked down at Lou who just shrugged.

"He's been doin' that all day long. Just fallin' dead asleep right in the middle of talking."

"And you two here with him?"

Lou smiled. "Oh, he'd wake up in a flash if Brandon started fussin' or something. He just keeps dozing on and off. Grandpapa used to do that too, but his snore was a whole lot bigger than Daddy's."

"Your dad doesn't need to be alone without someone to help him."

"But he ain't alone, Ms. Doc." Lou's dark brows scrunched together. "You're here."

Dee stared at Reese Mitchell's sleeping face, tenderness tugging at her smile. She *was* here. And, to her surprise, even with a snoring grizzly on the couch and two needy children, *here* was exactly where she wanted to be. She touched Reese's hair, dampened and curled from sweat.

Light his fire, indeed? She snickered and studied his peaceful countenance. Even with the bear-like snore and the general discomfort of being sick, gentleness remained. It blended as much a part of him as his smile. She nestled up a little closer.

"Why are you smilin' at my sick daddy, Ms. Doc?"

Dee pulled her body to attention and fought the flush of warmth in her cheeks. "Happy thoughts always cause me to smile. Don't they do the same for you, sweetie?"

"You're smiling because he's sick?"

"No." Dee chuckled, face growing warm at the direct attention. "Because it's nice to be here with you."

Lou's grin spread and she released a large, contented sigh. "It sure does make me happy to think about being a princess."

Dee knelt forward and stared into Lou's cherubic face. Ah, the sweetness of a little girl. "A very happy thought."

"I'm going to be a princess that fights dragons. Ain't no good to sit up in your tower and watch the prince have all the fun."

"Smart thinking, Lou. Who's to know when the prince may catch a bad cold and you'll have to save *him* from the dragon."

"Ain't no matter how sick daddy is, Ms. Doc." Her eyes grew wide. "If there was a dragon trying to skeer us, he'd use all his muscles to help fight, even if he had to cough through it."

Dee looked back over at her sleeping knight-in-overalls and agreed. A protector. The caution in her heart melted a little more and she turned to give Lou's curls a pat. "You're right, Lou. I think you can count on your dad to do whatever it takes to keep you safe." She almost leaned her head over on Reese's shoulder to take in some of the protection Lou felt. It was a novel idea, being protected and perhaps … loved?

Dee pushed the thought aside, patted her knees, and stood. "Well, Lou, let's get you some dinner and make sure car seats are hooked up in my car, so we'll be ready to take your daddy to the doctor as soon as Brandon wakes up."

"I ain't going to no doctor," Reese murmured, eyes still closed.

Dee didn't miss a beat. "And on the way to the doctor's office, we'll give him a good lesson on how the words *ain't* and *no* never go in the same sentence."

"Everybody's in bed." Dee walked in from the kitchen and took roost on the chair next to him like she'd done all evening long. "I called your mom and she's sending Emma up to stay overnight."

"I don't need—"

"Are you really going to try and argue with me again?" Dee leaned forward and raised both brows, her eyes large and dark in the lamplight. "You are so stubborn. Do I need to threaten to drive your truck?"

He slammed his hand against his chest. "Right where it hurts, woman."

A soft smile lit her face—the kind of smile to stir all sorts of things in a man's mind. He'd been wrong to think she was like Jana, wrong to assume she'd be more concerned about her health than helping with a sick household, wrong about her being timid and fearful, wrong about a lot of things. And all the wrong-turned-right thinking sent his brain into forward motion. The kind that involved warm winter nights hugging and kissing by the fire … especially kissing.

He started coughing instead—and coughed until the pain in his head pushed all kissing thoughts right out. He dropped back on the pillowed couch.

"The doctor said to take a pink pill twice a day." She touched his arm. "Reese, did you hear me?"

He barely opened his eyes. The firelight played against her face and when he didn't answer she leaned closer until she knelt by him, hand gentled against his knee.

"Reese."

"You're one beautiful lady, do you know that?"

She smacked his leg. "Go to sleep—and don't forget to take your medicine."

"I like bossy women."

She rolled her eyes, but the smile stayed intact. "That's probably the only kind to put up with you. And you're a bad influence. I'm usually not this bossy."

"It suits you." He readjusted himself on the couch and his blanket scooted down to his waist.

Dee cozied up beside him, tucking it back into place.

"Thank you for helping me with the young'uns today."

"They're sweet children."

"You ain't … you've never changed a diaper before, have you?"

Dee began to stand, but Reese reached out and grabbed her hand. "You did a fine job."

She laughed and pulled against his hold, even in the lamplight a blush stole into her cheeks. "I put it on backward."

"But then you fixed it. That's a lot to learn when you got a squirming two-year-old."

She relaxed her hand in his. "Have you thought about the football game?"

He liked looking at her, but the heaviness in his eyelids took her out of focus. "Yeah. Your supervisor's going to be there?"

"That's right. She'll be interested in what I'm doing at Blue Ridge and since accent modification is where most of my research is, then your presence will—"

"I'll go." He couldn't even open his eyes when she let go of his hand.

"Thank you."

"Thanks for being here today, Dee."

"You're welcome," she whispered, or at least it sounded like a whisper to his muddled up mind.

The blanket shifted back around his shoulders, her hand smoothing it close to his chin. He tried to grin. "You tucking me in?"

Something soft touched his brow. Her lips, perhaps? Probably her hand. He tried to open his eyes to be sure, but they stuck tight. Sleep closed off his fight, a dragon too big for him at the moment. A dream stirred on the fringe of his subconscious about a dark-eyed city girl, a fuzzy-bearded country boy, and a kiss just waiting to happen.

THE WEIGHT of Dee's day hit her as she pulled her office door closed. Class and clinic ran back to back, followed by another meeting with Dr. Russell, but at least Dr. Russell didn't have darts shooting from her eyes like before. She actually seemed civil. Dee's stomach spoke to the lateness of the hour with a few growls to make the point clear.

As she turned the corner, she nearly fell over a cart of cleaning supplies.

"Oh, honey, are you okay?"

Grace Mitchell placed a steadying hand on Dee's arm.

Dee adjusted her bags on her shoulder. "Not looking where I was going."

"Aren't you workin' a bit late?"

Her gentle concern comforted like a hug. "I'm afraid so. But you're coming in late too.

"Making up for lost time. Since I missed work for my doctor's visit and then helped out with Reese this morning, I came this evening to do my cleanin'." She patted the side of the cart. "One of the benefits of a job with flexible hours, ain't it?"

"How is Reese?" He'd occupied her thoughts sporadically all throughout the day. She almost called to check on him, but couldn't work up an excuse to suit her.

But thoughts of his gentle teasing and tender looks poured over a parched place inside of her. She shouldn't feed the attraction but taking care of him and his children felt so right. Like a piece of her life's puzzle somehow fit into his.

"He was out feeding cattle this morning."

"No, he wasn't."

Grace shook her head slowly back and forth. "He's as stubborn as winter, but the man's worked so hard to keep the farm going, he won't give up easy." She smiled her pride. "The farm is Trigg's life, all he's ever wanted to do. He has it runnin' through his blood, handed down from his daddy. Reese loves it because it's family land, and because he loves Trigg, but he's put his dreams on hold for long enough."

"His dreams?"

"He ain't told you?" She shuffled through some of her supplies. "This job in Chicago ain't just a way to help out with our farm, it's a step back into helping other farmers. Ever since he got his master's degree, he's wanted to reach out to others. He got a chance at it in Charlotte and it fit him, dream and all."

"I don't think he was too thrilled with Charlotte."

Grace chuckled. "Naw, he wasn't too keen on the city, but he sure enjoyed his work. He was going to leave Ransom once things straightened out after his stepdaddy died, but ..." Grace's expression sobered. "Nothing worked the way he wanted. First his stepdaddy, then Jana."

Dee braced her palm to her stomach, absorbing the sting of Reese's loss. Death marked everyone, not just herself, but the Mitchells knew more than their fair share, yet they didn't wear their grief the same way she did. They still lived with joy and hope.

"And then Trigg," Dee stated the obvious.

"The timing ain't been on his side yet." Grace's face brightened. "But praise God, Trigg is on the mend. He's been taking over a few responsibilities more and more each week. If his report next month stays as good as his last one, maybe this Chicago job will put Reese back on track with his own dreams."

Could his dreams ever include Charlottesville? The question came out of nowhere.

"Why don't you come on up for supper tomorrow night? I'm thinking of making some chicken and dumplings."

"You feed me enough, Mrs. Mitchell. I don't want to trouble you even more."

The woman stared at Dee in silence, her wise gaze peering deep and wide. "Ain't no trouble, Dee." She stepped closer and placed her hand on Dee's arm. "We're glad to have you."

The words echoed inside of her. Would that statement remain true if they learned about her past? "You're very kind, but I think I'll pick up something from Daphne's and get some class preparation done tomorrow. I am giving a midterm exam and I haven't finished creating the test yet."

Grace's look held a depth of awareness, seeing much more than Dee wanted. "If you change your mind, come on by. There's always room at the table, sweetheart."

The woman disappeared around the corner and Dee made her way to her car. Always room? With her crinkled and confusing past, truth digested slowly. Once the wager ended, maybe she could fall into this attraction for Reese, cling to the warmth of the Mitchell family, and enjoy the ride for as long as it lasted.

But until then, she needed to keep a clear head. The wager nudged at her conscience with the gentleness of a carving knife. She wasn't free to care about Reese, even if she wanted to. If his family knew the truth, they'd push her away.

She needed to focus. Trial number one started in three days.

Football.

CHAPTER 11

You silly boy, of course she's not presentable. She's a triumph of your art and of her dressmaker's; but if you suppose for a moment that she doesn't give herself away in every sentence she utters, you must be perfectly cracked about her.
(*Pygmalion, Act 3*)

"Stop pulling at your collar," Dee whispered to him. Her hair fell over her shoulders, almost to her elbows, teasing the scent of apples toward him.

Reese clamped down on his teeth and tried a tense smile. "This ain ... this isn't the type of clothes a person wears to watch football."

"*These* aren't the types of clothes," she corrected, but kept her gaze on the game below them.

"Exactly."

"In the VIP box, a collared shirt is perfectly appropriate." She folded her hands in the lap of her fancy slacks—as ridiculous for a football game as his collared shirt.

Daggone it. There came Ms. I-don't-agree. He stifled a groan. "You didn't have to take my ball cap away. How are people going to know I'm for the other team since I'm sitting over here in traitor territory?"

"I'm pretty sure they'll hear you cheering." Her grin turned as treacherous as the colors flying for the opposite team.

He narrowed his eyes and inched close. "I must really like you to put up with all this."

Her gaze softened and she almost smiled, then he replayed what he said and he almost smiled too. He was goin' crazy—pure and simple. She'd worn her hair down, all of it, in a mess of deep brown around her face, which made her eyes seem big enough to fall into. When her expression turned all soft and sweet, the collared shirt lost a little of its discomfort.

"Adelina tells me you are preparing for a significant interview, Mr. Mitchell."

Reese looked up and nodded to Dr. Lindsay, plotting each syllable. "Yes, ma'am. I have an interview in a month."

"What will you do should you get the job?"

"Praise God, ma'am. That's the very first thing I will do."

Dr. Lindsay's light eyebrows shot north. Reese looked to Dee who wore the same expression. Now what had he done? He was pretty sure he said every syllable just right.

Rainey, in Tech colors from head to toe, interjected. "Tell them about the job, Reese. I think she wants to know what you will do in your job."

Well, if people said what they meant, it would make conversations a whole lot easier. He swallowed a lump of nervousness and plodded forward. "It's a consulting position. I will travel up and down the East coast to farms, auctions, wherever I'm needed, to lend a hand and chew the cud a bit, so to speak." His grin only lasted a second.

Dee's slight shake of her head caused him to replay his sentence.

"I mean, I'm going to give information on how to increase the productivity of their herds and businesses." That sentence sounded so good in his head, he thought he ought to continue. "Most folks in these parts struggle with irrigation trouble, feed problems, and cattle health."

147

"Fascinating." Dr. Lindsay's pale blue eyes sparkled. "So, you enjoy this sort of thing?"

"Studied for it." Reese nodded, confidence building. "I like taking farms dinged up after some rough weather or set back after a bad year, then get 'em up and running again. Building relationships is a first stop to making a difference."

"Sounds like a campaign slogan fit for a political run, Mr. Mitchell."

"Well, I ain—" He paused and rubbed his trimmed beard. "I'm a pretty simple man, Dr. Lindsay, but I believe I can help other simple men who are earning their living off the earth and cattle. It's a hard life, but rewarding. Why there was this one time—"

Dee cleared her throat. Reese reached to pull at his collar, but stopped in midair. This was *not* the way to watch football.

"It sounds intriguing." Dr. Lindsay seemed genuinely interested. That said a lot about her in Reese's book. Quality. "There are large farms in the Charlottesville area. I imagine you'd consult there as well?"

Reese shot a glance to the game as Tech stopped UVA's movement down the field with a first down. He peeled his gaze away from the activity and back to Dr. Lindsay. "Most likely. I'm interviewing for the Mideastern region. Pennsylvania down to North Carolina."

"Last week Reese told me about his research." Dee turned to Dr. Lindsay, her proud smile making him feel twenty feet tall. "He explained the facts and details about his work so clearly, I wondered about his teaching at a university level."

Reese sat so stunned he was pretty sure his mouth hung open like a dog's. Dee thought he ought to teach at a university? Him? His mind dug into the possibility for a minute and it didn't scare him half as much as it should have. Of course, he'd always liked teaching other farmers, but college students? He'd never put much thought to it.

"Really?" Dr. Lindsay's eyes grew wide. "Researcher and teacher? Those are fabulous qualities for university faculty. What do you think of the possibility, Mr. Mitchell?"

His attention bounced from Dee back to Dr. Lindsay, with another quick look to the field. Second down—UVA. "Well, I haven't turned my mind to the option before. I ain … I'm not saying it's a bad idea, just a new one, but I'm all for an adventure."

Dr. Lindsay continued with her slew of questions. "Would you stay in farming if you could choose?"

Ah, something he'd thought about aplenty. "I really like fixing problems for folks and teachin' them how to do things better. That's one of the reasons I got my degree. So the consulting job helps me feed the need to educate and help others. I don't know if I'd keep farming directly, but I certainly want to keep my hand in it in one way or other."

Reese caught a glimpse of the action on the field from the corner of his eye. Third down and ten yards. UVA. He jerked at his collar again.

"And Adelina has been," Dr. Lindsay raised her brow. "Tutoring you to help with the interview?"

Reese nodded, absently. "Yep, she's real good at her job." The quarterback sent the ball spiraling through the autumn air. Reese spoke, barely aware of his words. "She's great with her consonants."

Reese gripped his seat. A defensive end for Virginia Tech moved into play.

"Great with my consonants?" Dee's voice barely registered.

"I reckon your vowels are good too," he murmured, attention focused on the ball.

The defensive end intercepted the ball and started on a dead run toward the goal line. Reese jumped to his feet, leaning over the edge of the stand. "Quit runnin' like a granny."

Two UVA players closed in.

"Pick up your feet." Reese turned to Rainey, who stood next to him. "What's he doin?"

One of UVA's players nabbed the Tech player's shoulder, sending him off balance. What was wrong with that boy? He ran like rocks filled his pants.

Reese cupped his hands around his mouth. "You're runnin' slower than fog risin' off manure. Pick up your feet, boy."

The runner barely squeezed in a touchdown and Reese yelled a big *yahoo* before returning to his seat. Alex Murdock looked ready to laugh, both of Dr. Lindsay's eyebrows met her hairline, and Dee's mouth rounded about as wide as her eyes.

Hmm, something was stinkin' and Reese wondered if it had more to do with vowels and consonants than fog and manure.

REESE SENT RAINEY on home without him and walked Dee to her door, his feet about as heavy as his heart. Women shouldn't trust men around football, and that was the truth. "I'm real sorry, Dee."

"You don't have to keep apologizing, Reese."

Wind rustled Dee's hair and she wrapped her arms around her shoulders, head down as she walked. Silence passed between them, and then Dee chuckled. "I don't think I've ever seen Dr. Lindsay laugh so hard."

"At least I gave her a good laugh." Reese shook his head, hands jammed in his pockets. "Did I ruin your chances with your boss?"

Dee sat on the front porch steps and leaned back to stare up at the night sky. Her dark hair fell back, almost brushing the porch step behind her. "Of course not. She recognizes you're a work in progress."

"I'm a work in progress, eh?" He joined her on the steps. "Well, if that ain't ... isn't the truth, nothing is."

"It's difficult to remediate this particular dialect, especially for individuals who have never gone beyond it." She shrugged. "You did very well for a long time tonight. If you keep up this pace you'll certainly be ready for Chicago."

"Your dad was from the Blue Ridge Mountains, right?"

The pale light of the moon haloed the curiosity on her face. "Yes."

"Didn't he talk like me?"

She kept her attention on the stars, so the moon placed a spotlight on her face. Every soft feature highlighted and her eyes almost glowed. "Dad moved away from home for a while to attend college."

"What happened to your daddy?"

She leaned her head against the stair railing and fiddled with the edge of her sleeve, keeping her gaze down. "He died in a car accident when I was fourteen."

"That's a rough time for a tragedy."

She nodded. "After that my brother and I practically raised ourselves. Charlottesville was Father's biggest dream."

"And he wanted it for his kids too?"

"My brother never put much stock in Father's wishes." Sadness rounded her eyes. "He always cut his own path, you know?"

"Yeah," Reese ran his hand through his hair. "I was that brother."

"Why am I not surprised?" She smiled and looked back up at the sky. "Jason wanted the quiet, farming life. It suited him. Dad never understood his lack of motivation for school." Her brows wrinkled. "So he would berate Jay or make fun of him. Compare him to our ..." She released a deep breath. "Anyway, Father didn't want to sound Appalachian anymore. I'm sure his travels made all the difference."

Reese rested his elbows on his knees and braided his hands together in front of him. "You mean made him sound better?"

"He had different goals than just being a farmer." She snapped her lips closed as soon as the words jumped out. "I didn't mean that the way it sounded."

"It aint ... it's not what you have, but your attitude about what you have. I'm a farmer." He shrugged, searching for the right words. "I like my job, but it's not who I am. It's just my job."

"But it *is* your job." She turned to face him. "It's what you spent years studying and how you earn your living. That's no small thing."

He considered her a minute, the stubborn tilt of her chin, the independence in her stiffened spine. Her job meant a whole lot to her.

"I never said it wasn't important. I said it's not who I am. My life is made up of a lot more than just a job." How could he really explain it? "Something bigger."

Her lips turned downward into a grimace. Not a good sign. "You mean your faith."

"It helps put things into perspective for me. I know at the very bottom of what I have— all those journal articles, my education, even this farm—there's only one thing that lasts forever. If I hang all my hopes on those things, then I'd be in deep trouble because at some point they'll fail me, but God's given me his track record."

She looked plum doubtful. "His track record?"

Reese prayed inwardly for clarity, which had never been his strong suit. His spirit ached for her, for the loneliness haunting her life. "You like lists, don't ya, Doc?"

"Ha, ha."

"Do you always finish what's on your lists when you want to?"

"That's ridiculous. No one does."

"So, how often would you say you *don't* finish everything on your lists?"

"I don't keep track."

He nudged her with his shoulder. "Come on, once a day? Once a week?"

"I don't know." She nudged back. "Twice a week, maybe."

"So, you fail to do what you plan to do twice a week, every week?"

She tilted her head so her hair cascaded over one shoulder, her moonlit face nearly stealing his train of thought. "Is this supposed to make me feel better?"

"No, I guess not at first." He focused on the dark outline of the mountains in the distance to distract his mind off of her lips. "But you're not alone, Dee. All of us make mistakes. Lots of us more than twice a week. Sometimes big and sometimes small. We're all works in progress."

Silence hung between them for a moment, then she pushed herself to a stand. "Then why even try, Reese?" Her words edged with a sting. "What's the point? If you're never going to meet the standards your God sets up for you, it seems like a waste of time and effort to try so hard to please him. I grew up with God's expectations hammered into me. Why not just please yourself and die happy?"

He stood next to her. "Are you happy, Dee?"

She looked away and stomped up two more steps.

Reese followed.

"You know what? Week after week, I had God's platitudes quoted to me. Do this and God will bless you. Do that and God will give you what you want? He doesn't listen."

"Christianity is one big to-do list for you, then?"

"It's impossible." She turned on him, her voice hoarse, and eyes glassy with unshed tears. "My dad tried and still died with a broken life. If we're all going to fail anyway, then why even work to live up to some ridiculous standard?"

"*That's* the point, Dee." He took her arm and trailed his hand down until his fingers entwined with hers. "We're all going to fail on our own. You. Me. Your daddy. My mama. We can't meet the standards we even set for ourselves most days, let alone God's standards. We're utterly lost."

She pulled against his hold, but he held on and rubbed a thumb against the inside of her palm. Her resistance eased out with an exhausted sigh. Yeah, his mama had been right. Dee's past fed her a diet of lies and impossible rules.

"But we're never too lost, we can't be found. That's why we need Jesus."

"Isn't Jesus the one who gave us the impossible to-do list?"

Reese stepped closer and tilted her face up with a finger to her chin. "Here's the difference between how you see God and how I see him. To me, he's a loving Father, finder of the lost. God said if his kids couldn't keep His list on their own, he'd complete it for them. So even if they failed, it would be *His* list that counted, *His* track record, not theirs. No more lost kids. He came down to complete the to-do list to rescue us."

She lifted a doubtful brow. "God completed His own standard? What do you—" Her eyes widened. "Wait a minute. Do you mean through Jesus?"

"It's only when we toss up our hands and say *I can't do it* we realize He loved us so much He did it for us." Reese touched her cheek and whispered. "It's called grace."

"Grace," she said the word like a little prayer, as if the meaning bloomed fresh and deep.

Cool air whispered around them as Reese waited for her to make the next move, lost in her questioning gaze. As if something clicked inside of her, she halved the space between them with a single step. It was the only prodding he needed.

He slid his hand around her waist and then, slowly, like preparing to taste something new and delicious, he moved in. Her eyes flickered closed and her hand rested against his chest. The smooth skin under his fingers at the side of her neck warmed him all the way to his pulse and urged him to bring his waiting to an end. She released a tiny gasp just before his mouth touched hers. His body jolted alive at the touch of her soft lips, slow and easy, savoring their sweetness. He paused, but her hand didn't flinch, so he tasted her again. When he pulled back from her, she stood unmoving, eyes closed, as if frozen.

Maybe he wasn't as good a kisser as he thought, but since she didn't pull away ... third times a charm?

He brought his lips to hers again, longer this time, sliding his palm up her spine to her mid-back. Just when he readied to end the failed moment, she sniffed a sob and eased forward, melting into him like thawing snow. Their breaths mingled, the taste quenching a long thirst. She slid one free hand from his chest up to the base of his neck to finger his hair and the simple touch pushed him deeper into the kiss, bringing her with him.

He didn't have to hold to her anymore. One of her fists gripped at his shirt, the other at his hair, drawing him closer. Man alive, he could suffocate from the pure heat shooting from her body to his.

Daydreaming couldn't compare to the real thing. No, siree. She smelled like apples and tasted just as sweet, and hot. Like fresh apple cobbler. Her hearty response sure calmed any of his insecurities. After all, he'd been out of kissing practice for a while, but Dee didn't appear to notice. As a matter of fact, she seemed to like the practice as much as he did. Shoot, with this much practice, they'd become experts in no time.

DEE COULD COUNT her kissing experiences on two fingers, and neither ended well. Reese Mitchell's gentle introduction easily surpassed anything she'd known—much like everything else about him. Large and strong enough to break her in half if he wanted, he reigned in all that energy and eased it out in delightful dosages.

The emotions raining through her body overwhelmed her senses. She couldn't move, could barely breathe. Intoxicating tenderness poured from him, breaking her resolve and opening a swell of affection. Oh what a *gentle* man!

Cradling her face in his rough hands, her reserve vanished at the tenderness in his third kiss. He coaxed her to trust him. Urged her to believe in her deepest hopes, and fall, unafraid, into his arms. A tightened band around her will loosened and rested in the heady sensation of his touch. He gave and promised so much in a single kiss.

He drew back, keeping his hand against her cheek. His gaze swept over her face, cherishing her from brow to chin. She held her quivering breath, knowing the magical moment would break and shatter into another untouchable memory.

"Wow." His voice hummed into the silence.

Exactly.

"Now I can check that off my to-do list." His thumb skimmed across her lips as he cradled her chin in his hand.

"What," she whispered, tingles still hovering over her skin in pleasant waves.

"Our first kiss." He leaned down and kissed her again, sending another spray of heat across her body. She gripped his shirt tighter. "And second."

He held tight, his body a rock of strength and protection. She buried her face into his chest and sighed. "You don't keep to-do lists."

He inched back and lifted a brow. "Of course I do. Right up here." He tapped his forehead and offered a crooked grin. "Scary?"

His continued closeness did strange things to her clarity of thought and his warmth pressed into her heart, filling empty places she didn't even know she had. "Terrifying." Her grin spread wide. "I'm on a list along with fertilizer, overshoes, and cattle feed."

"There's no need to be jealous, darlin'. You're near the top of the list."

Her smile turned into a laugh. "How very comforting."

He entwined his hand through hers and winked. "I knew it would be."

As he pulled away the cool evening brought her senses to life. What was she doing? How could this be so easy and sweet? It was wrong. "We can't do this, you know? You're my client."

He studied her with crooked brow. "Now wait one minute, you told me we were just friends helping each other out. Being neighborly." He tipped her chin with his finger until she looked up at him. "Isn't that right? Or *was* right until about three minutes ago when we moved a step above just friends?"

"You're right." She nodded, trying to push the guilt aside and hold on to the moment. He never needed to know about the wager anyway. "You're a friend."

He cleared his throat and pierced her with an expectant look. "Friend?" He swooped her close again and kissed her long and deep, until her breathing came in fragments and her thoughts a faded blur. "You oughta know I don't make a habit of kissing the sense out of my friends."

"Okay," she whispered through a chuckle. "Maybe a little more than a friend."

And all those pretty plans for escaping backwoods Appalachia became *a little* more complicated.

CHAPTER 12

How can she? She's incapable of understanding anything. Besides, do any of us understand what we are doing? If we did, would we ever do it?
(Pygmalion, Act 2)

D ee managed to sneak into church late Sunday morning to see if the pastor told more about the lost son. Since the last sermon, the unfinished story tickled a question in the back of her mind about the truth behind this Finder of lost things. Combined with Reese's words from the night before, her curiosity pushed her to a senseless choice: church.

The pastor's words supported Reese's revelation. God was a God of grace? The notion beat against her hardened experiences. Grace? Sounded much too simple for the reward.

She sneaked out of church before any of the Mitchells could invite her for a meal, stayed huddled in the house with some leftover spaghetti from Daphne's and even brought Haus inside after she got home so everyone would think she was gone.

Logic told her the actions bordered on ridiculous. She liked Reese, a lot more than she wanted; and she'd fallen asleep with thoughts of their kiss still tingling on her lips the past two nights. But he had expectations, and she couldn't fulfill them. He was a dad. His kids needed wife and mother material. She couldn't even change a diaper properly, let alone help with the really difficult situations of family life. Rainey and Mrs. Mitchell gave her glimpses into a world of motherhood filled with laughter and hope—a sweet glance into what motherhood *could be*. Then there was Reese's touch, his gentle kiss, cherished her and drew her in with the addictive potency of a drug.

And Ransom? She didn't want Ransom to be home—not when Charlottesville fueled her dreams, but how could her heart and her head wrestle with a promise she'd believed in for years?

When she pulled into the parking lot at the university Monday morning, the last person she expected to see was Reese Mitchell, leaned up against his truck drinking coffee. Uncharacteristically, he'd left his hat off, probably to taunt her, and had worn the leather jacket she liked so much.

He walked toward her, an extra cup in his hands, his face unreadable, and her heart stuttered with nervous energy. Why was he here? What would she say?

Maybe she was a runner after all?

"Good morning," Dee offered first, before he could respond.

"Mornin'." He held out the other coffee cup, his gaze intense.

"You ... you're in town early." She took the proffered cup.

"Here's the thing, darlin'. At first I wondered if I kissed you so thoroughly it left you weak in the knees for two days. But then I caught a glimpse of you at church yesterday and realized my kiss wasn't quite as powerful as I thought."

"Reese, I—"

"Then I got to thinking on all the things you've said and ain ... haven't said about your life, and figured you might be scared." He sighed and tilted his head to study her face. "I come with a pretty big package already. And I'm not in a hurry, so you can take your time and sort this out. But I'm going to have to tell you one thing." He closed in and placed his palm on her shoulder to trap her against her little car. His deep rumble of his words cascaded down her neck in a pleasant tingle. "After Saturday night, if you're going to be close enough to kiss, I'm going to have to kiss you."

She stopped his forward momentum with a hand to his chest. "I don't know anything about being a mother." Dee pinched her eyes closed. Did she just admit it out loud? "Nothing good—which you probably already figured out from my poor diaper changing experience."

She squinted open her eyes.

Reese pulled back and scrunched his brows. "Alright?"

Might as well get everything out in the open. "And I really don't want to be a farmer's wife."

Instead of shock, like she'd expected, his lips spread into an easy grin. "I like your train of thought, darlin'."

"What?" She studied his face and then recognized her mistake. "I mean, not that you're even thinking of me as a possible wife, but if you were it could never—"

He closed off her words with a finger to her lips. "You worry too much, Doc." His thumb skimmed over her cheek, weighing her eyelids closed again. "How about we just take this one day at a time, instead of charging off into matrimony?" Oh sweet heaven, the man's voice held aphrodisiac qualities. "I'm not in a hurry unless you are."

Her eyes shot wide at the assumption. "I am not—"

He winked, clearly having way too much fun with her discomfort.

"No, I'm not in a hurry toward matrimony." She ducked under his arm marched to the trunk of her car. Her face cooled by slow degrees and … distance from the source of her constant hot flashes. "Nor am I in a hurry for frequent moonlit kisses."

"Well, I wouldn't agree with you there."

He stopped her against the car with a surprise kiss. If she'd been a sensible woman, she wouldn't have wrapped her free arm around his waist to ensure he finished properly. However, once his lips met hers, sensibility fled about as far as thoughts of Charlottesville. Well, she was tutoring him after all, and practice *did* make perfect.

The crunch of gravel of a passing car alerted her to the horrifying revelation that she still stood in a very public *university* parking lot with her lips locked to one of the local bachelors. She pushed Reese away, and shot a glance to the front of her department building. What was she thinking! Clearly, she wasn't thinking. The withering glance she shot to her charming assailant only deepened his self-satisfied grin.

She released an annoyed sigh as she slid past him and opened her trunk to block the view of his face. She needed time to slow down her rapid-fire breathing and act like the only adult in close proximity at the moment. With a renewed fervor to keep something solid between her and Reese, she heaved a crate of books from the trunk and peeked around the trunk. Reese's cockeyed grin proved he wore a shame proof vest and still had kissing on his brain.

Her face flushed with heat again.

"Well since you're so interested in my wants and needs right now, I can't carry a cup of coffee and hold this crate, so would you carry my coffee?"

Reese ambled forward, shaking his head. "Nope." He slid the crate from her hands with one arm and shoved his cup at her. "I'll get the crate and you carry the coffee."

Her slow smile answered his before he fell in step beside her. "You know, Dee, mothering can be a learned skill?"

She took a drink of her coffee, uncertain how to respond. What if she had a predisposition for being a poor mother? Exposure to the Mitchells cast a glaring light on her imperfections and assumptions. If she hurt one of his sweet children like her mother had done, she wouldn't be able to live with herself.

"And should something like matrimony *ever* happen." He lengthened the word *ever* to obviously get her attention. "I can already tell you're going to be fine. Just in case you're wonderin'. Children are just looking for someone to love them, not be perfect. They don't have much use for perfect parents."

Even with his tinge of humor, little comfort came from his words. The last few weeks brought her father's inconsistencies to light along with her mother's. Did Dee even know *how* to love anyone? Her father's lists of *rightness*. Her mother's obvious rebellion. Clarity nailed deep from the preacher's sermon. The *two* lost sons lived in her broken, childhood home. How could she possibly know where she belonged or how she'd respond when she found it?

Reese stopped her with a hand to her arm. "You don't have to keep runnin', you know? You can trust me."

She forced a raw reply, splintered. "I know."

He hesitated, as if gauging her sincerity, and then saved her from further embarrassment. "So, are we taking these to your office?"

Dee held open the door for him to pass, measuring her breaths to maintain control. Her heart rushed through enough emotions to fuel reality TV. Somehow between her job offer and the current moment, she'd resorted to the emotional level of a preteen during a sugar crash. A good cry and a box of chocolate fit the order for the moment. "Um … no, I'm donating them to the nursing department. They're collecting medical books. I had a few from college."

"Well, I'll take them on up then."

"I have some more in my bag here, so I'll walk with you." Dee bypassed the elevator and made a direct line for the stairwell.

"Whoa there, little lady. Nursing is on the fourth floor." Reese gestured toward the crate with his chin. "Let's take the elevator."

"I don't take elevators."

He settled the crate against his hip. "You don't take elevators?"

She proceeded to the stairwell without looking at him.

"Hey, wait just a minute." Reese caught up with her as she started up the stairs; his low tones reverberated off the walls. "What's the story? You're not skeered, are you?"

"Scared," she corrected, continuing up the steps.

"You *are* scared?"

She stopped and turned to peer down at him two steps below her. "I don't take elevators, okay?" Her voice broke. "I can't."

He moved to the step below her, putting them at eye level. "It's something serious. More things that keep you up at night, I'd wager?" His gentleness coaxed her to answer. "What is it?"

She pinched her lips together. The mention of a *wager* didn't help.

What did Reese care if her past lay in tattered pieces she didn't even understand? And how did she share those dark and shattered stories with someone? What man wanted a woman with *her* messed up past and confusing present?

"I can't."

She turned on her heels and almost ran the rest of the flights to the fourth floor.

Reese didn't push it. He dropped off the books for her at the nursing department's office and followed her down the stairs to the main floor.

"I'll see you later, alright," he said as they reached the waiting area where the hallway split toward clinic and faculty offices.

She touched his arm as he turned to go. "Reese, thank you."

He nodded a reply, gaze a riddle of questions.

"Maybe ... maybe we can talk about it later. When we're alone?"

He slid his hands into his jean's pockets, a soft grin emerging. "I look forward to it, Doc."

"Adelina?" A voice from her memories broke into their quiet conversation. "Adelina!"

Dee turned and gripped Reese's arm for support. A chill scattered down her spine as she turned to face her mother.

DEE'S FACE grew paler than snowfall, even her lips lost color. Her nail nipped into the skin of his arm and she shifted her weight against him as if she'd fall over. What on earth happened? A woman, face careworn and leathery, rushed forward, hands worrying her purse strap with the same energy as her steps.

Reese drew Dee closer to his side out of a sheer protective instinct.

"Do you realize how long it took me to find you, girl?"

The woman ignored Reese completely, narrowing the distance but keeping her near-scream volume. Half the building stood on alert.

"Six months." Her bony finger needled a point toward Dee's chest.

"You won't return my calls. You even gone and changed your phone number without letting me know about it."

Dee stood straight, but kept her hold on Reese. "Can we discuss this in a more private place?"

The woman's face crinkled even more and tears formed in her eyes. "I know you're ashamed of me. I know you've always been ashamed of me, but it was your daddy that turned you against me. He turned everyone against me."

The woman dropped her purse and buried her face into her hands. Loud sobs echoed off the sterile white walls and drew further attention from the clerical staff behind the counter. A mop of auburn hair frayed with gray curled on the woman's head, and the full content of her words slammed Reese's breath right out of him. Dee's mother.

"This is neither the place nor time to discuss our history, Mother."

Reese stared from Dee to the weeping woman, looking for some hint of resemblance without much luck. *This* was the mother who hurt her so much? This weeping, broken woman?

"When is the right place and time, then? Huh? You tell me, girl." The woman's voice grew to a new volume. "Tomorrow? Next month? When?"

"I'm at work right now." Dee's voice trembled ever so slightly, which was all Reese needed to hear.

"Hidee, ma'am." Reese lowered his free hand in welcome. "I'm Reese Mitchell."

The distraction worked. The woman wiped her face on an old handkerchief and turned pale blue eyes on him. She blinked, as if seeing him for the first time, and stared down at his proffered hand. Maybe once, Dee held some resemblance to her mother, but the years and perhaps her choices, stole health from Mrs. Roseland's skin and eyes. After a pause and a few sniffles, she took his hand.

"Marion Roseland."

"It's real nice to meet you." Reese checked on Dee from his periphery. She stared at him with a look of pure shock, and maybe a little fear. Well, if he overstepped his bounds, he'd step *all* the way over. "Where you from?"

"I ... I drove in from Johnson City last night." She shot Dee another accusing stare. "Once I finally got in touch with someone at UVA who knew where my girl was."

"You talked to someone at UVA?" Dee's hushed tones rose a little. "What are you trying to do? Ruin my career like you ruined everything else?"

Mrs. Roseland burst into another bout of loud sobs. This wasn't getting anyone anywhere. Maybe having two bossy sisters taught him something about solving conflict. High emotions and the same room mixed as well as oil and vinegar.

"Woowee, Mrs. Roseland, Johnson City is a good two-hour drive. I bet you're tired. Here's a real good idea." Reese stepped between Dee and her mother, keeping a calm voice and a gentle smile, or at least he hoped. "You can't get much talking done with Dee right here in the middle of a hallway. It's her job and she has people counting on her to do things the right way. I'm sure you don't want to make things look bad for her, do you?"

Mrs. Roseland's lips quivered, and she had the good sense to shake her head.

"Well, my mama's house ain't too far from here. She'd be glad for your company. You could stay with her until lunch." He gave Dee a pointed look. "Then Dee will come by the house and have a visit with you. How is that?"

Mrs. Roseland gave Dee a doubtful expression but turned back to Reese. "I don't want to cause any trouble. I just want to talk to my daughter."

"That's exactly what you'll get to do at lunch. Ain't that right, Dee?"

Dee glared at him as if she might chop his head right off. "Yes."

"Alright then." He offered his arm to Mrs. Roseland. "Let me walk you to the truck."

He glanced back at Dee and the hard look in her eyes softened. Tears blinked at the corners and his heart quickened with the pain from it. He wasn't the brightest bulb in the fixture, but based on the current clues, Adelina Roseland's story cut a deep hurt—and he was bound to find out about it today.

Mrs. Roseland wept almost the entire way to Reese's mama's house. In between the awful sobs, she murmured *thank yous* and *I'm sorrys* and quite a few other things that opened up Dee's story a little more. All Reese knew for certain was the water under this bridge waved in torrents, and a good dose of Ma Mitchell might do this woman a great deal of good.

DEE'S CAR pulled into the driveway of his grandfather's house about a quarter after twelve. Reese stood on the steps of his mama's porch and waited for Dee to take the footpath up to him, but she didn't even look his way. She walked inside the house and closed the door. He folded his arms across his chest and nearly prayed for heat vision to burn a hole in the side of his grandfather's house, but didn't have the heart to lose such a pretty homestead.

What was she doing?

Blasted woman. He'd lost an entire morning taking care of her mama and there was no way she'd get out of it by hiding away. If he had to suffer through an entire truck ride with a weeping woman, Dee owed him an appearance, if nothing else.

He poked his head inside his mama's house. "I'll be back. Going to go and get something right quick."

Mama looked up from her conversation with Marion Roseland and nodded. Reese stepped off the porch and marched down the hillside, annoyance growing with each step. Stubborn woman. She needed a good spankin'. Nope. He shook his head. She needed a good shakin'. *Right.* Much better.

Dee stepped out on the porch before he even made it to the first step.

"I was coming."

"When?" He rammed his hands on his hips to show just how mad he was. "Tomorrow?"

"You don't understand." She ran a palm over her eyes and sighed. "This is not easy for me."

"I might not be the smartest man in the world, Dee, but I figured that one out on my own."

Dee's hands jammed on her hips, matching him, narrowed eyes and all. "You think you understand a lot about me, but you don't. You can't. Look what you've had." She gestured toward his mother's house on the hill. "A loving family? A happy home? You haven't any idea what I've been through, so don't patronize me and pretend you do."

"It ain't a wonder you've been hurt, Dee. Having a parent with a drinking problem isn't easy, but ignoring someone who's come to seek your forgiveness ain't right either. She's your mama."

"My forgiveness?" She responded with a humorless laugh. "She doesn't want my forgiveness. She wants money. That's all she ever wants." She stomped her foot against the porch. "And *ain't* Mr. Mitchell, is not a word."

"Listen, I don't know what all's happened with the two of you, but I *do* see the pain you're carryin' because of unforgiveness. Even if she doesn't want it, you need to give it—for your own sake. Your anger is tearing you apart on the inside, darlin'."

"That woman doesn't deserve it." She pointed up toward his mama's house, eyes wide and red-rimmed. "You want to know why? She's the reason I don't have a father. Did you know that? Did you know she killed my father?"

Air shot out of Reese's lungs. He leaned forward from the impact. "Your mama killed your daddy?"

"She might as well have. Because of her problems, Daddy had to collect her from the local bars. She'd find a ride with some loser and then stay in the horrible place until Daddy or Jay picked her up."

Reese took a few steps forward. "Oh Dee, honey. I'm sorry."

"One day, he got a call about her right after he'd picked me up from school. He usually didn't take me with him to those places, but it was on the way. He had to carry her out because she couldn't walk on her own." Tears slid from beneath Dee's closed eyes. Reese made it to the top step and took her hand.

She looked up at him, the anguish of the memory telling more than her words. "We were hit, ironically enough, by a drunk driver."

Dee's voice broke but she cleared her throat. "The car hit the driver's side and sent us into a roll. Daddy took the brunt of the impact and when ambulances arrived he was unresponsive."

Reese stood transfixed by the pain in her eyes, a pain he knew too well.

"I rode in his ambulance, bleeding from a few scratches and shaken up. When we arrived at the hospital, I wouldn't leave his side and stayed with him as they wheeled him into the elevator. That's when he opened his eyes."

The tears spilled faster. A sob shook her shoulders. Reese reached out and she stepped into his arms, resting her cheek against his chest. "He looked at me for a few seconds, never saying a word, and I watched the life drain out of his eyes. I watched him die and …" Her voice caught. "And I was trapped in that elevator with him and death."

She turned her face into his shoulder and shook them both with her sobs.

"That's why you don't take elevators."

Dee nodded against his chest.

"Oh honey, I'm so sorry." He stroked her head, loosening her bun until her hair dropped around her shoulders. Cool and soft against his fingers, he caressed her head until her sobs stilled and her grip on his jacket loosened.

"I hate her, Reese. I hate her."

Reese drew back and tipped Dee's chin. "Hate is a strong word."

"It's the truth."

"Honey, this hate is eatin' away at your life. Don't you see? All this worry and fear you carry?"

She shook her head like a little girl, eyes wide and watery. "I can't."

Reese's heart broke for her.

"Unforgiveness is a sickness." He used his mama's exact words from two years before. "It takes up the space in your heart meant for better feelings, until there's no room for good things. It causes you to mistrust people, fills your mind with negative thoughts, and hardens you into somebody you don't want to be. You've gotta forgive her so you can live."

"How can I expect you to understand?" She pulled out of his arms and turned her back to him, shutting out his argument. "You've had a golden world compared to mine. You've never been hurt like this."

Reese strung his thumbs into his jeans pockets and leaned against the porch post. "You sure about that?"

"Look at your life. Look at your family. You may understand the grief of losing a father, but you have no idea what it's like to feel betrayed—from someone who is supposed to take care of you and have your best interests at heart." She swung to face him. "If she'd just thought of others instead of herself, then none of this would have happened."

"Dee, I'm sorry you've been hurt. I'm sorry your mama had a serious prob—."

"*Has* a problem. It's still there. Did you see her eyes?"

"Alright, I'm sorry she *has* a problem, and that she's brought her problems to your door. But bitterness isn't hurting her as much as it's hurting you. You've got to let go or you're going to get hard inside and no one will get in."

"Let go?" She sent a dry laugh into the cool air. "Let go! Let go of years of living between an absent mother and a verbally abusive one? Of proving I can rise above the life *she* chose? Of fearing an ounce of her blood in me might damage my future as a wife and mother? Years of wondering if my father will ever be proud of me?"

The lostness in her eyes drew him closer, until his hand caressed her damp cheek. "I hate to say this, but you need to take this pressure off yourself about your dad and look at what you've already accomplished. Your past is chasing you like a hound."

"And I can't outrun it." Her bottom lip quivered again and he drew her back into his arms. "I just want to rest. I'm so tired."

Her declaration nearly brought him to tears. Years of working so hard for things that could never feed her hungry heart, and trying to live up to the wishes of a ghost? Yeah, she probably was exhausted. "Let it go, Dee."

She shook her head, unable to grasp the concept of letting go. She understood how to work and prove, but bitterness tangled truth into a murky mess. The idea of releasing something she'd gripped so long wasn't bound to happen in one conversation—not without some Heaven-help. "She ripped my childhood apart. I don't even know how to do this." She waved a hand between the two of them. "Don't spout off forgiveness to me."

Reese wanted to beat sense into her head. "Is playing the victim working for you, Dee? Thinking nobody else can hurt like you?" He shook his head. "That kind of thinking keeps you in the sad state you're in. You're trapped, Dee. With or without elevators, you're trapped on the inside."

"I know that. I feel it every day of my life," she nearly screamed it at him. "How on earth am I supposed to just let it go?"

"I understand what it's like to be so angry you think you're going to burn from the inside out. Furious enough to tear a person apart with my bare hands." He fisted the porch railing, pouring his reserved anger into it. "It's not about being hurt, because bad things happen to everybody. It's about what you do with the hurt and what you allow the hurt to do to you." He stepped forward and took a hold of her shoulders. "You want to know how well I understand."

Her gaze shot wide, stunned silent. Good. She needed to shut up and listen for a while.

"My wife of ten years had a two-year affair with my brother-in-law. Right under my nose." He held up his fingers to prove his point. "Two years."

Dee's quiet gasp fueled his argument.

"Bad enough for you? Well, let me see if I can make it worse. Not only that, she became pregnant with my brother-in-law's son."

Dee's mouth dropped open. "Brandon?"

"That's right. My sweet boy isn't my biological son at all." Reese spit the sour words out, fire burning deep within him like an angry cat fighting to claw its way out. "It gets even better. You ready for more?"

"Reese, I'm sorry. I—"

"When Brandon was two months old, she ran off to find my sorry excuse for a brother-in-law. After six months of trying to work through her betrayal, after I'd brought her back into our family to make things work, she upped and left us to meet Rainey's husband. I had the whole countryside out looking for her. Tom was the poor man who found her."

"The car crash ..."

"Yep, she got out of it all, didn't she? Took a good man with her." Reese drew in a deep breath and shoved the anger back into its hiding place. The hurt never left completely, but he could calm the flame to a simmer. "I hated her for a long time, but all the hatred ate me up inside. I became a person I didn't want to be. A person God didn't want me to be. An angry, hateful person."

Dee's expression softened to wonder. "So you forgave her? Just like that?"

"No. It took a year and a half of praying and crying out to God before my heart started changing. It's not something you can do by yourself because it goes against every human emotion we have." He took her hand and smoothed his fingers over her knuckles. "Only God can help heal a wound like yours, darlin'."

Dee looked up toward his mama's house. Her shoulders straightened and chin tilted upward as if she was getting ready for battle. "I'll go and talk to her, but I don't know how I can ever forgive her."

With those chilling words, Dee stepped from the porch and trudged up the path. Reese gave her a good head start, hoping the cool air might drive some of the rage away. She carried so much hurt, he could practically see it tying her spirit in knots. Reese offered a quick prayer up to heaven and then followed along, keeping a slight distance.

Her pace slowed. She finally stopped midhill and turned to him, round gaze crying out for a rescue he couldn't give ... no matter how much he wanted to. Her pain had brewed years longer than his and braided into the person she'd become, into her very definition of truth and life. The thought of suddenly releasing it had to be terrifying.

Yet, underneath it all slept a confident and compassionate woman. He'd caught glimpses in her interactions with him and his family, but the hidden woman remained shoved into a safe box away from sight. Maybe waiting too? For the right kind of healing?

"How could you forgive her?" The edge in her voice had disappeared. "She betrayed you in the worse possible way. How could you?"

It would sound too simple. Too easy. But he didn't know another answer. "Jesus."

She lowered her gaze to his chest and spoke with words barely audible. "You preach a different Jesus than my father." Her watery gaze met his, confused. "And I'm really not sure who to believe."

He didn't know what to say, so he stuck his hands in his pocket like an idiot and shrugged. She searched his face, intent on an answer he didn't quite know how to express. How did he tell her that her daddy was wrong?

With a heavy sigh, she started walking again, but he stayed close, watching the play of emotions across her face and praying for a revelation, for both of them.

Just before they reached his mama's porch, Reese leaned over to her and took her hand. "Maybe it's time you figured out what kind of Jesus is the real Jesus. Not mine or your daddy's or anybody else's. You like research, right?"

She offered a slow nod.

"Then do some research on your own to find your answer."

She blinked away her tears and took in a deep breath. "Maybe so, Reese."

Reese followed her into the house and prayed the Finder of lost things would bring Dee home.

CHAPTER 13

As if I ever stop thinking about the girl and her confounded vowels and consonants. I'm worn out, thinking about her, and watching her lips and her teeth and her tongue, not to mention her soul, which is the quaintest of the lot. (Pygmalion, Act 3)

Dee's mama sat at the kitchen island, coffee mug in hand, with Grace Mitchell nearby. Two years and untold poor choices deepened the wrinkles on her mother's face and the silver in her hair outnumbered the auburn. As Dee entered the house, her mother's red-rimmed gaze met hers, drawing Dee back years to a time of harsh words and harder experiences.

A cold swell of hate almost frightened her as readily as the flash of countless memories.

Fist fights, screams, blubbering tantrums, and a constant state of chaos littered her past. If her mother wasn't losing her temper or getting drunk, her father expressed his anger or withdrew into work. Then the façade followed—the game her father taught them to prove to outsiders they weren't a broken family. Certainly none of his friends at UVA knew the truth. But the painful evidence that both her parents lived lives of lies brought her own present to a sharp realization in her mind. She didn't want a story like theirs. She wanted something good and real … like the taste of it she'd seen with the Mitchells.

"I didn't think you'd come."

"I almost didn't." Dee refused to flinch at her harsh tones.

"Well, I'm glad you did."

Dee turned to Mrs. Mitchell, "Thank you for your kindness to my mother," words as stiff as her spine.

"Ain't been no trouble at all, Dee. I reckon this visit for the two of you is long overdue." Mrs. Mitchell moved around the island and came to place a gentle hand on Dee's shoulder, strength and compassion in the simple touch. "But your mama and me's had a fine talk."

"Two years overdue," came her mother's terse reply.

Dee stiffened, but Mrs. Mitchell patted away the tension and whispered. "Show her grace, Dee. She is your mama." She leaned in closer, her face sober. "You'll be the one to change, not her. Remember, honey, you ain't alone no more."

Mrs. Mitchell's gray-blue eyes filled with compassion, and … promise. For the Mitchells, Dee might bear her mother's behavior for a while longer and maybe …see how their God could help. Maybe.

"What do you need, Mother?"

"We'll leave you to visit." Mrs. Mitchell looked to Reese and started for the door.

Reese held Dee's gaze, infusing strength into her weariness. His compassion fueled hers, and almost emphasized Mrs. Mitchell's final words. *You are not alone.* How could he or Mrs. Mitchell still want to help her after all they'd learned today? After how she'd treated Reese?

"Thank you," she whispered, hoping he heard the apology in her words.

He paused, hand on the door. "I won't be far."

The door snapped closed. Dee drew in a deep breath, and turned to face her mother. "It has been a long time."

"Do you know how worried I've been? Last phone call was six months ago. Last visit almost two years?" Her mother slammed her hand down against the counter. "I'm your mama, Adelina. I need you."

Anger found its familiar place in her chest. So much for changing. "You *need* me? I *knew* it."

"I ain't got nothing left. Jay's stopped helping me. Won't offer one red cent. Say's I need to clean myself up." She spat the words. "How dare he talk to his mama that way?" She set her fiery gaze on Dee and stood. "I don't have nobody left. You're my flesh and blood. You have to help me. I can't keep going on like this."

Dee's jaw tightened, stepping back from her mother's closeness. "You came for money."

Her mother's entire countenance transformed into pure sweetness. "Just a little. Enough to tide me over until my next check." Mother's gaze darted away. "I have this new job, you see. All set up. Then I'll be alright."

Heat roiled from the pit of Dee's stomach and exploded in her face with a passion. Fiery tears burned in her eyes, but she kept them on hold. Her mother didn't deserve her tears.

"Do you realize … for one moment, I thought maybe you came to see *me*, for me? Your daughter? For a second I actually hoped you'd realized what it was to be a mother." She shook her head. "How could I have been such an idiot?"

"You don't know what it's like, Dee. You've never known. You only saw your father's goodness, but I knew the truth. I bore the brunt of his meanness. I protected you and Jay. The least you can do is help me out now."

"You protected me?" A humorless laugh filled the momentary silence. "You protected me? I think all the alcohol's skewed your memory, Mother. All you ever did was lecture, scream, or try to hit me. I needed protection from you, not from Father."

"I couldn't take it no more. I'd lived with your daddy's anger for years so you wouldn't have to see it. His high opinion of himself. His haughty goodness. It was all a joke. He was nothing but a hypocrite. It got to a point I just didn't have the strength to live it anymore." She narrowed her eyes. "Blame me all you want, Dee, but if the truth be told, you're pickin' and choosin' the memories you want to keep. I've made my fair share of mistakes and I don't expect you or Jay to forgive me, but I wasn't the source for all your hurt. You just don't want to see the truth."

"Oh, I see the truth. It's painted in your bloodshot eyes."

Her mother's eyes rounded and then she dropped to a nearby chair and started silently weeping. Strength to fight seeped from Dee's body. It was the same argument. The same set of lies. Stuck—again. "How much do you need?"

Her mother's head perked up and she quoted a large sum.

"Then promise me one thing."

"Anything you want."

Dee ached everywhere. "If I give you this money, you will not speak to me again unless I contact you first."

Her mother's lips quivered and a look of pure grief distorted her face. "I never wanted to hurt you, girl. Never."

A sudden surge of compassion took the edge off Dee's anger and shocked her quiet for a moment. Perhaps the counselor's words stung true—there lived a little girl inside Dee longing for a parent's love and acceptance. Could her mother change?

She pulled out her checkbook, scribbling out the sum. Maybe, observing the beauty of true love set a new standard for her? Grace Mitchell came to mind, urging her to follow the softer part of her feelings. Reese's gentle persistence, even when she deserved much less than his pursuit, tempered the edges of her hate with a newfound touch of gratitude. Dee handed her mother the check but didn't let go immediately.

"If you are truly sorry, Mother, take this money and find some help."

Her mother's eyes widened.

"If your memories are anything like mine—if you feel lost like I have for so many years, don't stay where you are. Find help." Dee leaned in, almost reaching to touch her mother's wrinkled hand. "I'll pay for it, if you'll go."

Her mother pulled the check free from Dee's hold and stood, head bent low and hands shaking. "I will. You wait and see."

The hollow words hung in the silence as her mother walked to the door. With barely a good-bye, her mother left, and a strange sense of peace blended with a wave of sorrow. Dee lowered herself into a chair. Anger ebbed to its constant ache and a swell of sadness took its place. She tried to hold on to the peace a little longer, the sensation an addictive calm in the storm of her heart, but it drifted beyond her grasp. What would she have to pay or face to find it again?

Mrs. Mitchell stepped into the house and sat down in the chair Dee's mother had occupied only a few moments before—the two women a stark contrast of lost and found. Mrs. Mitchell's soft hand covered Dee's. "I told your mama I'd drive her to the bus stop." Mrs. Mitchell patted her hand.

"I'm sorry. I didn't know she needed—"

"I think I can do her some good." Mrs. Mitchell gave Dee's fingers a squeeze, her rosy cheeks dimpled. "Every moment is an opportunity."

"Thank you for being so kind to her … and to me." Dee wiped a hand across her misty eyes. "She needed money, as usual."

"She needs a whole lot more, but trying to help her out of her predicament was a start. People like her, they've been wearing the same old clothes so long, they don't even know how to buy new ones no more." Mrs. Mitchell stood and brought Dee with her. "You saw her. It ain't easy, but she needs your compassion a whole lot more than your anger."

"I feel like she's jerked me around for so long. She zaps any happiness right out of my life."

Mrs. Mitchell brought Dee into a hug so precious, the tears spilled over.

"Oh, sweet girl, your Mama only has the power you give her." Mrs. Mitchell stepped back and cradled Dee's face in her hands. "You've carried anger around for a long time, and what good has it done? It ain't going to provide any happiness either. Don't let the pain of your past steal this hope in your present."

Mrs. Mitchell wiped Dee's tears with her thumb and shuffled out the door, as if it was the most natural thing in the world to give a lost woman a sense of coming home.

TIME AND TEARS passed as Dee found control again. Mrs. Mitchell's calm and Reese's words mingled in with her fresh self-awareness. Who was she and what did she want? She looked out the window at the blue-hued skyline. Love. She wanted to know what love really looked and felt like. She dried her face and stepped out on Mrs. Mitchell's porch, scanning the yard and field.

Reese sat on the hay bailer, Brandon perched on his lap, the little ball cap on his blond head lopsided. The ache left from her mother's visit dimmed at the sight. The afternoon sky behind them shone a patchwork of sun and cloud and painted the ground with rosy hues to the distant mountains. Dee looked from Brandon to Reese, and tenderness squeezed in her chest. No, she wasn't alone anymore and maybe … maybe love was closer than she thought.

She glanced up at the sky and then started a slow walk toward the adorable pair down the hill.

Could she ever have a family like that? She didn't expect an answer really. She hadn't talked to God in years so why would he answer, but the vastness of the sky held her captive in thought. *The hope in her present* Ma Mitchell had said. Hope?

As if in silent answer, Brandon's giggle brought her attention back to the two on the bailer. Reese looked her way, tipped the bill of his cap and followed it with a wink. He pulled the machine up beside her and turned off the engine.

"I don't have any more cows to birth right now, Dee, but if you've come out to help put up hay, I can fix you right up." He examined her suit from top to bottom, and focused on her heels. "And I see you came dressed for work."

"You're a regular joker, you know that?" Dee shaded her eyes from the sun and looked up at him. "As tempting as it is, I have to get back to my nice, clean job at the university."

Reese leaned toward Brandon. "Did you hear that, son? Dee thinks we're a dirty pair."

Dee shrugged and scanned over Reese's clothes, then looked at Brandon. "Dirt never looked cuter." She held Reese's gaze, her pulse tripping to a new rhythm, and *hope* marked the theme. "I have a favor to ask."

"Do you?" Reese rested his elbow up on the steering wheel.

"I'd like to thank you for helping me this morning. For taking Mom." Dee swallowed down the lump of fear. "And was wondering if you'd let me treat you and the kids at Daphne's tonight?"

"Well now." Reese leaned back, his smile spreading to a full white-toothed grin. Sneaky. "Do you mean a date, Doc?"

Dee ignored the heat in her cheeks. "I don't think it's called a date when there is a seven-year-old and a two-year-old along."

"Aww, hadn't you heard? That's the new type of family date. Besides, I'll take it any way I can get it."

The warmth in her cheeks upped a few notches, but she didn't mind. In fact, she kind of liked it. "Then I'd advise you to meet me there after work. Maybe 5:30?"

He touched his finger to the bill of his cap. "You got it, Doc."

"Good."

"Now, I need you to do *me* a favor." Reese tapped Brandon's nose. "Could you get this young'un up to the house? I just saw Emma's car pull in. The boy's about wore my leg out with all his wiggling."

Dee stepped forward and opened her arms. "Okay. But the correct phrase is *he's worn out my leg* not *he's about wore out my leg*, Mr. Mitchell."

"Either way, my leg will be obliged to you if you take him."

Reese lowered the boy and he wrapped his little arms around Dee's neck in complete acceptance. His soft curls tickled her cheek and she hugged him close for a second. Poor, sweet baby. Left by his Mama? She buried her face in his curls and breathed in the scent.

"Hey, sweetheart," she whispered.

She looked up to see Reese watching.

"And another thing," Dee added, trying to distract her heart from the pitter patter Reese's presence caused. "We need to go through your closet and figure out what you're wearing for your interview. It's a little over three weeks away."

"You're going to correct my clothes too?" He raised his hands in mock exasperation, but the slight tilt of his lips contradicted his overreaction. "Isn't there anything about me you don't want to fix, woman?"

She adjusted Brandon against her hip and examined Reese, taking her time to see if she could make him squirm a little. "Well, there's a lot of work to do."

He groaned.

"But, I wouldn't change a thing about your eyes."

His gaze met hers.

"Or your smile."

He adjusted his cap, chin at a proud tilt. "At least there's something."

Dee controlled her laugh. "But if you could mow some of the hair around your face, I'd get a much better view of your smile."

"First Emma, now you?" Reese gave his head a severe shake. "No doin', Doc. I've had this beard so long, I don't even know what my face looks like underneath."

"Maybe it's time to find out."

"Nope."

Dee sighed and pulled Brandon closer. "Fine." She turned to make her trek back up to Mrs. Mitchell's house.

"See you tonight, Dee."

She tossed him a grin over her shoulder. "It's a date."

REESE TOOK a good look in the mirror and then ran a hand over his freshly trimmed beard. Shave it off? The very notion pounded a shudder through him almost strong enough to make his teeth chatter.

It'd take a whole lot more than trying to impress a woman for him to remove a nearly permanent fixture like his beard. How would he keep his face warm in winter?

Brandon sat on the sink cabinet, chewing on his toothbrush and trying to reach for Reese's deodorant bottle. In one quick move, Reese swung the boy up in his arms, popping the toothbrush from his mouth and attacking the boys' face with a washcloth. Brandon's giggle warmed him all over. Oh, he loved that boy.

Lou appeared in the doorway and posed, pink from chin to shoelaces.

"Do I look ready for our date, Daddy?"

Reese about dropped Brandon. A sudden vision of Lou ten years in the future branded terror in his mind. Good heavens, he needed to get his guns prepared for perspective suitors as soon as possible.

"You look beautiful, Lou."

She crossed her arms and stared at him like he was ridiculous. Great. How did she get from seven to seventeen since breakfast? "Daddy, when I'm dressed up like a girl, you're supposed to call me Louisa."

"Is that right?"

"Yep, it sure is." She danced into the room with her pink dress flapping around her. "Do you think Ms. Doc will like my dress?"

"Well, I don't see why she wouldn't. You're the prettiest girl around."

"You think Ms. Doc is pretty?"

Reese swallowed the tension in his throat. "I can't think of any reason not to."

"I want my hair to grow long like hers."

Reese expected Lou to want to be like Dee. She'd copied Emma for the past year, as Emma went through all her weird fashion trials, but Lou's desire to be like Dee brought his thoughts to pause. Dee carried a pretty heavy weight with her. A past still controlling her life and a heap of unfinished business in her heart.

He needed to take things a little slower, for his sake and the kids. Lou might remember her Mama a little, maybe even the blessed few times Jana took an interest in her little girl, but most of her girly memories had been spent with Emma, Rainey, and Mama long before Jana ever died.

And Dee had never disguised her desire to move away from Ransom. Maybe Reese needed to slow way down and stop thinkin' with only his heart and hormones, instead of his head. Experience gave him a tough lick, and one he needed to consider before diving headlong into a relationship, especially since he went into any romance with a long-term view.

Dee wasn't like Jana—unfeeling toward her children, emotionally unpredictable. Old fury and memories simmered beneath the surface of his skin searching for a place or time to explode. Dee wasn't like Jana. He tamped down the pain and wondered for half a second about Charlottesville. With its Mennonite community and wealth of farmland, it was ripe for his type of work—or at least the work he wanted to do.

Slow down. He blew out a slow breath. *Be smart. And think about more than dark eyes, long legs, and moonlit kisses.*

He sat down on the closed toilet seat and pulled Lou up into his lap. "You remember, honey, Dee is only here for a little while, right? She might not be in Ransom for a long."

Lou ran her hands along her dress and nodded. "That don't bother me none. I'll just do what you told me when my new teacher came."

"What was that?"

Lou's brows crinkled and she took on a serious tone. "You said, 'If we know Ms. Cooper's leavin' next year to get married, then we best enjoy her while we got her.'"

Reese laughed. "Yea, I reckon I did say that."

"'Course you did. I ain't lyin'.'"

Well, he'd enjoy Adelina while she was here, and when the time came for her to fly away? Reese inwardly groaned and hugged his young'uns close. Dee wanted Charlottesville. His home was in Ransom. He'd trust the good Lord for a third option.

CHAPTER 14

Have you ever met a man of good character where women are concerned?
(Pygmalion, Act 3)

As Reese walked into Daphne's, Brandon on his hip and Lou sashaying her pink skirt at his side, awareness dawned crystal clear. Dee found a new dream. One growing as sturdy and homespun as the cornstalks lining the road between town and the Mitchells.

Home.

The hint of its sweetness lingered like an unsung melody, waiting for the first strum.

As Brandon Mitchell tried to feed her ketchup-drenched French fries or Lou stole the conversation to discuss the best way to climb a tree, or Reese cherished her with a single look, her dreams shifted to unfamiliar territory—uncertainty. His easy conversation welcomed her into his world of little girl frustrations, farm chat, and family warmth. It all added up to some homegrown food for her starving heart. She sat among them as if she belonged—an idea battling against Charlottesville with powerful force. How could she rectify the two?

Emma took their orders with a grin on her face as if she'd planned the entire *date*. Loneliness bowed to this sense of belonging. Thoughts of snuggling up with Lou, Brandon, and Reese to watch a movie or read a story by the fire quelled the dissonance of years of loneliness and fear. Everything about the Mitchells redefined her understanding of family.

Their table received lots of attention from the locals who visited Daphne's. Small towns worked the same way everywhere. One change in the routine rippled through the entire population within a few hours. No use hiding her feelings for Reese now. If the local tongue waggers proved efficient, they'd have Dee and Reese married by the weekend.

"I think our date is causing quite a stir."

Reese looked up from his cheeseburger and Dee gestured to the tables nearby. He didn't take his eyes off her to confirm her claim, only tilted a slow and steady grin. Her entire chest erupted in a warmth of beautiful tingles at the sight.

"I'm not so sure it's the idea of the date as much as it's the glob of ketchup hanging from your chin."

Okay, confidence died a painful death. She snatched her napkin from her lap and shot him a narrow-eyed complaint in an attempt to hide her embarrassment. "Great."

"One of the hazards of having a two-year-old." Reese ruffled Brandon's hair and lifted his gaze back to Dee. "Not for the faint of heart."

She noticed his hint of challenge. "What about the teachable heart, then?"

"That's the perfect kind." Reese nodded. "And patient too. And a little crazy."

Emma sidled up to the table, teeth in full gleam, earrings dangling a rhythm with her walk. "You guys like dessert? Aunt Daphne whipped up some of her signature chocolate chip cake." She leaned forward and cupped a hand around her next words. "But...if you're a little adventurous, I added an Italian mocha pound cake." Her brows wiggled with mischief. "Or an almond panna cotta with mocha sauce. We're learning Italian desserts this month."

"You know the young'un's will want some cookies with a scoop of vanilla, Em." Reese rubbed his jaw. "And I think I'll just stick with Daphne's best."

Emma's smile fell. She turned a hopeful gaze Dee's way. Tough sell for the dreamer.

"Which of those new recipes would you suggest, Emma? Do you have a favorite?"

Emma's grin returned with added sparkle. "Well, a few people ordered the Italian mocha cake because it had the words *pound cake* in it so it seemed less intimidating to them. I even sent a slice to Dr. Elliot from Amory Lennox, just to see if I could sweeten up their budding romance a bit. But my favorite is the almond panna cotta because of its unique, rich flavor." She drew in a wounded breath. "No one's tried it yet."

"Then I'd love to be the first."

The lilt in her step as she nearly ran back to the kitchen provided all the thanks Dee needed. Life existed in beautiful array outside of academia. Full and even bigger than she'd allowed herself to experience. She held on tight. It took a charming cattle farmer to open her eyes and her heart to what she'd missed for years, maybe even her whole life.

"I think you might be Emma's favorite person now."

Dee adjusted her napkin in her lap, a bit overwhelmed by the sudden crash of emotions inside her heart, not to mention the earnest admiration from Reese. Success and the joy of meeting her own goals certainly carried an element of pride, but compared to a genuine sense of belonging, her former life sat in a superficial heap. Like comparing a generic chocolate bar with Aunt Daphne's chocolate cream pie. Good, but nowhere near as great.

"I like prodding her dream along. Dreams are important things."

His brow crinkled. "Yes, they are. Powerful."

His nebulous answer needled a twinge of doubt, and perhaps

distance? A country music ringtone went off and Reese reached for his phone.

"It's Rainey." He shrugged and placed the phone back on the table without answering it. "She can wait. I'm on a date." He chuckled. "And reciting poetry like Wordsworth or something."

"That type poetry has a more Seuss-ish flair, Mr. Mitchell."

His head fell back in a full laugh. "Yep, that's me. Romance with a flair of Seuss. No wonder the women keep flocking my way."

His phone buzzed again and a message popped up for them both to read: *Do you think I would text you during your date if I could get anyone else to answer? Pick up the stupid phone, brother, or ballet is in your future.*

"Gotta love Rainey's sweet subtle ways." Reese murmured and picked up the phone.

"Ballet?"

He pulled at the collar of his polo and cleared his throat. "Yeah, she drives Sarah and Lou to ballet practice every week. She likes to threaten me with having to sit through a full hour of pink tutus and *happy* music practice." He shuddered. "No man should have to go through such torture." He sent a reassuring look to his daughter. "But I love watching you dance, honey. You know I've not missed one performance."

"I know Daddy. It's a girl thing."

"Like nothing else in the world." He rolled his coffee brown eyes up to Dee. "I'm going take the phone outside so I can talk. Would you mind keeping an eye on the kids?"

"I might even spare both eyes."

"That would be wise. Two-year-old boys are notorious for being rascally now and then." He shrugged, gaze darkening with mischief. "Thirty-three-year-old boys can be too."

The heat in his gaze transferred to her face and she swallowed a giant size lump of *heaven help me.*

"Daggone it, woman. You make it real hard for a man to even think of slowing down when you act all sweet-like." He stood and leaned close. "I'm trying real hard not to be a rascally thirty-three-year-old."

185

Dee didn't have a clue to what he referred, but she enjoyed the teasing and mischief accompanying his humor as much as the way his shirt hung over his broad shoulders. He walked away and as if magnets were attached to her pupils, her rebel gaze appreciated each step he took to the restaurant door. Jeans never looked so good.

Reese caught her watching and heat reignited in her cheeks at the easy smile spreading full on his face. Obvious? Thy name is Adelina. She reached up to check her mouth wasn't hanging open, and then jerked her attention back in the direction of the kids, just as Emma came to the table with desserts.

"Sweets for the sweet." Emma lowered the dishes and the kids gave responsive squeals. "This is my favorite part." Her nose wrinkled in a grin. "I'm always the good guy when I bring dessert."

She lowered the foreign dish in front of Dee and leaned close. "I'll be back in a few minutes to see what you thought."

No pressure.

Reese walked through the door, his frown a clear contrast to his previous mood. "Rainey's got a flat tire out by the Old Peterson Place and had to walk a half mile to get reception to call."

He ran a hand through his hair and the curls sprung loose. Dee's fingertips tingled a little.

"Is she all right?"

"Ornery as hornets, but what's new?" His lips quirked. "She's driving on her spare or would have changed it herself. Mama's at her painting class and Trigg ain—isn't answering the phone." He scanned the table, face falling. "And the young'uns just got their ice cream?"

"I can take them home."

Then the thought sunk in followed by a healthy fear. She looked from Brandon to Lou as if seeing them for the first time. She'd take them home? Alone?

Lou smiled. Brandon beat his spoon against the table. Dee's pulse skittered up a beat. How hard could it be, right? They liked her. She liked them. It was a fifteen-minute drive home. No problem.

Reese seemed about as certain as she did. "You sure about that?"

The actress emerged in full glory. "Of course. Unless you *want* them along to help change a tire?"

"Not really. It's gonna be at least two hours. You sure?"

"Yes." She accepted her mission with the sanity of a loon and shoved his arm. "Go."

"Bedtime is in about an hour. Could you take them on up to the house? I'll put the car seats in your car. Door's unlocked and Lou'll be a big help."

Okay. Now she'd added a bedtime routine to her benevolent act? She drew in a breath of confidence and smiled. She'd earned a PhD for goodness sake; surely she could take care of two children for two hours. How hard could it be? "Got it."

"And I'm a great bath helper," Lou added with part of the chewed up cookies in her mouth showing. She wiped a sleeve across her lips.

Dee cringed and snatched a napkin. "Ladies in twirly skirts use a napkin, sweetie."

Lou wiped her face and then Dee took the napkin, folded it, and arranged it in Lou's lap to match hers. Lou's partially toothless grin spread as wide as her Daddy's. "I'm learnin' to be a lady, Daddy."

"Well, I can't think of no better teacher for the task, Lou*isa*." Reese's appreciative gaze spiked Dee's hope, a little. "If you're sure, darlin', I'll head on to fetch Rainey before she gets too antsy."

"Better hurry along."

"Thanks, Dee." He lowered his lips to her cheek and left a kiss, his soft stubble introducing a tingle to her neck. "And I'll walk real slow so you can enjoy the view."

A rush of fire coursed into her face. She pushed him away with a huff, making sure to keep her gaze fastened on her dessert. Reese's deep laugh taunted her all the way to the door. She refused to look … much.

"You sure do have Daddy laughin' a lot, Mrs. Doc."

Dee placed a cool palm to her face and focused her attention on the adorable seven-year-old. "Do I?"

"Yeah." She raised her sleeve.

Dee cleared her throat. Lou caught the hint and picked up her napkin instead. Smart girl.

"Ain't you gonna eat your dessert?"

Definitely. She needed something to cool the embarrassment alive and well in her bloodstream. A strawberry garnished the top of the chocolate gelatin dessert tempting her from a fashionable glass. Dee dipped her spoon and took a bite. Cream, chocolate, and coffee smoothed together to form a tantalizing combination. She took another taste and a moan of delight escaped. Heaven help her, food wasn't supposed to be so good.

"So?"

Emma's sudden closeness nearly sent Dee clear out of her leather Liz Clabourne's. "Emma, oh my." Dee pressed her hand against her chest. "It's fantastic."

"Really? You think so?"

"Definitely." Dee reached over to wipe a dribble of ice cream from Brandon's chin. He offered her a heart-stopping grin, wrinkled his nose, and took another bite. Blood-related or not, he had his Daddy's charm.

"I'm so glad." Her smile turned conspiratory. "It's the easiest recipe I've been taught so far. And you can change up the ingredients." She flapped her hands in excitement, her writing pad bouncing along with her. "Now to talk Aunt Daphne into advertising new dishes. She's not too fond of recipes she can't pronounce."

"Mrs. Doc." Lou's warning came too late.

Dee turned in time to see an entire scoop of vanilla go from Brandon's spoon directly into his lap. She gasped, so did Emma. Lou helped it along with a giggle. Brandon looked up, green eyes rounding, and then with the glint of adventure dimpling his cheeks, he grabbed the ice cream with both hands.

Or tried.

He had the entire scoop halfway to his mouth when it slipped between his chunky fingers.

"Brandon, let me—"

Vanilla splashed into Dee's face and slid off her chin to splat against the table. Another dollop of it clotted against Emma's apron before it made a slinky move to the floor. Maybe TV and movies didn't clearly prepare her for two hours alone with Brandon Mitchell.

ALL REMNANTS of vanilla ice cream washed away during Brandon's bath. However, no one, movies, Google, or anything else, prepared her for wrestling a slippery toddler into a bath full of bubbles, washing a mass of gold curls, and then trying to catch the true-born rascal to get him out. The aerobic activity proved as effective as catching raindrops in a sieve. The sweetness of giggles and joy soaked as deeply into Dee's heart as bath water into her drenched white blouse.

Lou put in her best attempts to help, but the seven-year-old hadn't made it out unscathed either. After Dee helped wash her beautiful dark hair, they both slipped on the linoleum and put their ballerina poses into practical use with near-splits, finally landing in unladylike positions on the puddled floor.

By the time she'd given them both their cups of milk, brushed out Lou's hair, and read them a bedtime story, every ounce of tension in the day rested firmly on her shoulders. She closed Brandon's door to the sound of his jabbering to himself and smiled. Despite the near-flood in the bathroom and the battle with a squirming naked boy, she'd discovered a new fascination with baby toes and powder. Oh, heavens, she wanted to pinch each one of his little piggies and snuggle a full half hour with him smelling of baby shampoo and wrapped in a fuzzy towel.

It was the oddest contradiction of emotions she'd ever known. Maybe Appalachia truly made people crazy. She grinned as she snuck one of Reese's flannel shirts from the laundry room and threw her soaked blouse in the dryer while Lou put on her pajamas. The flannel shirt carried the thick and welcome fragrance of spice and wood.

She massaged a kink in her neck and stepped into Lou's room. Butterflies hung from the ceiling in rainbow colors and a pair of pink camouflage boots stood at the end of the bed—a wonderfully perfect combination of tomboy princess. She mentally kicked herself. Yet another false assumption. When would she stop identifying the Mitchells with all of her broken ideas of truth?

She sat on the edge of Lou's bed and pulled the blankets up to the little girl's chin. Her bright eyes sparkled in the lamplight, creating another beautiful new memory to replace her old broken ones. Dee waded into the tender memories with sweet abandon.

She smoothed back Lou's hair, nurturing the swell of protectiveness and affection this evening birthed. "Good night, Lou."

"Night, Ms.—" She crinkled her brow. "Since your tuckin' me into bed and all, can I call you something besides Ms. Doc?"

Dee twisted one of Lou's dark curls around her finger and bathed in the tenderness of the moment. "If your daddy doesn't mind, why don't you call me Dee?"

She grinned and snuggled down into the blankets, eyes fluttering closed. "Good night, Dee."

Dee pushed off the bed.

"Wait, Dee." She emphasized the name as if she liked using it. "Ain't you gonna say prayers?"

Dee's feet halted on the carpet. She made a slow turn, trying to sort out how to answer. Pray? Her mind drew a complete blank. How long had it been since her last prayer? The hospital with her father? The weekend after when mother disappeared? Dee clasped her hands together, words coming painfully slow for a speech-language pathologist. "Okay ... um ... what does your dad usually do?"

"He gits down on his knees and thanks God for things. Then he asks God to give us sweet dreams."

Didn't sound too complicated. Dee lowered herself to her knees. Lou's hand emerged from the covers to take Dee's. Words knotted in Dee's throat and the fourteen-year-old girl hiding behind years of hurt peeked from her soul into a prayer. God? Are you there? She pinched her eyes closed.

"Um ... dear God." *Thanks, first.* Got it. "Thank you for this day and the great dessert at Daphne's." Her thoughts turned to Reese and Ma Mitchell's kindness, and Brandon's giggles, and Lou's voice. Nothing in this day came on a schedule. The bad …. and the endearing. "Thank you for friends who help when tough things happen and for … happy memories." She paused, tears pricking the backs of her eyes. What next? "Please help us to have sweet dreams so we'll be ready to have a great day tomorrow. Amen."

"Amen," Lou echoed.

Dee walked from the room, legs as unsteady as her heart. She clasped her fist to her chest and collapsed on the couch as tears squeezed from beneath her closed eyes. From the visit of her mother to a wild night with two children, her emotions swung from one side of the pendulum to another.

But the good outweighed the bad. For the first time in her life, tomorrow wasn't clouded with the hardened push for Charlottesville or the nagging denial of her hateful past. Her heart's wearied rhythm steadied into a quiet beat, even tinged with a sense of rare peace. And her prayer? It sounded painfully simple and trite. Did God even listen to lost women like her? Was the temptation of peace a byproduct of her little prayer? Hadn't the pastor called him the God of lost things? Her thoughts blurred as sleep crowded in with a perfect mix of baby giggles, butterflies, and a dark-eyed cattle farmer.

REESE STEPPED into the quiet house, weary from his hour-long battle with Rainey's tire. One thing led to another, and he had to drive all the way back to Rainey's house for a different tire. What a stupid way to end a first *real* date. He succeeded in getting Rainey and Sarah off Peterson road alone at night. That held some satisfaction, at least.

The lamplight sent long shadows across the kitchen into the living room, the house quiet. Reese's soft footfall from years of hunting in the woods helped him slip down the hall and peek into each room without a squeak from the floorboards. The scent of baby powder and bubbles greeted him from the bathroom as he passed. Both kids slept as sweet as puppies, but there was no hint to the whereabouts of his cute little sitter. Lou wasn't conniving enough to tie her up or anything yet, was she? He'd heard tales about such mischief—even been accused of it himself as a boy.

A grin slid wide. Good times.

Surely Dee wouldn't have left them on their own. After all, her car sat in his driveway.

As he walked back down the hall from the bedrooms, a soft whistling stirred from the living room. It drifted toward him in a gentle rhythm, like breathing. A few extra steps forward answered his curiosity, and much more.

Dee's hair fell in waves of dark and medium brown over the pillow on his couch. An afghan tucked tight against her chin and spread the length of her body, except for a bare foot with red toenails peeping from the bottom. He tiptoed closer, holding his breath, and enjoying the view. He hadn't laid eyes on anything so beautiful in a long time.

He touched her hair and it slipped between his fingers, soft and silky, calling for another touch. Thoughts of taking it slow died with the same success as they had in the restaurant. Wonder switched with the flint of desire. Heaven help him, the woman slept on his couch, in his house, at night, and smelled like baby powder and apples. Best combination he'd sniffed in years.

His body warmed with the memory of their last kiss and his mind followed suit with new memories he'd like to add. New ones meant more for a wedding night.

One of them needed to get out of the house, quick, or there was sure to be disapproval from The Almighty. He stood and took a step back ... for her own good.

"Dee?" His voice barely created a whisper.

She sighed and stretched her arms up, a smile spreading across her sleeping face. His blood shot from simmer to boiling faster than any microwave.

"Woman, you sure ain't making things easy on this man."

Her brow puckered and she yawned. "Ain't is not a word, Reese Mitchell." She murmured and sat up on the couch, rubbing at her eyes, the blanket fell away to reveal her wrinkled slacks, *his* green flannel shirt, and a whole lot of pretty white skin from her neckline down to the first button. "And I just took care of your children for you, in case you forgot, so I think I probably made things a whole lot easier for you."

He jerked her up from the couch and attacked her with a kiss that spoke volumes about his difficulty at the moment. His hands got tangled in her mess of silky hair. Her mouth tasted like coffee and chocolate —definitely not helping his self-control. The way he kissed her should have sent her bolting for the nearest door, but she didn't seem to understand, because she smiled a lazy smile and slid her hands right around his waist like she wanted more. "You shouldn't fuss at me about making things more difficult for you. I only wanted to help."

"I wasn't talking about the children, darlin'."

She tilted her head to see him better, the lamp light deepening her eyes. She didn't have one clue the power she possessed. Praise God for small favors.

"What do you mean?"

He kneaded the flannel against her back and sighed. "I come home and there's a Sleepin' Beauty on my couch dressed in *my* flannel shirt?" He snuck in another kiss then followed her sweet scent down her neck. Embers stirred to heat in his chest, blazing to full fire. Yep, she was lighting his fire alright. White hot!

Her gasp nearly undid him. He gripped her shoulders and held her at arm's length.

Her brow puckered till she looked like she might cry. "You think I'm beautiful?"

To be such a smart woman, she sure was stupid sometimes. "So much I'm close to sinning."

His expression must have cleared things up because her little grin perked up—and rekindled the inferno under his skin. Thankfully, her mercy and good sense kicked in because she pulled away from his grip and pinched the top of his flannel shirt closed around her neck.

It helped—a blessed little. But at the moment, every little bit counted.

"I'm sorry." But her eyes didn't hold a hint of apology. "After I gave the kids baths, my blouse was drenched." She backed toward the hall, expression finally sobering enough to cool down his heart rate from a stampede to a more sensible gallop. "I threw it in the dryer while I waited and ..." She shrugged and pushed back a handful of her chocolate-caramel-colored hair. "Fell asleep, I guess."

He shoved his hands in his pockets to keep from grabbing her again. "That's fine. Why don't you wear it on home and give it back to me tomorrow." Because the idea of her changing clothes in his house kept a fire burning fairly bright in his chest.

"Got it." Her grin returned and she nearly ran down the hall to the laundry room. In a second she returned, white shirt draped over her arm and shoes in one hand. "I'd better go."

"Out of sheer mercy if nothing else."

Her eyes twinkled in response and she made a beeline for the door. He followed behind, careful to keep his distance, but his traitor-eyes noticed each step. "Thank you for taking such good care of the young'uns."

She turned in the doorway, face lit by moonlight. "Thanks for letting me help. They're great kids, Reese."

"I'm a blessed man."

"Yes, you certainly are." She sighed as big as the sky, a frown pouting out her lips. "And an incredibly honorable one. I really can't understand why I'd be a temptation for you at all."

There she went being stupid again. "Clearly you don't see what I see, then."

She studied his face, his eyes, her gaze roving over each feature with a sweet appreciation. A soft glow spilled over him at her gentle expression, no question about her affection. Sincere and ... grateful?

"No, I guess not." She shrugged. "But I think I'm starting to understand why my vision's so foggy. I don't think anyone in my family had a clear view of life." Her gaze flew back to his. "Or love."

His breath came to a lurching halt. Love? Now that's not a word he'd heard from a woman he wasn't related to in a real long time.

She pulled her blouse into her chest and squeezed tight. "Or truth."

The events of the day crashed in on his wayward thinking and knocked some of the hormones into submission. The bonfire in his chest cooled to a fireside chat. He braided his fingers through hers and tugged her closer, but not too close. "You are a whole lot more than what you think, Dee. Smart, a hard worker, caring, teachable."

She looked disappointed at his words, so he added a few more compliments. "You're kind, grateful, and have a deep compassion to do the right thing."

Now she looked plum sad. He didn't just need accent lessons, he needed training on how to talk to a woman. But what man didn't. "Sorry, you've had a tough day and here I am saying something wrong."

She faced him and took a step closer. "It's not you." Without warning, she touched his cheek, her cool fingers soft, like the look in her eyes. "I have a lot on my mind to sort out, but it's not you." She rose on tiptoe and rested her lips on his. His entire body tensed with the effort to maintain control, but her vulnerable expression gave him the needed nudge. "Thank you."

"Why are you thanking me?"

Her fingers slipped from his reach and she stepped onto the porch before turning his way. "For just being who you are, Reese Mitchell."

She smiled up into the cool night and walked, barefoot and red toes, to her car. It was like getting a glimpse of the little country girl hiding behind all those fancy clothes and wrong presumptions. He could almost envision long pigtails and a snaggle-tooth smile, until he focused on the flannel shirt and the heated kisses.

His pulse stampeded off again. Her car door closed and the engine roared to life.

He locked his door, turned to the living room still floating with the smell of apples and baby powder, and stomped directly to the bathroom with one purpose in mind.

Cold shower.

CHAPTER 15

Oh, I didn't mean it either, when I was a flower girl. It was only my way. But you see I did it; and that's what makes the difference after all. (Pygmalion, Act 5)

Dee's week tumbled forward at breakneck speeds with a wild mix of mid-term exams, clinic, and a much-too-brief session with Reese at the university. Of course, they'd engaged in some texts and phone calls, even caught lunch together two days, but nothing of any length. Her mind buzzed with Reese's reference to her as Sleeping Beauty, his rock star evening kiss, his disheveled appearance as she walked out his door with shoes in hand ... and the beauty of his self-control! Her one boyfriend from graduate school never used such restraint, but she'd excused his behavior as part of a man's genetic makeup. Born predator. She'd misinterpreted so many rules and relationships and become devalued and proud in the process. Reese proved respect held deeper than passion, though passion provided a lovely after-dinner feature. Oh, man, she could get used to dessert like that on a regular basis.

Her thoughts ground to a halt. She glanced at him across the cab of his truck, Lou and Brandon crammed between them. Could she? The battle raged between her heart and head, without an easy answer in sight. She'd plowed into Ransom over two months ago with an escape plan burning a path to Charlottesville and now she longed to dress in flannel and appear on Reese's couch again. Clearly, she'd lost her mind … and wanted to stay there if it meant Reese, the kids, and feeling of being cherished by a good man.

Her finger moved a slow line across her lips, replaying a lovely memory. Simply ridiculous to melt over a man's kisses … but oh so sweet. She snuck another glance at Reese and studied his lips through his closely trimmed beard. The heat in her face spiked. He caught her look and his smile turned roguish.

Charlottesville? What was Charlottesville when a handsome man, cute kids, and a Saturday brunch with the Mitchells waited? It seemed so right. How had she spent her weekends before the Mitchells swept into her life? Her thoughts took a downward turn.

Alone.

And she didn't want to go back.

Dee's phone buzzed into the unusual quiet, drawing her from contemplation.

Lou lifted her head from Dee's shoulder and frowned. "You're buzzin' like a bee, Dee."

Dee grinned down at Lou's easy use of her name and reached for her phone. Alex Murdock's number popped onto the display window, an unwanted intrusion. It buzzed in her hand and she pushed the *ignore* button.

"Everything okay?"

"Fine." She shrugged to ease the tension in her shoulders. "Just Dr. Murdock. Probably calling to check up on the status of my research." *Well, that was partially true.* Oh what a tangled web we weave …

A cloud passed over Reese's face. "He sure does keep close tabs on you. Seems to me, you're doing a fine job."

"Thanks." Dee weighed her next words; one slip of the tongue could unravel more than her career. Telling the truth was tricky business and she desperately wanted to fix things without hurting anyone in the process. "We have some shared projects and he's anxious about the … um … outcome of those."

She should confess—honestly confess her part in the wager with Alex. Riding in a crowded truck to a family gathering probably wasn't the best time or place, but maybe later. *After* the Autumn Leaves Ball?

Coward.

"I do need to talk to you sometime though."

He lifted a brow and glanced sideways. "How about we send the kids inside and we can talk about it now?"

Air lodged in her throat. Now? When she hadn't sorted out a logical, convincing, heart wrenchingly honest explanation? "Sure," she squeaked out the word, brain rushing through a plan, or confession, or both.

Reese unbuckled Brandon from his car seat and sat him on the ground, followed by Lou. "Will you help Brandon get inside, Lou? We'll be there in a minute."

Lou gave him a warning look. "Don't be too long. Granny's tater-cakes don't wait for nobody."

"Tell you what." Reese looked to Dee as he spoke. "I'll just blame it on the city girl so Granny will feel sorry for me."

Lou's expression turned doubtful. "She won't buy it, Daddy. Granny can sniff out a fib faster than Haus can tree a coon."

Lou walked toward the house, urging Brandon to follow, and Reese climbed back in the truck. He trailed his hand along the back of the seat until his fingers came in contact with Dee's hair. She instinctively slid a little closer, even though she shouldn't, for clarity's sake. He threaded her hair between his fingers and gave her a look of complete trust. She was the worst human being in the world.

"What did you need to say, darlin'?"

The truth lodged tight, anchored in place by six hard years of graduate school. *Just say it.* Confession won top spot on her list for two weeks. Every ounce of confidence fled. He cared about her. It shone in his eyes and whispered in his touch. And the truth? His wife broke his heart with her deceit, and though Dee's offense couldn't compare to unfaithfulness, she'd used him for her own gain. Like a pawn.

"You look mighty intense. Something wrong?"

Her gaze went to the source of his words. His lips. Which caused a whole new dilemma. The idea of kissing him combined with pure cowardice distracted her from her well-meaning confession.

She looked up and fumbled around in her thoughts for a little too long.

His grin hitched up on one side. "I think I know what you have on your mind."

"Um, you do?"

"Yeah," he nodded, his expression growing serious. "Scootch over here a little closer and I'll tell ya."

She wasn't sure how it happened so fast, but before she slid more than a few inches, he had her in his arms. His lips, warm and wonderful, covered hers and sent the fire in her cheeks spreading through her entire body.

He didn't seem to mind her limited practice—and she certainly didn't mind the idea of practicing, especially with the marvelous side effects. He drew back, but she kept her eyes closed, allowing the memory to settle deep, in case her confession stole him away. His breath brushed against her cheek and his lips followed.

"Did I guess right?"

"Good guess." She opened her eyes, breath tripping into a staccato rhythm. "That *was* one thing I had on my mind."

"As I said before, I like your train of thought, darlin'. I've been thinking about it all week."

Her smile broke free. "Me too and now I might have trouble remembering what I was going to say."

"That's okay. I have a one track mind anyway."

She put a hand to his chest to stop his forward momentum and laughed. "If you keep distracting me, I'll never remember."

"Alright. I'm listenin'." He focused on her lips again. "Mostly."

She slid her hand to his cheek and took a deep breath. "Well, I have this fairly important engagement to attend next week. It's a large party in Charlottesville called the Autumn Leaves Ball."

Reese's gaze came up to hers and his moustache twitched. "A ball? Like in Cinderella?"

"Nothing as grand as that kind of ball, but it is a fancy affair, with music and an extravagant dinner and—"

"Dancing?" He pronounced the word like it hurt.

She bit the inside of her cheeks to control her grin. "Probably."

"Oh." He groaned. "It's *that* kind of party. I'm more of an outdoor-barbeque-type fella."

She studied his grimace, working up the courage to ask … or worse, confess. His honest, brown eyes had become a regular fixture in her dreams. He harnessed power and strength into the gentlest touch to cherish her. She'd never understood the true meaning of the word *cherish* before, but cocooned in the haven of Reese's arms, her mind awoke from a long, lonely solo into a full symphony. Charlottesville and all its splendors dimmed to the backlight in an instant, and she knew. *Home wasn't about a place or time—it was about relationships*, and there was no place like home. *Right here.*

Her will wrapped around the awareness like an iron fist. She wouldn't hurt Reese or his family, even if Charlottesville offered grand prize. She *loved* home too much.

"Dee? Do you want me to go with you? Is that what you're saying?" Reese searched her face.

The fact he offered to go secured her decision. The wager was over. Alex's win held no prize greater than the one holding her. She loved Reese Mitchell. Relief swelled at the inner declaration and inspired a ridiculous giggle. "You are so sweet. Did you know that?"

He raised a brow. "Are you just figuring that out?"

"I'm a slow learner." She placed a gentle kiss against his lips and then rested her forehead against his chin, an overwhelming sense of gratitude shaking her to her core. Love? The fragile and mysterious melody hummed beneath her skin. Amazing.

"So about your Cinderella Ball?"

His fingers sifted through her hair and she snuggled closer into his strength. Home never felt so good. "I just wanted you to know I'd be away." She swallowed the brief edge of disappointment. "Would you mind feeding Haus for me?"

"Is that all?" His voice rumbled in his chest and his arms tightened around her. "Old Haus has grown on you a bit?"

"There's something catchy about Ransom." She kissed him, long and tenderly with all the freedom running through her veins. She'd totally underrated lips. Though great for eating and using certain speech sounds, they reached their functional pinnacle in kisses, or at least in the right kind of kisses.

She savored the afterglow of loving him, acknowledging it, and reached for the truck door. No more wager. No more lies. She'd earn her own way to Charlottesville, in her own time. "Goodness gracious, Mr. Mitchell, we'd better get inside before we miss out on those tater cakes."

"You can share a little more dessert with me first." His grin turned wicked. "I'm not in a hurry for lunch unless you are."

She slid to her door, slapping at his hand and turning up her best Appalachian accent. "We'll be in a heap of trouble from one hawkeyed Mama if we don't show up for her vittles."

He laughed and sent her a look with *hungry* written on each sparkle in his eyes. Her misconceptions about mountain people, the Appalachian culture, and true love fell over and over again, but not without being rebuilt into the possibility of a new dream, a new understanding. Now all she needed to do was call Alexander Murdock, and forfeit Charlottesville.

Dee closed her front door and leaned her back against it with a content sigh. Lunch with a loving family, snuggles with two cute kids, and an afternoon kiss from her handsome farmer? *Stellar day.* The warm fuzzies hitched on one thought: Charlottesville, and the call she needed to make. Haus' paws clipped across the wooden floor and followed her to the couch, where she collapsed. Her unlikely companion settled on the rug near her feet and smiled up at her.

She scratched him behind an ear. "It's been a good day, boy, but I think it's about to get harder."

His grin didn't change.

"I'm serious. Charlottesville was so close and now?" She shrugged, the weight of a dying dream throbbed into a deep ache. "Not impossible, just a longer wait."

She stared at her phone in hand, the heaviness landing with full force in her mind, but she wouldn't turn back now. One click of a button rang Alex's number. Waiting worried a hole in her stomach. One ring. Two rings. Three. Pride pinched to the stinging place. Admitting failure to anyone else would have been three times easier, but to Alex Murdock? Four. Five. An automated voice opened his voicemail. Leaving a message was the way of cowards.

Beep. "Hey Alex, it's Adelina. The wager is off. I'll bring my research to the ball. Bye."

Haus tilted his head with a look as if he knew a whole lot more than a dog should. .

"What? I could have texted it. That would have been worse." She stood and walked to the fireplace, arranging new logs into place. "Something I need to work on if I'm going to have people take notice of my work, I guess. I've never been all that good at self-promotion."

Haus yawned. Dee chuckled. "Or interesting conversation with a dog, I guess."

The fire bloomed to life, embers from the morning catching new flame. Gold flickered across the darkening room, highlighting the cherry hues of the dulcimer's grain. It waited in its usual spot, taking her mind back to a time when Appalachia held a sense of wonder and fascination ... and good memories. Her smile bloomed. Kind of like now. Old sparks and new life.

She lifted the dulcimer from the mantel. A pale cloud of dust scattered in various directions, confirming the instrument as underused as her skill. The scent of cherry and wood stain breathed from the flower-carved tone holes. She cradled the dulcimer's long, teardrop-shaped body, smoothing her fingers over each turning peg to the tip of the peg head. Silence waited in anticipation, but could she fill the quiet room? Years and forgetfulness filled the space of time since she played it last. Would she remember?

She shifted the dulcimer in her arms and took the almond-colored pick from the mantel. It was a finer instrument than her granny's. Smoother, with a polished elegance. Her fingers trembled as she sat back on the couch. Haus' head popped up from its resting position, curious and maybe aware of the magic this instrument possessed. A sound as mysterious and old as the mountains. A sound to draw a hidden piece of her life to the surface.

She rested it onto her lap and strummed a line across the four strings on the stringboard. Someone must have replaced the strings before she moved into the house, because they shone with new silver. An awed touch of her Granny's presence filled her movements as she adjusted the turning pegs until the strings blended in tune. The simple strum soothed a lifelong ache and urged her to continue, a simple thrill rolling down her spine. Here was something wholesome and good from her past. Something beautiful, even. What tune did her fingers remember? A rusty hinge of notes pieced together, crowding in various refrains of chorus or verse, until one tune broke free of the rest.

She chuckled at the irony. "Amazing Grace." Her Granny's favorite song and a reflection of her personality. How had her father gone from the tender instruction of Granny Roseland's faith to the hardcore pressure of a truth built on an unattainable to-do list? What situations and circumstances curled his teaching into a knot of self-determination and righteousness?

Amazing Grace? Grace Mitchell's face inspired a smile—a woman of grace? What made this grace so amazing—that made forgiveness a possibility? The limited visits to Reese's church offered insights into the God she'd blamed for years—insights which roused unsettling results.

She started slowly, the melody unfolding in scattered halts and misfingered strums, until on the third time, it flowed. The words to the song remained lost in time, but the melody rang all around and through her, painful and healing.

The magical strain held her in such captivity she didn't hear the knock at her door until Haus jumped to his feet in response. In her defense, it was a little knock. When she opened the door, Lou peered up at her, basket in hand.

"Hey Dee, was that you playin' music?"

She opened the door wider, welcoming the little girl. "I was trying."

Her eye grew wide. "Well, it sounded a whole lot better than Daddy tryin'." She offered the basket. "I can't stay. Granny's in the car waiting on me."

Dee followed her gesture to the gray car in the drive. Mrs. Mitchell gave her signature wave, rosy smile intact.

"We gotta go pick up Emma from the restaurant cause her car's in the shop, but Granny wanted you to have some yummy leftovers from lunch." Lou stepped closer, dark brows wiggling. "And an extra strawberry pie just for you."

Dee shot a grateful grin to Mrs. Mitchell and took the offering. "Now what did I do to deserve such a present?"

Lou's double dimples emerged with her smile. "You're family."

The impact of her simple statement brought the last few days to full circle. *Home.*

"Hey, Lou!"

The little girl turned on the step.

"Do you know the song Amazing Grace?"

She placed one hand on her hip and took a sassy pose. "Well, of course I do. We sing it nearly *every* Sunday."

Every might have been a stretch, since Dee couldn't remember hearing it once in the last month of her visits. "Do you remember the first line?"

Lou drew in a deep breath, like the effort wasn't even worth the time. "Amazing Grace, how sweet the sound that saved a wrench like me. I once was lost but now I'm found. Was blind but now I see."

Dee replayed the words. "A wrench?"

Lou nodded, completely confident in her answer. "Yep. I ain't never understood why God thinks we're tools or something, but there are lots of words I ain't too sure about in church. Last Sunday my teacher kept talkin' about going fast." She shrugged and dropped down a few steps. "I still can't understand what's wrong with going slow when you eat, but she was plum fixed on fast eatin'."

Dee caught her laugh in her hand at Lou's description of fasting. Combined with the idea of God saving a wrench, by the time she closed the door, she'd buckled over laughing, nearly dropping her pie on the floor. She sat the food on the counter and sliced a piece of pie, replaying the other words from Amazing Grace.

I once was lost, but now I'm found.

Found? The lost son. This lost daughter? Maybe there was much more to grace—and she wanted an answer.

CHAPTER 16

Hit you! You infamous creature, how dare you accuse me of such a thing? It is you who have hit me. You have wounded me to the heart. (Pygmalion, Act 4)

Dee's phone buzzed as soon as she and Reese pulled into the church parking lot for Sunday service. She shot him an apologetic look and glanced down at the number. A groan rolled from her mouth before she could stop it. Alex? On a Sunday morning? Was he only now getting her message?

"I'm sorry, Reese. Why don't you and the kids go inside and I'll be there in a minute."

Reese's brow crinkled into worry lines. "Everything okay? Is it your mama?"

"No, it's my supervisor."

"That Alex Murdock character?"

Dee grinned at the description. Character was one way of putting it. "Yes, the very one."

"He sure does make a fuss over you, doesn't he?"

Dee couldn't look at him, afraid he might recognize a liar when he saw one. "We have a fairly pressing situation to rectify. It will only take a minute or two."

A storm brewed on Reese's countenance and he jerked his chin down in a nod. "Alright. I'll leave you two alone." He slid from the truck and turned to unhook the children. "Come on young'uns. Dee has an important phone call to make."

The edge to his voice stung like a slap to her face. Angry? She'd never seen him really angry before. And at her? Dee slid the phone back in her purse. "What is that supposed to mean?"

"I may not speak clearly all the time, but I can read nonverbal communication loud and clear. I've been duped before."

"What? Duped?" Her first thought teetered toward the wager and then spiraled to his wife. "You wait one minute. What are you suggesting?"

Reese didn't answer until both kids stood outside the truck. "Private talks? Lunches together? Visits?" He propped his hand on the top of the door and leaned inside the cab, jaw wound tight. "He needs to talk to you an awful lot. That's all I'm sayin'." He slammed the door.

Oh, no, he didn't! Dee jerked off her seatbelt and met him around the front of the truck, her heels clipping across the uneven asphalt. "You were saying a whole lot more than that." She dug her finger into his chest. "Jealous, are we?"

"I ain …" He growled and watched the kids run up the church steps. "I'm not jealous. I don't have no reason to be jealous. If you want Mr. Big hair and plastic face, I can't compete, and I *ain't* going to."

"Reese Mitchell." He marched toward the church, but she grabbed his arm. "What is all this?" She waved a palm toward him and lowered her arms, bewildered. "Have I ever given you reason to think I care about Dr. Murdock? Any justification for you not to trust me?"

Her question stopped her cold. Her stomach tangled into a knot, heat draining from her limbs. Trust her? No, she wasn't trustworthy. Her entire relationship with Reese hinged on a lie, a trick. The shadow of the church's steeple fell across the asphalt in front of her like a sign from God. Wasn't there something in the Bible about no liars in the kingdom of Heaven?

Reese's shadow moved forward to block the steeple, his voice low. "The two of you seem awful close. He calls you all the time. Comes to see you. He's acting like—"

"Acting like what?"

Reese's eyes narrowed. "Like he's a whole lot more interested in you than for research and Charlottesville."

Dee laughed. "I can assure you, Alex Murdock is only interested in my research. The visits? The calls? They're part of his job."

Reese's expression wrinkled with doubt and the realization gave her self-scrutiny another kick. His wife broke his heart through deception, but Dee wouldn't be compared to her. She'd offer Charlottesville as payment for the wager. The consequences of her forfeited dream hurt her alone.

"I care about *you,* Reese." She squeezed his arm. "I'm not interested in plastic."

The thundercloud in his countenance dimmed and his lips twitched on one side. "So, are you saying you're into a more organic kind of guy? Home grown?"

A twinge of guilt still gnawed a worry pain in her stomach, but a smile won the battle on her face. She'd make it up to him. The whole wager. He never needed to know. "Mr. Mitchell, I don't believe in wasting time or energy on anything. And I think we've already established at heart I'm a country girl, so homegrown suits me just fine."

"I like hearing that a whole lot, darlin'." He took her wrist, thumb skittering over her palm. "And I'm sorry for jumping to the wrong conclusion. Sometimes, I just—"

She raised her hand to stop him. "Just because you've forgiven someone, it doesn't mean the memories are gone, right?"

Reese rubbed his jaw, squinting. "That sounds familiar."

"I heard it from this cattle farmer I know."

"I don't think his vowels and consonants were as eloquent as all that." He placed his arm on her back and steered her toward the church. "He's a little slow up here sometimes." Reese tapped his forehead.

Dee looked up at the sky as if considering his statement, then she linked her arm through his. "Better to be slower up here." She tapped her head. "Than here." She placed her palm on his chest. "And that's certainly not the case with you."

He opened the church door for her and leaned close. "So you're saying I'm thickheaded but warmhearted?"

She laughed. "Definitely. And good."

Too good.

Suddenly her feet grew sluggish. She didn't belong in a church or with someone as generous as him. She was blatantly living a lie. To a great guy. Why would Reese want someone like her and why would God ever let a liar into His Heaven?

DEE ASKED Rainey to drop her off at the end of Mrs. Mitchell's driveway so she could use the walk to call Alex in privacy. He'd texted her three times during church with enough exclamation marks to impress a *Calvin and Hobbes* comic strip. The quote for the day further humiliated her by reminding her about wishing for the impossible. Which is exactly what she'd done the entire church service. Wished for a wholesome past to match Reese's, wished for a clean slate to offer God, wished the wager was nothing more than a happy memory, but no. The sting of her own conscience paired with Alex's annoying texts reminded her of her broken past and current poor choices.

The phone barely rang before his voice came on the other end. "Where have you been?"

"In church."

"Wh—" The statement caught him off-guard. Good, she needed the upper hand for this conversation.

"Listen Alex, I'm finished with the wager. Whether you like it or not, I just can't go through with it. It's wrong to use some innocent person to promote myself."

"That's the problem, Adelina. You're not taking opportunities when they arise. You'd be a perfect match for Charlottesville, and now's the time to take advantage of your success." His voice held a frantic quality, pleading. Very strange. "Do you realize what sort of team we could make up here?"

"I'm finished." Her feet dragged along the gravel, heavy with the effort of fighting him—and herself. "If I can't prove myself in the usual ways, then Charlottesville isn't for me."

"That could take years. This is your opportunity to jump above the curve."

"I won't do it." She stared down at the phone a minute, frustration with herself morphing into an Alex attack. "What is it with you and this wager? It's *my* choice. You win. You should be thrilled to steal my research."

"Adelina, I don't want *your* research." The panic in his voice chilled to anger. "I'm not trying to steal anything. I'm trying to help you."

Help her? By taking her research and using it as his own? By pushing her so hard she agreed to a ridiculous bet which could ruin her relationship with Reese?

"Our conversation is over, Alex. I'll see you on Friday." She hung up on him mid-sentence.

She turned her phone off to remain blissfully unaware of Alex's attempts to call back. From this point on her efforts and energy stuck to building a future out of a desire for relationships and love not fueled by guilt and control.

Reese's grin came to mind. Her quality of life tripled with the proper priorities ... and influences.

The aroma of brown sugar and butter drew Dee through Mrs. Mitchell's front door. Heaven in a kitchen. Mrs. Mitchell offered a toothy grin and a brimming spoon. Family, romance, food. One of the best lists she'd made in a long time.

"Perfect timing, Dee. I need a taste tester."

Dee liked the idea of providential circumstances all the more.

"What am I testing?"

"Blackberry cobbler. I'd frozen berries earlier this year and decided we needed something different than apples for a change." She nodded toward a barstool. "Sit on down here and let's see what we got before the rest of the folks come in from church."

Dee followed her directions and took the heaping spoon. She closed her eyes and let the wonderfully warm blend of sour and sweet melt over her tongue. The sugar coated bread made a slight crunch before softening into the juices. "Mmm … I think you have another winner."

Mrs. Mitchell's wink emerged. "I reckon a little ice cream wouldn't bother it none, would it?"

Dee laughed, the homemade charm in this woman even more appealing than the desserts. "Not a bit."

"Reese and Trigg stayed behind to help Pastor with unloading the new hymnals?"

"Yes." Dee relaxed back onto the stool. "Rainey should be here any minute, though. She dropped me off and went to her house for a casserole."

"Oh good, that will give us a little time to talk."

Tension spiked up through Dee's spine. Her phone conversation with Alex ended well before she came into earshot of the house. Hadn't Lou said something about Mrs. Mitchell sniffing out fibs? Oh where were her lucky rocket underpants when she needed them?

"Now, now, honey, there's no use gettin' your back up. I was just wondering if you'd heard from your mama?"

Dee released her held breath on a sigh. "She called last week to tell me she's enrolled into a program." Dee added in a lower voice. "For the twelfth time."

"Well, you never know when the twelfth time will be the one that matters most." Mrs. Mitchell stuck a serving spoon in the cobbler and set it up on the bar. "God's timin' doesn't always suit us."

The truth of those words reverberated all the way to her PhD. Much too long. Or was it? If she had graduated two years earlier, like typical a student, she wouldn't have come to Ransom. Never met Reese or his kids. And if Alex hadn't wounded her pride, she wouldn't have agreed to the wager, then … Clarity nudged her begrudging acknowledgement. Alex Murdock helped her fall in love with Reese Mitchell? The thought nearly brought a chuckle.

"I guess we realize it in hindsight."

"Most of the time it's a bit clearer that way, ain't it?" Mrs. Mitchell tossed her towel over her shoulder and peeked into the oven. "God brought you to Ransom, and to our family."

"I think you have things the other way around, Mrs. Mitchell. There's nothing I can bring to your family, but your family have certain brought so much to my life."

"Are you saying helping Reese with an opportunity to save this farm isn't big? Or being a friend to my daughter isn't important?" She approached the counter, brow as pointed as the fork she raised. "Or that big ol' smile on my son's face every time he talks about you—don't mean nothing?"

Emotions swelled to a knot in her throat. "I ... I never thought about making any sort of difference like that? I've always thought—"

"You know, I read this quote one time from Mother Teresa and it made good sense to me." She plunged a serving spoon into the pan of cobbler. "I think it went something like, *we can't do great things, only small things with great love.*" Her smile creased. "I like that. Sometimes we get so caught up in the *great things* we forget about the big differences we make in the small things." She slid a dish of cobbler across the counter to Dee. "One ingredient at a time."

Dee looked down at the delicious offering, two seconds away from bawling like a baby. How any of the Mitchells accepted, or even saw, anything beautiful in her, let alone God, she couldn't understand. How could she pay them back for such a love?

"Your family ..." Dee stopped and considered her words as Mrs. Mitchell stirred something in a large pot. "I've never known a family like yours. You really live what you believe." She shook her head, the grandeur of their faith as out of reach as half the dulcimer tunes from her past. Lost to time and trouble.

"Sounds like you ain't too sure about your place in our family or God's?"

"I haven't really talked to God in so long." Her words disappeared into a sigh, her failings a giant weight upon her shoulders. "If you knew the truth about me. Really? I don't think I deserve either family."

Mrs. Mitchell stopped stirring. "Seems to me God takes a special interest in the undeserving. And besides, I think you're trying to measure goodness in a twisted-up way. You keep boucin' between trying to prove yourself through good works and beatin' yourself up because you never make the mark. How's that working out for you, sweetheart?"

Dee gave her a sad chuckle and played with the fork on the dish. "Not so good. It's pretty exhausting."

"I think the problem is that you're missing the secret ingredient."

Dee swiped at a rebel tear. "What?"

"My Aunt Lynn cooked the best peach pie this side of the Mississippi. It was like takin' a taste of summer. I spent five years trying to make that pie. Took every recipe I could find, and then some, but none of my peach pies ever tasted like hers. I did everything I could, but nothing worked. It wasn't 'til I asked her about it, did I realize what was wrong."

"What was it?"

"The secret ingredient. The one thing my aunt added to her pie to make it unique. I could keep trying everything else, working so hard to get it right, but without the secret I'd always be trying ... and failing. Seems to me, Dee, you're trying all the wrong things to find the right answer, but you're missing the secret ingredient."

"Faith?"

"Jesus."

Dee nodded, ticking his name off her list. "But then what else?"

Mrs. Mitchell's eyes widened. "What else?"

"Yes. Confess. Believe." Dee mentally ticked them one by one. "What else? Feed the poor? Serve the hungry? Be a good neighbor? Never lie? And what about white lies? How many of those do I have before I am completely kicked off the Heaven list?"

"Whew, that's one big list, ain't it? No wonder you've worked up a lather." She chuckled and set down her stirring spoon. "Only Jesus.

He's the secret ingredient that holds all the other stuff together. The secret ingredient that makes everything else worthwhile."

Only Jesus? But what about all the work she'd done? All the money she'd given, back when she actually went to church somewhat regularly? And all the wrong things? She needed to pay some sort of penance for those. "Only Jesus? You're telling me that if I just ask Jesus to save me, that's it? That gets me into Heaven?"

"That's it."

Dee stood slowly, digesting the new information. "But that can't be right. Anybody could be a Christian. Anyone could go to Heaven."

Mrs. Mitchell's eyes lit, point made. "Exactly. You can't do nothin', Dee, good nor bad to get into God's Heaven. It's all about Him. His love. His grace."

Dee slid back into her chair, legs weak, and the inner skeptic offering an objection. "Sounds too easy."

"Does it?" Mrs. Mitchell's smile softened. "Not if you really think about it. It takes a divine change of the heart to humble us enough to bring empty hands to God. We all want to be good enough by ourselves so we have braggin' rights, but nothing else will fit through the door of Heaven but Jesus. He's all you need. He'll right your wrongs *and* make you good enough for His family all at the same time."

A car door outside alerted them of a break in their private conversation.

"Thank you, Mrs. Mitchell."

"Grace." She corrected and patted Dee's hand, her name more apropos than she realized. Or, maybe from the glint in her eyes she knew exactly how appropriate.

"Thank you, Grace."

Reese liked the feel of Dee's hand in his.

They'd spent a long time talking at his mama's house the day before and added another few conversations at lunch the next day, then a date night followed. An actual date—one where two-year-olds didn't throw ice cream and sisters kept their tires on their cars.

A place where dinner involved higher class food than hamburgers and professional casual was the preferred dress. He planned on showing Dee Roseland his classy side, or at least the less grungy, kid-stained side. He did have one, it just took a little while to grease up the hinges of his memory to find it.

She sat across the candlelit table at Rossi's, the only high-end Italian restaurant in Ransom, wearing some blue, shiny blouse and looking like a princess. After over two months of knowing her, he recognized with more clarity the various emotions she tried to hide, but even more he saw the change in her. A softening, or maybe a release of the beauty she kept hidden behind a heap of hurt. She needed love more than anyone he'd ever met, and the call to meet that need pulled like a magnet.

Jana swept into his life like a dream—all certain, gorgeous, and demanding. Starstruck wonder and pure stupidity at her interest in him blinded him from her self-centeredness and need for change. She'd never been broken, and even when the ugly truth about her adultery bled into knowledge, she refused to admit her wrongs, blaming her choices on everything and everyone else.

As Dee smiled at his crazy attempt at humor, he realized the difference. Humility and gratitude. Maybe he'd changed on the outside a little, with nice clothes and fancy talk, but she'd blossomed like a spring flower with a little bit of love for rain. His chest expanded with purpose. If all she needed was love, well, he grew up with the right preparation, family, and faith to meet her need.

"I never noticed this place before." She glanced around the room, smile growing.

"Charlottesville quality?"

"Oh yes." She took a drink and lifted a one-shouldered shrug. "Not exactly what I expected from little Ransom."

"Now, Doc, there are all sorts of little surprises in Ransom if you take the time to look."

Her gaze leveled on him, seeming to take in his deeper meaning. "Kind of like you ... and your entire family."

"I think my family might come as more of a shock to one's system than a surprise."

She laughed. "Well, they've been both to me." Her gaze grew serious, focused. "You certainly have." Dee pushed her hair behind one ear and stared down at her plate. "About the time I think I have you figured out, you do something else to surprise me."

He leaned forward, lowering his voice, knowing full well he planned a huge surprise for her in a few days. "Do you like surprises, Dee?"

She looked up, dark gaze glittering in the candlelight. "I do now."

He patted the table in his signature move to add emphasis. "Well, I'd rather you think I'm surprising than a lost cause."

She took his hand and squeezed his fingers, gaze softening. "Not you, Reese."

Her unspoken admission softened his heart even more than the pudding it already was. If this romance continued long-term, would she be content to stay in Ransom? With him? He knew his care only touched the tip of her longing, but not the deepest need of her heart. He couldn't breathe life into her soul or provide healing for her lostness or give her a dream job in Charlottesville.

"You know, I wouldn't be surprised if Ransom didn't hold a few more surprises for people with big-time dreams but smalltown hearts."

The fact she took a drink before responding gave him more of an answer than her words. Nope, her heart still belonged, at least partially, somewhere else. "Some dreams are such a part of who you are, it's hard to see past them, but ... I think I'm beginning to understand."

"And what's that?"

"I only knew my story, this small little piece of life, and it painted a pretty drab picture." She met his gaze, earnest and questioning. "I ... I never knew how it could really be."

"Appalachia?"

"No." She shook her head. "Family."

If he didn't lighten the mood he'd end up as teary-eyed as her. "Crazy, loud, with enough twang to fill up your entire list?"

"Exactly." Her grin curled wide. "And more than enough love to make me believe that any dream can come true."

CHAPTER 17

I did it because we were pleasant together and I come—came—to care for you; not to want you to make love to me, and not forgetting the difference between us, but more friendly like. (Pygmalion, Act 5)

Adelina toyed with the chain around her neck and watched the refined procession of faculty from various departments around Charlottesville's campus saunter into the Grand Ballroom. Standing in the Hall among the elite beat new energy into her love for the place, and renewed her wish to someday follow in the footsteps of so many professors she admired. Maybe her father pushed the dream her way, but a part of her took hold on her own.

Someday, maybe.

Alex Murdock hovered nearby, like a migraine in autumn, but he'd not spoken to her once. He kept sending her a giddy grin, almost like a kid at Christmas, but otherwise hadn't spoken to her. *Strange man.* And stranger by the minute. He nearly glowed with unspoken glee, but even his irritating unpredictability didn't bother her as it used to months ago. Why?

She'd changed. Her reformation put Reese's accent modification to shame because hers transformed at the heart-level. Priorities rearranged. People replaced things. Family filled up lonely nights. Hope beat the rhythm of her dreams with something more long lasting than white stone columns and award-covered walls.

She belonged.

She smiled to herself, tender thoughts of *home* a welcome addition to her inner world. What a difference belonging made.

The atmosphere around her buzzed with life and prestige, sparking a tinge of regret in her choices. *But only a tinge.*

She made the right decision.

"Adelina?"

She turned at Alex's voice, his dashing appearance only enhanced by the sleek tux. Oh, if she didn't know him so well, she might feel some attraction to him, but no way. Her heart beat constant for a farmer tucked away on a lovely hillside in Ransom. She looked at her watch. Seven thirty. He was probably finishing up Brandon's bath.

"You're glowing." He edged closer, hands sliding into his slacks' pockets. "Glad to see me?"

The arrogance nearly dripped off his Grinch-like grin. "How are you, Alex?"

"Fantastic. I feel a little like Santa Claus." He rubbed his palms together.

"As I recall Santa is in the habit of giving gifts, not taking research away."

"Oh, Adelina, if you only knew." He shook his head in a consolatory way. "I never really wanted your research. I only wanted you to prove yourself." He glanced away toward the door, not making any sense at all. "And now I have the perfect surprise to make sure you're noticed."

Her smile faded one degree at a time and fingers of cautions pinched her spine. Why did Alex's plans and immediate terror come in a pair? "You do?"

She followed Alex's gaze to the entry stairs where a magnificent specimen of manhood entered. A particularly familiar magnificent specimen of manhood.

The confident walk, the dark hair, the broad shoulders? Knowledge and reality crashed head-on. It couldn't be … The classic tux hugged his body in all the right places, his dark curls lay tamed and trimmed, even his walk matched the elegance of the atmosphere, but what took her breath away was his clean-shaven face. Not even a shadow. Her whole body froze, except her mouth, which dropped open. She forgot how to breathe.

Here? He was here? And he looked like a dream come true.

A sudden wave of reality hit the spin cycle toward panic. "Oh no! What have you done?"

"Just finishing what I started." Alex's words drew her attention back to him, his clueless smile still firmly implanted. "If you won't make Drs. Lindsay and Franklin aware of who you are and your excellent skills, then I will. And since the wager fell through, I thought I'd bring your success to Charlottesville one way or another. You deserve this."

"You planned the wager?"

He nodded with the same excitement as Lou when she'd displayed her pizza-sized mud pie last week. "Since you wouldn't freely give over some aspects of your research so I could show it to the Department Chair, I had to think of something off the cuff to get it. Mr. Mitchell came at the right time."

Or wrong time, as the case may be. Alex Murdock wanted to promote her? Had planned the entire wager for her own advancement? The information halted and spun in the processing phase. Had her pride blinded her so thoroughly? Another kick to her assumptions.

"The last professor we hired to work alongside me made my life miserable. Plus, she was old enough to be my mother." Alex shuddered. "But you'd make a perfect fit for this world. This department. I had to find a way to get you here. It wasn't too difficult to get Mr. Mitchell's phone number and give him a call. I respect your hardwork and determination, but sometimes you have to put yourself out there to make things happen." His gaze sobered, almost sweet. "One insecure soul can recognize another."

Insecure? Alex Murdock? The world must be coming to an end— or she'd truly stepped into an alternate dimension. Or perhaps, her prejudice against him kept her from seeing all the signs.

The crazy pieces to the puzzle left a difficult picture to believe if she kept Alex in the box her prejudice placed him, but now? Maybe she'd been wrong about him all along too. Wow, hindsight was a killer. "You did this all for me?"

He nodded and his smile turned sheepish. "With a little selfishness peppered in. I hoped getting you to Charlottesville as my colleague would …" His gaze, unswerving, sincere. "Tempt you toward a relationship?"

Her brain took a full ten seconds to register it all. Alex's diminished distance and expectant stare shocked her back to the present. "Sorry, Alex. Not going to happen."

"Don't sugarcoat it, Dee." His hand flew to his chest and he feigned a wound, stepping back. "What about that insecure soul thing didn't you hear?"

She didn't have time to work out all the weirdness of the moment because Reese's gaze found hers across the room and his beautiful smile spread unhindered by his beard. Her brain struggled to match the man before her with the grungy, single dad covered in tractor oil she met her first day in Ransom. With his smooth walk and suave appeal, he could have stepped out of a magazine or off a movie set, but no—he was stepping directly toward her.

"I'm going to find Dr. Lindsay."

No! She didn't grab Alex in time to stop his exit. Was it possible to play the whole thing off as the surprise it was supposed to be without anyone else knowing about the wager, especially her Prince Charming? Because if he discovered the initial reason for their relationship, he'd hate her.

"You look beautiful," he said as he closed in, his words honed with such pristine articulation it brought music to her ears, her PhD, and her heart. "You should wear purple more often."

If breathing had been difficult before, it turned nonexistent as his hand reached her waist and he placed a kiss on her cheek. The musky scent of his cologne enveloped her in daydreams and spice, stripping words from her mind. Nothing prepared her for this.

"You told me you'd changed your thoughts about surprises." He tilted his head ever so slightly, searching her face. "I hope this is a good one."

Prince Charming had nothing on Reese Mitchell. She swallowed and drew in a deep breath of his cologne, forcing her vocal folds to produce at least one word. "Amazing."

His lips looked fuller than she'd imagined and they quirked into a fuzz-free heart-stopping grin. "I don't think I'm going to miss that beard half as much as I thought." He leaned close again, his cheek almost touching hers. "If I have to dress up every once in a while to keep that look in your eyes, I'll do it. Maybe even buy another suit."

Tingles spread from his whisper down her neck and coursed through her chest like fire. She closed her eyes and pressed her cheek against his—smooth and soft. Oh Heavens, time to find some privacy because her lips needed to explore the feel of his cheek too.

"I don't know if I could handle it on a regular basis." She pressed a hand to her chest. "I'm having a hard enough time trying to string words together to make sense. I ... I can't believe you're here."

"All you had to do was ask, you know?" His fingers twisted a lock of her hair around a stray curl, tugging her forward. "I like your curls. I've never seen your hair this way before."Her eyes drifted closed at the tingle his gentle touch to her hair caused. "I can't believe you came, especially since Alex is the one who asked you."

Reese slid his palm down her naked arm until his fingers closed around hers. "I care about you, sweetheart, and this is important to you." His grin bloomed with little-boy mischief. "Add a wholesome dose of jealousy to the mix and a man will do all sorts of things."

"Even don a tux." Dee gave him a healthy appraisal, appreciating each inch, before meeting his gaze again. "And did you notice how well I appreciated every inch?"

He squeezed her hand and released a shaky breath. "Woman, the look on your face was worth every hair on my chin." He tugged her closer, gaze intense. "Do you think all this work will be good enough for your supervisor?"

"Oh Reese, I don't care about what my supervisors think, but I know you're a great deal too good for me." *The truth shall set you free?* She loved him, and love demanded her honesty, even if the possible results knifed fear through her heart. Reese deserved the truth. From her. "We should talk."

"We're both getting pretty serious all of a sudden. Didn't you call this a party?" He looked around the room and rubbed his bare chin. "All those fancy people on the dance floor don't look serious to me. Besides, if I'm going to get all gussied up like a penguin..." He rolled his eyes and sighed. "If I'm going to dress up, you'd better have fun with it. Mama said she didn't think I got this spruced up for my own wedding."

"And you look fantastic." Her gaze swept another appreciative look from his shoe tip to black mane. "But, I never planned on this." She waved between them. "When I first arrived in Ransom, I wanted to run away. I wanted to find any possible means of escape. Whatever it took. I believed my job would fill this great void in my life." She stared at him, pleading for understanding. "But Ransom proved to be so different. Nothing matched my expectations."

The smile on his face stilled. "Why are you talking about this right now?" He tilted his head, confusion wrinkling his brows. "Are you afraid I'm going to embarrass you?"

She squeezed his arm, hoping it conveyed some of her emotion. "Reese Mitchell, you could bring a whole herd of cows into this ballroom right now and use as many 'ain'ts' as you want, and I would gladly kiss you right in the middle of the dance floor."

"Is that right?" His low soft tones sent a trill of warmth over her. "Where are the cows when I need them?"

"And there's no one else I'd rather have with me than you." She fulfilled her own wish by touching his smooth cheek for a brief moment. "It's taken me a long time, years in fact, but I've finally begun to realize what matters most."

"One shave of a man's face and you get all sentimental, darlin'?" He paused. "Do high society gentlemen say *darlin*, or should I have said *my dear?*"

The warmth in those chocolate-colored eyes reminded her she'd come home. "I don't care which one you use, as long as you'll keep saying it to me for a long time." Her hand tightened with the tension in her throat, preparing her confession. "Reese, I need—"

"Let's dance."

His words knocked her out of focus and nearly off her heels. "What?"

He took her hand and drew her toward the floor where a handful of other couples moved to the slow music, his face set with purpose. "But I can't talk and dance at the same time. I don't think I can listen and dance at the same time either, but we'll see. Less hair on my face does not mean more rhythm in my body."

A shocked laugh bubbled out. "We really don't have to do this, Reese. I'm as happy to stand aside and hold your hand."

"I paid good money for lessons." Reese brought her to him. One hand rested at her waist the other stayed entwined with her fingers. "Might as well make some use of them."

"You paid for lessons?" Dee stared at him, feet frozen in place. "Really?"

"Yes, ma'am." His brow furrowed, focused on his newfound skill. "The fastest dance lessons in history."

He looked at her so intensely she could almost see him counting his steps in his head. She moved along with him and marveled at yet another way this man treasured her. He hadn't wanted to dance, or dress in a tux, or shave his beard, and yet he'd done it all. For her.

Love.

"Don't you dare start crying on me, Dr. Roseland," he said in his best Standard American Dialect, which made her tear up even more. "I know for a *fact* I can't dance and watch you cry at the same time."

"Why would you do all of this?"

He stopped in the middle of the floor. "You don't need me to use words to figure that one out, Dee. You have a PhD, remember?" His grin almost emerged and then he sobered. "You're more than worth it to me." He cleared his throat and started dancing again. "But stop asking questions so I don't have to listen or we'll never finish this dance."

A few tears slipped down her cheeks. She wasn't worth it. He could do much better. *Oh dear Jesus, I'm so sorry. Please help Reese forgive me.*

She pinched her lips together to keep the prayer inside and not distract Reese, but her heart pumped an erratic rhythm. She didn't deserve his kindness and patience. His sacrifice and tenderness. His laughter and family. She didn't deserve any of it—but she craved it to her core, to her soul. Her mind paused a moment on the thought. She didn't deserve his love? Just like God's love, but God gave it anyway? Completely. Exactly as Mrs. Mitchell tried to explain.

Dee's throat tightened as an unexpected rush of tears burned her eyes.

Grace.

The music ended and sweet revelation took hold. *She belonged.*

Reese breathed a sigh of relief. "Next time I do that, could we make it a private dance? Then I might can dance and listen all at once. Maybe even talk too."

She pulled him into a hug. "Whatever you want, Reese Mitchell." Her words snagged on the tears gathering in her throat. "I'm overwhelmed and humbled to have someone like you do all this for me."

His brows crashed together. "Someone like me? Cattle farmer widower with two rotten kids, a raft of misused consonants, and a pair of stinking farm boots?"

"I was thinking more along the lines of a kind, tenderhearted, funny man who has swept me off my feet with his charm."

"And roguish good looks?"

She examined his face. "Definitely."

He drew her into his arms and rubbed his cheek against hers. Knees softened to jelly, but his arms tightened around her, body warm and wonderful. *Thank you, God.*

The prayer shoved her into motion. "But *I'm* not worth it, Reese." She shook her head and stepped back, hands resting on his arms. "I need you to understand, it didn't start this way. The right way."

"Whoa now," his voice rumbled low and soothing. "I think you're worth whatever Charlottesville needs and all your supervisors can see it."

"No, it's not them. It's you. And me." Tears clouded her vision. "I've made a horrible mistake. We need to find a place to talk, because I can't do this here." She swept a glance around the room, a frantic attempt among the masses of faculty and guests. "I need to make you understand. I'm so sorry—"

"Dee!" The voice froze her in place. Alex swooped up behind her, his presentation as perfect as if it had been scripted, Drs. Lindsay and Franklin on his heels. "Dr. Lindsay and Dr. Franklin have come to meet your guest."

Oh, no, Alex. One slipped phrase before she explained the entire ordeal to Reese might ruin everything. One misplaced word.

Reese offered his hand and a full-fledged grin. "Dr. Lindsay, it's a pleasure to see you again."

His articulation would have impressed Dianne Sawyers.

Dr. Lindsay's pale blue eyes grew wide as she swept Reese a look. "Mr. Mitchell?"

"And this is Dr. Henry Franklin," Alex added, moving aside for the older, and much more serious, gentleman to take Reese's hand.

"You've been receiving accent modification from Dr. Roseland, Mr. Mitchell?"

"Yes, sir. For three months." The professional emerged and caused another wave of shock. He really should be a professor one day. Back straight, expression confident, and a hint of charm to quell anyone's discomfort. She filled her lungs with a satisfaction. "Dr. Roseland has helped prepare me for a job interview as a consultant for McCready Agricultural Firm in Chicago."

Not one slip of the tongue or mutilated vowel.

"And you're from Appalachia?" Dr. Franklin obviously had his doubts.

Reese shot Dee a smirk. "I was born and raised in the Blue Ridge Mountains my entire life, sir. It's a nice place to call home and I'm quite proud of it, but I'm open to the possibilities of experiencing new opportunities."

"I can vouch for it, Mark. I saw him a month ago at a football game." Dr. Lindsay's smile bloomed. "And his heritage was quite apparent, but what a splendid transformation, Mr. Mitchell. Are you happy with the outcome?"

"I will be if all the hard work pays off next weekend." He stood a bit taller. "But even if it doesn't, I know the skills Dr. Roseland has reinforced will only expand my marketability and professional options."

He sounded like the author behind his research articles. Consultant for the East Coast. A swell of pride distracted her from her previous panic.

"I can't believe you are from Appalachia. There isn't a hint of accent, not even in your vowels." Dr. Franklin's gruff reply brought a smile to Reese's lips.

"Well, I am being particularly careful right now, Dr. Franklin. If you forced me into a long discussion of cattle feed or irrigation systems, I might give a truer hint to my heritage."

"I've known several Appalachian businessmen, and few cloak their accents as well as you, let alone hold themselves with an air of sophistication."

"His confidence was all his own, Dr. Franklin." Dee interjected. "And he's a fast learner with the proper motivation."

Reese's gaze took on a heartwarming glint. "The proper motivation does make all the difference."

A smile waited behind his remark. He held her attention beyond social protocol, but neither her scattered pulse nor her roasting cheeks minded. Let the world know, and laugh if they wanted. She was in love with a wonderful guy!

"It seems highly improbable." Dr. Franklin's gruff reply brought a smile to Reese's lips.

"Dr. Roseland has the perseverance of a hunting dog. She's skilled, talented, and a hard worker. You couldn't find a more focused or honorable person to bring into your department."

His unfettered admiration broke through the attraction with the knife of conviction.

Dr. Franklin stared at him in wonder. "I must introduce you to Charles Lennox. He'll be shocked."

Dr. Franklin took Reese by the arm and, with Alex at his other side, disappeared into the crowd. As soon as he returned, they should leave. Quickly.

"Adelina, I'm happy to have this opportunity to talk to you in private." Dr. Lindsay's kind expression softened even more. "Alex provided some of your research for me to review and I must confess I am impressed by the work of someone with your limited experience. Even though his name is listed as a coauthor, he affirms you are the lead researcher on the projects. You are quite accomplished. I believe there is a future for you here, perhaps even sooner than you realize."

REESE WOULD NEVER REMEMBER ALL the people Alex and Dr. Franklin introduced him to. Dr. this or Dr. that. And Alex kind of grew on him, in a shiny-penny-that-needs-a-home kind of way. Reese wasn't ready to become great friends with him or anything, but Alex displayed more selfishness and youthful arrogance than any underhandedness or harm. But, as interesting as the last fifteen minutes had been, meeting one person after the other, Reese wanted to get back to his beautiful date. He grinned. God allowed him a front seat view of His work in her life, bringing her into family and love. What a show.

He caught sight of her across the room and something akin to fireworks started shooting off in his chest. Man, she was gorgeous. Purple dress loose to the ground, tight around her waist, and showing off one bare shoulder. Wonder what it would feel like to kiss her without a beard?

Hopefully it wouldn't be too long to find out.

He couldn't deny taking a strong liking to the dazed look of admiration on her face when she saw him. He'd felt that way about her plenty of times, but turnabout suited him just fine.

Reese turned his thoughts back to the discussion with Alex Murdock. "Guess I'll have to come down to Ransom this week to help Dee prepare for her grand presentation."

"Well, she's seems to be managing fine on her own. My sister says she's a great teacher."

Alex smiled. "Oh no, I don't mean her teaching. I know she's an excellent teacher. She taught several classes for me while she was in graduate school. She's only proven her competency and determination even more tonight."

"Has she now?" Reese started to walk across the room, hoping Alex might take the hint and stay behind. No such luck. The guy kept right on following him as if he'd decided they were going to be family or something.

"Of course. You're a walking research project." Alex spread his hands in the air like he was making a headline. "A new accent in ninety days or less?" Alex grinned. "I never thought she'd be able to pull it off."

Reese caught Dee's gaze as she spoke to another woman. Her smile flickered enough to let him know she liked what she saw. Well, that made two of them. "She's a pretty remarkable lady."

"You have that right," Alex said. "I couldn't have lost the bet to a better person."

Reese stopped and turned to face Alex, sure the guy was talking crazy. "The bet?"

"Yeah, you know. Accent modification of a severe Appalachian accent? National Convention presentation?" Reese's smile faded as Alex kept talking and he darted a deer-caught-in-headlights look to Dee. "Nothing important. A harmless wager among friends."

The fireworks in Reese's stomach dropped like coal. "A wager that involved me?"

"Nothing serious, really." Alex took a deep breath and hooked his hands on his hips, eyes focused anywhere but on Reese. Reese's jaw tightened. "It was really about Dee's success in her first job. How well she'd make the adjustments, a little nudge for her career. How long it would take her to hone her skills—"

"How long it would take to turn a country boy into a city one?" Reese thundered his consonants with purpose. Pain drilled a line directly to his heart. He focused the fire inside on the brunette staring back at him. Fooled by another woman. When would he ever learn?

IN ONE GLANCE Dee's world started crashing. Reese's gentle expression transformed from one of confusion, to hurt, and then hardened into anger all within a ten second span. Those same dark eyes that fifteen minutes ago had melted her with compassion now regarded her with utter mistrust. And why not? She'd tricked him. Of course, she'd never expected to fall in love with him during the process of her little wager, but that was no excuse. The beautiful bond of home and belonging severed with the fire in his gaze.

A staggering jab of loss nearly buckled her.

She'd unintentionally toyed with his emotions, but never to hurt him. Oh, how could she make things right and rescue the beautiful sweetness between them?

Reese turned to Alex and made some quick response then started for the door, one of his strides taking two or three of hers.

"Reese, wait please."

He didn't so much as pause, but kept marching forward out of the ballroom and down the hall, a man on a mission to leave his liar-of-a-girlfriend far behind.

"Please, let me explain." Her voice echoed off the tiles, coming back to her in full desperation.

"I've done nothing but listen to your lies since I first met you, Doc." He turned as he pushed open the doors to the cold November night, the breeze brushed gooseflesh up her bare arms. "I'm not listening anymore."

"They weren't lies. It might have started out as a game, but that was only—"

"A game?" He seared her with a look before stepping out into the night. The door slammed behind him like an exclamation mark. *Thoughtless choice of words.* She jerked open the door and quickly followed, tripping along the lamp lit path.

"No, not a game. Not now. I had no idea I'd grow to care for you and your family so much. It was only supposed to be a business opportunity, not—" The internal chill met the external one and she shuddered. "Everything changed. Everything."

He waved her away, but his pace slowed. "Get back inside, woman. If you don't catch your death, you're gonna fall over and kill yourself. We're finished with this, Dee."

"I am not leaving until you listen to me." Dee ran to catch up but her heel caught in a crack of the sidewalk. She released a cry as her ankle crumbled beneath her.

Reese's caught her before the pavement did. His warm palms ran down the length of her arms to steady her and the pain in his eyes forced her tears to the surface. "I'm so sorry."

He released her and stepped back. "Get back inside, Dee. Now."

His harsh words rasped with hurt.

She whimpered as it stung. "Oh Reese, I never meant to hurt you." She'd heard that phrase before, but not from her own lips. Her mother? Pain knifed a fresh wound. "It all started as a simple bet. That was all. I never imagined falling in love with you."

"Love? This is what you think love is like?" He stepped back and shoved a hand through his curls. "Love has nothing to do with a wager or a bet—and it sure don't have an accent. Love isn't about yourself, Dee or what you can get from it."

"I know that."

"Do you?" Reese shook his head. "What happened if you won the wager?"

Dee bit her lip.

"I know it has to do something with your research. Does it mean a promotion? Charlottesville?"

Her expression must have given the answer because he sighed and looked up at the sky. "Fix me up and you get a one way ticket to

Charlottesville? Is that what you wanted all along?" He moved close again and took her by the shoulders. "Is that all I was? All my family was to you? A climb up the success ladder?"

Tears snatched at her voice. "No. That's not true."

He let go, his gaze smoldering. "I've been used enough. Whatever you thought this was, it wasn't love. Love doesn't play games with a person's heart." He stepped back, his beautiful lips curled into an unfriendly snarl. "Enjoy your win. I hope it keeps you warm at night."

Reese marched down the path without a glance back. The night air pricked at the tear trails on her face and she stumbled back to clutch a lamppost for support. She watched him walk away, until he disappeared into the shadows, hoping … praying he'd turn around and forgive her.

What had she done? Music and laughter drifted out to her, an ironic taunt. The life she wanted? She wiped at the tears and stepped back through the door, familiar voices and a long-coveted dream calling her to accept her success. But the ache of Reese's pain, pain she'd caused, dulled her senses. Lost—she'd lost him. A comfort and joy which spread beyond the reaches of the walls of UVA or the promises of the past beat hollow in her chest. How could she go back to her past life without the Mitchells as part of her future?

"Adelina," Dr. Lindsay's voice called Dee back into the façade of belonging, but she knew the largest piece of her dream rode in a pickup truck back toward Ransom. "Where is your friend?"

Adelina swallowed the lump in her throat and searched for her voice. "He had to leave."

"How unfortunate. He was such a pleasant person." She offered a small shrug of her shoulders, smile warm. "But I hope it will not dampen your spirits too much. Your research and work ethic coupled with Dr. Russell's adamant praise makes you the perfect candidate for us."

Dee's muddled thoughts reeled to a stop. "Dr. Russell's praise?"

"She wasn't too keen on you to start, but her comments over the past month have secured the reasons I chose you as the initiator in this new program. Dr. Russell spoke of how you've become part of the community, expanded your clinical interest to involve child therapy, and your initial student rankings have been exemplary."

Dee forced a plastic smile. "Thank you, Dr. Lindsay. I am grateful for the opportunity."

"We need professors who connect with students well, and Dr. Poe is retiring midquarter due to health concerns. He leaves a vacancy of experience in both child and adult speech disorders." She inclined her head. "Someone with heart."

Dee's gaze zeroed in. Dr. Lindsay was asking *her* to leave Ransom midyear and come to Charlottesville? Not Alex Murdock?

"Hasn't Charlottesville always been your dream?"

Dee looked back at the closed door where Reese disappeared. Charlottesville had always been her dream, long before Lou's hugs, Brandon's giggles, and Grace Mitchell's cooking. Long before Rainey's friendship and Reese's kiss.

Her eyes warmed with fresh tears. *Someone with heart?*

"Adelina?"

Dee blinked. "Yes. Charlottesville has been my dream job ever since I was a little girl."

"It looks like your dreams are coming true. I will send you a letter with all the particulars. You can expect it next week. Enjoy the spoils of your success."

Dr. Lindsay shook her hand before returning to the ballroom.

Success?

She glanced at the beauty and glamour of the hall. Upper class academia in its entire splendor. Tinkling glass and murmured voices floated a welcome melody above the strum of a string quartet. Everything about it promised prestige, and a shadow of happiness.

Her father would have been so proud.

Then why did she feel like such a failure?

Dee stepped away from the ballroom and pressed her fist against her chest. Grace Mitchell's words mingled with Pastor Brian's sermons spun over and over in her mind. She'd witnessed love and family over the past few months. Grace and acceptance.

And though the dream of Charlottesville gleamed beautiful and good, the comparison to what she knew with the Mitchells fell surprisingly empty. Tears swelled anew, escaping her fragile hold on them and spilling down her face.

She couldn't stay here like this. With a last look toward the ballroom, she retrieved her coat and marched out the door into the night. A second-best dream proved better than no dream at all. When Dr. Lindsay's offer arrived, Dee would accept it. And if all went well, by Christmas Break, she could leave the past and all of her failures in Ransom and start afresh in Charlottesville ... with everything but her heart.

CHAPTER 18

I'd like to kill you, you selfish brute. Why didn't you leave me where you picked me out of—in the gutter? (Pygmalion, Act 4)

Reese stomped through his mother's door first thing Saturday morning to pick up the kids. His head pounded like a hungry herd of cattle toward their feed. It'd taken him five hours to get home from a three-hour drive due to road construction, plus he'd gotten his first speeding ticket in ten years. From bad to worse.

All because of a woman.

He'd gone right to his barn and worked two hours on his broken-down lawnmower, using vowels and consonants he was pretty sure God never wanted to hear again. He didn't want to talk to anybody—but worse, he didn't want to listen. Dee proved his deepest fears—he was an idiot and women were liars. Every single, last one of them—except his relations, and a few seniors at church. And Meg, who was practically his sister.

He all but slammed the screen door to his mama's kitchen, but years of habit and the fear of Mama curbed the impulse. His chest ached with pain and longing, so deep it stirred up every wound Jana left behind. Every memory. Each and every broken promise.

His teeth ground to the hurting place. He needed … he wanted …

What *did* he want?

To beat some nails in a fence. Chop enough firewood to get three families through winter. Get Adelina Roseland's beautiful face out of his thoughts. The first two he could do without a bit of trouble. The last—easier said than done. Stupid man. Hadn't he learned his lesson?

Evidently he had a bad case of short term memory loss. Stubborn and stupid. Dee played the game of life with the ease of a pro—and won. He pressed his palms against the kitchen counter, his eyes closed to stay a sudden warmth behind them.

"Reese, is that you?" His mom called from down the hall and he braced himself for the admission.

He'd screwed up again.

Mama emerged from the hallway, pink curlers and a smile her hallmark morning features. "You sure are comin' over early. I figured you wouldn't even be back from Charlottesville until this afternoon."

Reese rubbed at the heat creeping into his neck. "Yeah, well I decided to get on back. Not exactly the fancy ball sort and all."

The look she sent him drilled through his excuse better than his Craftsman cordless into a two-by-four. He focused his whole attention on the cookie jar, even decided to snatch one. *Empty.* He groaned. His kind of day.

Mama flicked on the stovetop, her morning hum obviously absent. She was on to him.

"Besides, I have a lot of work around here."

"Mmmhmm." She placed her cast iron skillet on the stove with a clink and added a dollop of butter. Her pointed look confirmed she doubted any story he conjured up.

Reese paced from the front window to the counter and back, trying his best to keep his eyes off his mama's. The butter sizzled in the pan and a crack of an egg followed. Might as well give it up altogether and go for a change of subject.

"The kids awake yet?"

"It's six thirty on Saturday morning. What do you think?"

"Right."

Three more eggs cracked.

"Answer me this, Reese. Did you spend thirty dollars a lesson this past week trying to learn how to dance?"

Reese reached up to rub his jaw, shocked by the smoothness of his face. No wonder he was so cold this morning. He clamped his lips tight. *Women.*

"And ain't you the man who drove three hours to Charlottesville yesterday to attend some high society party as a *big* surprise for someone you care about?"

Cared about. Past tense. He didn't have any use for liars. Reese shoved his hands into his pockets and cleared his throat. Anything he said at this point could be used against him. And probably would.

"And, if I recall rightly, you ain't shaved your face since you started growing hair on it. But unless my visions going along with my memory, your face is just as smooth as this eggshell." She cracked another egg against the pan, and tossed another Mama-look over her shoulder. "Seems strange you'd spend such a short time with the lady who inspired such a transformation."

"I needed to get back." Yeah, he knew it was stupid to say it. *He* didn't even believe it.

His mama just raised an eyebrow and started scrambling up the eggs.

With a sigh he pulled all the way from his boots, he straddled the stool at the counter. "I'm stupid, Mama. Plain ol' stupid."

"Okay, I really must be dreaming," Rainey walked into the kitchen, red flannel pajamas and wild mess of hair a before breakfast welcome. "Did Reese admit he was stupid ... out loud?"

Oh great. His shoulders sagged. Now he had to elaborate in front of two people? "What are you doing here?"

"Did shaving off your beard take your good mood with it?" Rainey rolled her eyes. "Sarah wanted to have a sleepover with your two. So we stayed here. What are you doing back so early?"

"That's exactly what he was fixin' to tell me." Mama stared at him and he squirmed in his seat.

"She was using me." Reese pushed the words out through gritted teeth. "She had been all along, ever since the first day."

Rainey joined him at the counter. "Using you? What on earth are you talking about?"

Reese took in a deep breath and told his mama and Rainey what happened at the Ball as plain as he could. It hurt just as bad the second time through as it had the first, especially when he piled it up against the hundreds of sweet moments he'd shared with Dee over the past three months.

His brain hurt as badly as his heart. No clues. No hints to her duplicity. He was the biggest idiot on the face of the planet.

Not even the Trigg-in-his-head was laughin'.

Rainey's chin rested on her hands as she listened, looking like a little girl, scrunched brow and all. "So, she agreed to fix your accent for free so she could impress the professors at Charlottesville with her skill and fulfill her lifelong dream of getting a job there?"

"Exactly," Reese answered, and then played her phrase back in his head. "No, wait, it ain't that simple."

"She didn't agree to fix your accent for free?"

"Yeah, but—"

"And she told you she wanted to move to Charlottesville?" Rainey's brows rose.

"Well, sure, but—"

"And she even mentioned that you were part of her research, didn't she?"

Reese slammed his palm on the table. "Now Rainey, you're making it sound a whole lot simpler than it really is. She made a bet about me. All the time she spent with me, with us," he waved his hand around the room to remind both women how Dee had tricked *them* too. "It was all part of a game to her. We were all being used."

The truth should make them as mad as he was.

"Taking care of you when you're sick isn't a game I ever want to play," Rainey's frown made him madder. "And weeping to Pastor

Brian was probably part of her conniving plan to use you too, right? When you weren't even around to impress?"

"She made a fool of me, Rainey. Made a bet with her little uppity friends and used me to get what she wanted."

"Would you listen to yourself?" Rainey pushed herself away from the counter and rolled her eyes. "Reese Mitchell, what's hurt worse? Your heart or your pride?"

"Now Rainey," his mama's words were soft. Caring. She understood, of course. "Don't be too hard on your brother. He's never been real good with women."

Reese shot up from the table. "Listen here you two. This ain't got a thing to do with me and women. It has to do with right and wrong. I'm not the one who pretended to be nice to somebody, pretended to love somebody, just to win a bet. I'm not the one who put on a sweet face to the children when all the while lying to us. I didn't betray anybody."

Mama stepped to Reese's side and rested a hand to his arm. "Is this about Dee? Or Jana?"

Reese blinked against the blow of her words. "Jana's been gone for over two years, Mama. We're talking about the present."

"Are we?" She squeezed his arm. "You're a smart man, Reese. Think."

He pulled away from her. "Mama, I don't—"

Her sharp squeeze stopped him. "Don't talk. Think. All you're seein' is red because you're so mad. But what are you really mad about?"

"I've already told you? I told you the whole story."

"Who said *yes* to Dee's therapy?"

Reese pointed his finger. "You told me to do that."

"And who reached out to help her—be neighborly."

"You did too, Mama. And so did Rainey."

"And who started a romantic relationship with her? Took her to the café? Walked with her in the moonlight?"

"You were watching that?"

Rainey raised her hand. "I told her about that part."

"You what?"

Rainey shrugged. "I can see her house from my back porch."

Reese closed his eyes, but even with Rainey and Mama's faces blocked out, he still felt them staring with the *I told you so* kind of look. "I don't believe this."

"Seems to me, son, you're trying to blame Dee for all the hurt you've held onto since Jana. You've tried to pretend it was gone, but it ain't. It's eating away at you."

"This isn't about Jana. It's about Dee."

"No, son, it's really about you and this anger inside. You're trying to find someone to blame and Dee hit a nerve. You can't see the present because your mind's still fogged up with the past. And you're so stuck in the past, when Dee makes one wrong move, she gets all Jana's blame."

"What do you expect me to do, Mama? Just forget it. Forget the fact my wife snuck around behind me and slept with my brother-in-law? Bore his child? Practically threw my worthlessness into my face." He raised his arms in the air, eyes stinging. "There are just some things you can't forget."

"Nope, you probably can't forget it, but you can forgive it."

"Forgive?" Was his Mama crazy? "I was a good husband to her. I took good care of her." He felt his chin quiver and it made him madder. "I've done enough."

"She's dead, Reese." Rainey's blunt response caught him off-guard. All he could do was stare at her. "They were both wrong, but the longer we hold onto anger, the longer their betrayal hurts us. Over and over again. Jana can't hurt you anymore if you give all your anger up to God."

He shared this same conversation with Dee, hadn't he? Back when he thought she cared about him? Back when she wasn't so conniving and …

His chest hurt, and he hated eating his words. Sour.

"I did forgive her." Reese throat tightened around his words. "And she betrayed me again."

"Forgiving doesn't mean you say what she did was okay. It means you don't let it control you anymore." Mama stepped close again and placed her hand on Reese's arm. "Dee ain't Jana. They're as different as peanut butter and corn on the cob. But until you get the anger against Jana out of your heart, there ain't no room for all the love you have to give to somebody else, or receive. That anger will flare up every time Dee does something that looks anything like Jana. She don't deserve to bear the sins of somebody else's past, and neither do you."

"Jana doesn't deserve my forgiveness."

"It's not easy, Reese. I know." Rainey's understanding pierced his heart. "Better than anybody else. I know."

"And you're worth so much, boy. To us, to God, and, if you think about it, to Dee."

"What if you're wrong, Mama? What if she's exactly like Jana? What if—" He paused to find his voice. "I can't do this again. I can't."

His mama shook her head and gave his arm a squeeze. "No, you can't." Her smile flickered. "But God can."

Reese jerked from his mother's hold. "I can't. It's too close. Too hard." He shook his head. "I don't care what the preacher says, Mama. Do you realize what she took from me?"

"Nothing that God can't restore, Reese."

Words burned in his throat and seared a path down to his chest. Forgive Jana? How could God even ask Him to? He'd taken her back in throughout her pregnancy with Brandon. Cared for her. And she'd tossed him off as nothing more than an old jacket, stained from her misuse.

He wiped a sleeve across his eyes. "I can't."

Without another word he marched from the room and out into the cold morning air, almost running from their compassion, their faith in Dee, their expectation to forgive Jana. Dawn barely hinted an orange hue over a horizon framed in by clouds that promised snow. His vision blurred. How could they expect him to forgive all she'd done? How could God expect it?

Jana had taken the one thing he held above everything else, family, and twisted it until it limped into an unrecognizable form. He'd pieced back together what fragments remained of their life, but underneath it all he struggled with questions and fear. Deep inside, in a place he didn't visit often, he knew he just wasn't good enough for the likes of her ... or Dee.

How could his mother and sister take her side? Wasn't the truth plain enough? The obvious patterns? Was he the only one seeing things straight?

He marched down the hill in the direction of Dee's house, a stack of logs calling for a good beating. He'd oblige. His muscles ached to beat something. The cool wind brushed up against his bare face and sent a shiver through him. Stupid. He'd even shaved a perfectly warm beard for the likes of that woman.

His mind flitted to Dee. The look in her eyes when she'd seen him at the party sure didn't look like the eyes of a two-faced liar. In fact, there seemed to be a whole lot more between them than an accent, with or without the hair on his face. Idiot. She'd acted so well, he couldn't even figure truth from pretend anymore.

And her kisses? All the more proof he wasn't thinking with his brain, but something altogether less trustworthy.

Haus welcomed him into the yard with a grin. The dog looked plum happy ... and clean? He stared at the grinning, clean dog for the longest time, until Haus must've got tired of grinning, because he turned around and walked to the house. Without another look back, he curled up on the porch and Reese did a double take. Was that dog sleeping on a pillow?

Who on earth bought Haus a dog pillow? Mama was too levelheaded to buy something so fancy for a dog, and Rainey would have laughed at the notion. Emma might consider it. She was sort of prissy that way, but it didn't seem likely on her waitressing pay.

And Trigg? No.

Dee's scent drifted on the breeze toward him. Dee? She hated dogs, didn't she?

He looked back down at Haus, who nuzzled the pillow. *Traitor.*

Reese stepped into the garage in search of his grandfather's axe, but stopped. On the shelf stood a bottle of dog shampoo, a dog brush, and a little book entitled *How to Take Care of Your Dog*. The hard edge on his emotions shifted a little. Slips of paper stuck out from the book in all directions, very uncharacteristic for the tight-lipped professor. The thought of her lips distracted him from his anger for a moment and he flipped through the book. His name on a page caught his attention.

Reese says Haus likes bacon. Try some bacon-flavored dog food.

He looked at the dog food bag nearby and sure enough, bacon-flavored. He huffed in annoyance and went back to the notes.

Lou said it would be nice if Haus had a collar so he would feel like a real somebody. Reese leaned back out the door and sent a glance to the porch. A blue color snugged in against Haus' dark fur. Reese's smile unhinged and a different kind of warmth rumbled in his chest. He stepped back into the garage. Crazy woman, spending good money on a dog pillow and collar.

He flipped the page of the notebook and a thin slip of paper feathered to the floor. More notes, except these didn't have anything to do with Haus. It looked like one of Dee's familiar to-do lists.

1. Send a thank you note to Grace Mitchell. That woman is amazing.

Well, the notion was common knowledge, but at least it showed the good sense Dee housed in her pretty, conniving brain.

1. Make sure Brandon has a new stuffed monkey. His old one has a hole in the back.

Reese had tried to replace the monkey three times without success, but the fact she wanted to take care of his boy stretch the warmth through his body and made him about cry. Stupidity jumped right back into his head – and it's what got him into trouble in the first place.

1. Buy Rainey lunch as a thank you for the clinic work. I've never had a friend quite like her.

I guess that's something to thank God about like the pastor said.

Reese coughed through the tightening in his throat. Was God answering his prayer for Dee? Through all of his crazy life and even in the middle of his hurt, had God found Dee?

His name on the next line caught his attention.

1. Work up the courage to tell Reese the truth.

Reese reread the statement. All that anger he'd aggravated to volcanic proportions suddenly puttered into embers. She'd planned to tell him ... like she'd tried to say last night. What started as a silly game for advancement turned into something deeper.

He blew out a long breath and hitched a hand at his waist as he looked upward. "Is that what you've been up to all this time, Lord? Trying to force me to see what an idiot I am?"

Rainey and Mama had been right. Of course there was no need to admit it out loud to feed their egos, but in the quiet before God, he humbly accepted the truth. Clearly, Reese wasn't good at playing God?

He shook his head and gently placed the paper back in the notebook. A mist gathered in his eyes. He'd stuffed the anger so deep, it only took the right trigger to boil ignite. No, he'd never really forgiven Jana. He'd said all the right things in church and covered it over with smiles for the family, but old scars waited for the right moment to reopen and spill out on the woman ... he loved.

Unshed tears blurred his vision and he sighed, releasing the hurt along with the last threads of his anger. God was trying to get him to see straight—and he needed to start looking in the right direction. *Heavenward.*

Scenes and conversations rammed through his head from the past three months. He couldn't match her actions with Jana's. The arrogance wasn't there or the selfishness. The wager wasn't Dee's best choice, but it didn't deserve his outburst at the Ball or his leaving her alone on the sidewalk. She wasn't a manipulator or heartbreaker. She was a kind, beautiful, smart, lonely woman trying to find her answers, her peace, in the wrong ways.

One scene shot to full screen in his mind. She'd told him she loved him. He groaned. And he'd thrown in right back in her face like it didn't mean anything. He couldn't … no, he wouldn't lose this chance, because she did deserve better—and he'd give it to her.

Reese tossed another look heavenward. "Well, what do you want me to do, Lord?"

Energy swelled within him, energy and hope. His gaze fell to the axe across the room. He needed to think some more, especially with an ax in hand. Maybe beating out the frustrations would help clear his mind … and his heart … and then? Well, by then maybe God would help him figure out how to keep Dee Roseland in his life.

CHAPTER 19

You see, really and truly, apart from the things anyone can pick up (the dressing and the proper way of speaking, and so on), the difference between a lady and a flower girl is not how she behaves, but how she's treated. I shall always be a flower girl to Professor Higgins, because he always treats me as a flower girl, and always will; but I know I can be a lady to you, because you always treat me as a lady, and always will. (Pygmalion, Act 5)

Dee's body ached all over, from the inside out. Tossing and turning through the night, a battle of guilt and regret, marked wounds much deeper than sore muscles. She'd lost something far greater than a promotional step up the academic stairway. She'd lost her home. Failure never burned with such raw, spirit-scarring depth before. She sat up in bed and rubbed at the remnant of tears on her cheeks. Her pasty face evidence of a night of weeping.

The sun's light spread through the blinds of her hotel window and warned of late morning. She placed her elbows on her bent knees and covered her face with her hands. If only it all had been a nightmare.

Reese Mitchell proved to be the perfect knight in shining armor, not because of a tux or a beard, or any of those things—but because he loved her, and taught her how to love. She replayed the moment he'd entered the ballroom in her mind and her face flushed hot.

Drop-dead gorgeous.

And though looks weren't everything, Reese Mitchell showed off a side of him, fuzz-free, she'd never imagined, as amazing on the outside as the inside. She touched her lips, memories of his kiss lingering. Fresh tears pressed through her closed eyelids and took familiar trails down her face. And what had she done to that amazing man?

Alienated him. Hurt him.

Crying began anew, quivering her body. She slid from the bed and fell to her knees with an anguished sob. She finally learned what mattered most, only to lose it?

"I'm sorry, God. I'm so very sorry."

I am with you.

The words pealed through the pain, light piercing her darkness and beckoning her to follow. A simple whisper threading beyond her sorrow. Something in her soul sprung open, welcoming the voice and the hope into her brokenness—a gentle touch sifting beyond the wounds. *I have loved you with an everlasting love.*

Her spirit clung to the promise, to the light. Amazing Grace? Oh please, she needed grace. She yearned for forgiveness, wholeness, but didn't deserve it. She'd done so many things wrong, allowed bitterness and pride to feed her selfishness, lied, hated, judged. She didn't merit something as beautiful as the light of grace spilling through her—yet it came, flooding with quaking force. She couldn't stop it. She didn't want to.

You once were lost.

Her past of poor choices, her fear and blindness, even her deception of Reese or her hateful pride wasn't too big for God's grace. He loved her anyway and always.

"But now," her voice caught. "I'm found."

Found. Home. Hope swelled a melody of thanksgiving, along with an entire chorus of tears. Truly home.

Time passed in a blur of joy and gratitude as she lay with her face to the floor. Sweet relief. Amazing love. And, as the tears cleared, and out of the throes of her first real communion with her Heavenly Father, she devised a clear plan.

Reese had trusted her, believed in her ... cared for her? Oh yes, she knew the look in his eyes, the sincerity in his touch. He cared, far deeper than any man and despite her many failings, she'd never given up a dream without a fight. Even if she had to fight against Reese's memories and his deceased wife's betrayal, she'd attempt to show him the truth. God brought him and his beautiful family into her life and she would not give them up without another chance to prove she was not a liar.

No dream fell too far from God's hand, just as no soul grew too lost for Him to rescue.

Like her.

A splash of water to her face teased a mild chill and complete alertness. Her reflection produced a moan. Pale face, dark rings under her red-splotched eyes, and a remarkable glow in her wobbly smile.

She pulled on jeans and a sweater, tossed her hair in a ponytail, and rammed the remainder of her things into her bag. If she had to swallow every ounce of pride, or beg on hands and knees, or ... she zipped her bag closed and sighed. No matter the cost.

Her cell buzzed to life and drew her attention to the nightstand. Eleven-thirty? Unbelievable. She frowned. Much later than she'd hoped. She reached for the mobile and Alex Murdock's number lit the display screen.

She ignored it and tossed the phone onto the bed. Hadn't Mr. Tricky done enough?

Her shoulders slumped forward and she buried her face in her hands—but it wasn't Alex's fault. In his own strange way, he'd attempted to promote her and fulfill her dream. It was kind of sweet, in a weird sort of way.

A knock sounded at her hotel door. "Adelina, we need to talk."

Alexander Murdock? Really? She glanced around the room and then bent low as if he could see her through the solid door. She didn't have time for this. She needed to get to Ransom. *Stupid wager.*

"I know you're in there." His muffled voice grew louder. "Open the door."

Dee stared at the closed door with every desire to burn a whole through it and right into Alex's perfect forehead. He probably wouldn't feel a thing.

She sighed and slit a glance to the ceiling. "Sorry, Lord," she whispered. "It just comes so easily with him."

"I'm not leaving until you—"

Dee jerked the door wide. "What could you possibly have to say to me this morning, Dr. Murdock?"

He wore a guilty expression, which suited his features quite well, but the rest of him looked downright haggard. Wrinkled clothes? Sloppy hair? Evidence of a night similar to hers. Her frustration spun a decrescendo into mild annoyance.

"I wanted to apologize about last night. I didn't mean … I didn't know your friend wasn't aware of our wager." His expression softened more. "It was an unintentional blunder."

Alex leaned against the door frame, his gaze searching hers—no pretense or arrogance. Somehow, he reminded her of a lost little boy. A rare glimpse of the man behind the façade? The hard edge of her annoyance ebbed even more. Last night shone a lot of truth, even on Alex Murdock, and underneath all the arrogance beat the heart of a good guy. Misguided and superficial at times, but good.

"I know."

He looked down, kicking his foot against the carpet. "It wasn't hard to tell how much you cared for each other." His less-than-perfect hair made him more approachable. He ran a hand through it to upset it even more. "I'm sorry, Adelina." He shook his head a moment and met her gaze, expression brightening a little. "But it sounds like Dr. Lindsay wants you in Charlottesville sooner than you thought? January?"

"Looks that way. Dr. Lindsay said I should know something for certain in a few days, but I'm not sure I want it now."

"Because of Mr. Mitchell?"

Dee closed her eyes, a vision of Reese in his tux, his lips near her ear pushed her fear aside for a split second. "Yes." She met Alex's gaze. "Definitely."

"He's a lucky guy."

Dee's stomach roiled the guilt back into existence. "No, I'm the lucky one." Her eyes misted over and a sweet peace dulled guilt's sting. "I've made such a big mistake, but I'm going to try and make things right."

Alex stood up straight, a daring smile on his face. "Then go talk some sense into that farmer. You're a speech-language pathologist. Talking is what you do. Why are you still here?"

Dee leveled him with a challenging look. "Because you're still talking to me."

Alex stepped back, hands up in defense. "You don't have to tell me twice. Good luck, Dee. With the farmer and with Charlottesville." He winced. "I think you're definitely going to need it with the former."

"Thanks a lot," she said to Alex's retreating back.

She slid the last of her things into her computer bag and said a little prayer as she clicked the door closed behind her and started for her car. Halfway down the flights of stairs, her phone buzzed.

She'd give Alex kudos for persistence. She almost shoved her phone back into her purse, but the number caught her attention.

Reese.

She stopped her decent and clung to the railing as she opened up his text message.

We need 2 talk. Daphne's at 6?

She released her breath in a whimper and typed her reply.

Yes.

She'd never had a prayer answered before—and certainly never so quickly. God *was* listening. And maybe, miracles still happened? She certainly needed one.

She sent a look to the ceiling, warmth gathering in her chest and tingling in her eyes. "Thanks for that second chance."

You are mine.

The words reverberated through her, calling her from some deep place within her soul and reminding her where *home* really was. She shook off her contemplation, closed her phone and finished the stairs, hope fueling each step. God? Speaking to her? She wasn't quite sure how it all worked, but she had a three hour drive to figure out how to speak back.

THE ROAD CONSTRUCTION during her drive from Charlottesville left little time for Dee to change clothes at her house before meeting Reese. However, her drive provided lots of thinking time and even a little bit of prayer time. Could road construction be God's plan too? She cast a doubtful look to Heaven and shrugged. Didn't Pastor Joe say something about providential appointments, the good, the bad, and the crazy? The thought of His continual presence awakened awe all over again. Wow, each breath proved amazing.

Wisps of snow danced in dusk's fading light. God brought the snow. She grinned, the child in her heart giggling in complete wonder. She checked Haus' food. God brought Haus for company. She patted him on the head and he smiled. Was God in everything? How had she not seen it before?

The forest-framed road shadowed the gravel drive from Dee's house, making it appear later than 5:45. Snow drifted in a thicker pattern, showering a chorus of white against her windshield as she slowed to reach for her phone. She'd be a few minutes late at this rate. Would Reese wait? She sent a quick text.

On my way. 5 min late. B there soon. D

She tossed her phone in her purse and upped her speed. A ribbon of fear knotted in her stomach. What if he left? What if he didn't forgive her?

Help me, Lord.

The winding road narrowed along with her visual field. She slowed a little more. A white wonderland emerged through the crystalized trees and sparkled against her headlights. She grinned. God washed her sins white as snow? *Certainly apropos, Lord.* Everything appeared new, not only because of the snow, but because she *saw* them with new eyes. Is that what the songwriter of "Amazing Grace" meant? Blindness to God's work, but then sight to see Him everywhere? In everything?

A movement to her right drew her quick attention. A deer bounded forward, directly in her car's path. Reflexes kicked in. She swerved to miss the frozen animal and slammed on her brakes, sending the car into a half spin. Loose gravel popped underneath the car, giving poor assistance to slow her slide. The river ledge edged closer. A sudden clunk jolted her to a stop and then the car swayed forward in a strange seesaw movement.

Dee tightened her hands on the steering wheel and closed her eyes. The gentle tilt slowed to a fragile stop. She'd never liked seesaws. Her body quivered as the initial rush of fear subsided. She held her breath and peeled open her eyes. At the scene in the dimming light, her blood ran cold and her pulse took off at a frenzied pace. The front of her car dangled over the edge of the embankment, locked in place by some unknown catch of wood or shrub underneath?

Her headlights shown ahead into blackness, the river somewhere below.

Dee didn't move. She couldn't move. Every muscle tightened with the icy sting of terror. Would one movement break her precarious roost and send her plummeting into the river? Like Reese's wife? Dee's breath lodged in her dry throat, mind clicking into motion. Okay, if she fell into the river, she needed a way to escape, right? Holding her breath, she slowly slid her hand to the door and pressed the button to roll down the window. She twisted to unhook her seatbelt, but the car shifted underneath her, dropping forward another foot or two.

Dee gripped the steering wheel again and stared ahead into the blackness of the water. *Dear Lord, please help me.*

A buzz nearby alerted her to a message on her phone. She blinked aware.

Reese.

As if in slow motion, she inched one hand away from her hold on the steering wheel and reached for her purse. Nothing else moved except the inch by inch progression of her fingers toward the passenger seat. Her body tightened like a statue while her hand sifted through the top of her purse finally coming in contact with her phone.

The car shifted on its perch, thrusting another foot closer to the river. She stifled a cry and blinked at the burning of tears. The phone buzzed again in her hand and she jumped. Just as she dialed Reese's number, something cracked beneath her car. The uncertain grip the vehicle held on the ledge gave way. Dee screamed and braced her hands on the wheel. Tree limbs crashed against the windows and she careened uncontrollably toward the dark river, as she desperately listened for the words: *I am with you.*

SOMETHING WAS WRONG. Dee's last call ended in silence and now she was late? Reese's stomach squeezed into a knot. It didn't add up. First she texted she was running five minutes late, then she called with no answer, and now … a no show?

Emma reached for his glass to give him a refill, but he waved her away.

"If she said she was coming, then she's coming, Reese." His little sister shifted a stubborn tilt to her chin.

"I wanna believe that's true, Sis, but I'm not sure of a whole lot right now." He reached into his wallet and threw a few bills on the table. "If she shows up, would you tell her to stop by the house?"

Emma touched his arm. "I don't know what's happening between the two of you, but I do know she cares about you. It's as plain as Haus' grin. You've made a difference in her life."

Reese offered a humorless laugh, but his little sister squeezed his arm tighter.

"I see a lot of people come in and out of this restaurant, Reese. And I have the chance to watch them over time. Dee came into our family as a sad and lonely person, but she's not the same anymore. She's found a family. Her brain might not realize it yet, but her heart does. She's too smart a woman to throw it all away."

The earnest look on his sister's face almost made him smile. "I'm sorry to burst your bubble, but all those fairytales you love don't happen in real life, little girl. And just because something is the best decision, doesn't mean a person's going to choose it."

His baby sis quirked her brow, smile growing. "Skeptics are nothing more than people who are afraid of big dreams."

Reese shook his head and stood. "Right." He patted his sister on the shoulder. "So maybe she's been delayed by all the traffic we have here in Ransom."

"I'm sure there's a good reason. Maybe she's not used to driving in snow." She nodded toward the door. "But I'll give her the message *when* she shows—"

"*If* she shows up."

"*When* she shows up, big brother." She tossed a wink over her shoulder. "I dream big."

He chuckled and walked out the door. The tension in his body, which had eased a little while he talked to Emma, returned as he drove home. He'd spent the day coming to terms with his unforgiveness of Jana and replaying his time with Dee. Apart from the Autumn Ball, there wasn't a scene in their relationship where she'd shown anything but genuineness. So what happened tonight? Was it as simple as a natural delay? She'd returned his text so fast; it encouraged him of her sincerity.

Worry gnawed at the back of his mind. Dusk filtered dark shadows across the snow-dusted road toward home. His headlights blared through the darkness, revealing the path ahead. He instinctively slowed as the curve appeared. *Wait.* Snow skimmed over a fresh tire tread trail of a car's path off the road. His breath stuck in his throat.

He slowed his speed, his gaze following the trail to the roadside. A break in the brush drew his attention to the steep embankment. His stomach knotted with a sudden awareness and he slammed on the brakes. No.

He parked the car, headlights blaring over the ledge, and reached for his flashlight in the glove compartment. Its solo glow sliced into the evening hues, revealing the vehicle's erratic turn off the road. Energy pulsed through him with each step he took nearer the embankment. Not another victim of this ravine, Lord. And please not … He stopped his mind from going there.

The light pierced beyond the shrubbery and down the thirty foot drop of gray dusk toward the river. As the pale glow glided over the water, the scene knocked the air out of his lungs in one rush. Reflected back to him tipped the crippled remains of a silver car nose down in the river. He couldn't tell for certain whether it was an Accord, but his heart already knew the answer.

COLD CHILLED Dee from her chest down. She tried to shake the ice-prickles from her fingertips, but her hands moved slow and stiff. Why wouldn't they work properly and why was she so cold? She attempted to open her eyes, but they weighed too heavy for the act, along with her useless arms. With another effort she forced them open and blinked her surroundings into view. Darkness swelled a foggy picture. Her thoughts moved in a discoordinated dance, sliding just out of reach for her to take hold of them. Where was she?

The dark surroundings combined with her muddled thoughts made it difficult to process everything. So cold and … stings of pain spiked up her legs. Her head ached. She looked down. Water? How did she—?

Clarity pierced through the fog. Reese! She had been on her way to meet Reese. Pieces of memory filtered in. A deer? The cliff? She blinked again and looked around as if for the first time. Oh no, she was in the river. Water poured in through the broken glass of her passenger window and pressed up against her chest. She sat at an angle, her right side deeper into the frigid liquid, numb and useless. The snow filtered down in soft, gentle flutters as the sky began to clear with frosty moonlight.

She shivered.

Then the pain came. Throbbing pulses of it traveled from her foot up her leg. Something warm trailed down her face. She freed her left hand from the icy hold of the river and reached to wipe it. Her quivering fingers showed blood in the pale moonlight. Another hard shiver shook her body and sent a shock of fresh pain surging up her leg and wrapping around her right wrist. She cried out and her stomach roiled. No, she couldn't get sick here. Not with the water floating all around her.

She bit back the pain and tried to open her door, but either from the car damage or the water pressure, she couldn't get it to budge. Could she climb out the window? One pull split blinding pain up her leg, she almost lost consciousness again. Her foot pinned tight somewhere underneath the murky water.

Trapped.

Her rasped breaths sped into panic. Trapped in a car filling with freezing water? How long had she been here? Was she going to die?

She searched for an answer, a way to escape or find help. The lighter contents of her purse floated around her, but her cell phone certainly lay somewhere beneath the water, if in the car at all. She was utterly alone with no way to find out. Lost?

I am with you ...

A voice, almost audible, caressed her spirit, with warmth.

She looked around her as much as her aching body allowed, but only the coming darkness greeted her. Her breathing stilled and she closed her eyes to listen. God's presence broke into her panic with peace, peace like she'd never known.

Certainty filtered through her, dousing fear with a Presence. Not alone. He held her. Even now. Whispers in her spirit urged her to believe in what she couldn't see and faith rose to the challenge, calming and sure.

The water swirled a little higher now and shook a tremor from head to aching toe, but a growing fire flickered into flame in her soul. Even now in the middle of her dying moments, God took the opportunity to remind her of his love—of His presence. No matter what the future held, she belonged to Him.

"You are with me." The words came hoarse and raw, but brought a smile.

Awareness clung to her newfound faith with a confidence beyond her understanding. She released her fear and gave way to the growing numbness of her body. An internal light shone to such a point, she thought she almost saw it, shimmering off the water and highlighting the inside of her car. Was this what dying felt like? Was God sending His angels for her even now?

The shaft of light spread around her, spotlighting her window and falling on her face. She supposed angels had to be bright to come into dark places like riverbeds at dusk to take God's kids home. How sweet.

"Dee."

And the angels even knew her by name.

"Dee, honey, answer me?"

Why did the angel sound like Reese Mitchell? She smiled. A farmer-angel. About as cute a knight-in-dirty-overalls.

A shadow appeared by the glowing light and a voice spoke from it. "You're alive."

Dee blinked against the light. "Reese," her voice croaked his name.

"Praise God, you're alive."

Dee looked up into his worried face, mind fuzzy and slow. "But Reese, you're not an angel."

Not an angel? What was the crazy woman talking about?

It didn't matter if she'd lost what little sense she still held, as long as she lived. He would have kissed her until she *knew* he wasn't an angel, if she hadn't looked fragile enough to break in half.

Reese adjusted his flashlight so the glow shown less directly. The fact she talked to him, even if she talked crazy, was a good sign, but as her image came further into light, his stomach wrenched tight. Water covered her to the collar bone on her right side, a glob of blood puddled on her forehead, and her nose looked busted.

And her crazy talking would have been fine on a normal day, but not after sitting in freezing creek water for over half an hour. However, crazy or not, talking was a whole lot better for her than sleeping.

"I've never been mistaken as an angel before, darlin'."

"Calling me darlin' sounds so sweet. Makes me think you like me."

Her voice sounded strange, drowsy and distant. He had to get her out.

"Like you?" His hands went to the door handle and he pulled on it without success. "Why on earth do you think I'd get all gussied up, shave my favorite beard, and overlook you standing me up for our date, if I didn't like you?"

Dee shivered. "I didn't st … stand you up." Her teeth chattered. "I tried n ... not to hit a d … deer."

Reese pulled at the door one last time and gave up. He had one more hour, at the most, to get her out of here before the water raised high enough to cover her face. But the freezing temperatures would kill her first.

His gut twisted. Dee wouldn't die.

Not if he could stop it. How long until the ambulance he called arrived? Too long from the look of it.

"Dee, can you climb out this window?"

She shrugged her left shoulder, almost like she wanted to lift an arm, but couldn't. Then she yawned. "No. My foot is stuck. I think it might be broken or something." She shook her head as if to clear it, her speech sluggish. "I'm rrreally cold, Reese, but I'm not sad about it."

Reese felt his brows rise and reached in to shine his flashlight round the inside of the car. "Of course, you're cold. You're in river water in November." He stuck the flashlight under his chin and cupped her face with his hands. Her cheeks were ice cubes.

"I'm real glad you're not sad about it, darlin'." He pushed back her hair, sticky from the blood on her forehead. "Lots of people would be scared to death down here all alone."

"B ... but I'm not alone."

Her words came softer, fading. She was losing consciousness. He worked to keep the conversation going, even rubbed her cheeks and neck, while eyeing the inside of the car for his next move.

"And just who was down here in the freezing river with you?"

"God."

Her simple answer nearly made him break down and cry like a baby. Was God going to take her too? Like his father and grandfather. Even like Jana? Please, not again.

Sirens blared from the distance. His phone call at work. Her head dropped forward.

"Stay awake, Dee. Come on, darlin', talk to me."

She murmured an incoherent phrase.

He ran his hands up her shoulders and face, trying to increase the circulation on skin not submerged in water. She nodded, but her eyes dragged closed.

"Dee, honey, wake up."

Old fears strangled him. He'd cut off her foot before he'd let her die in this car. The sirens blared through the night, still minutes away. *He didn't have minutes.*

"Dee, help is here." He shook her. "Dee, I'm going to get you out, darlin'."

No response. Her face shone pale as death.

"Dee."

Nothing. Previous talks from Nurse Meg warned him not to move a patient, but past experience overrode the warning. He wouldn't watch her die.

He flipped open his pocket knife and sliced through the seatbelt, allowing her head to rest against his upper arm as he worked. The sirens moved closer, but he knew they were still on the other side of the hill. Sound carried well along the river and blared *too late* for Dee.

Risk her leg to save her life?

With a deep breath, he reached in and grabbed her body. She barely whimpered as he jostled her into his arms and leaned her toward the open window. With a quick prayer for help and one strong motion, he pooled every ounce of strength. She cried out as he jerked her from the car, a deadening crack in series with her cry.

He stumbled back through the river, barely keeping his balance as he splashed toward the bank. His legs moved slowly, the cold water already taking its toll on his senses. Exhausted, he collapsed on a flat rock along the side of the river and pulled Dee to him, rubbing her shoulders and back. He'd lost his flashlight in the pull, but his truck's lights only made her look closer to death than she was—or he hoped she was.

Her arms flung lifeless at her side. He jerked off his jacket and wrapped it around her shoulders, pulling her tight against his chest and begging God and all of those angels watching, to keep her alive, even if he had to give her up.

CHAPTER 20

The great secret, Eliza, is not having bad manners or good manners or any other particular sort of manners, but having the same manner for all human souls: in short, behaving as if you were in Heaven, where there are no third-class carriages, and one soul is as good as another. (Pygmalion, Act 5)

Dee's head ached and her body protested every movement. Her eyes refused to open and a sudden sense of déjà vu tickled her thoughts with out of reach memories. A low hum of voices blurred around her, nudging the ache in her head. Two men mumbled through bass tones and a woman's treble interjected. There were familiar rings to the frantic lilt of the woman's voice? Who was she?

Dee ordered her fingers to flex and they seemed to obey, her right accompanied by a deep throb.

She moved her right foot, but as she turned her left, pain spiked up her leg, and she moaned. Where was she? Light seeped beneath her eyelids and the voices began to clear.

"As far as we can tell the hypothermia caused minimal damage to her phalanges … her toes and fingers. The metacarpals of her left foot are broken, but given the circumstances, she's a miracle. No internal bleeding. No other broken bones."

Miracle. It hurt to smile so she stopped. She'd prayed for a miracle.

"What about her head?"

She knew the smooth tones of that deep voice. Reese. Was he supposed to be here? Another attempt to pry her heavy eyelids open failed. What was wrong with her head?

"We won't know the extent of her concussion until she wakes up. Her scans come back clear, not even mild swelling. Although, she may have some temporary confusion, sensitivity to light or sounds, and perhaps some concentration or balance issues, we have no reason to suspect anything worse. Like I said before, Mr. Mitchell, this lady is a miracle."

"Will she know us? Will she remember me?"

Dee's ears perked at the sound of her mother's frantic questions. She clenched her teeth and squeezed at the blankets at her sides. Why was her mother here? Why was she in the hospital? Head injury?

A ray of comprehension dawned. The car accident!

"Now, now, Ms. Roseland," Ma Mitchell's soft voice poured out the words like warm honey. Smooth. Gentle.

If her face wasn't so sore and her head didn't hurt pound the mamba, she'd grin over at that sweet woman—once she could see her.

"The doctor didn't see no cause for concern from her brain scans. Let's not worry where there's no cause for it."

"But I can't take her home and care for her. Mitch would never let me."

Dee's heart rate doubled at the mention of her Mom's newest boyfriend. The consistent beeping in the room sped up too. Her mother? Take care of her? Oh, no, Lord. I know you're working on my pride, but Mother?

I am with you.

As if a hand of comfort rested on her shoulder, the words ushered renewed calm. *Wait.*

She wasn't alone anymore. Warmth and peace filled the empty

places inside of her she used to know. The dizzying need to worry and fight ebbed.

She fumbled through her thoughts to recall what happened before the hospital scene. Blurry pictures of Reese's concerned face came into view. Had he been with her too? At the crash site? A shaft of joy overflowed from her heart into her face.

It stung, so she tried to stop smiling, but the thought of him coming to her rescue sent another ache through her cheeks.

"As I said earlier, Ms. Roseland, we cannot draw any certain conclusions about her mental status until she wakes. I will check back in a few hours. The nurse should be in shortly."

A door opened and closed.

Another attempt to open her eyes succeeded. She squinted against the florescent lights and the blurry surroundings. Even her eyes felt bruised. Her forehead throbbed from movement, but eased a little as her vision adjusted to the light.

A face cleared before her, a wonderfully familiar face. Reese. Awareness dawned in his mocha eyes, followed by his tender smile. Oh how she loved him. Of course he'd be here—even for a liar.

"Well now, Sleeping Beauty decided to wake up for us." He took the chair by her bed. "Good to see those eyes."

Her smile hurt. Her cheeks hurt. Even her chin hurt, but she couldn't resist returning his grin. He pushed tendrils of hair away from her face and tears pooled in her eyes. So gentle. An avalanche of memories spilled into her mind. The Ball? The argument. The hurt she'd caused. Why hadn't she been honest with him from the start? He wasn't like other men. He understood brokenness and forgiveness. He wouldn't trample over her weaknesses, but protect and care for her in them. How could she have known there was such a man?

"You found me." Her words didn't reach above a whisper. "I'm sorry."

"Oh, baby, look at Mama. Come on now. Look here at your mama." Dee's mother crowded between them and leaned so close Dee smelled her cigarette-laden breath. A strange calm curbed the usual edge of annoyance. Was that part of belonging to Christ too? Even her emotions? "There is no need for you to apologize for Reese finding you. He should have found you. Heaven knows, he has a better sense for Ransom than you do."

She searched Reese's gaze again.

He understood and leaned down for a whisper. "It seems like Somebody a whole lot better than me found you first."

Tears pricked at her eyes and her face ached from another smile. "Lost sheep."

"Never too lost, darlin'. He's better than any old GPS."

"What are you two talking about? GPS? Sheep? What?" Mama came nearer, hands shaking. "Do you know who I am, honey? Do you remember me?"

She raised her gaze to her mother. Deepset wrinkles framed her blue eyes and spoke of concern. Dee's heart softened. "Mother."

"Oh, baby." Her mother fell forward and sobbed into Dee's shoulder, shaking the entire bed. Dee winced. Reese took charge.

He placed his hands on her mother's shoulders and gave her a gentle tug. "I know it's a relief, Ms. Roseland. We're all real glad, but do you think Dee might be a bit sore?"

She shrugged off Reese's hands and took a step back. "She almost died."

"But she didn't and we're all grateful." Reese patted her arm. "See, she's lookin' better and better each minute."

Her mother stared up at Reese as if he'd lost his mind. "Better? She looks horrible. Pale, bruised. Her nose is the size of a fist."

Dee raised a weak hand to her cheek and allowed her fingers to investigate her face and hair. How bad did she look? What day was it? Monday? Tuesday?

"My classes?" Dee's voice grew in frantic volume.

"Rainey cancelled them for you. It's alright," Reese said.

Dee thoughts sped through her schedule. "Haus?"

A grin spread wide on Reese's face, like he wanted to laugh. "Just fine, Doc. Lou even gave him one of those dog treats you had stashed away. The kind that make his breath smell better?"

Pain stung her forehead as she scrunched her brow. "Nothing wrong with taking care of a dog's breath."

Reese shook his head, pacifying her. "Naw, nothin' at all. Especially for someone who doesn't like animals."

"What are the two of you talking about?" Mother looked between them. "You're not making any sense. Dog breath? Haus?"

Reese's eyes never left Dee's face. "Just talking about surprises, is all."

A tremor of hope moved through her. Obviously he'd discovered her little secret about taking care of Haus, but it couldn't be enough to help him forgive her, could it? He didn't look angry, but maybe he realized a romantic future with a liar was out. Could she be content with friendship? Her gaze fluttered to his lips and the heart monitor staggered back up a speed.

"Marion." Ma Mitchell moved forward and took Dee's mother's arm. "Now you have a chance to get that drink of water you wanted a few minutes ago."

A look passed between Reese and his mother. Ma Mitchell smiled at Dee. "I'd imagine Dee would like something to drink too, wouldn't you, sweetie?"

Dee offered a slight nod, hoping her face expressed her gratitude. The nod wobbled her vision for a moment and encouraged a hint of nausea. Oh man, she was probably irresistible right now.

Ma Mitchell sidled up next to Dee's mother and placed a gentle arm around her. "Will you help me find a nurse, Marion, and we'll be right back with something."

"Do you want something to drink, baby?" Dee's mom squeezed her hand. Thankfully it was the right one. "Are you sure you'll be okay if I leave."

Dee swallowed through her dry throat and nodded. "Yes, please."

"I'll be right back. Don't you worry." Her mother scuttled out the door, but not before looking back over her shoulder at least four times. Dee wasn't sure what was worse—having an absent mother or this present one.

Ma Mitchell offered a wink before the door closed behind them, providing yet another contrast between the two ladies. Maybe with Grace Mitchell around to ease her mother's rough edges a few more miracles awaited.

If ...

Dee pushed a shaky hand through her hair, looking anywhere else but at Reese. "I probably look like I've been in a fight, don't I?"

"You had a fight between life and death, darlin'. It ain't pretty."

"Fantastic." His words registered and she shot him a look, then relaxed back onto the bed, exhausted from the slight movement. "Ain't is not a word."

Reese leaned forward, his dark eyes a chocolatey pool of compassion and warmth. "Now I *know* you're going to be alright." His grin broadened. "So if I stick around and use bad grammar long enough, I reckon we'll have you out of this hospital by tomorrow."

"I hate hospitals."

His expression gentled with understanding. "Yeah, that's how I feel too. Bad memories."

They sat in silence a moment and she studied him. "You need to shave."

"I'll make a wager with you." He took a deep breath and ran a hand over his chin. "I'll shave my face as soon as you can go home."

She tried to smile but wasn't sure it worked. Her eyes proved heavy all over again. "I don't make wagers anymore. They only hurt the people I ..." She swallowed and avoided looking at him again. "People I love."

He hesitated, then sat down in the chair next to her bed. "How 'bout we make a list, then? What do you say about that?"

She adjusted herself in the bed to sit up straighter and winced at the pain in her foot, her head throbbed in time with the pulse in her leg. Oh, the humility!

His hand smoothed against her shoulder. "Easy now. Doc said you had a broken foot."

"I'm not the best patient."

"Now, ain't that shocking?" He couldn't hide his sarcasm, not that he tried too hard.

She raised an eyebrow to him in warning. "What kind of list do you suggest, Mr. Pleasant?"

He leaned in close again and pushed back another errant piece of hair. She must look frightful, but the sweet look in Reese's eyes never let a clue of it. Hope turned a whirl in her stomach, right next to the nausea.

Reese held up one finger. "Number one, you need to eat something. It will make you feel better."

"You sound like your mom."

"Smart woman."

"Number two?"

"You get some good rest tonight so you can get to number three. Going home."

Her dry mouth became dryer. "And after that? After I get home?"

"We have the talk we meant to have before you decided to drive your car into a river." One side of his lips inched back up.

"I was on my way to you." She pressed forward, words breaking apart and tears blurring her vision again. The beeping in the room sped up too. "Reese, I'm sorry—"

He stopped her words with a finger to her lips. "We can talk about it later, Dee. No need for you to get upset. Right now you need your rest."

Upset? Did she have a second chance with him? Was he only there because of his kind nature, nothing … more?

His finger slid to her chin. "We need to talk, but we can't have a proper talk right this minute."

Dee's mother burst through the door, two bottles of water in hand. She looked back to Reese, who stood and stretched out his long lean body. How could she have been so careless to risk his heart? God, please don't let it be too late.

"Well, Mama, I reckon I should get you back home and pick up the kids from Rainey's." He turned to Dee. "Unless I can help you with anything, darlin'?"

She loved the way her called her *darlin'*, teasing her hope a little more. "Will you come back?"

He slapped his cap back on his head. "You can bet on it." His gaze held hers. "Until you order me and my farm smell to take a permanent break, I plan to be here as often as I can. Neighborly, you know."

Not exactly what she wanted to hear, but she'd take it. "Thank you, Reese. I do want to talk, about the Ball and the accident."

His brow raised, but before he could say anything her mother broke in. "What? You don't need to talk about that nasty accident. It can't be good for you. Here." She shoved the straw from a hospital cup. "Right now you drink this water and rest.

"We'll come back and check on you." Ma Mitchell waved a hand her way. "And I'll bring something tempting to eat. Heaven knows the hospital food won't do it."

An overwhelming sense of gratitude forced a new swell of tears, and another solid pain in her head. She took a sip of water and relaxed back against the pillows, her swollen nose tingling. She'd thought she brought something special to Ransom with her expertise, but all along God was bringing something … or someone to her. An entire family in fact. A healthy, wholesome family with so much love it spilled over into strangers' lives and made them want to stay.

Just like her.

REESE slid into the room without making a sound. Dee's dark hair fell across the pillow, framing her pale, bruised face. But the bruises had lightened from two days before and her nose wasn't as swollen. He still shook inside at the recurring images of her trapped in the sinking car, her pale, bloody face, and the lifelessness in her cold body. His fists tightened against the handle as he gently brought the door to a close.

The crash, her brokenness, and the little surprises of her care found in the garage, affirmed his feelings for her. He loved her. Plain, but not quite so simple. Doc meant to leave Ransom. He'd known it going in, headstrong and heart-crazy. Would she stay with him? Charlottesville waited a good six months away, at least.

Out of the corner of his eyes he caught sight of another person in the room. A man.

Dr. Alex Murdock.

Not exactly as he'd been before. Dark circles shadowed his eyes and his hair sprayed out like he'd forgotten to comb it. Reese straightened and backed away from Dee's bed, but Alex looked up, noticing him, and greeted him with a sad smile. In fact, he looked plum disappointed.

"She didn't sleep last night. The nurse said she was in a good deal of pain." Dr. Murdock's voice stayed low. "They gave her something about an hour ago to help her rest. The doctor wants to keep her for two more days to make sure all signs of the concussion have subsided."

Reese nodded and took a seat. He left for Chicago tomorrow. "Did you just get here?"

"About a half hour ago. I came to see how she was doing." He gestured toward Dee and sighed. "And to congratulate her on her new position. She's worked hard for it."

A knot twisted tight in Reese's throat. "UVA?"

Dr. Murdock nodded, his expression a wounded riddle.

"When does she start?"

"January, unless she chooses to wait until the fall." Dr. Murdock grimaced. "She's wanted to be there for a long time. I can't imagine prolonging her stay in Ransom."

"No, I'd reckon not." Reese studied her peaceful face, the sense of loss deflating his chest.

"She will do well for herself there." Alex's voice spilled into the silence. "She's always had more talent than she realized."

Reese stared down at Dee and the knot closed around his heart. What had he been thinking? She'd give up her lifelong dream for his little farming family? And would he even ask her to? He shook his head and pinched back the uncomfortable warmth closing off his throat.

Another loss. One woman he'd lost to another man and this one he's losing to a dream. Why couldn't he meet someone who saw him and his family as her dream? He shoved his hands into his jean pockets and jabbed at the sadness with common sense.

Why should he be surprised? She'd known him and his ornery self for a grand total of three months—how could that be enough to change a lifetime of dreaming? His life, and the giant shift from singleness to readymade family, was a giant pill to swallow too.

And if he tried to convince her to stay, and she said yes, would she live to regret it later? His will stiffened at the thought. *No*, regret pushed people into foolish choices. He'd learned that lesson the hard way. Love didn't take from people. It gave. He wouldn't be the one to stand in the way of her dreams.

"I guess your rental house will be available in the spring?"

Alex's question interrupted Reese's musing. "You in need of one?"

Dr. Murdock's smile turned downward. "I'm Adelina's replacement here in Ransom. " He shrugged. "Sorry about that."

Reese blinked to full alert and stared hard at the other man. Poor guy got hit in the pride with a two-by-four, no doubt. Rainey wasn't going to like this news one bit. "Well, that'll be a big change for you."

Dr. Murdock stood. "You have *no* idea." He shook his head as he walked passed. "I have the unique ability to sabotage my own life. It's a gift." He pushed his hand through his hair with the force of frustration. "And a pattern."

Reading between the lines, Reese's compassion grew toward the misfit. Sounded like his good intentions turned sour more than not.

"Maybe the mountain air does things to people, but I can tell Adelina's changed. Even at the Ball."

Reese's face relaxed into a smile. She wasn't the same person she'd been when she first came to Ransom. If nothing else, at least he knew she wasn't a lost sheep any more. Maybe that's the only reason God brought her into his life—to bring her peace.

And maybe Alex needed a good dose of Ransom's magic too.

"I guess I'll get to find out about that mountain air soon enough. See you later, Reese."

The door opened and closed at Dr. Murdock's exit. Reese sighed into the stillness of the room and sat down next to the bed. He collected Dee's fingers into his hand and rubbed the soft flesh of her wrist. A smile flickered over her lips. Maybe it was a sign of sweet dreams. He hoped so.

His flight for Chicago left first thing in the morning so their conversation would have to wait until he got back. But what was the use? He knew what she wanted most and he couldn't give it to her.

He released his hold on her hand and wiped a hand across his eyes.

"Dear Lord, help me let go. Help me trust you." He looked up at Dee's serene face. "And help Dee live out the dreams you have for her life without me getting in the way."

I give my dreams to you, Lord.

At least Dee was safe. A miracle, like the doctor said. He could live with that knowledge and be content.

Mostly content.

HE GOT THE JOB. They offered it to him on the spot. As Reese drove from the airport home, he replayed the moment in his head. The two businessmen told him his résumé and presentation were the best they'd seen from the two hundred candidates. Once they heard about his vision for farmers in his region, they didn't even hesitate to let him know his status as their top candidate.

He sat shocked by God's goodness. He got what his family needed with the most ease of any interview he'd ever experienced … and one of his own dreams began to open before him. If only Dee's vision shared a similar future. If only she would stay.

But he couldn't ask. Wouldn't expect it. He knew too well the gnawing ache of a curbed dream.

The closer he got to home, the more certain he became of his decision to step away. He had a farm to save and a family to tend. The old resolution he'd cultivated for years moved back into his mind with the comfort of familiar boots, well familiar boots with a rock in them.

He entered Mama's house to the sound of a full room of laughter.

Dinner, something salty, distracted his senses and led him to the dining room, where a table of family greeted him.

"Congratulations," Emma yelled, jumping up from the table to give him a big hug. "Do you feel more prestigious?"

"Good grief, Emma, don't praise him too much. We'll never hear the end of it." Rainey tossed him a grin, complete with a proud tilt to her stubborn chin.

Reese rubbed his smooth jaw and smiled at his baby sister. "Grateful and relieved are more like what I feel, little sis. I'm a far cry from prestigious."

"Come on in and sit down. I even made apple cake to celebrate." His mama waved him to the table.

"Daddy," Brandon's sweet voice rang out over the welcomes.

"Hey, buddy," he tousled the blond curls and took his seat. Reese pulled at the collar of the oxford he still wore. "Sounds mighty good. Thank you, Mama." Reese scanned the faces and stopped at his brother. "How'd your appointment go today?"

Trigg's lips cocked to one side. "Clean bill of health. Told me to get back to work."

"As if he ever stopped," Rainey added popping Trigg on the arm. "He listens worse that you do, Reese."

"Slow and easy back to work," Meg reminded, the nurse's look brooking no argument.

Reese about thought he'd cry. Sure sign of an emotional day. He ignored Rainey's teasing and appreciated the healthy smile on his brother's face. "Well, praise God." He locked gazes with his brother, sending him a certain message of gratitude. "I can finally get some worthwhile help from somebody around here."

"Hey, now," both sisters said in unison.

"But," Rainey interjected, her finger pointed directly at Trigg's chest. "The doctor said it's going to take another six months for Trigg to be back to full strength."

"Or more," Meg added, shooting Trigg a sharp look. "I tried to get the doctor to tell Trigg it would take him a full year to keep the mule of a man slowed down, but I couldn't convince him."

Trigg's lopsided grin grew into full-fledged pride. "Looks like Meg's out of a job."

Meg didn't even flinch. "Trigg Mitchell, the only payment you've ever given me is a hard time. I gladly relinquish my job as your overprotective and underpaid nurse."

"You really do bring out the worst in her, Trigg. She's usually so mild-mannered and gentle." Rainey laughed and picked up her glass of tea. "I guess fifteen years with this family is enough to try anyone's patience, including Mother Margaret over here."

Meg's sweet smile encompassed the room. "You all are the best family I've ever known." She slit Trigg a sideways glance. "Well, most of you anyway."

"God knew she needed the older-brother sort." Trigg took a healthy bite, eyes brimming with laughter he wouldn't shed. "Toughen her up."

She sent a *help me* look to Mama. "How on earth did such a grumpy man come from such a jewel of a woman?"

Reese sure did love this family, adopted ones and all. His thought turned to Dee. When he'd called the hospital earlier she was in the dining hall, most likely fussing about having to use crutches. He scooped some mashed potatoes and chicken on his own plate with a little too much force. The potatoes splattered onto Brandon's high chair.

"Whoa, Reese, are you trying to start a food fight?" Emma laughed and wiped at Brandon's chair.

"Sorry." He shrugged off his clumsiness. "I reck … I am pretty hungry."

He felt his Mama's stare more than he actually saw it. "Heard from Dee today?"

"No." He took a bite. "Her mama said she was down at the dining room for the first time. Said she wanted to go off on her own." His grin lifted. "Stubborn woman."

Mama chuckled. "We wouldn't know nothin' about stubborn women in this family, would we?"

"All I know is they've been giving her meds for sleeping better at night because her foot is causing her some pain. I think she's supposed to be discharged tomorrow morning."

Rainey poked him with her fork. "You two need to talk."

A twinge of pain knifed at the edge of his forehead and he rubbed at it. "There's not much to talk about. She's leaving."

The room fell silent except for Brandon's fork scraping the last bit of mashed potatoes off his plate.

Emma found her voice first, of course. "Leaving? She still has a whole spring before her school year is over."

"It seems an opening came available early and she impressed her supervisors enough." He kept diving into his potatoes, not wanting to face them. "She's going to Charlottesville in January."

"January?" Rainey nearly stood from the table. "That can't be right, Reese. What about her classes? Her clients? She might be desperate for Charlottesville, but she's not a quitter."

"They've already found a replacement, I believe." Reese didn't even look at Rainey. If she knew the chosen replacement, she'd probably blow a fuse right out of the top of her ponytail.

"Well, we all know she's wanted this." Mama sat back in her chair, fingers patting a soft rhythm on the table edge. "I imagine she'll be happy about it, don't you?"

The room fell quiet again, except for Brandon beating his spoon against his empty cup like a drummer.

"Your Uncle Ralph's farm ain't thirty minutes from Charlottesville," Mama said, slicing a piece of apple cake onto a plate and handing it to Reese. "He could sure use some help up that way come summer." She shrugged and looked up at him. "If not longer."

Reese about choked on his potatoes.

Emma must have caught on to his mama's madness. "Oh, right." An elfish gleam tipped off her grin. "And since he and Aunt Libby don't have any children to help, they've kind of adopted us as their own."

Rainey smacked her forehead. "Let's be subtle, shall we? Men and subtlety works about as well as rain boots on a dog." She focused those sneaky blue eyes on him. "Reese, you have family near

Charlottesville who've been begging for company. It wouldn't be too farfetched to think of moving in that direction."

He stared at his mama and sisters like they'd been into Lizzie's mama's homemade wine. Move? To Charlottesville? Even if he thought the best of Libby and Ralph, moving seemed a big jump in decisions. "What?"

"Uncle Ralph and Aunt Libby are family—and they *have* asked for us to move closer," Rainey shrugged. "It makes a lot of sense."

Not in his brain.

"And the schools are great," Emma's smile never wavered. Imp.

"Are you listening to your own craziness? Move away?" He looked over at Lou. "What about the young'uns?"

That should pull at the womenfolk's heartstrings.

"Three hours away isn't forever, Reese." Rainey cut a slice of cake too as if her statement was the most common sense thing in the world.

Evidently the notion of the kids leaving didn't pull quite hard enough. Reese gave the cake a suspicious look. Maybe it was the cause of all the craziness.

Emma nodded, reaching for the culprit-cake. "Wouldn't Ralph and Libby just love some quality time with Lou and Brandon? Plus, they have horses."

"Horses!" The crazy bug bit his little girl. She stared up at him, bright eyes pleading. "Horses, Daddy? I love Aunt Libby's horses."

He hated horses.

"And they live right next to a lake." Lou clapped her hands together. Brandon must have thought it was a good idea, because he followed suit—mashed potatoes splashing over his tray.

"Trigg, set them straight." Reese was drownin' in a sea of women-sense.

His brother looked up from his plate, as if he just entered the conversation. "Charlottesville would be a more central location for your new job, wouldn't it?" Trigg's question shot through the silence. "It's right near all those highways that run north and south. Good location for somebody who is going to be traveling up and down the east coast."

He stared at his quiet, unassuming big brother as if seeing him for the first time.

"And with Trigg's recovery, you could get back to what you love best. Training other farmers." Rainey lifted her fork to her sneaky lips. "Maybe even teach as an adjunct at UVA, with another instructor we know."

"You've always been a good teacher," Trigg added, then took a bite of the cake.

His entire family tripped right off the deep end. His gaze searched out his mother's. "Come on, Mama. Aren't you going to say anything to help me out here?"

She perked a weathered brow and hesitated, taking her time to sweep the table with a glance. "Well, now, Reese, what is it that you want?"

"I don't think it has a lot to do with what I want. What about Trigg? What about the farm?"

"We have until summer, Reese." His mama took another bite of cake. "A long time for healing and change. Besides, if you still want to help out financially, you can do that from wherever you are, right?"

"Trigg don't mind sharing you with Ralph and Libby," Emma added with a wicked grin. If pixies were real, she'd be one.

"Are you afraid your young'uns will have bad influences in Charlottesville?"

He frowned at Rainey's stupid question. "No, of course not."

"Are you afraid of the change?"

He stuffed down any hint of fear of uprooting his family. "That ain't it."

"Is it because Dee can't cook?"

All eyes went to Emma, who shrugged. "Just wonderin'. A man's happy stomach is real important in these parts."

"Her cookin' doesn't have nothing to do with it. I just … I don't …" He slammed his palms against the table. "She's getting her dream job, okay. I'm not a part of that dream."

"I don't know if I'd be so sure, son."

He couldn't answer. In fact, he wasn't sure of anything at the moment, except the fact he wasn't touching the apple cake. Safety lived in Ransom. Safety and the familiar. Jana moved to be with him in Ransom, would it really be possible to uproot his family to follow Dee? Start brand new? He swallowed his fear. Try out his dreams?

"I reckon dreams can change with the right motivation and heart?" Mama's voice softened.

"For both of you," Rainy added.

Reese looked over at his little girl, then stared at Brandon, and emerging out of the insane conversation and broken heart came the lightning flash of understanding. His dreams waited for the taking too. Would God give him Dee *and* his love for teaching too? He slumped back in his chair, overwhelmed.

All eyes waited for his response. He sat up and looked around the room. "Well, I think I have a few plans to make."

CHAPTER 21

I can't turn your soul on. Leave me those feelings; and you can take away the voice and the face. They are not you. (Pygmalion, Act 5)

Dee opened her eyes, heavy and fighting to close again. The hateful side effects of her medication took their time releasing her mind and body from their hold, even though she'd been off them nearly eight hours. It took a full thirty minutes to wake up in the morning, and another thirty minutes to get her brain in gear. She'd never been a fan of pain meds and certainly not mild concussions.

She'd already weaned herself down to one pill before bed, but it still sent her mind into Wonderland. She stretched her body, the sudden realization she sat fully clothed and sitting in the chair beside her bed coming slow and confusing.

What was she doing here? The sleepy fog of her brain cleared to a syrupy clarity.

She was being discharged. Right. It was Thursday morning. She breathed a sigh of relief. Time to go home, with the comfortable red couch and the dulcimer over the fireplace, and a grinning hound.

She pushed herself up to a stand and grabbed her crutches, permanent fixtures in her life for the next six weeks. A small price to pay after her near death experience. Or new life experience, maybe? She smiled. The Ball and the car crash revolutionized her life, eternally. Now she needed to find Reese Mitchell and plan a future.

On the phone last evening, Dr. Lindsay gave her an extension to this afternoon for a definitive answer about the job. One conversation with Reese Mitchell would clear up her answer one way or the other. If she won back his trust and his love, then she'd give up Charlottesville without a second glance … well, maybe without a third glance.

The welcome quiet of the room must have lulled her to sleep as she waited for the discharge papers. There'd been little quiet since she'd come to the hospital. Her mama hovered like a shadow, listening to every conversation, talking almost incessantly. No opportunity for private conversations with Reese, even when he did visit.

It was infuriating—and yet, a touch of gentleness cooled her anger with new understanding. A remarkable peace stilled her heart and nerves, curbed her anger, and touched each emotion with a sense of His presence. Words she'd heard growing up took on a whole new meaning, and the small bits of Bible verses she'd read while in the hospital sunk deep and provided a great deal of clarity and conviction.

Leah, the young morning nurse, bustled in with a glass of water. "Did the nap help?"

Dee rubbed the back of her neck and returned her smile. "Was I asleep long? I have no sense of time."

Leah retrieved the cup after Dee's drink and then handed Dee a clipboard with a few last papers to sign. "Only long enough to miss your visitor."

"Visitor?" Dee signed the last form and handed back the papers, working her way to a precarious stand. She balanced herself with her crutches. "Do you mean my mother? She left to bring the car around."

Leah's brow quirked. "Not your mother. Your not-so-secret admirer."

Dee stared at her, confused. A secret admirer? Surely the side effects of the meds hadn't made her *that* forgetful.

Leah sighed. "Reese Mitchell."

"Reese was here?"

"Not two minutes ago. Said something about a new job in Chicago?" Leah shrugged and handed Dee her purse. "Crazy man. I went to high school with his brother. Neither one of those farm boys could survive in Chicago."

Dee froze, pen in hand. Chicago! How had she forgotten about his interview yesterday? He accepted the position? He was leaving her? She had to talk to him. Convince him to stay.

"Two minutes ago? Then maybe I can catch him." She reached for her new phone, but one look reminded her of the hospitals poor connection.

Leah sent a doubtful look to Dee's casted foot, but it only fueled her determination. She hobbled past the skeptical nurse holding the room door open and then lobbed along the hallway as fast as her untrained crutched arms carried her. Oh, what a thought! Reese walks in to talk to her and she's probably snoring with drool dripping from her mouth. Definitely a reason to drop Chicago!

She rolled her eyes heavenward. And he was moving to Chicago? Her heart quivered. Did any of the universities in Chicago have a Speech-Language Program?

The exit sign shown to her left at the stairwell door. The elevator waited directly in front of her. Her gaze volleyed between the two. She was on the eighth floor. Tenth! That meant eight flights of stairs? With crutches? The truth kicked her hope into frustration. How on earth would she get to him this way?

The elevator doors opened wide, inviting her forward. She froze and stared at the gaping metal mouth. Her muscles congealed to unmoving. Thirteen years of stairs. Thirteen years since she'd witnessed her father's death trapped inside one of those steel coffins.

She took a step back, visions of her father's unseeing eyes pushing her away, gripping at her determination.

I am with you.

Fear gripped deep. Grace clutched deeper.

If God could save her from a sinking car and from the crushed weight of her past, couldn't he save her from the ghosts in the elevator? With another look toward the stairs and back to her casted foot, she stepped to the steel doors. Her throat constricted and her breath stalled to an arrhythmic pattern. She took a deep breath and walked into the metal box, forcing the sound of her father's labored breathing from her mind.

I will never leave you.

She repeated those words like a mantra in her mind and pushed the *close door* button, her palms cool and sweaty.

With eyes pinched closed, her father's face flew to the forefront of her thoughts. Lifeless eyes haunted her, squeezing breath from her body in puffs. A wave of panic spun her motions into a frenzy, but she gripped a prayer as tightly as she held the crutches. Would God take her fears too? Her heart cried for help and peace tumbled over her fears. Breathing came easier. The thudding of her heartbeat in her ears slowed. She loosed her grip on her crutch and stretched her fingers wide. Then the most amazing thing happened.

The door opened.

And she'd survived.

A weak laugh quivered from her, and the cool rush of air on her face alerted her to fresh tears. She wiped at her face with her fingers and readjusted her crutches to ease out of the elevator. Strength poured back into her steps and propelled her out of the elevator. She'd survived, and not only that, but overcome. Another weakening blow to the fears. *Thank you, Jesus.*

She glanced back at the empty elevator, a new tilt to her chin, and tossed a thankful glance toward Heaven. Her past closed behind her. Now for her future.

The hallway gave a direct line to the exit doors ahead. Could she catch Reese? Probably not, but she had to try. She moved through the lobby and paused outside the front doors. Finally, some bars and a signal. She texted him a quick message then hobbled forward.

People moved out of her way, avoiding the clop of the crutches against the sidewalk. One quick scan of the front of the hospital gave no sign of Reese.

More waiting?

She sighed and leaned against her left crutch, pulling her phone back out. Two missed calls flickered across the screen—both from Reese and both timed over an hour ago. No text.

If he left the hospital a few minutes ago, he had to be close. What did she have to lose? She dialed his number.

Two rings.

"Hey," his deep voice melted through her.

She closed her eyes and smiled. "Hey."

"Good nap?"

Every morning, Lord. She wanted to hear his voice every morning. Pretty please, with Ma Mitchell's sugar cake on top? "I'm sorry I missed you. Why didn't you wake me?"

He chuckled, the bass note vibrating in her heart. "I tried once, but I don't think you heard me over your snoring."

She gasped. "I was not snoring."

"Mmhmm."

Her eyes settled closed again, enjoying the touch of his warm voice, like finding home and enjoying Ma Mitchell's chicken-n-dumplings all rolled up into one.

"Where are you?"

"Not too far." His voice answered close, strangely close. "You got down here awful fast."

Her eyes flew open and she turned to see him standing behind her, phone to his ear and lips angled in a grin. His clean-shaven face still surprised her. Clean-shaven and gorgeous. Her heart thumped faster for a totally different set of reasons than a childhood trauma. He had one hand tucked into his snug jeans, and his brown leather jacket brought out the deep caramel of his eyes. Movie material right here.

Heated cheeks and roving eyes were becoming a way of life. Her stomach tightened. Or she hoped they were—for him only. Please, God.

"W ... were you expecting me?"

He stepped closer and slid his phone into his pocket. "No, just trying to figure out what to do next. I didn't want to go far."

"You didn't?"

He took another step and tilted his head to one side, studying her so intensely she froze in place. "You got down here awfully fast. Did you take the elevator?"

She couldn't stop the nervous laugh in reply. "I heard you were offered the job."

"And that was important enough to take the elevator?" He stepped closer, now only a touch away. "I didn't think you took elevators."

"We need to talk." She gripped her crutches until her fingers hurt.

"We sure do."

"And I couldn't let you walk away when there was so much to say." Even though, at the moment, she had a hard time remembering what those things were. Who knew Reese Mitchell's heart stopping grin caused the same type of confusion as a concussion?

"That sounds mighty desperate, Doc."

Desperate? *Desperately in love.* All reserve flew away with her inner declaration. "You don't have to go to Chicago, do you? Can't you stay in Ransom ... with me?"

His brow wrinkled. "But you're moving to Charlottesville."

"Not if you won't move to Chicago."

He shuffled a step closer, gaze intense. "Sounds like a wager to me."

"No." She shook her head. "No more wagers. I can't move to Charlottesville without you."

His next step brought him directly in front of her. "You're not giving up your dream, Dee. Not for me."

Tears tightened her voice. "What if I've found a new dream?"

His smile spread across his face and the look he gave her almost made her forget she had a broken foot. She wanted to jump into those strong arms. He cupped her cheek and slid his thumb to rub away a tear.

"A new dream?"

She pressed her cheek against his warm palm. "You."

He raised his other hand to brush a stray hair from her cheek and then, ever so slowly touched his lips to hers. "I'm not moving to Chicago."

"But Leah said you took the job."

He nodded, his thumb caressing her cheek. "That's so, but it's a consulting job. I travel the east coast and train other farmers. I'm not moving there." His brow scrunched. "I'd die in a big city. You know that."

Her jaw swung unhinged. For someone who specialized in speech clarity, she'd been speechless around Reese Mitchell more times in the past three months than in her entire life.

"You're not moving to Chicago?" Her eyes leaked again. "You'll be in Ransom?"

"But you ain't giving up your dream."

"I called Dr. Lindsay and begged her to extend my stay in Ransom for the full school year. There's no way I'm moving to Charlottesville if you want me to stay."

"Well that's too bad, 'cause I happen to be moving there."

"What?" She grabbed the lapel of his jacket to support her weakening legs. Were the pain meds affecting her hearing too? Goodness gracious, she was falling apart.

He snuck another kiss directly on her open mouth. His arms came around her waist for extra support, so she let one crutch slide to the ground. It freed up an arm to wrap around his neck.

"We have family up that way and they've got a little house just outside of Charlottesville waiting for us. It's a more central location for the consulting, plus Uncle Ralph could use some help with his cattle."

"What about Trigg?" Her eyes flickered closed as he threaded his hand through her hair.

"Since Trigg got a clean bill of health from his doctor, I figured the young'uns and I could move on up there this summer." The rogue arrived in full grin. "Ain't that a nice coincidence?"

Dee almost caught the sob before it wracked her body, but Reese was there, holding her in his strong arms and letting her cry all over his cedar-smelling shirt. Home in his arms—her earthly example of a Godlike love? "I can't believe it. You're going to move to Charlottesville? Lou, Brandon, and you?"

"Plan to. If you'll have us."

His strength breathed into her, warm and welcoming. She'd done nothing to deserve such sacrifice. Nothing. She hugged him close and lifted her face to the sky. Amazing Grace brought this lost child home.

At the thought she laughed and hugged Reese tighter. It was overwhelming—a love like this. So free and genuine. She leaned back, still supported by his arms, and cupped his face in her hands. His dark eyes red-rimmed with unshed tears and her heart swelled with another wave of gratitude.

"I'll have you, Reese Mitchell." She nuzzled his chin, reveling in his embrace. "You, and Lou, and Brandon. I'll gladly have you." She sniffed, voice hoarse with emotion. "But you need to remember one thing."

He lifted a brow. "What's that?"

"Ain't is not a word."

He laughed and hauled her close for another kiss, right there in front of the hospital stairs, God, and everybody.

And she kissed him right back.

Finally home.

EPILOGUE

The dinner table at Grace Mitchell's house nearly bent under the weight of food. The Mitchells knew how to celebrate Christmas with Lampoon flair and enough chaos to leave Dee in no question she was part of a *gang* as Grace called her family. Wrapping paper strewn from one side of the living room to another, the Christmas tree tilted at a dangerous angle, and joy filtered from every corner of the house, especially her heart.

Even her brother Jay came, observing from a safe distance and wearing a smile tinged with fear. Yeah, it might take a while for him to *get it*, but he would. Hope pumped a new song into her life and encouraged dreams of her own family—or her own readymade family.

She carried a pot of green beans to the table, wading through the masses of birth family, adopted family, neighbors, and friends all piled together in Grace's house.

"Hey, Dee," Rainey shouted from behind. "Don't forget the serving spoon."

Dee reached around Shaye Russell's back to pluck the spoon from Rainey's hand, the sweet bond of friendship an added bonus to her life in Ransom. The friendship between she and Rainey continued to grow and provide as much entertainment from Rainey's vibrant, and somewhat rebel personality, as it did encouragement.

Lou sat in the middle of the breakfast nook, one of the lone areas not occupied by a herd of people, trying to piece together a horse stable Aunt Libby bought her. Her cherubic face gleamed with a halo of smiles. Uncle Ralph's laugh boomed through the whirr of chatter in the next room as Grace hummed "Joy to the World," apparently unaware of the happy bedlam on all sides.

It was complete insanity—and absolutely wonderful.

Dee completed her task and returned to the kitchen for her next assignment, careful to swing through the living room to sample the bluegrass quartet of Trigg, Emma, and a couple other cousins, who gave background music to Grace's quiet voice.

Dee slid around the corner of the fireplace and turned to enter the kitchen, just in time to see Reese gather up Brandon from the floor.

"Daggone it," he groaned and shot a glance over his shoulder to Lou. "Hey, Lou, could you grab the diaper bag and bring it to the back bedroom. Brandon just poured a glass of eggnog down the front of his clothes."

Lou fastened a longing stare at her lovely horse stable and then looked to her Dad's retreating back. Dee caught her attention. "I have it, Lou. No worries. Okay, sweets?"

Lou's smile returned in full bloom and she focused on her gift with the wonder only a seven-year-old could show. Dee scooped up the backpack and followed Reese's path down the hall, his sweet scent of spice and leather leading the way.

Brandon stood on the bed, jean overalls around his ankles, and dimpled cheeks offering her a smile as she entered.

"Dee," he announced and her heart skipped into a staccato rhythm.

"Hey there, darlin'." Reese wrestled the shirt over Brandon's curly head. His gaze raked over her, appreciation growing with his smile. "It's a shame it takes a rascally boy to give us alone time."

Dee set the bag on the bed and took out an extra set of clothes for Brandon. Oh, fuzzy snowman pajamas. "I think that goes along with the territory, don't you?"

He took the clothes from her and nodded his thanks. "It's a package deal for sure." He tickled Brandon's naked belly and his giggle trilled directly to Dee's heart.

"Tis the season for packages from what I see." Dee bumped him aside with her hip and snatched the snowman pajamas from him. Placing fuzzy pajamas on a cuddly toddler definitely made it on her Christmas list. Right next to snuggling up by the fire with his fuzz-free Daddy.

Reese took the freedom as opportunity to come behind Dee and wrap his arms around her, which made it incredibly difficult to focus on inserting the squirming boy's feet into the footie part of the p.js.

"You like packages, do ya?"

His voice warmed her ear and sent responsive tingles coursing down her neck. "If it involves something as cute as this package." She zipped Brandon's pajamas from his feet to his chin. "Then I'm all for it."

Reese squeezed her closer and pressed a kiss to her neck. She nearly melted to the floor. Merry Christmas to me!

"I think I have the perfect gift for you then." He turned her around and took Brandon from her arms, one palm up. "Wait right there."

The red polo brought out the umber hues in his eyes, but the mischievous glint remained a fixed feature. After another month with him, and more time with his family, God continued to shock her with his blessings. Faith? Family? A man like Reese? She didn't need one more thing for Christmas. God's dreams for her life proved much bigger than her wildest ones.

And Reese's new job gave her opportunity to hone her parenting skills a little. During his first weekend gone, when she stayed overnight with the kids, no one died—which was a definite plus in her favor. How much she'd grown to love these kids over the past month! The dream of motherhood niggled away at her previous doubt. The idea still scared her, but it was a healthy respect for the massive responsibility—not the gnawing anxiety of recreating her past. And Reese's encouragement and love made her believe in all sorts of dreams she'd discarded as impossibilities.

"Alright, I have something for you." Reese stepped forward holding a giant box wrapped in candy cane paper. "Go ahead and open it now."

A thrill spiked her smile as she took the gift. "It feels like cheating to open it on Christmas Eve instead of Christmas Day."

Reese glanced up to the ceiling in thought, and then added his signature wink. "How about this? You open it today, but don't tell anybody about it until tomorrow."

"Okay." She released the word, slowly, measuring his response. "But I'm not giving you a gift until tomorrow."

The new pair of cowboy boots wrapped under her Charlie Brown Christmas tree came to mind. His old ones had lived a long and painful life from the look of them, and after a little brainstorming help from the mastermind behind the Mitchells—aka Mama Grace—Dee made her purchase with the giddiness of a love-struck teen.

Reese's brows puckered. "I thought you already gave me your gift."

"I did not."

He swooped in and branded her with a kiss which took her breath away. "Well, now you did."

She pressed a hand to her chest and sighed against him. "I think I benefited from that gift much more than you did."

"Doubtful, but I can try again if you want to fuss about it." His palms ran down her arms and rested against her hands on the gift.

She offered a sassy look. "That kind of argument might take a long time, and your Mama said we only had a few minutes before dinner."

He groaned, having an obvious battle with his smile. "We better not get Mama riled. It's a scary sight." He nudged the gift forward. "Go on and open it."

She pushed up on tiptoe and stole a kiss before delving into unwrapping the large box. The paper tore away to reveal a pair of her very own, brand new, overshoes. She tilted her head back in a full laugh. "You don't think my heels are conducive to farm life, Reese Mitchell? Are you afraid I'm going to hurt myself without the right footwear?"

He stepped back, eyes lit with a look of childlike anticipation.

"Now, Doc, I do care about your safety—that's a fact, but I had a whole different reason behind getting you those overshoes."

She examined the unflattering and highly practical shoes, then met his gaze. "And that was?"

"Everybody in my family has a pair of overshoes by the back door." He kept his eyes locked on hers and dropped to one knee. "Except you."

Dee nearly tipped the box right on Reese's head, but caught it in time to see him unveil a stunning, white gold, floral-shaped diamond ring. Tears blurred her vision and a gasp stuck in her throat.

He stayed on his knee, the tenderness in his expression bringing tears to her eyes.

He slipped the box from her hands and placed it on the bed, and with his free hand he took one of hers. "I love you, Dr. Adelina Roseland, and I want to see you every morning when I wake up, hold you every night as we go to sleep, and set those overshoes right beside mine wherever our home might be."

Dee laughed through a sob and dropped to the floor in front of him, cradling his smooth jaw. "Yes, Mr. Mitchell. Your family will be my family, and where your overshoes are?" She ran her thumb over his cheek. "That will be my home."

He slid the ring on her finger and grabbed her up in his arms, pulling her to a stand while he kissed the breath out of her. "Sounds like the perfect fit. You, me, Brandon, Lou, and …" His gaze left the possibilities wide open.

She sighed into his embrace and allowed gratitude a firm hold. There was no place like home.

ACKNOWLEDGMENTS

Every book takes research of some amount or other, even contemporary books, and I couldn't have finished this story without certain supports.

To my crit partner, Amy Leigh Simpson, you were the first to read through this entire story and fall in love with it! Thanks for the amazing feedback and encouragement.

To champion blogger and encourager extraordinaire, Carrie Booth Schmidt, who pumps endless amounts of support my way on a daily basis. So thankful for her faith in my writing... and me.

To my dear friends and former colleagues, Teresa Boggs, Lynn Adams, Lindsay Greer, and Marie Johnson...thank you for being readers, brainstormers, and tireless encouragers on this journey.

To Buford Harmon, his invaluable personality, knowledge, and love for 'home' provided great information about cattle farming.

To my parents who have tirelessly believed in my 'call' of story-creating...and who are probably the BEST marketing team on the planet.

To my Granny Spencer, who provided a beautiful example of God's grace in the joy she found in her faith, family, home, and community. She was an amazing Christian matriarch and her influence touched so many lives. I am beyond grateful to have known her.

To my daughter, Lydia, who is so proud of my writing and is the coolest teenage girl I know because she 'gets' the fact that I still talk to imaginary friends.

To the Giver of great and life-changing stories. May our hearts always find a place called 'home' in the assurance of His love.

Made in the USA
Middletown, DE
17 April 2023

28987404R00179